The Girl on the Bridge

Also by James Hayman

The Cutting
The Chill of the Night
Darkness First
The Girl in the Glass

The Girl
on the Bridge

A McCabe and Savage Thriller

JAMES HAYMAN

WM

WILLIAM MORROW
An Imprint of HarperCollins*Publishers*

HarperCollins books may be purchased for educational, business, or sales pro-
motional use. For information, please email the Special Markets Department at
SPsales@harpercollins.com.

FIRST EDITION

Designed by Diahann Sturge

Library of Congress Cataloging-in-Publication Data has been applied for.

ISBN 978-0-06-266133-3

17 18 19 20 21 LSC 10 9 8 7 6 5 4 3 2 1

Once again, to Jeanne.

"In a real dark night of the soul, it is always three o'clock in the morning."

F. Scott Fitzgerald, *The Crack-Up*

Prologue

October 2001

WINTER COMES EARLY to northern New York State. By the third Saturday in October nighttime temperatures on the Holden College campus in Willardville had dropped to well below freezing. A light snow was falling and a thin coating of white covered the lawn and brick path leading to the elegant Georgian mansion on Sycamore Street. Greek letters over the door announced that this was the home of Alpha Chi Delta, Holden's first and, arguably, most prestigious fraternity. By ten P.M., the silence of the night had long since been shattered by the amplified blast of guitars and drums that even through tightly closed windows could be heard blocks away. On the semidarkened ground floor, strobes lit a mass of bodies glowing red and green. Dancers gyrating to the sound.

Outside on the sidewalk, Hannah Reindel, a petite and exceptionally pretty seventeen-year-old freshman, stood, arms folded tightly around herself. Ignoring the white flakes floating down onto her head and shoulders, Hannah looked up at the thin boy next to her who was only a few inches taller than she was.

"I'm *not* your girlfriend, Evan." The words were spoken firmly, but with a gentle smile. "I don't want you . . . or them . . . getting the idea I am."

Evan sighed. "I know that. I never thought you were. But you are my friend and I need you to help me get into the party."

Hannah pulled the collar of her sweater more tightly around her neck in a vain attempt to stop melting snow from dripping down her back.

"I already told you," Evan went on, "the rules of the invite state it very clearly. Any freshman guy who wants to attend the rush party is required to bring a good-looking girl—well, actually, the word they used was *hot-looking*—or they wouldn't be allowed in."

"And I'm hot-looking?"

"Yes, you are and don't pretend you don't know it."

"I'm a short brunette. All those guys are interested in is tall blonde cheerleader types. Not a nerdy grind like me."

"Hannah, you're the best-looking girl I know."

"Thank you." Hannah sighed. She couldn't bring herself to tell Evan he'd never in a million years be asked to pledge a house like Alpha Chi Delta. He was too sweetly goofy, too physically clumsy and much, much too serious about his studies even to be considered by the alcoholic preppies and oversized jocks Alpha Chi was known for. Even if he somehow did manage to get a bid, she couldn't imagine why he'd ever want to open himself up to the vicious hazing every Alpha Chi pledge was supposedly put through. Probably he just needed to belong and figured he'd start with the house everybody on campus said was the best one to belong to.

Hannah shivered and told herself for about the fifth time she should have worn a real coat instead of just the totally uncool knee-length black woolly thing she had on. But she hadn't and now she was shivering in the gusty wind that was blowing the last of the autumn leaves from the branches of the tall trees that had given Sycamore Street its name. She figured she might as well go inside to a warm room or risk catching pneumonia. But Alpha Chi? With Evan?

Oh, what the hell, she finally told herself. *Maybe it'll be more fun than I think and they can't* all *be assholes.* And at least it *would* be warm in there. From all the body heat being generated on the dance floor if nothing else.

"Okay, let's go," she told Evan, "but remember, do not tell them I'm your girlfriend. This isn't a date."

"I know," Evan Fischer replied with more than a hint of regret. "I wish you were and I wish I was. But I understand. You're just my admission ticket. Period. End of story. Once we're inside you don't have to hang with me. You don't even have to talk to me. Talk to whoever you want. Dance with whoever you want."

"Fine," she said. "Let's go in. But if I decide I want to go home you have to promise you'll drive me. It's too frigging cold to walk."

"Yes, I promise. I won't leave without checking with you. Now let's have a little fun."

"Right. Fun. Okay. Let's go. I'm freezing my butt off hanging around out here."

With that, Hannah Reindel and Evan Fischer started up the path to the door.

A guy about six-four who looked like he weighed at least two forty was sitting on a stool just inside the front door. A tackle on the football team? He looked it. Tackle or not, he checked Evan's name against a list, then gave Hannah the once-over. He must have thought she looked sufficiently hot because he waved them in. They went from the vestibule into a large room where the furniture had been pulled back to the walls and piled up in order to create a dance floor that was crowded with at least fifty or sixty gyrating college kids. Between the fire burning in the oversized fireplace and the effect of body heat, the room felt warm and welcoming to Hannah compared to the biting cold outside. She began to relax.

Evan asked Hannah if she wanted a beer. She shook her head no and he headed toward the bar. Within seconds she lost sight of him.

Almost involuntarily she started moving to the rhythm of the music. A hand touched her shoulder. She turned. A tall, good-looking guy dressed in black jeans and a black sweater was looking down at her. He was sipping from a bottle and smiling. "Hi, I'm Josh. Welcome to Alpha Chi. You look like you could use a beer."

"I don't drink beer."

"Everybody in college drinks beer."

"I don't."

"Don't you get ever get thirsty?"

"Not for beer. Actually, I don't drink alcohol at all."

Josh cocked his head to one side and winked. "Got it. No problem. We've got an excellent alternative we call our Freshman Punch. The college requires us to have plenty of nonalcoholic drinks available."

"How did you know I was a freshman?"

"It's a small campus. If you'd been here last year, I'm sure I would have noticed you. Besides, this is a rush party. You must have come with a freshman guy. What's your name?"

"Hannah."

"Hello, Hannah."

"So, what's in this 'Freshman Punch'?"

"Mostly fruit juice. We make it especially for folks who don't want to get drunk. And to satisfy the admins who say we have to have something appropriate for the underaged. Wait here and I'll get you a glass." Josh disappeared into the crowd, heading, presumably, to the bar. While she was waiting, Hannah kept moving in time to the music, which was both good and loud. She allowed herself to relax and smile. Suddenly she really felt like dancing. She recognized one or two faces but didn't see anyone she knew by name.

"Here you go." Josh handed her a tall frosted glass filled with a clear pink liquid.

"No alcohol?"

"Not a drop. Scout's honor."

Hannah took a sip. It was cold, a touch salty and just slightly sweet. "Umm, I love it. What's in it?"

"About six different kinds of fruit juice. And a couple of secret ingredients." Josh winked again. She wished he'd stop winking. She was tempted to ask him if there was something wrong with his eye but she was pretty sure he wouldn't find that funny.

Hannah took a few more swallows. Licked her lips.

Josh finished the last of his beer and took her hand. "C'mon, drink it down so we can dance. This band cost too much to waste."

Hannah shrugged, drained her glass and deposited the empty on the mantel next to about ten others. She kicked off her shoes, pushed them into a corner where she figured she could find them, took Josh's hand and followed him to the dance floor. After about five minutes of going full speed, the loud music was replaced by something lower and slower. Josh smiled, moved closer and put his right arm around Hannah's back.

The band was good, the dance floor too crowded for much movement. Josh and Hannah swayed softly in the middle of the throng.

It only took a couple of minutes before she started feeling woozy. She figured it had to be the warmth and the closeness of the room. "I don't feel so good. I think I better sit down."

"Oh geez, I hope you're not getting the flu or something."

"Nothing like that. I just feel a little dizzy."

"Come with me. We'll get you out of this crowd."

She didn't think she ought to follow this Josh guy, who she didn't even know. "Where's Evan?" she asked. She was having trouble getting the words out. "The guy I came with."

"Probably upstairs. That's where we interview the wannabe pledges. I'll bring you to him. Come with me."

Hannah tried to puzzle out how Josh could know Evan would be up there. She felt him take her hand and pull. She stumbled along till they came to a wide set of stairs; the music, loud again, was pounding in her head.

Hannah looked up. She felt like she couldn't even walk let alone climb what looked like an endless flight of stairs. She mumbled something but what came out didn't make sense. Didn't even sound like real words.

"Come on, let's go." Josh started pulling her up the stairs. No, *pulling* wasn't the right word. Dragging was more like it. A couple of times she felt her knees banging against the treads but Josh kept pulling. She tried and failed to shake off the fuzziness in her head as she stumbled up after him. A bunch of kids were on the landing at the top. She wanted to call out for help but her voice didn't seem to work and most of them were too involved in making out to notice her anyway. Two couples lay sprawled on either end of a beat-up couch. Others stood squashed against each other along the wall and in the corners. Each so focused on the other's face and body there was no way they'd notice anything or anyone else. Hannah tried to pull away from Josh. Somewhere deep down she was sure she didn't want to be going where he was pulling her. But somehow she couldn't summon the energy to resist. She looked desperately down the long hall. No sign of Evan or anyone else she knew. Not anywhere.

Josh opened the door to a dimly lit room and pushed her in. Hannah tripped over something and slipped to the floor. Someone's hands pulled her to her feet. She fought to keep her eyelids open. Fought to understand what was going on. With her head drooping down, all she could see were a sea of legs in front of her. She looked up and saw a bunch of guys smiling down at her. The one in front happened to be totally naked. Before her mind could make sense of that, she heard the click of the door being locked behind her.

Chapter 1

Durham, New Hampshire
December 2013

Evan

THE OTHER SIDE of the bed is empty when I wake in the early-morning darkness. The bedside clock tells me it's ten after three. This is not unusual. My wife sleeps poorly and often leaves our bed in the middle of the night. She always has in the eight years we've been married. I know it's the illness that makes sleep so hard for her.

Even when she takes a double dose of the meds her doctor prescribes to calm the anxiety that keeps her awake, she sleeps only fitfully. And when she does the nightmares wake her. The panic can strike at any hour of the night.

I know the middle of the night is the worst for her. It has taken her from our bed more nights than I can count or care to remember. And at this time of year in New Hampshire the darkness will remain for another four hours or more.

A dozen times I've asked her doctor what more we can do. A dozen times the doctor shrugs and says continuing with the drugs and her therapy are the only things she can think of.

"This is always going to be with her," her doctor tells me, and sadly I agree. "She won't ever be able to pretend it never happened or put it totally behind her. But I'm hopeful between drugs and therapy we can make the flashbacks and bouts of terror less frequent and maybe less immediate."

The words upset me though I try not to show it. Her friends, what few she has left, often tell her to try not to think about it. "Can't you just put it behind you? Get on with your life?" several have asked. The answer is no. The horror of what happened that night in the fraternity at Holden College will always be part of who she is and friends who don't understand that, well, it's usually what leads to the end of the friendship. What's past is never past for Hannah. It will always be as real and immediate as the night it happened. As a psychologist myself I know better than most that there is no way the woman I love, the woman I feel so guilty about, can ever "put this behind her." There is no way she can ever talk it away. It will always be there. Always waiting to suck her back into the vortex of that night. I feel helpless there's so little I can do. Other than to love her. To listen to her. To comfort her. To let her know how precious she is to me.

I listen for her footsteps in the living room. When she leaves our bed she sometimes spends hours in the living room pacing back and forth. Passing time and again through the light and long shadows the fire in the stove throws across the room. The stove burns day and night. It's the only source of heat we have in the cabin.

I get up and leave the bed. The floor is cold under my bare feet. I walk to the bedroom door and open it. "Are you all right?" I ask.

She turns at the sound of my voice. When she looks at me like she does now, with fear in her eyes, I know she's no longer here with me in the present but back in that filthy room where it all happened twelve years ago. She never escapes the room entirely but sometimes the flashbacks are worse than others. When she has the look I now see on her face I know she's reliving every hideous moment of the night that changed her life. And, in the end, changed both our lives.

I can't count the number of times I've tried to bring her back from that place. Sometimes I'm able to. But mostly I simply have to stay with her and wait it out. It is my job to do that not only because I love her and have always loved her but because of the guilt I've carried from that night. It was for me that she agreed to go to that party in the first place.

She's dressed for the outdoors. She wears jeans and a sweater. Boots. A heavy down parka. She has a woolen cap that she knitted herself pulled down over her ears.

"Where are you going?" I ask.

She doesn't answer, just looks at me standing there in the long-johns pants and the heavyweight New England Pats sweatshirt I sleep in on winter nights. It's as though she doesn't know who I am or why I'm there. I've seen the look before and as always it makes me anxious.

I turn and hurry back to our bedroom. I grab my clothes and pull them on as fast as I can. As I lace up my boots I hear the door to our cabin open. It doesn't close and I can hear the wind whipping through the opening. I finish dressing as quickly as I can. Hurry back into the next room. Of course she is gone. I swear under my breath and grab the big yellow flashlight off the shelf. On the way out I glance at the thermometer nailed to the tree just outside the window. Eighteen degrees. Not too bad for a New Hampshire winter night, but with a strong wind blowing, the windchill will be considerably colder than that.

I peer into the darkness outside the cabin door. There is no sign of her. She hasn't taken either of the vehicles. Her ancient Jeep Wrangler sits where it has been parked for the last week next to my only marginally newer Dodge Ram pickup. She's going on foot and I think I know where. I turn on the flashlight, go around to the back of the cabin and point it down the snow-covered trail. There's been no fresh snow for a couple of weeks so it's not easy to make out any tracks she might have left tonight. Differentiate them from those of other days and other nights. Still I'm sure she's headed to the old rusty railroad bridge that spans the Lamprey River. I debate whether or not to take the truck and drive the long way around. It will get me there faster but not much faster because the path is a much more direct route. Also there is no way to know for sure that the bridge is where she's headed. The path gives her choices. I decide to follow on foot. I start after her. I want to run but the uneven ice makes running or even walking with any kind of speed difficult. Even dangerous. If I trip and twist or sprain an ankle, I'll never catch up to her.

I call her name as loudly as I can. "Hannah! Come back! Hannah!" But even if she's within the sound of my voice I know she can't hear me. In the middle of a flashback she wouldn't hear me even if I was standing and shouting right next to her. In the middle of a flashback she isn't here. She's back at Holden College in Willardville, New York, and it's twelve years ago. Nevertheless, I shout again and then again as I follow. Once I think I see her briefly on the path ahead of me. But the moving thing is not her.

Just a good-sized doe darting across the path. Followed by two or three others trying to find something green for their breakfast.

The path forks more than once. Each time, unlike the poet Frost, I take the path more traveled by. The one I fear most. The one that leads to the bridge.

After a two-mile hike the pine and spruce become sparser. I climb the short steep rise that leads to the tracks that cross the bridge. I see her almost immediately. She's standing in the middle of the bridge, holding the rusty guardrail, looking down at the water that's rushing below carrying large chunks of ice with it.

"Hannah," I call out.

She turns her head in my direction. "No!" she cries. "Please no! Please let me go!"

I'm afraid to come any closer. She's balanced precariously on the edge of the rail bed looking down through the rusting steel crossbeams of the bridge. I want to rush toward her but I'm afraid any sudden movement will panic her. Send her over the side and into the freezing water twenty feet below. I'm even more afraid that it's her intention to let herself fall into the water on purpose. Not to hurt herself but to avoid being raped.

"Hannah, please come to me." I say it just loudly enough for my words to reach her ears. I hold out my hand. "Please. We'll make it all right. I promise. We can make it all right."

"I want it! I want it! Please fuck me!" she screams into the night, and I know that no matter what I say she isn't here in this place on this night but in another place I have never forgiven myself for bringing her to on a night twelve years ago when we were both young and hopeful. Looking forward to happy and fulfilling lives stretching endlessly before us.

With a last cry of pain, she climbs over the low guardrail faster than I can move to get to her. She falls and disappears into the darkness. Then I see her. Her arms, trapped inside the heavy parka, struggling against the flow. I watch the icy, fast-moving water carry her under the bridge. I run to the other side and jump in myself. My flashlight goes out. I lose sight of her. I become disoriented turning this way and that in the water. Once or twice I think I see her and try swimming toward her. But my heavy jacket pulls me under. As I struggle to get back to the surface, I look everywhere but I know that she's gone. I pull off my jacket and manage to swim to the side and scramble up the bank. I'm freezing and I know I won't last long at eighteen degrees, soaking wet and without a coat. I force myself to jog the quarter mile or so to the main road. I wave frantically at the first pair of headlights I see. Thank God they belong to a police cruiser. A sheriff's deputy I've seen before pulls up. Practically incoherent I babble, trying to tell him what has happened. Trying to tell him to hurry. He calls it in. Sends for help. He turns the car's heater on high, flips on his siren and flashers and drives me to the emergency room at the Wentworth-Douglass Hospital in Dover eight miles away.

Hannah's body washed up after daybreak some two hundred yards downstream from where I emerged. The medical examiner lists hypothermia as the cause of death. Perhaps I'm the only one who knows the medical examiner is wrong. I am the only one who knows that the true cause of Hannah's death is what happened twelve years ago in a filthy room at Holden College. And at that moment I swear to myself I will take the lives of those who took hers.

Chapter 2

Portland, Maine
March 2014

FOODIES HAVE LONG considered the Port Grill one of the best restaurants not just in Portland but in all of New England. During high tourist season reservations have to be made weeks in advance and even in winter the place is jammed just about every night. However, by ten o'clock on this particular Tuesday night in early March, the last of the diners have finished their desserts and coffee, paid their bills and cleared out. Except for the remaining kitchen and waitstaff, the restaurant was nearly empty when a single woman walked in, hung up her coat and found her way into the small, cozy bar. She looked around. A pair of twenty-somethings occupied a small table to her left, each apparently enthralled with the other's questionable charms. Ahead, alone at the far end of the bar, sat Joshua Thorne.

He was sipping a martini and chatting up the female bartender who, judging by the rapt expression on her face, seemed to be buying whatever Josh was trying to sell. And why not? At thirty-four, he retained the trim athletic build of the star quarterback he'd been twelve years earlier at Holden College in upstate New York. A Division III star but a star nonetheless. Given that he was even better-looking in person than he was in his photo, and since he seemed to be telling his tales with an easy, attentive charm, a lot of women no doubt bought his bullshit. And yes, the bartender definitely seemed to be one of them.

The woman's eyes took in Josh's broad shoulders, flat stomach and slender waist. Her briefer told her he worked out strenuously and regularly and it showed. His dark hair revealed a few hints of gray around the temples. These lent his face a kind of youthful gravitas that she guessed helped make him as successful as he was.

Walking across the room, she could feel his eyes slide from the bartender to her. Could feel him studying her as she climbed onto a stool. Not the empty one next to him but three down. Not so close as to seem obvious. Not so far away as to seem distant. She acknowledged his look with a glance and a perfunctory smile, then turned away.

He continued watching with obvious interest as she took off her jacket and hung it onto the back of her barstool, revealing a creamy silk blouse, one selected to show her nearly perfect figure to best advantage. And to offer Josh, at this angle, just a modest hint of cleavage.

Aware that he was still studying her, she found herself thinking she might just allow herself to enjoy a side benefit or two. Why not? No one ever said she couldn't have a little fun on the job.

Like her, Josh had hung his suit jacket on the back of the barstool. Even from three stools away its soft, dark gray pinstripes looked well-cut and very, very expensive. She'd been told Josh had his suits custom-made, *bespoke* as the Brits called it, by a London tailor named Henry Poole at number 15 Savile Row. More than five thousand bucks per suit. And why not? Why shouldn't someone like Josh spend that kind of money on himself? He worked insane hours and earned a generous seven-figure income. With all that dough who could argue with five thousand dollars for a suit? Josh, no doubt, figured he deserved the best, not just in clothing but in whatever interested him, most particularly in the women he liked to spend his nights with. And if he wanted the best, well, for tonight at least, that was unquestionably her.

The woman took note of his shirt. Blue and white striped cotton. French cuffs riding just high enough to reveal a gold Rolex. The cuffs themselves held together by a pair of gold cuff links, which, from where she sat, looked like they had his initials engraved on them. His shirt was set off by a dark red tie with a small diagonal pattern running upwards from left to right. Hermès, she thought. Or perhaps Ferragamo. Attached to his trousers, a pair of suspenders in the same shade of red. She wondered if Josh called them braces. Probably. One of the affectations guys like Josh made part of their persona after hitting it big on Wall Street.

As the bartender approached to take her order, she could feel his eyes still focused on her. He seemed to like what he saw. No surprise there. She had shoulder-length blonde hair. A more than pretty face and a body to match with slim shapely legs set off tonight by a black pencil skirt and a pair of Christian Louboutin shoes. She'd chosen the shoes because she suspected Josh would recognize the trademark red soles and appreciate the thousand dollar price tag. Her only jewelry was a simple, gold Elsa Peretti open-heart pendant around her neck and a $38,000 diamond studded Patek Philippe watch on her left wrist, which, sadly, she'd been instructed to return after the job was done. Her fingers were bare, adorned neither by elaborate diamonds nor simple gold bands.

"What can I get you?" the bartender asked, looking a little grumpy at being aced out of her evening with the QB.

"Vodka martini," the woman said. "Extra dry. Double Cross if you have it."

"We do," said the bartender, "but I should mention we'll be closing in twenty-five minutes."

"More than enough time for one martini."

The girl nodded and went off to mix the drink.

Joshua Thorne was still looking at the woman with obvious interest.

"Double Cross?" he asked from his corner seat. "I don't know that brand."

She turned her head and smiled. "You should. It's very good. Very expensive but very good." She didn't add she enjoyed the irony of the brand name given the nature of the occasion.

The bartender set the drink in front of her.

Josh drained the remaining drops from his own glass. Rose and moved toward her. "Mind if I join you?" he asked, indicating the stool next to her.

She paused for a moment before responding. "Not at all." She smiled. "In fact, I'd enjoy the company."

He signaled the bartender. "I'll have what she's having," he said.

The woman's smile morphed into a soft throaty laugh. *"When Harry Met Sally?"* she asked.

Josh's face betrayed no recognition of the film, the line or even Meg Ryan's famous fake orgasm. Perhaps he had no time for old movies. "I guess that depends if your name is Sally," he said.

She shook her head. "No, 'I'll have what she's having' is just a classic line from an old movie. My name is Norah. You're not, by any chance, called Harry, are you?"

"No. I'm Josh." He offered a hand. She shook it.

As she did, she glanced down at the fourth finger of his left hand. No ring. No surprise. After all, why give the game away when you're so obviously on the prowl?

"So shall we call this particular movie *When Josh Met Norah*?" he asked.

"Why not?"

"So what kind of movie shall we make it? A romantic comedy?"

"A bit soon for romance." She smiled. "As far as comedy goes, who knows? Are you funny?"

"Oh, absolutely. A regular Woody Allen."

"A little taller, I think."

"Yes, just a bit. Though for a funny-looking short guy he certainly attracts some interesting-looking women."

"That's what being a powerful director will do for you." She decided to change the subject. "Do you live in Portland, Josh, or are you here on business?"

"Business. I live in New York but I come to Portland quite often. I have a client here."

"I see. And does your wife come with you?"

He held up his left hand with its ringless finger. "Divorced. Three years ago," he said with the practiced ease of the habitual liar. "How about you?"

"No. Never married."

"Why not?" he asked. "Haven't met the right guy yet?"

"It's more that I don't put much faith in long-term relationships."

"Probably wise."

The bartender returned and set Josh's martini in front of him. "Your Double Cross, Mr. Thorne."

"Thank you, Andie."

"It's my pleasure to serve you." The girl's sarcastic tone betrayed the irritation she felt at Josh's interest having shifted so quickly from herself to this last-minute replacement. She went back to the task of getting the bar tidied up for closing, now only fifteen minutes away.

"Andie? I guess you're a regular here."

"Not really. She told me her name earlier. As in 'Hi, I'm Andie. What can I get you?'"

"And you told her your name?"

"I did."

They raised their glasses, clinked and sipped.

"Umm, you're right," said Josh, "this is good. Very smooth. So do you live in Portland?"

"No, I live in New York as well. Lower East Side. But I come to Portland quite often. I keep a house here in town."

"Oh really? And why is that?"

Before she got a chance to answer, Josh's phone vibrated. He pulled it from his pocket, glanced at the screen, then put it back in his pocket.

"I'm sorry. Just a text from an old friend."

"Oh, do you need to answer it?"

"Nah. Nothing urgent. I'll take care of it later. You were telling me why you keep a house in Portland."

She shrugged. "Nothing mysterious. I'm from here. It's the house I grew up in and it holds a lot of memories. So when my parents died and I inherited the house I decided to keep it."

"And what do you do in New York?"

"I work for an ad agency. Account management. How about you?"

"Wall Street. I'm with a small investment bank."

"A *small* investment bank? Now would that mean you make small investments? Or that the bank is small?"

Josh thought that was funny. "No, our investments are mostly quite big. Very big, in fact. It's the bank that's small. Just a couple of hundred employees."

"Sounds big to me. My agency only has a dozen or so."

The bartender came over and handed them each a check. "I'm very sorry but we'll be closing in a couple of minutes," she said, now eyeing Norah more with resignation than hostility. "You can finish your drinks but I'll have to cash you out."

Norah reached for her check. Josh's hand got there first. "Please let me."

"There's no need."

"No, but I insist." As he signed the bill, he said, "Listen, this has been fun. I'd love to have a little more time to chat. Maybe get to know you better. I'm staying at the Regency up the street. Their bar's open late. Why don't you join me there for a drink?"

Norah wrinkled her nose. "Hotel bars are boring," she said. "I have a better idea. Why don't we go to my place? It's only a few minutes away and not only is it more comfortable than a hotel bar there's also a whole bottle of Double Cross in the freezer just waiting to be opened."

The surprise on Josh's face was subtle, but definitely there. Norah wondered if she'd been too aggressive. Made the invitation too obvious too soon. Would the fish slip the hook and swim away? Or was Joshua Thorne so eager to get into her pants that directness didn't matter? She suspected that was the case.

"Works for me," he said, sliding off the barstool. "Not only good booze but I get to see where you grew up."

They put on their jackets and retrieved their coats. Norah led the way out of the restaurant onto a wet, chilly and totally empty Fore Street. They turned left and went down a short flight of stairs to a parking lot reserved during dinner hours for the restaurant's customers. Norah's rented Nissan Altima was the only car still in the lot. They climbed in; she pulled out and turned right onto Commercial Street.

"You said you come to Portland often?" she asked.

"Quite often. Particularly in the last six months. I've been working on financing a deal for a company called Trident Development and there've been a bunch of glitches delaying closure."

"What kind of glitches?"

"Mostly political. Your hometown's planning board is frankly a humongous pain in the ass. But I think we've overcome most of the problems. With any luck the deal should be signed and sealed by tomorrow or the next day at the latest."

"I'm wondering," said Norah, "if you're talking about that huge condo complex Trident wants to build on the waterfront? Down at the foot of Munjoy Hill?"

"Yup. That's the one."

"I'd be careful who you mention that to," Norah said with the barest hint of a smile. "There are people in this town who'd stone you to death if they found out you were the guy financing that one."

"Really? I'd be stoned?"

"Stoned."

"I've always kinda liked getting stoned." Josh grinned. He seemed pleased with his own questionable wit.

"Sadly," she said, "the stoning I was referring to would be more biblical in nature."

"Ah, I see. And are you one of the ones who'd be stoning me?"

"If that monstrosity ever gets built, it's certainly a possibility. I like this town the way it is."

Norah decided it was time to change the subject and started pointing out the sights of the city as she took a series of rights and lefts. A little more than five minutes later she pulled the Altima into the driveway of a modest wooden house that looked like it had been built during the Eisenhower administration. She clicked a remote control. The door to an attached garage rolled open and the interior lights went on. She drove in. The garage door closed behind them.

Chapter 3

RACHEL THORNE CHECKED the time on her phone. Nearly two in the morning and she still couldn't sleep.

It had been more than an hour since she'd gotten into bed. More than three hours since getting home from a depressing Chinese dinner and a stupid rom-com she'd bullied Annie Jessup into seeing because she, Rachel, thought she needed both company and distraction. And maybe she did. But, as it turned out, Annie wasn't the best choice. During dinner she wouldn't stop bitching about her latest boyfriend, who seemed more interested in her as good-looking arm candy and a more than willing fuck-buddy than as a serious and complex human being with many admirable traits and a worthwhile career of her own.

Join the club, honey, was Rachel's first thought but she didn't say anything. She hoped the movie would serve to cut off Annie's bitching. Which it did. Unfortunately, in spite of praise from the *Times*'s reviewer as a "light, frothy feel-good confection," the film turned out to be a cloying two-hour bore filled with stupid sight gags and unfunny bathroom humor.

When Rachel finally got back to the apartment she was feeling both on edge and not in the least sleepy. Instead of going straight to bed she poured herself a large glass of red wine. A fifty dollar Cabernet from a vineyard that Josh had proclaimed "really exceptional." She plopped down in her favorite oversized easy chair, tucked her legs beneath her and sat, sipping wine that, as it turned out, was okay but in no way exceptional. Rachel drummed her nails impatiently on the table next to her chair. She so wanted this day to be over. But it wasn't. At least, not technically. As she sipped she looked out over the spectacular view of the lower Manhattan skyline through the floor-to-ceiling living room windows and tried to clear her mind of ugly thoughts. She briefly considered trying the *ohm, ohm, ohm* chant Annie told her would help but decided not to. That kind of woo-woo stuff never worked for Rachel. Probably because she thought it was all kind of stupid anyway. She finished the last few drops of wine and decided a second glass wouldn't hurt. She poured it, returned to her seat and dug her phone from her jeans pocket. Still nothing from Josh. Maybe there wouldn't be anything, but she supposed it wouldn't hurt to go on record as trying again.

She spent the next ten minutes sending him one more e-mail and another text. That made a total of two e-mails and three text messages since seven o'clock when she left the apartment to meet Annie. That seemed like it should be enough. Of course, it wasn't like she ought to treat Josh's lack of response as any kind of surprise. He frequently didn't return her texts or e-mails when he was off on a business trip. Too busy making money. Or picking up strange women in bars. She rolled that around in her head for a while until she finally said the hell with it. *Que sera sera.*

She got out of the chair, walked to the window and stood looking across the water at the spectacular view of lower Manhattan and, off to her left, Lady Liberty. The condo occupied the top two floors of a six-story building on one of Brooklyn Heights's best streets. They bought the place two years ago just weeks after Josh banked his fourth consecutive seven-figure, end-of-year bonus. He'd been working for HBC, Harris Brumfield Capital, since earning his MBA at Columbia nine years earlier. He'd been making good six-figure salaries plus generous bonuses right from the start. But the really big money, the extra zeros kind of money both Rachel and Josh lusted for, had only started coming in four bonuses ago.

The apartment's location provided Josh with a dead easy commute to his office on Broad Street. When the weather was nice he could even walk it. Conversely it forced Rachel into an hour and then some haul up to the Charlton School building on East 84th Street. The black car Josh urged her to take was usually even slower than the subway. She'd complained about the unfairness of that when they'd first looked at the place and Josh had declared he wanted to buy it. But as usual, whenever any disagreement arose between them that involved spending money, especially a lot of money, Josh won and Rachel lost. Josh's trump card in these arguments was always the same. Since he made the big bucks and she only made a "paltry" $75K a year, he got to make the decision. Still, if she was going to be fair, aside from the pain of the commute, she loved the apartment.

She drank the last few drops of wine, went upstairs and changed into her standard sleep outfit. A Charlton School soccer team T-shirt size XL and men's boxer shorts size S. She washed her face, brushed her teeth and climbed into bed.

An hour later she was still lying there, eyes wide open. For about the hundredth time, she went over all the possible reasons other than the one she hoped for that Josh might not be getting back to her. Too many, she told herself, to be certain of any of them. Life was a gamble. The results unknown until the dice were tossed.

Hours passed. By three A.M. Josh still hadn't called or texted and Rachel still couldn't sleep. Finally, she figured she might as well get up, go downstairs and get some work done. Even before it started getting light she'd go for her run and then take her time getting showered and dressed before leaving for school at seven o'clock.

Chapter 4

THE FIRST THING Joshua Thorne became aware of as he began the long, slow climb back to consciousness was the drumbeat of pain inside his skull. A throbbing so insistent it was hard to think about anything else. It felt like someone pounding on his brain with a hammer. Possibly several hammers.

Jesus, he wondered, had he gotten himself so crazily drunk that he was now suffering the mother of all hangovers? No. He was pretty sure that wasn't it. He'd been drunk a million times in his life, suffered a million hangovers. None of them remotely as bad as this.

He realized he was naked and lying on what felt like a bed. Whose bed? He wasn't sure. But wherever he was, it wasn't the Regency Hotel. There was no sheet under him and the bare mattress felt damp and smelled like somebody had taken a piss on it. His own piss? He didn't know but he kind of hoped so. The idea of lying on somebody else's piss was even less appealing than the possibility that he'd peed himself in his sleep. There was a bare pillow under his head, but no blankets or sheets covering his body.

Josh tried opening his eyes but something seemed to be holding his lids in place. This puzzled his jumbled brain for a few seconds before he realized it must be a blindfold. He tried to reach behind his head to pull the thing off. But his hand was stopped well short of its mark. He tried the other hand. Same result. Both wrists seemed to be tied tightly to the bed frame. He tried drawing his legs up. They too were restrained.

Josh lay still, trying to figure out what was going on. Had he indulged in fun and games that ended with somebody tying him to the bed? It seemed unlikely. He'd never gone in for whips, chains, bondage, any of that shit. The kinky stuff was strictly for weirdos and no way in hell was Joshua Joseph Thorne any kind of weirdo.

"Hello," he called out. His voice was croaky with phlegm. He cleared it and called again. "Is anyone here?"

He listened hard. There was no answer to his question.

He called again, this time louder.

Still no response.

All he could hear was the occasional clank of what sounded like a radiator and, distantly, some music. Classical music. Mozart or some such.

The music made him think about Rachel, who was home, probably still asleep in their condo in Brooklyn Heights. An unwanted thought popped into his head. He had no idea how long he'd been lying here. No idea what time of day or night it was. He might have been conked out so long it was already morning and, back in Brooklyn, Rachel had already completed her morning run, taken her shower and left for school. Or, Jesus, even worse, maybe it already was the middle of the day and he'd missed his wrap-up meeting with the Tridents. He had no sense of time. No clue as to how long he might have been lying here dead to the world. Even worse he had no memory of how he'd gotten here. Or how he'd allowed himself to get tied up and blindfolded.

Josh lay still for a moment. All right, he told himself with as much calm as he could muster, this wasn't a calamity. All he had to do was figure out how to untie his hands and feet, get dressed and get out of here. Wherever here was. Josh tried to ignore the pain still pounding in his head and concentrate his brain on remembering.

Slowly, by small degrees, memory returned. A fuzzy image of dinner at the Port Grill with people from Trident. He searched for their names and was pleased when they came to him without much effort. Joe Bonner. Tom Evans. Ryan Fundaro. Josh transported himself back to the table in the back room. The one he'd chosen because it was quieter than the main room and where it would be possible to hear and be heard. Slowly his mind began filling in details of the conversation, which was mostly about Trident's future plans. The image of Joe Bonner popped into his head—Joe going on about how Josh was "part of the Trident team" and how this deal and others to come would make them all rich. Hell, they were already rich. All of them richer than 99.99 percent of the poor schmucks in the world. Richer even than the not so poor schmucks seated around them. The not so poor schmucks who could afford dinner at the Port Grill.

Josh smiled to himself. The slow return of his memory seemed like kind of a victory and victories were good. He lay there trying to reconstruct the rest of the evening in detail. After dinner, he remembered asking if anybody wanted to join him for a nightcap. As expected, nobody did. They left. He headed into the nearly empty bar. He saw no available attractive women so he schmoozed with the bartender who, while no great beauty, was kind of cute and would do just fine for a one-night stand if no one better turned up.

But then someone better did. Norah. Elegant, sexy Norah. And just like that, the game changed. But Norah what? She'd never told him her last name and he never asked. He hadn't told her his either, had he? Why bother with last names when it seemed perfectly obvious Norah wanted the same thing Josh did. Safe, anonymous one-time sex with somebody more than a little attractive. He bought her a drink. They talked for a while. Some silliness about a line from a movie. *When Harry Met Sally.* When Josh met Norah. Then what? Then the weird shit started. Or what he should have realized was weird shit. The fog lifted and Josh remembered it all in exquisite detail.

Instead of going to the Regency, elegant, sexy Norah suggested driving back to her house. Really? A woman like that asking him to come home with her instead of going to a nice safe hotel after just twenty minutes bar chatter? That should have been a red light right there. Warning bells should have been clanging. But as usual Josh's cock outranked his brain and made the decision for him. Schmuck that he was, he let her lead him on like a horny teenager. Or maybe more like an eager lamb to the slaughter.

He remembered driving to her house. A crummy house. Especially crummy for somebody wearing a forty thousand dollar watch. The house was maybe a ten-minute drive from the restaurant. On the way he remembered telling her about the project and she had said something about getting stoned. Stoned? Jesus, was that it? Had she given him some drug that had knocked the shit out of him?

When she opened the door from the garage and they dashed into the house it had been like a race to see who got their pants off first. They'd both kicked off their shoes. They stumbled around while she pulled down her thong and he pulled down his boxers. Then he grabbed her ass and pulled her to him, the two of them teetering around like a pair of clowns, both with their underpants down around their ankles. They stumbled in tandem from the kitchen into what must have been the living room and fell onto a grubby carpeted floor. Orange shag. Shag for shagging. Somehow Norah must have managed to kick off the thong completely because he remembered her wrapping her long legs around him. He pushed into her. She pushed back. Both their hips thrusting hard at each other. There was a lot of gasping and groaning and finally shouting as she came only seconds before he did.

Afterward she slid out from under, stood and smiled down at him.

"Baby, you really are good," she said. "What a waste."

What a waste? He wondered briefly what she meant by that but, at the time, he was too focused on watching her pull off the rest of her clothes to think too long or too hard about it. Then she stood there for a minute posing naked for him. Gorgeous body. Tall. Slender. Perfect boobs. Perfect everything. Not a Brazilian, just a regular bikini wax that left most of the hair between her legs and proof, had he needed any, that she was a natural blonde. She walked naked into the kitchen. As Josh took off the rest of his own clothes and tossed them on the floor, he heard the fridge door open and close. A clatter of ice cubes dropping into a cocktail shaker.

"Martini?" she called out.

"Of course," he answered. At the time a postcoital drink seemed like an excellent idea.

He heard rattling and pouring and a minute later she came

out holding two oversized martini glasses. She handed him one and they sat, facing each other, still naked, their backs resting against the opposite arms of the brown corduroy couch, their bare legs intertwined, her big toe, its nail covered with dark green polish, between his legs teasing his cock, trying to arouse another erection.

He leaned forward to clink glasses.

"To your health," she said with what could only be described as a mischievous smile.

They sat quietly and sipped for a while and, when they'd finished the drinks, Norah said, "C'mon. Let's go upstairs."

Josh remembered thinking that sounded like a really good idea. He also remembered feeling wobbly as he got up and started for the stairs. Even more wobbly climbing the steep narrow steps. She held his hand and led him to a bedroom, urging him along. *"C'mon, c'mon, Josh, you can make it. Don't crap out on me."*

By the time he flopped down on to the bed, the room had begun growing darker and darker. Soon everything was black. The last thing he remembered her saying was, *"Now you can tell me how much fun you're having."*

That's where the memories stopped.

Josh took a deep breath and tried to force himself to calm down. It was the drink. It had to be. The Double Cross martini. A double cross, all right. The bitch had drugged him. Rohypnol? Maybe. Or maybe not. Josh had enough experience feeding roofies to coeds back at Holden to know it'd take a double dose, maybe even a triple, to knock him out like that. So maybe it was something else. In fact, he was sure it was.

What he couldn't figure out was why in hell she would want to drug him. Couldn't have been for sex. She knew Josh was more than willing to let her go at him as many times as she wanted any way she wanted. Up, down, sideways or with both of them standing on their heads if there was any way they could manage it. After their first go last night he was already thinking about signing her up for a long term fling either here in Portland or down in New York, or even in fucking Timbuktu if that's where she wanted to go. So what the hell was the deal? Why the drugs? Why the fucking drugs? That's the question that weighed on him. There had to be a reason.

Maybe she just got her jollies fucking guys, then drugging them and tying them up. Mistress Norah and all that kind of shit. If that was what she wanted he was ready for more. Let her come on up and climb aboard. He pictured her straddling him and the picture was strong enough to start giving him a hard-on.

On the other hand maybe it didn't have anything to do with sex. But what, then? The project? Could this whole little adventure have something to do with the project? He tossed that one around in his mind for a while. She'd pretty much admitted that, if she had the chance, she'd stop the project. What was it she'd said in the car? *"There are people in this town who'd probably stone you to death if they found out you're the guy financing that one."*

Stone him to death? That's what she'd said. The thought flitted around in his brain. It seemed preposterous, but could she have meant that literally? Was the woman a killer? A pro hired to . . . what did they call it in the movies? *Ice* him? *Whack* him? *Feed him to the fishes?* Maybe this *was* a movie. Maybe he was lying here with his goodies hanging out so she could film the whole fucking thing. To do what with? Post it on the Internet and get his ass fired? Could that be it? He tried to imagine Floyd Brumfield's reaction to seeing "the movie." Probably laugh his ass off and show it to his buddies. But fire the firm's number one rainmaker over some stupid sexual peccadillo . . . or was it a pecker-dillo? Josh found himself giggling at the pun. No way Floyd would toss his ass out. Rachel might. But Floyd? No way. Besides, if sweet little Norah really did want to fuck him over on the Internet she wouldn't have covered half his face with a stupid blindfold, would she? There was no way anyone except maybe Rachel and possibly half a dozen other former and current girlfriends would ever recognize him just from his body. On the other hand maybe they'd been on camera the whole fucking time. As in the whole time they were fucking. If so, she'd also be one of the stars of the show and somehow she didn't seem the type to want that.

His mind went back to the project. How was fucking him and drugging him and tying him to a smelly, bare, pee-soaked mattress supposed to affect the project? He had no idea. Maybe her plan was to make him miss the meeting. Maybe she was stupid enough, or maybe someone who'd hired her was stupid enough, to think missing one lousy meeting would screw up the deal. If Norah thought that, well, she was dumber than she seemed. Yes, the Tridents would be pissed. And yes, Joe Bonner had a short fuse. He'd probably been calling Josh all morning. All afternoon if he'd really been conked out that long. Josh wondered if his phone was ringing away in the pocket of his suit jacket, which, as best he could recall, was last seen downstairs on the floor by the couch. Either way missing a meeting was no biggie. Bonner would be pissed off but clients got pissed off all the time. Being pissed off didn't mean walking away from a hundred million dollar deal that was almost done. All it'd take to put things right would be a whole bunch of *mea culpas* and a lot of sucking up.

Maybe Norah realized it wouldn't stop things altogether. Maybe she just thought having him miss the meeting would hold up financing long enough for the locals to get their shit together and put more pressure on the politicians. That seemed more likely. Jesus Christ. Was all this shit he was going through just her idea of what she said in the car? *Stoning him in the biblical sense?*

It was ridiculous. Too fucking stupid for words. Josh felt an angry storm building inside his gut. He willed it to stop. "Stay calm," he whispered. "Lie still and stay calm." He sucked in long slow breaths through his mouth and then slowly let them out through his nose.

When he was about as calm as he figured he was likely to get, Josh tested the knots that held his wrists. There wasn't much play. His wrists were squooshed right up against the bed frame where the rope was tied and pulling just seemed to make the knots tighter. Not likely that he could somehow slip his hands out of the restraints. Still that was the only thing he could think of so he started working his right wrist. He wriggled it first this way, then that. He squeezed his fingers tightly together, trying to make them as narrow as possible. After what must have been twenty minutes or maybe more, it was obvious he was getting nowhere. No way the fat part of his good-sized throwing hand was going to slip through this rope. He wondered if the damned thing might even be cutting off the flow of blood and what would happen if it did.

Finally Josh gave up and he dropped his head back on the pillow. It was time to put an end to this stupid fucking game.

"Hey!" he called out. "Get me out of here. You've had your fun now get me the hell out of here."

He waited. There was no response.

"This isn't fucking funny," he yelled louder. "Untie these goddamned ropes and get me out of here!"

Still nothing. He wondered if maybe he was alone in the house. He listened for the sound of another human being. Footsteps. A voice. Anything. But all he could hear was the same clanking of the radiator and, very faintly, the same kind of classical music as before.

He lay there thinking about the stupidity and injustice of what Norah had done to him and the more he thought about it, the angrier he became. He started screaming incoherently, yanking his hands against the restraints. Swinging his body hard. First to the left. Then to the right. He pulled his legs up toward his chest, muscles straining to break the rope.

Finally when it was clear there was no way he'd ever be able to escape this pee-soaked prison on his own, he lost it altogether and an uncontrollable rage took over. "Norah!" he shouted as loudly as he could. "Norah! Get me the fuck out of here or I'll fucking kill you, you fucking bitch!"

When there was no response, Josh yelled louder. "Get me the fuck out of here, you fucking bitch," he screamed, "or I'll cut you into fucking dog meat!"

But no matter how hard he struggled, no matter how loudly he yelled and screamed, the restraints held firm and his pleas and threats went unanswered. Finally, exhausted, he fell back, his heart pounding, his lungs sucking in foul-smelling air as fast as they could. The struggle had made the throbbing in his head worse than before. At this point his brain was banging so hard he thought it might literally explode.

That's when the door opened. "Now, Josh, I'm afraid we can't have you making so much noise, yelling and screaming like that," said a voice. Norah's voice? He was sure it was. "I mean, you'll wake the whole neighborhood. What will people think?"

Josh forced himself to calm down. He had enough self-discipline to do that. The most important thing right now was to convince Norah to let him go. He'd never be able to do that yelling and screaming like a crazy man.

"Norah," he said as calmly as he could. "You've had your fun and games and now it's time to cut these ropes and let me go. If you don't I can promise you'll live to regret it."

The only response was the feel of a cold hand taking hold of his bare leg and turning it slightly to one side. And then, unexpectedly, a painful sting as the hand plunged what felt like a needle deep into his thigh.

After a few seconds of growing dizziness, Josh's head fell back helplessly onto the pillow. Blackness enveloped his world once again.

Chapter 5

RACHEL CHECKED HER phone for messages and e-mails before she left the apartment for the subway and then again after she arrived at school. That was at 7:25 A.M. Still nothing from Josh.

She'd tried repeatedly to reach him last night and added an e-mail when she got up this morning explaining that she wanted him to do her a favor before he left Portland. *A bit of a pain for you I'm sure*, she wrote, *but I'd really appreciate it if you can find the time. If not, I'll understand (I guess).*

The favor she had in mind was for Josh to take the ferry over to Harts Island when he was done with his meetings to check out a possible summer rental she'd found online. She made the request even knowing that for Josh the idea of spending a summer vacation in Maine was only a couple of steps up from spending it in downtown Detroit. Okay. Maybe that was an exaggeration. Still, he'd told her ten times if he'd told her once that he wanted to rent the same cottage in East Hampton they'd taken last year. And the year before that. In fact, he'd been talking about buying the place if they could get it for a decent price. Buy it even though he knew she hated all the summer bullshit you couldn't avoid in the Hamptons. Of course, the bullshit she hated most of all had nothing to do with the house or the beach or the crowded restaurants. Rather, it was watching the gaggle of rich divorcées and trophy wives fawn and drool over hunky Josh every time they laid eyes on him especially on the beach with his shirt off. Well, too damned bad. They couldn't have him. Not anymore. Not now. Not ever.

The house Rachel had picked for Josh to look at was pretty damned nice. A gorgeous contemporary sitting all by itself right on the water on the back side of Harts Island a mile and a half across the bay from the city of Portland. The photos in the ad showed large open rooms. Floor-to-ceiling glass on the ocean side. Every conceivable amenity including a heated lap pool.

It seemed, she wrote in her e-mail, like a reasonable request. As a teacher she got the whole summer off. While Josh would never take more than a couple of weeks away from work, he could always fly up weekends. She reiterated that Portland was an easy one-hour hop from LaGuardia or JFK, not much longer and a hell of a lot cheaper than the sea plane service Josh liked taking to East Hampton on summer Fridays to avoid the crush on the Long Island Expressway or the crowds on the LIRR.

Rachel checked her watch. Still twenty-five minutes before her first class. She figured one more e-mail wouldn't hurt. She poured herself an extra big mug of coffee and started typing, determined to keep the tone light and friendly. Not to reveal the anger she was really feeling.

> *To: ThornyJ@gmail.com*
> *Joshua.Thorne@harrisbrumfield.com*
> *Subject: Next summer*

Darling,

She paused, wondering for a minute if "Darling" might not be laying it on a little thick. She decided it wasn't and started typing again.

Darling,

I've tried reaching you a couple of times. Maybe you're not checking your phone or e-mail or maybe you're pissed off for reasons that escape me. Either way, would you please get back to me when you get this or any of my other messages? Maybe you've just lost your phone but I hope not. That would be a huge pain. Even if you have, I'm pretty sure you'll be checking e-mail on your computer at some point.

PLEASE do me a favor when you're done with your meetings and before you fly home. Like I said in the previous messages I saw a great ad online for a summer rental on Harts Island that I'd love to take for July and August. I'm attaching the link (again). Check it out.

Yes, I know you'd rather have East Hampton but frankly spending an entire summer cheek by jowl with the ladies who lunch (especially Melanie Bitchface Harris and Trudy Brumfield) is more than I can handle.

If you TRULY, TRULY object to Maine maybe we can have it both ways. A month here. A month there. I hope you'll be at least willing to take a look at the house on Harts (only $5,000 a week—would be at least $20K/week in EH, probably more).

Please respond!!!!

R.

Rachel read the e-mail over. Decided the tone was perfect and hit Send. She still had fifteen minutes before she had to head over to her first period class teaching English to seventeen AP seniors at Charlton, a posh private day school for girls over by the river on East 84th Street.

Today her students would be analyzing the narrative structure of Henry James's *Portrait of a Lady*. Rachel had never cared for James so she'd never taught his books before, but this year the department head decided as a great American novelist James should be required reading. Rachel was sure half her students, even the most diligent, would sleepwalk their way through the book. It had bored her to tears the first time she read it so she couldn't imagine the kids sticking with it. She spent the next quarter hour sipping coffee and trying her best to think up interesting discussion points about Isabel Archer's endless waffling about who she should marry and where she would live and God only knew why so many men seemed to fall head over heels in love with her. Then she got up and headed for her class.

After Henry James, the school day progressed normally until the middle of her third period class with her sophomores. That's when she felt her silenced cell phone vibrate on her desk. She glanced down. Caller ID indicated Josh's direct line at Harris Brumfield.

She was tempted to answer but decided to let the call go to voice mail. Calling back would have to wait until after the period ended. For another twenty minutes Rachel led a discussion about the relationship between King Lear and his three daughters. Having already taught the play a bunch of times she could handle this one on automatic pilot. Finally the buzzer rang and the girls packed up their stuff and walked out.

When the room was empty, Rachel checked voice mail. The call had come from Josh's assistant, Roseanne Mezzina. *"Rachel, this is Roseanne. Could you please call me as soon as you get this message? It's important."*

She tapped the "call back" number on the screen.

Roseanne picked up immediately. "Rachel?"

"Hi, Roseanne, what is it?"

"Have you heard from Josh this morning?"

"No. Should I have?"

"Do you have any idea where he is?"

"What do you mean? He's in Portland. I mean, he is, isn't he?"

"That's what we thought too. But I've tried calling and texting half a dozen times and I just can't find him . . ."

Rachel said nothing.

"Rachel? Are you there?"

"Yes. I'm sorry. I'm here. He didn't respond to my texts either. I'm just really puzzled."

"I'm puzzled too, but worried as well. Floyd got a call about forty-five minutes ago from the people Josh was working with at Trident. He was a no-show for this morning's nine-thirty meeting. He didn't call. He didn't text. Just didn't show up and they're not sure whether to be worried or pissed off or both. Neither am I. They were supposed to finalize the contracts on financing a major construction project this morning and Joe Bonner, the Trident CEO, wants to know what's going on. Floyd told him he'd find out. Meanwhile, Floyd's flying up to Portland himself to make sure the deal gets done. And then to see if he can find out where the hell Josh is."

Rachel glanced up. The girls from her ninth grade class were filing into the room and taking their seats. She turned her back and lowered her voice to a whisper. "That's crazy, Roseanne. Josh doesn't just *not* show up."

"You know that. I know that. More importantly, Floyd knows that. But I guess the people at Trident don't."

"They saw him yesterday, didn't they?"

"Yes. Bonner told Floyd yesterday's meeting went according to plan and after the meeting Josh took him and a couple of Trident's other top people out to dinner at a place called the Port Grill."

"Josh says it's his favorite restaurant in Portland. Plus it's near the hotel. He always goes there."

"I know. In fact, I made the reservation myself. Bonner said everybody left the restaurant around nine-thirty except Josh. He told them he was going to head into the bar for a quick nightcap. He asked if anyone wanted to join him. The guys from Trident declined. Said they didn't want to drink anymore since they all had to drive home. Everybody shook hands and said goodnight. That was the last anyone saw of him."

"Wasn't Josh staying at the Regency?"

"Yup. I made that rez as well."

Rachel took in a deep breath. Let it out. Watched her fourth period students taking their seats. "Okay," she said, "so Josh would only have had a short walk back to the hotel. Or a short stagger if he had more than one nightcap. No big deal since he wouldn't have been driving."

Rachel looked back at the class. The girls were all in their seats, watching her and, no doubt, trying to eavesdrop as well. "Hold on a second," she said to Roseanne. She held the phone against her leg and told the class she had some personal business to attend to and would be gone for a few minutes. "In the meantime, I want you all to start writing a short essay, three hundred words, on the meaning of Robert Frost's *Stopping by Woods on a Snowy Evening*. I want you to prove to me that you not only read the poem but that you understood what it was about. If you don't finish your essays before I get back you can finish them tonight."

The class moaned at the unexpected assignment. Rachel ignored the collective moan, went out into the hall and closed the door behind her. "I'm back," Rachel said into the phone. "Is there anything else?"

"No. Just that Floyd asked me—I guess, ordered me is more accurate—to track down Josh '*fucking now*' as he put it and to find out what's going on."

Rachel let a few seconds pass before responding. "What do you mean 'what's going on'?"

"Rachel, I'm sorry. Like I said I'm worried. Now I've got you worried as well. But I think we *ought* to be worried. When I call, his cell goes straight to voice mail. He hasn't returned any of my texts or e-mails. I asked the people at the Regency to check his room. They said his suitcase and briefcase were there but the bed hadn't been slept in. I'm sorry to have to tell you that. The manager asked if they should check him out of the hotel. I told them no. Told them just to hold the room for him until they heard otherwise from me and charge the company credit card."

"Jesus. Maybe he was in an accident?" said Rachel. "Hit by a car? Had a heart attack? Or a stroke? Or maybe got mugged or God knows what. Did you call the hospitals?"

"Not yet," said Roseanne. "I thought it'd be better if you did that. Hospitals are happier providing medical information to wives than to executive assistants. There are two of them in Portland. Mercy and Cumberland Medical Center. I can get you the numbers if you like."

Rachel ignored the offer. "What about the police?" she asked. "Did you call them?"

"I tried them. Woman who answered the phone said no serious accidents were reported in Portland last night."

"And no murders or muggings?"

"Oh my God, Rachel. No. They didn't mention anything like that."

"Well, something's happened," said Rachel. "And I'm damned well going to find out what. If you hear anything in the meantime, anything at all, please phone me right away."

Rachel Thorne broke the connection and walked to Karen Abernathy's office. Karen was the head of school and one of Rachel's biggest supporters. A close friend, though she was twenty years older. She didn't want to tell Karen too much but she could tell her that she needed some personal time off from school. Maybe just a day or two. Maybe longer. And that it was a very important but very personal matter she couldn't talk about. She hoped Karen would understand. If she didn't, well, too bad. Josh came first.

Chapter 6

AT A LITTLE after two o'clock on a cold, overcast Wednesday afternoon in Portland, Detective Sergeant Michael McCabe's phone buzzed. Dispatcher Kelly Haddon was on the line.

"What do you need, Kelly?"

"I'm not really sure. Some lawyer from New York says he needs to talk to you. Name's Mark Christensen. Says he thinks a violent crime might have been committed in Portland last night."

"Oh yeah? News to me. Unless he's talking about that little dust-up on Riverside?" The dust-up in question involved a couple of local drunks who had words in the parking lot of a topless "gentlemen's club" called Diamonds after enjoying their respective lap dances. For reasons as yet unknown, one of the "gentlemen" pulled a knife and stabbed the other. The victim was currently recovering in the ICU at Cumberland Med and the knife wielder was under arrest and awaiting arraignment in the county jail. Carl Sturgis, one of McCabe's senior detectives, was handling the details. No reason for a New York lawyer to be interested in that.

"I don't think that's what he was talking about," said Kelly.

"All right, then. What *was* he talking about?"

"He wouldn't tell me."

"Wouldn't give you any specifics at all?"

"Nope. Just said it was urgent."

McCabe sighed. This so-called lawyer could be some kind of nutcase. On the other hand, all McCabe had on his plate at the moment was another day of trying to keep from dozing off while catching up on a desk full of paperwork. He was thinking about requesting a transfer to Narcotics. The detectives there were always busy chasing down one scumbag or another.

"Okay if I put him through?"

McCabe generally disliked calls from lawyers, especially New York lawyers who tended to be even bigger pains in the butt than the locals. The primary exception being his brother Bobby, who practiced personal injury law in the city, and if McCabe was honest, there were times he wasn't so happy about hearing from Bobby. It was usually bad news about their mother's rapidly progressing Alzheimer's. He'd been telling himself he should put in a visit while she still recognized him. If she still recognized him.

McCabe finally said, "Sure, that's fine. Put him through." He picked up the other line. "This is McCabe."

"Sergeant McCabe?"

"Yes."

"My name is Mark Christensen. I'm an attorney practicing in Manhattan."

"Criminal law?"

"No. General practice. Mostly personal injury. I got your name from your brother Bob."

"Really? And how do you know my brother?"

"He used to be my boss. Hired me out of law school. Now he's just a friend. Back when I worked for his firm he mentioned you a couple of times. Said you were a detective in Portland. I spoke to him this morning and when I told him what it was about he suggested I give you a call."

"Okay, you told our dispatcher you *thought* a violent crime *might* have taken place. Did it or didn't it?"

"Right now, *might* is the operative word. But—and I don't want to say this in front of my sister—I don't think it'll stay that way for long."

"Okay, why don't you just tell me what it's all about?"

"I'd rather do that in person if you don't mind. Also there's something we need to show you."

"We?"

"My sister Rachel—Rachel Thorne—is with me."

"And you're both here in Portland?"

"Yes. Just up the street at the Regency Hotel. We flew in from New York. Landed about an hour ago. Rachel needs to be present when we meet. The case concerns her husband. My brother-in-law."

"All right, come on over," said McCabe, feeling suddenly grateful for a reason to ignore the forest of papers strewn across his desk.

"109 Middle Street?"

"Yup. Corner of Franklin. Fourth floor. Ask the woman downstairs at the reception desk to buzz me directly."

A little more than five minutes later the elevator doors slid open and a slim balding guy about forty stepped out accompanied by a tall dark-haired woman who looked to be in her late twenties or early thirties. McCabe couldn't help looking at the woman a little longer than he should have. To say she was gorgeous would have been a serious understatement.

"Detective McCabe? I'm Mark Christensen. This is my sister."

"Rachel," she said with a thin smile, reaching out her hand. "Rachel Thorne."

Christensen was outfitted in the standard big-city lawyer's uniform. Black cashmere overcoat. Blue pinstripe suit with a white handkerchief neatly folded and tucked into the breast pocket. White shirt. Blue and yellow striped tie.

For her part, Rachel was dressed simply. Gray slacks, gray cashmere pullover, low-heeled black shoes and a dark blue leather jacket that looked expensive. Her shoulder-length hair was neatly tied back. He estimated her height at about five-nine.

McCabe signaled Maggie, who was watching from her desk, to join them. "This is my partner, Detective Margaret Savage," he said. "I've asked her to sit in on our conversation."

"That's fine," said Christensen.

The two detectives ushered brother and sister into a small interview room. McCabe and Maggie sat on one side of the plain wooden table. Christensen and Rachel Thorne on the other.

"Before we start," said Christensen, "I should mention that I'm not here as Rachel's attorney but rather as a concerned family member."

"Okay. That's fine," said McCabe. That, at least, suggested there shouldn't be any irritating issues of attorney client privilege. "And I will mention that we're videotaping this discussion. That's standard procedure. The camera's hidden up there in that light fixture."

Christensen glanced up at the light. "Okay. No problem."

"All right," said McCabe, "we're on your dime, Mr. Christensen. Why don't you tell us what's going on?"

"I think I'd better let my sister do that."

Rachel Thorne took a deep breath. "My husband has disappeared," she said. "He may have been kidnapped. But I have a horrible feeling it might be something even worse."

Rachel spoke in a quiet but breathy voice, sounding to McCabe like she was working hard to keep herself under control.

"I see," said McCabe. "I'm very sorry to hear that. What's your husband's name?"

"Josh. Joshua."

"Joshua Thorne?"

"Yes, I took Josh's name when we got married."

"And when you say he disappeared, was that from Portland?"

"Yes." Rachel let out a breath she'd been holding in. "As far as we know, the last time anyone saw or heard from him was last night at the Port Grill where he had dinner with his clients. Since then, he hasn't answered any phone calls or texts or anything either from me or from his office and he didn't show up for an important business meeting this morning."

"I see," said McCabe. "You mentioned possible kidnapping? Have you received any demands for money?"

"No. Nothing about money."

"Does Joshua have access to enough money to make ransom demands worthwhile?"

McCabe studied Rachel Thorne as she pondered how to answer his question. Large brown eyes. Sculpted cheekbones. Perfect skin. No two ways about it. Even with the anxious expression drawn across her face, or maybe partly because of it, she really was incredibly attractive.

"I suppose so," she finally said. "He works on Wall Street and makes a lot of money."

"How much?"

He half expected her to say, *"None of your business,"* but she didn't. "Nearly three million last year. Also his firm, Harris Brumfield, has pretty much unlimited amounts of money."

"And your husband's important enough to them that they would bail him out if necessary?"

"I think so. Yes, I'm sure of it. He's their number one deal maker."

"All right, Rachel," said Maggie. "Is it okay if I call you Rachel?"

"Of course."

"Okay, then, why don't you give us a little background on Josh and yourself so we'll have some idea about what might have happened and how to go about looking for him."

"I'm not sure where to start." Rachel Thorne's eyes were starting to well with tears. Christensen pulled the handkerchief from his pocket and handed it to her.

"Just start at the beginning and tell us what you know," said Maggie.

Rachel nodded. Wiped her eyes and nose with the handkerchief. She took a deep breath. Let it out. "Okay. Josh works for a small investment bank in New York called Harris Brumfield. They have their offices in downtown Manhattan on Broad Street. It's a boutique firm specializing in real estate investment. At least, *boutique* is how they like to refer to themselves. Josh flew to Portland yesterday at noon on a quick business trip. Two days and one or possibly two nights tying up details on financing a large residential development. According to his assistant at the office . . ."

"Can you give me the assistant's name?" asked Maggie. "And phone number?"

"Roseanne. Roseanne Mezzina. Josh's direct line is 212-555-6741. Roseanne answers it."

THE GIRL ON THE BRIDGE 53

Maggie jotted the information down. Blessed with an eidetic memory, McCabe would remember it without having to make a note.

"According to Roseanne, Josh got to Portland a little after one yesterday afternoon. He took a car from the airport and went directly into a nearly three-hour meeting."

"Did he rent a car?"

"I wouldn't think so. He usually just takes Uber."

"Do you know the name of the client?"

"Yes. A company called Trident Development."

Maggie and McCabe exchanged glances. The Trident name was familiar and not in a good way to just about everyone who lived or worked in Portland. Both the company and its CEO, Joe Bonncr, had been in the news a lot lately. Trident was planning to build what many Portlanders considered a wildly oversized condominium complex right on the waterfront on the city side of Ocean Gateway. The proposed cluster of three ten-story buildings, which the *Press Herald* editorial page had called "a cancer on the community," would block a lot of people's views of the water and was way out of keeping with what many considered Portland's, and particularly the waterfront's, historic architectural heritage and charm. To say there was a lot of anger about it in the city would be a major understatement. Especially when the planning board, after rejecting Trident's plans twice in two years, suddenly flip-flopped even though the only changes the company had made to their proposal was reducing the height of the buildings from twelve stories to ten.

No one could prove anything, but whispers around town suggested that several big buckets of money had suddenly found their way under the mattresses of a few city bigwigs. The level of public anger alone made the sudden disappearance of the guy financing the deal look suspicious. It also raised another interesting question. Were any of the Trident executives also in danger of not turning up for work? Personally, McCabe wouldn't give a rat's ass if the whole lot of them were suddenly run over by a large truck. But, as the Portland PD mission statement declared, his job as head of the department's Crimes Against People unit was to *protect and serve*, even if it meant protecting and serving a bunch of money-grubbing bloodsuckers.

"Do you know where Josh went after the meeting?" asked Maggie.

"Yes. Roseanne told me everything she knew. At about five o'clock he left the Trident offices . . ."

"The ones at 3 Portland Square?"

"If that's where they are. After leaving the meeting he went to his hotel."

"The Regency?"

"Yes."

"Do you know if he walked there?"

"No. But if the offices are close by he probably would have."

"They are. It's an easy walk."

"Mark and I talked to the people at the hotel before calling you. They told us Josh checked in at five-fifteen, went to his room and then ordered a drink from room service. He called Roseanne a little before six to catch up on the day's goings-on at the office. He probably left the hotel at seven-fifteen or so. He had a seven-thirty reservation to meet Joe Bonner and two of the other Trident people for dinner at the Port Grill restaurant. Roseanne told me that Joe Bonner confirmed that they all arrived on time and that they finished eating at around nine-thirty. Bonner and the others went home. Apparently Josh went into the bar for a nightcap. Nobody's heard from him since."

"I see," said Maggie. "So you haven't communicated with Josh in any way since then?"

"I've tried." Rachel described how she'd called, texted and e-mailed her husband both last night and again this morning and gotten zero response.

"Is that unusual?" asked McCabe. "Him not responding when you try to reach him?"

"Unusual, yes. Unheard of, no," said Rachel. "Sometimes his mind is somewhere else. Sometimes his phone is. So I wasn't particularly worried until I got the call from his office about ten o'clock this morning."

"Okay. Keep going."

She then took them, chapter and verse, through her phone conversation with Roseanne Mezzina.

"After talking to Roseanne, I was obviously very concerned. I told my boss some personal issues had come up and I needed a couple of days off. Then I called Mark and told him what I knew." Rachel reached over and took Mark Christensen's hand. "I know I can always rely on my big brother when I need help," she said with a faint smile. "After I told Mark what was going on he called your brother Bob. Bob suggested we come up here and talk to you face-to-face. So we did. Same flight Josh took. Only twenty-four hours later."

"We would have called you from New York," said Christensen, "but we had to scramble to make the flight."

"When we arrived in Portland," Rachel continued, "we took a car over to the Regency just in case he'd shown up there in the meantime. I spoke to one of the assistant managers."

"Name?"

"John Travers. We were hoping if Josh wasn't at the hotel that at least we might find some clue as to his whereabouts. He wasn't and we didn't."

"Did you ask to see the room?"

"Yes. Travers was reluctant, worried about privacy concerns and whatnot, but Mark threatened him with some legal mumbo-jumbo and he finally took us up."

"Describe the scene."

Rachel Thorne shrugged. "It was just a hotel room. Kind of upscale but nothing special. There was a *Do Not Disturb* sign hanging outside the door. Inside, the empty martini glass was still on the tray with a small bowl of nuts. Josh's Dopp kit was open on the bathroom sink and some towels had been used so it looked like he showered and shaved before going to dinner. His overnight bag and briefcase were in the room. The bed hadn't been slept in."

"Did either of you touch anything?"

Brother and sister looked at each other. "Yes. We both did," said Mark Christensen.

"All right, before you leave, we'll want to get a set of both of your fingerprints. Also cheek swabs for DNA."

Rachel looked at him questioningly.

"If we decide to check the room for prints or DNA we'll need to be able to distinguish yours from anyone else's."

"That's fine," said Christensen.

"Did you look inside the briefcase?" asked McCabe.

Rachel Thorne shook her head. "No."

McCabe wondered if Josh Thorne's laptop might still be there. Or any pertinent papers. Without probable cause to believe a

THE GIRL ON THE BRIDGE 57

crime had been committed it might be tough to get a judge to sign off on a warrant to open the briefcase. Thorne had only been unaccounted for for eighteen hours or so. Not nearly enough to classify him as a missing person. Even so it seemed like it might be worth trying.

"Was there any indication anyone else had been in the room at any time?"

"Not that I could see. I suppose the room service person who brought him the drink might have gone in."

"Did you check to see if he'd been involved in an accident? Or maybe suffered a health emergency of some kind?" asked Maggie.

"Yes. Mark called both the hospitals in Portland from New York. Josh wasn't at either one and Roseanne said your people didn't know of any accidents."

McCabe raised a finger to signal a time-out. It wouldn't hurt to double-check. He called Kelly Haddon, who confirmed what Rachel Thorne had said.

"Okay. So nobody knows where Josh is," said Maggie. "Does your husband have any long term health issues, either mental or physical?"

Rachel Thorne looked puzzled. She shook her head. "No. Josh is fit and healthy. Why do you ask?"

"Only because in the absence of any other supporting evidence such as a ransom note or a body turning up, one or even two days is not considered a particularly long time for a healthy functioning adult to be out of touch. Are you sure your husband isn't just . . . how shall I put this delicately? Maybe taking a sabbatical from your marriage? Or from his job? Or maybe from both?"

McCabe watched a frown line form between Rachel's eyes.

"Yes, I'm sure. Josh and I love each other. We love being together. And while he wouldn't necessarily respond to calls or e-mails from me when he's away on business, there's no way he wouldn't show up for a critical meeting or not take calls from Joe Bonner or Floyd Brumfield or leave his briefcase in an empty hotel room. It just wouldn't happen."

"Besides," said Mark Christensen, "I'm afraid there *is* supporting evidence."

"What kind of supporting evidence?"

"Show them the e-mail, Rachel."

Rachel Thorne closed her eyes, took a deep breath and then opened them again. "I'm afraid this is more than a little embarrassing but I received an e-mail that came in this morning while Mark and I were in the process of boarding the flight. It was written by somebody named Norah Wilcox and sent from an e-mail address I didn't recognize. NWilcox@yahoo.com. And the subject line, *Support the Fight Against Rape*, wasn't something Josh ever would have sent out. Or even forwarded. I assumed it was spam. A plea for a donation. But instead of deleting it I opened it after we'd taken our seats on the plane. When I did, what I saw made it obvious Josh is in terrible trouble."

Chapter 7

RACHEL THORNE REACHED into her leather shoulder bag and extracted a mini iPad tablet.

She hesitated before sliding the tablet across the table.

Maggie and McCabe placed the tablet between them and studied the screen. It showed a photograph of a nude man lying on a bed, hands and feet tethered to an old-fashioned iron bed frame with what looked like clothesline. His legs were spread, genitals prominently displayed. His eyes and the upper part of his nose were covered with what looked like a necktie serving as a blindfold. Propped on his chest was a white cardboard sign with black hand lettering that read *Rapists Get What Rapists Deserve.*

The most curious part to McCabe was the blindfold. If the purpose of the picture was to destroy Thorne's reputation by accusing him of rape and posting it on the Internet, or even just sending it to his wife, why cover half his face with a makeshift blindfold? That made it a picture of an anonymous male nude bound to a bed. Again it didn't make much sense.

"This is your husband?" asked Maggie.

"Yes."

"You're sure?" asked McCabe, picking up the tablet and tapping it to enlarge the image. "With his eyes covered like this is there any possibility it might be someone else?"

"To anyone else, it might be. To me it's Josh. I know the shape of his head. His nose and mouth. I know his hair. And we've been married seven years. I know his body as well as I know my own. I don't need to see his eyes to be sure."

"Does he normally wear a wedding ring?"

"Yes. It's not there. I noticed that as well."

"Any other jewelry?"

"A gold Rolex. Which isn't there either. But that tie covering his eyes looks an awful lot like one I bought for him last year."

McCabe gave Rachel both his own and Maggie's e-mail addresses, handed her the tablet and asked her to forward the picture to them.

After she did, he held up one finger to signal a time-out and went back out to the squad room and found one of his senior detectives, Bill Bacon.

"Bill, I want you to try to track down somebody named Norah Wilcox. Norah with an *H* at the end. E-mail address NWilcox@ yahoo.com but that's probably a phony."

"You got anything else on her."

"Only that she's probably good-looking enough to interest a successful, young Wall Street banker named Joshua Thorne. So it's likely she'd be in her twenties or early thirties. Possibly lives in or around Portland. It's a good bet he picked her up in the bar at the Port Grill last night. There's no hard evidence but consider it a possibility that she killed this Thorne guy after snapping this picture."

McCabe held up the tablet. Bacon leaned in and looked. "Charming."

"At this point it's all we've got. I'll let you know when there's more but, in the meantime, start looking."

"Will do. Anything else?"

"Yes. Check ViCAP and see if you can find any accusations of rape or complaints of sexual assault against this Thorne guy. Thorne with an *E* on the end."

McCabe returned to the interview room in time to hear Maggie ask Rachel Thorne, "I'm sorry to have to ask, Rachel, but is your husband a rapist?"

There was a look, a pause, a brief fluttering of long dark eyelashes. "No. No. He's not."

To McCabe, both Rachel Thorne's tone and physical manner seemed appropriately anxious for someone whose husband had disappeared and is being accused of serious sexual crimes.

Maggie continued. "To your knowledge has he ever been accused of rape?"

This time she responded more quickly. "No. Except for that sign on his chest."

"Has he ever forced himself on you?"

"Would that be considered rape?"

"Yes. Spousal rape is a crime."

"The answer is no," she said. "Josh can be sexually aggressive. I sometimes call him Mr. Testosterone. But . . ." She paused again. "But I'm usually okay with that. And if I tell him I don't want to, he usually backs off."

"Not always?"

"Not always. But I'd never call it rape."

"Have you ever known him to be unfaithful? For example, when he's away on a business trip?"

McCabe found himself wondering how far a wife might go to protect a cheating or even a rapist husband's reputation. How far she'd go to deny to herself or to others what she might suspect or perhaps even knew to be true. After all, McCabe couldn't count the number of times he tried to deny what he knew to be the truth about his own ex-wife's sexual indiscretions. Denied them supposedly for the sake of their daughter, Casey, who was then only eight years old. Kept denying right up until the day one of Sandy's lovers, one with a lot of money and no current spouse, asked her to marry him.

"I urge you to be honest about this," Maggie told Rachel. "It could be important in finding your husband. Finding out what might have happened to him."

"Josh isn't a rapist," said Rachel.

"You told us he could be sexually aggressive," said Maggie.

"I also said he takes no for an answer."

"With you he does," said Maggie. "But maybe not with other women. Say, for example, a woman he picked up last night in the bar at the Port Grill. And let's also say this woman—we'll call her Norah Wilcox—showed enough interest in Josh to invite him back to her place and when they get there maybe Josh is a little too quick on the draw and she tells him no. But Josh decides not to take no for an answer."

Rachel sat silently staring at Maggie and McCabe, elbows on the table, hands pressed together under her chin almost as if she were praying. Or maybe just thinking how much she wanted to tell them. For well over a minute the loudest sound in the room was Maggie's plastic pen tapping against the wood.

"Mark," Rachel finally said, turning to her brother, "please wait for me outside. I appreciate your help, but I want to keep the rest of this conversation between me and the detectives."

"I'm not sure that's a good idea, Rache," said Christensen. "In fact, I'm sure it isn't."

"Please, Mark. I'm sure it is," Rachel responded.

"Rachel . . ."

"Mark, please."

The brother nodded reluctantly and rose. "Okay. Your call."

"You can wait for your sister in the conference room," said McCabe. "Or if you'd rather there's a coffee shop right up the street. Corner of Exchange."

"Okay. I'll head up that way."

"Okay, but before you go, please ask Detective Bacon, the tall thin guy sitting out at the first desk there, to take a set of your fingerprints and a DNA swab."

Christensen nodded. "Okay. Fine. Rachel, call me if you need me to come back."

Rachel waited until her brother shut the door before turning back.

Chapter 8

"YOU ASKED IF I thought Josh might have picked up another woman. Given this picture, it's obvious I have to stop lying both to myself and to others about the fact that my husband isn't always faithful. I've suspected it for a long time and he's even admitted to what he calls straying once or twice. I'm sure that's pretty common among husbands who travel a lot for business and I've decided I can live with it. But rape? We've been married seven years. I know Josh better than anyone else and, even with his fooling around, I find rape hard to believe."

"If he's never raped anyone," asked McCabe, "what do you suppose motivated this Norah Wilcox, or whatever her real name might be, to tie him to the bed and put that sign on his chest? And cap it off by sending you this picture?"

"I don't know . . . Maybe I'm wrong . . . Maybe he's not the man I thought he was. Jesus Christ, this is awful." She lowered her head and put her hands over her face.

"Has Josh ever hit you?" McCabe asked when she finally looked up, breathing deeply, eyes moist and red.

"No."

He waited, hoping silence would prod Rachel into saying more. After a minute it did.

"Well, actually, yes. Only one time."

"With his fist?"

"No. He slapped me. With his open hand."

"Why did he slap you?"

"I slapped him first. We were having an argument."

"About what?"

Rachel's brown eyes studied McCabe in a way that suggested she was still debating the wisdom of providing a pair of strange cops even more intimate details of her marriage.

"About sex," she finally said. "It was last September. I teach at a private girls' school in Manhattan and I'd just gotten home hot and tired from a tough day and a long smelly subway ride. I still had a bunch of papers to grade before I could quit. When I got home Josh had already had a couple of drinks."

"Was he drunk?"

"A little. He wanted to . . . to have sex. I said no. I had work to do and I didn't feel like it anyway. I tried to leave the room. He grabbed me, pushed me up against the wall and said, as my husband, he could fuck me any damned time he wanted."

"Are those the words he used?" asked Maggie.

"Yes. Pretty much verbatim. No. Exactly verbatim. I called him an asshole—again verbatim—and told him to back off. He didn't. Just started fondling my breasts and trying to pull my clothes off. I got angry and I slapped him. He slapped me back, hard enough to bloody my nose. Might have landed me on the floor if I wasn't propped up against a wall. I thought he was going to haul me into the bedroom, pull my clothes off and—I may as well use the word—fuck me. It certainly wouldn't have been making love. Instead he pushed me away and slammed out of the apartment. He got home about two in the morning smelling of booze. And of another woman. He obviously found somebody more willing than his wife."

"Is there anything else about Josh's behavior you haven't told us we should know about?"

Rachel sighed. "Detective, with all his faults, and I'm the first to admit there are many, I love my husband. He's smart, funny and often very generous. Yes, he sometimes goes after other women. Even so, I don't want our marriage to explode." Rachel was weeping openly now, her tears, stained black by mascara, sliding down her cheeks.

McCabe repeated the question. "Is there anything else about Josh's behavior we should know about?"

"Yes." Rachel caught her breath. "Maybe this has something to do with that sign on his chest. When Josh was in college, a young woman, a freshman, accused Josh and some of his fraternity brothers—all members of the football team—of drugging her with roofies, rohypnol, at a fraternity party, then dragging her upstairs to a bedroom and taking turns raping her."

"Rachel, you told us not ten minutes ago that Josh had never been accused of rape," said Maggie, an angry edge to her voice, "and that you just couldn't see him raping anyone. Now you're telling us he took part in some gang-rape in college?"

"He swore it wasn't rape. I believed him. I still believe him."

"Well, you'd better give us the details."

"It's just these things are incredibly hard to talk about to a couple of cops I met less than an hour ago. And I guess I don't want some ancient accusation to become, I don't know, part of the public record. Part of—" Rachel tilted her head, indicating the camera hidden in the light fixture "—your video up there. I don't want my husband being charged with sexual assault by some bimbo for something that supposedly happened twelve years ago."

"You'd better tell us about it, Rachel."

Another brief silence. Another deep breath. "I have a hard time dealing with this let alone talking about it. But what I was told was that Josh and five of his fraternity brothers supposedly had sex with this girl one after the other. Josh swore the girl was both slutty and drunk and that the sex was consensual. That no roofies or other drugs were involved."

"What college? What fraternity? What year?" asked Maggie.

"Holden College. Alpha Chi Delta. Happened in the fall of 2001. About a month after 9/11."

"Did he tell you the girl's name?"

"No. I'm not sure he even knew it. He just said she had sex with him and five other guys. But he swore the sex was consensual. She was asking for it and egging them on."

"And you believed him?"

"Yes."

"Why?"

"I guess partly because no charges were ever filed. Maybe even more because I don't see Josh as a rapist. If Josh wants sex there's no reason he'd ever have to resort to rape. Not now. Not back then either. He's a very good-looking guy. Very charming. Intelligent. Successful. He knows I hate it when other women come on to him, but it happens all the time. He can have all the sex he wants whenever he wants it."

Maggie didn't bother getting into the reasons for rape. How for some men, usually insecure men, it was more about demonstrating power and domination. For others it reflected a deep, possibly hidden misogyny. But most commonly, at least in the rapes Maggie had investigated, when it was about sex, it usually came down to a simple sociopathic indifference on the part of the rapist to the pain and trauma suffered by the victims. The guy wanted sex and saw an opportunity so he took it. In those cases the rape meant no more to the rapist than jerking off. Except for him it was more fun. "What else can you tell us about this rape?"

"Alleged rape."

"Okay, alleged rape."

"Not a lot. Like I said I only learned about it a few months ago."

McCabe squinted at her. "How did you learn about it?"

"By accident. I overheard Josh talking on the phone with another man who was involved. Apparently the girl who was supposedly raped that night recently committed suicide and the supposed rape was the cause of her killing herself. I heard Josh say to the other guy, *'I'm sorry she's dead but you can't blame yourself for that. And I'm sure as hell not blaming myself. What happened happened. The suicide wasn't our fault. She killed herself. We didn't.'*"

"Did you know who or what he was talking about?"

"No. Not at the time. When he got off the phone I asked him what was going on. He tried brushing it off. Telling me it was nothing important. Just a business deal that wasn't going right. But I told him I heard him talking about somebody committing suicide as a result of a rape. I heard him say he wasn't blaming himself. I told him he needed to tell me what it was all about. He tried stonewalling, but I kept at it until he had enough of my haranguing.

"He finally said, 'Okay, you really want to know?' I said, 'Yes, I really want to know.' Hell, I *needed* to know. He went to the liquor cabinet, made himself a strong drink and asked me if I wanted one. I said no. He sat down with the drink and told me about the rape allegations. He said he and some of his fraternity brothers did have sex with this girl but it was totally consensual. He said he could prove it. I asked him how. He said he made a recording of this girl saying yes, that she wanted them to fuck her."

"A recording?" asked McCabe.

Rachel shrugged. "Yes."

"Why did he make this recording?"

"I guess to prove the sex was consensual."

"Audio or video?"

"I'm pretty sure there was no video. Kids weren't posting stuff like that to the Internet in those days."

"Did you ever hear this recording?"

"No. I didn't want to. But Josh swore you could definitely hear this girl's voice shouting, 'Yes. Yes. Please fuck me.' Stuff like that."

"Did it ever occur to you," asked Maggie, "that Josh or maybe one of the other guys forced this girl to say that stuff, recording it to cover their asses? Claim consent if she ever tried charging them with rape?"

"Oh God, I don't know. How do you force somebody to say stuff like that?"

"Does Josh still have it?"

"I don't know. He might have it somewhere in our apartment. Or maybe in his safe deposit box."

"Did he tell you anything else about the incident?" asked McCabe.

"He said the girl was drunk and wanted to take on everybody. She was lying there naked inviting guys, as Josh put it, to climb aboard one after the other."

"Do you know if this girl was conscious when all these guys were *climbing aboard*?" asked Maggie.

Rachel looked momentarily puzzled. "She must have been if she was inviting them to do it."

"Did Josh seem upset by what he was telling you?" asked Maggie.

"More like angry."

"At you?"

"Yes. For insisting that he tell me the story. But he seemed much more relaxed after he finished. Maybe the booze relaxed him. Or maybe just telling it and getting it out of his system."

"What happened after the rape?"

"Alleged rape."

"Alleged rape."

"Nothing. Not for four months. Josh said he even asked the girl out on a date but she told him no."

"Josh told you this?"

"Yes. Said he thought she didn't want to go out with him because she was probably ashamed of what she had done that night."

"What happened after four months?"

"Out of the blue, winter semester, this girl goes to the dean of students and accuses this whole bunch of guys of gang-raping her that night. Said she only knew two of their names. Josh and Charlie Loughlin."

"Keep going."

"Josh and Charlie were called in by the dean and questioned by him and a group of other college administrators. They both insisted the sex was consensual and Josh played the recording to prove it. He told the dean that four other guys who hadn't been named would corroborate their story if any action was taken.

THE GIRL ON THE BRIDGE   71

There were no other witnesses. No videos. No anything except
the audio recording and all the guys swearing that the girl had
been asking for it. According to Josh, the college administrators
strongly advised the girl not to pursue rape charges with the police. Told her there was no proof. Just was a case of 'he said, she
said.' Except there were six *he saids* and only one *she said* and, in
fact, she hadn't said a word until four months after it supposedly
happened. A week or so later the girl dropped out of school. Josh
never heard anything more about it until he got the call from
Charlie."

"Did he tell you the victim's name?"

"No."

"Did he tell you anything else about the suicide?"

"Just that Charlie Loughlin told him the girl had killed herself
by jumping off a railroad bridge up in New Hampshire. Josh said
he told Loughlin the suicide just proved what he thought at the
time . . . that she was mentally unbalanced."

"Have you ever met this Charlie Loughlin?" asked McCabe.

"Once at a college reunion. And a couple of times for dinner
when he came down to New York on business."

"Do you know where he lives?"

"Connecticut somewhere. West Hartford, I think. He's in the
insurance business around there."

"Have you ever met any of the others who were supposedly
involved in the rape?"

"I don't think so."

"How did Loughlin hear about the suicide?"

Rachel shrugged and shook her head. "I don't know. Maybe he
read about it in the papers and recognized the girl's name."

"But he did tell Josh how this girl killed herself?"

"Yes. She jumped off a bridge into a river. I don't know if it was the fall that killed her or if she drowned."

"You don't know her name?"

"No."

"But Charlie and Josh must have known it?"

"I guess so. If Charlie saw it in a newspaper he must have recognized her name."

"When did this phone call take place?" asked McCabe.

"I already told you. A few months ago."

"Can you be more specific than that?"

Rachel leaned her head back and closed her eyes. "It must have been right after the holidays. Our tree was still up and school hadn't started yet. So I'd say late December or maybe the first few days in January. It was probably a Saturday or Sunday afternoon since Josh was home and it was still light out."

McCabe said he'd be right back. Went out to the squad room and found Connie Davenport, Crimes Against People's newest detective. Told her to drop whatever she was doing and see what she could find out about a roughly thirty-year-old woman committing suicide by jumping off a railroad bridge in New Hampshire. No, he told Davenport, he didn't have the victim's name. The only other information he had was that it had probably happened around Christmas and that she had attended Holden College.

McCabe returned to the interview room. Rachel was pointing to the photo of her husband. "You two keep talking about rape because of the sign on his chest, but does that look like a man who just raped somebody? Looks to me more like it was the other way around."

McCabe had to admit Rachel had something there.

"Aside from anything else, Josh is big and strong. Six foot three.

Two hundred and ten pounds. How would some woman—Christ, any woman—get the better of him? Get him tied up like this?"

McCabe could catalog dozens of ways smaller women could incapacitate bigger, stronger men. From holding a gun on them, to slipping them drugs, to waiting until they'd passed out from booze, to one memorable instance back in McCabe's NYPD days when a rejected Park Avenue matron got even with her cheating husband by whacking him over the head with a rare Ming Dynasty vase. The husband survived the resulting skull fracture, but the insurance company refused to pay the wife's sixty thousand dollar claim for the broken vase because they said the damage had been intentional. The wife insisted she'd never intended to damage the vase. Just the cheating bastard who was her soon-to-be ex-husband.

"How would it be possible for any woman to do that?" Rachel persisted.

"I don't know," McCabe responded. "Is Josh into bondage?"

Rachel stared at him curiously. "Bondage? You mean like whips and chains?"

"No. More like being blindfolded and tied up. Like in the picture."

"God, no. That's what's so weird about this. He hates anything even slightly kinky. That's the last thing he'd want to do. He's a Republican, for Christ's sake."

McCabe swallowed a strong desire to laugh and instead went back to trying to construct a likely scenario. What seemed certain was that Joshua Thorne met a woman last night whose name may or may not have been Norah Wilcox. They ended up going somewhere. Maybe her house or apartment. Maybe a short term rental. Maybe even a cheap motel. One unanswered question was why?

The Regency was a luxury hotel just a short walk from the Port Grill and Thorne already had a room. But instead of going there, he . . . they . . . went to a place where Thorne ended up tied down on a bare mattress that looked like it had been dragged in from a homeless shelter.

The first question was where. The second was what happened when they got there? Given the sign on Thorne's chest, the obvious answer was he raped the woman he picked up and taking and sending the photo to Rachel was her revenge for what he had done. A second possibility was that it was revenge for the college rape that recently resulted in the victim's suicide. A third was that Thorne was a habitual rapist and some past victim was getting back at him.

So how'd it happen? The woman does whatever she does to render Thorne unconscious, though probably not by whacking him on the head with a Ming Dynasty vase. Once he's out she ties him down on the filthy mattress, puts the sign on his chest, takes his picture and sends it to his wife.

How does she get Rachel's name and e-mail address? From Thorne's smartphone? That seemed reasonable. No pass code necessary. These days all you do is press the owner's thumb against the phone and it opens right up. Okay, so she e-mails the picture. Then what? Does she untie him and take off into the night? Or possibly into the morning?

No, McCabe decided, that didn't make sense. Josh would have gotten up, gotten dressed and gone to his meeting. Or at least called his clients when he woke up to explain why he missed it. Unless he was still unconscious, which seemed unlikely since it was already nearly three in the afternoon.

Okay. Scenario two. Norah doesn't free him from the ropes.

Just leaves him tied up and takes off. What would he do? Yell and scream till somebody hears him and rescues him. Unless she put some duct tape over his mouth to shut him up.

Scenario three was, in McCabe's view, the most likely one. That the reason nobody heard Joshua Thorne screaming and yelling was because he was already dead and everybody knows dead men have a hard time raising a ruckus.

McCabe got up. "Nature calls," he said. "Be back in a minute."

Chapter 9

McCabe headed across the floor to the small conference room. Once inside he flipped on a monitor. Rachel Thorne's face filled the screen. He muted the audio and called Dispatch.

"How can I help you, Sergeant?"

"Any excessive noise complaints come in last night?" he asked. "Somebody yelling and shouting in a residential neighborhood in the middle of the night?"

"Hold on, I'll check."

A minute later Kelly Haddon was back. "Yes. There was one," she said, "a woman named Joan O'Malley called 911 at 2:14 A.M. Complained about some guy swearing a lot and screaming about wanting to kill someone. She thought the noise was coming from the house next door and that bothered her because the owners don't live there anymore and she thought maybe some homeless drunks had broken in and gone off the deep end."

"Address?"

"O'Malley lives at 337 Hartley Street. About halfway between Forest and Stevens. Next door is 339. Both houses back up onto

Baxter Woods. The far side of 339 is also open to the woods."
Baxter Woods was a small patch of undeveloped parkland on the
north side of the city. Named after Percival Proctor Baxter, a former mayor of Portland and governor of Maine.

"Who investigated the complaint?" asked McCabe.

"One of our rookies. Cathy Willetts."

McCabe had never met Willetts but he'd heard her name before. One of his younger detectives, Brian Cleary, told him she
was a good-looking twenty-something just a couple of months
out of the Academy. Brian had asked McCabe if he thought it was
smart for him to date another cop. He sure as hell was interested.
McCabe told Brian it probably wasn't a good idea. McCabe didn't
mention how he and Maggie had resisted similar temptation right
after McCabe broke up with his old girlfriend Kyra.

McCabe thanked Kelly for the information and called Willetts's boss, Sergeant Walt Ghent.

"The one and only Michael McCabe. To what do I owe the
honor?"

"Hiya, Walt. I need some input."

"Shoot."

"One of your people checked out an excessive noise complaint
on Hartley Street last night?"

"That's right. Rookie named Willetts."

"This rookie know what she's doing?"

"Yeah, she does. Gonna be a good cop, I think. I'm looking at
her incident report now."

"Okay, tell me about it."

"Not all that much to tell. Everything was quiet by the time
Willetts got there. She knocked on this O'Malley's woman's door.
Takes her a while to answer and when she does O'Malley starts

whining about how nobody, including the cops, ever let her get a decent night's sleep. Willetts apologized and said she was just responding to O'Malley's own complaint. O'Malley said to forget about it. Everything had quieted down. Willetts asked her if she really thought the noise was coming from the house next door and O'Malley admitted she wasn't sure. It might have been some kids raising a ruckus on the street. Or maybe some druggies doing their thing in Baxter Woods. O'Malley's thank-you took the form of telling Willetts, 'I don't know what takes you people so long to get here.'"

"Did it take long?"

"Nah. Willetts was there six minutes from the time Dispatch got the call. Not instant but not bad. Anyway, after getting the basics from O'Malley, Willetts went next door and rang the bell on 339. When nobody answered she went around back. Shined her light through the windows. The place was dark and quiet. No homeless guy. No druggies. No TV or radio left on. No car in the driveway. No nothing. Then, just to be thorough, she checked out the woods alongside and behind the house to see if any homeless people might be winter camping out there and maybe downing too much coffee brandy or whatever the hell they're drinking or shooting up these days. Maybe getting into a noisy scuffle while they're in the process."

"But she didn't see or hear anyone?"

"Nope."

"Okay. Thanks, Walt."

"YOU HAVE OTHER pictures of Josh on this tablet?" Maggie was asking Rachel when McCabe walked back in. He didn't sit. Just stood by the door listening.

"Yes, of course," said Rachel.

"Good. We'll need one that clearly shows Josh's face so we can distribute it and start a search."

Rachel took the tablet, flipped through a bunch of photos, settling on one of a good-looking guy wearing jeans and a sweater smiling at the camera from a park bench. Trees with red and gold leaves filled the background. "I took this last fall in Prospect Park in Brooklyn. It's a good likeness."

"Okay. We'll have to borrow your tablet and cell phone for a while to get an investigation under way. What's your pass code?"

" It's 1884. That's the year Charlton, the school I work for, was founded."

"The same for both of them?"

"Yes."

McCabe caught Maggie's eye and signaled with a tilt of his head that he wanted to talk to her.

"Okay," said Maggie, "there are some things Sergeant McCabe and I have to discuss right away if we're going to find Josh. In the meantime, please wait here for us. We'll need to ask you some further questions. It could be a while so I apologize but please don't go anywhere."

WALKING BACK TO the conference room McCabe filled Maggie in on Mrs. O'Malley's noise complaint.

"Could be unconnected."

"Maybe. Still worth a look-see."

They went in and closed the door. On the monitor Rachel Thorne's face still filled the screen.

"You think she's lying?" asked McCabe. He trusted Maggie's instincts on such things even more than his own.

"Lying about what?"

"The college rape."

"Maybe. What I do think she's doing is trying to protect her husband or maybe just her marriage to a guy who may screw around but also brings in the big bucks." Maggie studied Rachel's more or less expressionless face on the screen. "And who knows? Maybe she messes around as well. The proverbial open marriage. Either way, she looks to me like a woman who enjoys spending Josh's seven-figure bonus money. Anyway, if she is a liar she's a good one."

"She's got plenty of motivation," said McCabe. "If Josh gets outed as a rapist, from college days or otherwise, the money flow could dry up, and if rape can be proven, it might even land him in jail."

"I don't see how. Even assuming the college rape *was* rape, it happened twelve years ago. The statute of limitations on sexual assault is eight."

"In Maine it is. But Holden College is in New York State. No time limit on prosecuting rape in New York."

"Okay. Good for New York. But I still don't see how you'd prosecute. The victim didn't press charges back then and since she's currently dead she can't do it now."

"No. She can't. And if Norah tried to press charges she could be charged with kidnapping even if Thorne did rape her. I have Bill Bacon tracking down women named Norah Wilcox and Davenport checking for recent suicides by women who attended Holden College in 2001. In the meantime, why don't you see what Starbucks can get us on the Wilcox e-mail and photo."

Maggie nodded.

"Then maybe you could finish up with Rachel and then cut her loose."

"And meanwhile you're just going to stand there gazing at the beautiful but distraught wife?"

"Yeah. I wanna see how she acts when there's no one else in the room."

"She knows there's a camera focused on her."

McCabe shrugged. "People sometimes forget they're on camera."

"Maybe some people do. But not this one."

MAGGIE HEADED TO her desk where she e-mailed the Prospect Park photo of Thorne both to her own computer and to Dispatch with a note asking Kelly to send out an extended ATL—Attempt to Locate—for Joshua Thorne. Within ten minutes every cop in Maine, New Hampshire and eastern Massachusetts would be on the lookout for anyone resembling Josh. Within an hour they'd all have the Prospect Park photo taped to their dashboards.

She next took Rachel's iPhone and iPad downstairs to Starbucks, the Portland PD's resident computer geek. Whoever had shot the bondage picture of Thorne might not have been computer savvy enough to remove the EXIF code and other identifying metadata from the photograph. If that was the case Starbucks might be able to identify whatever camera or smartphone the picture had been taken with. And even if it was Josh's as she suspected, if it still contained its SIM card, they'd be able to pinpoint its location and, with any luck, Josh's location at the same time.

WHILE MCCABE STOOD watching Rachel Thorne, he called his boss, Lieutenant Bill Fortier. He knew Bill would be in the middle of his weekly status meeting with Police Chief Tom Shockley but figured by getting them together he could kill two birds with one stone. Fortier answered on the first ring. No greeting. Just an unusually brusque, "What's up, McCabe?" Something was pissing Fortier off.

"Missing person," said McCabe. "Possible kidnapping. Possible homicide."

"New York banker by the name of Joshua Thorne?"

"Yeah. How'd you know?"

"His boss just stormed out of the chief's office."

"Guy named Brumfield?"

"Yeah. Floyd Brumfield. Obnoxious New York type. You know, Master of the Universe and all that bullshit? He told us, and I quote, we damned well better pull our fingers out of our butts and find his boy Thorne or there'd be hell to pay."

"Nice. Did he happen to mention what kind of hell?"

"FBI hell. He said Deputy Director Jack Ellerbey is a good friend of his from East Hampton, and if we didn't find Thorne fast, Ellerbey's people would move in and take over."

"Think he has that kind of pull?"

"I have no idea. But when Brumfield stormed out, Shockley trotted after him like an eager poodle. I'm still sitting in the chief's empty office so why don't you just fill me in on what you know."

McCabe provided Fortier with a shorthand version of the interview with Rachel Thorne and her brother. He added that, at the moment, Maggie and Starbucks were trying to digitally locate Joshua Thorne's iPhone.

Fortier asked a few questions but not many before responding. "Okay, I got it. You know what you're doing. Forget Brumfield and his threats. Just keep me posted on any developments. Major or minor."

"I'm getting my people together at three-thirty. Small conference room. You may as well sit in."

"Will do."

The door opened. "How's the distraught wife doing? Make any on-camera confessions?" asked Maggie.

"Cool as a cucumber. Closed her eyes for a while. Like she was meditating. Or praying. I don't know. Got up a couple of times to stretch and walk back and forth. Opened the door once and looked up and down the hall."

"What's your gut on what happened to Thorne?"

"My gut says he's probably dead."

Maggie nodded. "Yeah. Mine too."

"You know what keeps running through my mind?" asked McCabe. "Remember that opening scene from *Basic Instinct*? The one where Sharon Stone ties the guy to the bed with silk scarves and then plunges an ice pick into his throat and about eighteen other places right in the middle of screwing him."

"Coitus interruptus?"

"Yeah. Interruptus in the worst possible way."

"Okay, so we both think Josh is dead," said Maggie, "and you think we're looking for Sharon Stone."

McCabe laughed. "Yeah. As played by someone named Norah Wilcox."

"Norah's motive being revenge for a rape?"

"She said so herself. Rapists get what rapists deserve."

"And rapists deserve to be killed?"

"It just occurred to me. If someone murdered Joshua Thorne for his role in the Holden College rape," said McCabe, "we could have another problem."

"Like what?"

"Like the other guys who were accused of that rape. Charlie Loughlin and the other four who supposedly *climbed aboard* after them. If this is revenge for what happened at Alpha Chi Delta that night there may ultimately be six victims."

"Joshua Thorne being the first?"

"Or, who knows, maybe the last."

Chapter 10

MAGGIE OPENED THE door to the interview room and Rachel Thorne looked up.

"I thought you'd forgotten about me."

"I'm sorry, Rachel, but there were a few things we had to do to kick the search for Josh into high gear."

"Where's Sergeant McCabe?"

"He's busy at the moment."

"I see." Rachel chewed on that for a moment. "Does that mean I'm being relegated to the second string?"

The insult seemed calculated. Maggie decided to let it pass. "Not at all," she said sweetly. "McCabe and I are partners. We work together. We're both trying to find your husband."

"Of course. I'm sorry I said that. I'm just a little upset. Actually, a lot upset. Can I go now?"

"In a little while. I need to ask you a few more questions first."

"Can't that wait?"

"No. I'm sorry, but it's important we move on something like this as fast as we can."

A long sigh. "Okay. What do you want to know?"

"Can you tell me where you were last night while Josh was here in Portland?"

Rachel frowned. The question didn't please her. "How is that pertinent?"

"Standard police procedure. Don't take it personally."

"I take it very personally."

"Fine. Whatever. Where were you?"

"Having dinner with a friend at a Chinese restaurant in Brooklyn called Fung Tao. Then we went to the movies."

"What did you see?"

"Something called *Love Times Two*, which was a complete waste of time."

"Oh yeah? I heard it was pretty good."

"Don't bother. After the movie I took a cab home. I got back to my apartment a little after eleven."

"Can you give me your friend's name and phone number?"

"Oh, come on. You couldn't possibly think I had anything to do with Josh's disappearance so why do you need to bother my friend?"

"Please just cooperate."

"Where's McCabe? I want to talk to him."

"He's not available. Now would you please just give me your friend's name and number?"

Another sigh. "Annie Jessup. She lives in Manhattan. You can find her number under contacts in my iPhone."

"Thank you."

"Can I go now?"

"Just a few more questions. How long have you and Josh been married?"

"I think I already told you."

"I don't think so."

"Seven years. We met at Columbia. He was getting his MBA at the Business School. I was getting my master's at Teachers College. We moved in together a couple of months later. Got married the following year."

"And you're teaching now?"

"Yes. At a small private girls' school in Manhattan."

"What school would that be?"

"I already told you that as well. The Charlton School."

"You and Josh have any children?"

"Not yet."

"You want them?"

"I don't see what that has to do . . ."

"Please. Just try to answer the questions."

"Okay. Fine. Yes, we've agreed on at least one and maybe a couple. We've been trying, but so far it hasn't happened."

"How does Josh feel about having kids?"

"He wants them too. He played football in college. Quarterback. He sometimes talks about someday taking his son to Prospect Park and teaching him the finer points of throwing a forward pass. He looks happy when he talks about stuff like that. I think being a father might help straighten out some of the other issues going on with him."

"Like the cheating?"

"Yes, that. Also the intense focus on making money."

"Do you and Josh have a prenup?"

"No. We were both broke when we got married. It didn't seem pertinent."

"I assume your husband carries life insurance."

"Of course. Two policies. One we bought. And one the company provides as part of Josh's comp package."

"How much."

"A million dollars for the one we bought. Five million for the company policy."

"Six million bucks. That's a lot of money. And you're the beneficiary of both policies?"

"Yes. But you couldn't possibly be suggesting . . ."

"And who's the secondary in case you both die at the same time?"

"You're scaring me, Detective."

"I'm sorry. I don't mean to. But it is background information we need to know. Six million dollars is a lot of money."

"Josh's mother gets the money if we both die. His father's already dead."

"Your parents don't get anything?"

"No. Josh bought the policy and paid for it. And my parents are well-off. Not rich, but certainly better off than his mom. Josh's dad died a couple of years ago. He was broke and then some."

"Debts?"

"Not anymore. Josh paid them off. He also sends his mother money every month to supplement her Social Security survivor benefits, which is all she has on her own."

"How much?"

"Three thousand dollars. Enough to allow her to live a little more comfortably."

"And how do you feel about his giving her that much money?"

"We have so much. I think it's the right thing to do."

"Where does his mother live?"

"South Carolina. Just outside of Greensville. Same house Josh grew up in. I'd just as soon you didn't say anything about this to her. She's not in good health and bad news like this could kill her."

"I'm sorry, Rachel. Unless Josh turns up in the next thirty-six hours, he officially becomes a missing person and we'll have to go public."

"I see. Any more questions?"

"Yes. You said a man named Charlie Loughlin called Josh about the suicide of the girl who was raped . . ."

"Who claimed she was raped."

"What do you know about Charlie Loughlin?"

"Charlie's one of Josh's old fraternity brothers and an ex-teammate. I wouldn't call them best friends, but they talk occasionally."

"One last thing. Does your husband carry a company cell phone, a personal cell phone or both?"

"He uses his own. The number's 646-555-7824."

"What's his pass code?"

"I have no idea. I never use his phone. I never asked him."

"Fine. We'll need to know right away if you hear from Josh or from anyone else claiming to know where he is. Especially if you get a ransom demand. Will it be possible for you to stay in Portland while this is going on?"

"I'm not going anywhere. Not until I know where Josh is. What about my brother?"

"He can head back to New York. We'll call him there if we need him. In the meantime, you and I are going downstairs to get a cheek swab and a set of your fingerprints."

"Anything else?"

"Yes. We'll need to keep your phone and tablet for a while."

"Is that necessary? I can't get by without a phone. I need to make calls."

"Get yourself a prepaid burner phone. You can find them in any drugstore. When you've got it call me and let me have the number. Also call me if anything else occurs to you. Here's my card. My cell number's on it."

"Shouldn't I call McCabe?"

"You can call me."

Once again Rachel didn't look pleased. Maybe she just preferred dealing with the boss. Or, more likely, dealing with good-looking men. *Well, Cutie Pie,* Maggie thought to herself as she ushered Rachel out the door, *tough shit.*

Chapter 11

McCabe was the last to arrive for the meeting. When he got there all eight of the detectives in his Crimes Against People unit were seated around the conference room table along with Fortier and the department's senior evidence tech, Bill Jacoby.

Maggie had also invited Aden Yusuf Hassan, aka Starbucks, to attend. A young Somali IT whiz, Starbucks had been serving as the PPD's resident computer geek for nearly eight years. The nickname Starbucks was based more on his addiction to endless cups of strong black coffee than for any resemblance to the Melville character.

As he walked toward the TV monitor McCabe could feel a palpable sense of energy in the room. Everyone was itching for a little action after a winter that had been unusually quiet. The only thing that had broken the monotony of cold empty days was the number of bodies discovered dead from overdosing on heroin. And finding ODs was more depressing than chasing down bad guys. With spring on its way the denizens of the fourth floor of 109 were itching for a little action, which meant they'd dive into the search for Joshua Thorne with enthusiasm.

McCabe slid the interview video into the box and pressed Play. Images of Rachel Thorne and her brother filled the screen.

"Good-looking babe," remarked Brian Cleary. "What's she done?"

McCabe hit Pause. The image froze. "As far as we know, nothing," he said. "The woman's name is Rachel Thorne. The guy next to her is her brother who, for better or for worse, is an attorney from New York. They came in this afternoon because Rachel's husband, a rich Wall Street banker named Joshua Thorne, went missing last night. Our job is finding him." McCabe pressed Play and took an empty chair in the corner to watch.

When the interview had played through, McCabe went back and played it again. Everyone in the room including the squad's two resident wise guys, Cleary and Sturgis, watched in silence both times. Just before the second run-through finished, McCabe hit Pause. The image of Rachel Thorne remained on the screen, mouth half open, frozen in midsentence, an expression of concern on her face.

Maggie grabbed an armful of photos she'd printed and went around the table handing everyone two. The first showed Josh blindfolded and tied to the bed. The other was the Prospect Park ID picture. "These are the pictures of Joshua Thorne that his wife showed us," she said. "The bondage shot was presumably taken by his captor and e-mailed to his wife."

"Pretty nasty," said Bill Fortier as he studied the picture. "My guess is 'what rapists deserve' is death. I've got a strong feeling we could be dealing with a murder case."

"We agree," said McCabe. "But we can't be sure it isn't just an attempt to publically humiliate Thorne. Not till we find his body."

"I agree," said Tom Tasco. "*What Rapists Deserve* may be nothing more than public exposure on TV and the Internet. Anybody post this picture online yet?"

"I've been looking," said Starbucks. "So far I haven't found it."

"How about any others like it?" asked Tasco.

"What do you mean?" asked McCabe.

"Well, if the goal is humiliating Joshua Thorne, covering part of his face with a blindfold doesn't make sense. Makes him just an anonymous naked guy."

"Okay. I agree with that."

"But who says this is the only picture that was taken?" Tasco continued. "Maybe the person, and I think it was probably a woman, who took this shot also took a bunch of others. Some without the blindfold on. Maybe a video as well. This one could just be a warning of more to come later. We have no way of knowing."

"They're not online yet," said Starbucks. "I've checked every search engine I know using Thorne's name, plus the *Rapists Get What Rapists Deserve* line. I also searched using Brumfield Harris and Trident Development as search terms. So far, nothing."

"What if it's a blackmail scheme?" asked Eddie Frazier. "Give us a million dollars or we'll post these pictures with your unblindfolded face, your name and maybe damning details proving some rape you committed."

"There are no money demands yet," said Maggie.

"Probably wouldn't be done as ransom," said Frazier. "Somebody collecting a bag of ransom money is way too easy to catch.

Better to have Rachel or maybe Brumfield Harris transfer money out of Thorne's account into an anonymous foreign account. When the transfer's complete delete the photos and let the guy go."

"Interesting idea," said McCabe. "Eddie, why don't you and Tom follow up on that? Check out where Thorne keeps his money. Maybe his wife knows. Maybe his assistant, Roseanne Mezzina, knows. Also talk with Floyd Brumfield. Ask him to alert us if any requests like that come in."

"Won't that just make Brumfield call in his FBI contacts sooner?" asked Fortier.

"We can't worry about that, Bill," said McCabe. "We gotta just keep doing our jobs as best we can. If the Feds come in, the Feds come in."

Fortier nodded. "Okay. You're right. We know anything else?"

"Yeah," said Maggie. "The photograph was taken and the e-mail sent with Joshua Thorne's smartphone. The metadata was left in place and Starbucks confirmed the source. We haven't been able to locate the phone yet. The photographer may have taken the SIM card out. Or it could be at the bottom of the ocean."

"One of the things that's interesting about all this," said Cleary, "is that this Norah Wilcox signed the e-mail, identifying herself to Rachel Thorne and, by extension, to us."

"Any idea why she'd want to do that?" asked Fortier.

"Only reason I can think of is misdirection," said Maggie. "Like maybe this Norah Wilcox doesn't actually exist and someone wants us to spend a lot of time chasing a ghost."

McCabe nodded and turned to Bill Bacon. "Bill, how're you making out tracking down Norah Wilcoxes?"

"Not great so far. Nothing at all on the ViCAP database for anybody with that name. I tried spelling Norah both with and without an *H*. Didn't help. A Google search turned up a couple of hundred hits, Facebook and LinkedIn a hundred or so more. For what it's worth, the name Nora without the *H* is more common than with. I ran through the whole bunch looking for youngish females attractive enough to interest a guy like Josh Thorne. That narrowed the field to just about zero."

"Just about?"

"One good-looking Norah Wilcox in Oregon, but she's only eighteen. Still in high school. Another one lives in the UK. Otherwise nada. The people search websites turned up a few women with the right name but only a handful are in the right age bracket and most don't live anywhere near here. None at all on the east coast. All that notwithstanding, I figure it doesn't really matter. Like Maggie said, the name's probably phony anyway."

"We can't assume that. I want you to keep tracking down every possible Norah Wilcox you can find, with or without an *H*. See if there's even one who's good-looking enough to attract a stud like Thorne. Get in touch with anyone remotely possible."

Bacon's expression made it clear he wasn't entirely happy with the assignment but he simply nodded and said, "Okay, boss, got it."

"Connie, I want you to handle the missing persons aspect. As soon as he's officially missing put out the word that we're looking for Thorne. Put his name and face on TV, radio, et cetera.

"Tom, I want you and Brian to head over to the Trident offices and talk with the guys who had dinner with Thorne last night. Joe Bonner's assistant should know who the other two were. Separate them out and talk to them one at a time. I don't want anybody holding back anything they might not want to say with the boss sitting right there."

"Anything specific you're looking for?" asked Tasco.

"Yeah. I want to find out if any of the three—or, for that matter, anyone else at Trident—might have received threatening e-mails or phone calls regarding the waterfront condo complex. We need to know if anybody's made any explicit or veiled threats against the company or its executives. Do the same with the people at Brumfield Harris.

"Okay. Anybody finds anything remotely pertinent, I want to know about it.

"Mag, like we discussed before, I'd like you to take on the college rape angle. Connie's looking for any recent suicides of females who went to Holden College. She'll let you know what she finds. Meanwhile, talk to this Charlie Loughlin guy. See what he knows about the suicide. What he'll admit about the rape at that fraternity party and then see what you can get from the people at the college."

"Okay. But I probably ought to go to West Hartford to talk to Loughlin. Also to Holden College, which is way the hell up in New York State."

"Bill, we'll need you to approve travel expenses."

McCabe knew budgets were tight and every time Fortier talked to Shockley they seemed to get tighter.

"You can't handle any of this via phone and e-mail?" asked Fortier.

"I don't think so," said Maggie. "Not if I want to get a real fix on this Loughlin guy. Or put any pressure on the folks at Holden."

"Okay. We'll cover mileage and expenses. But please, nothing extravagant. There's not a whole lot of blood left in the stone."

Maggie gave Fortier a look of wide-eyed innocence. "No problem, Bill. The West Hartford Four Seasons is only four hundred a night."

Fortier responded by giving Maggie the same evil-eyed expression her father used when she was sixteen and got home after curfew.

"No sweat," she told him. "I'll sleep and eat cheap. Like everyone's always saying, I'm the original junk food junkie."

Chapter 12

THE PORT GRILL was only a block and a half from 109 and, though freezing rain and snow showers were threatening, nothing had started yet, so McCabe decided to walk. The restaurant was housed in a squat nondescript redbrick building with only a pair of small, discreet bronze signs on either side of the door announcing the location. Given the place's reputation the owners must have felt there was no need to scream out its presence. At five in the afternoon McCabe found the doors still locked. He peered in and rapped on the glass until a young woman wearing a white shirt and black pants covered with a white apron noticed him. She pointed at her watch and waved her hands back and forth signaling the place hadn't opened yet. He held his gold badge up to the window and gestured to her to let him in.

She turned the lock and cracked the door a couple of inches. "We don't open till five-thirty. Is anything the matter?"

"I'm Detective Sergeant Michael McCabe. Portland Police. I need to talk with one of your staff members."

The woman frowned. "I hope no one's in trouble."

"No. Nothing like that. I just need some information for a case we're investigating. May I come in?"

"Yes. Of course. I'm sorry." She held the door open. McCabe went in and she relocked it. The empty bar where Josh Thorne had his nightcap was to his left.

"My name is Sarah Jackson. I'm the assistant manager. Who do you need to talk to?"

"Can you tell me who was tending bar just before closing last night?"

"Sure. That would have been Andie. Andie Barrett."

"Is Andie here at the moment?"

"Yes. She's eating dinner in back with the rest of the crew."

"Could you let her know I'm here? She's the one I need to talk to."

"Can it wait till she's finished?"

"I'm afraid it's urgent."

"Okay. Wait here and I'll get her."

A minute later a freckle-faced woman with reddish brown curls and an uncertain smile appeared. McCabe guessed she was in her mid-to-late twenties.

"Are you the police officer?"

"Yes. Detective Sergeant Michael McCabe." He showed her his badge and ID.

"I'm Andie." She held out her hand. He shook it. "Sarah said you wanted to talk to me."

"I'm sorry to interrupt your dinner."

"That's okay. I was pretty much finished anyway. What's going on?"

"I need to ask you about someone I think you served at the bar last night. Is there any place we can talk privately?"

"Sure." She led McCabe into the bar. "We can take that table in the corner there. That's about as private as it gets."

They went in and sat. McCabe slid the Prospect Park picture of Josh Thorne toward her. "Do you recognize this man?"

There was no hesitation. "Sure. He was in here drinking right up until closing last night. His name is Joshua Thorne. Called himself Josh. What's he done?"

"Nothing. We're just trying to locate him so we can ask him some questions."

"He said he was staying at the Regency if that helps."

"Was anyone with him last night?"

"Not at first. He came into the bar late. Nine-thirty or so. Sat over there." She pointed at a stool around a corner at the far end of the bar. "Ordered a vodka martini and we started talking. Is he a criminal or something?"

"Nothing like that," said McCabe. "What were you talking about?"

Andie shrugged. "Just stuff. He asked my name. Said he was here on business and asked me a bunch of questions. Like did I work here full-time or did I also do something else. I told him I'm studying nursing at USM but needed bartending money to help pay the bills. After we got past the preliminaries, he started hitting on me."

"Oh yeah? Hitting like how?"

Andie shrugged. "Nothing nasty. He just asked me what time I finished up and would I like to go over to the Regency and have a drink with him there. Said their bar closed later than we do, which I know is true because I used to work there."

"What did you tell him?"

Andie gave a sheepish smile. "Honestly, I was thinking about

it. I don't have a boyfriend at the moment and this guy was definitely good-looking."

"Did you notice if he was wearing a wedding ring?"

"Yeah, I noticed. He wasn't."

"Okay. So what happened?"

"Nothing. Before I even had a chance to say yes or no, he
dumped me for another woman."

"Really?"

"Yeah, really. Like, ten minutes after we started talking this
good-looking blonde walks in, dressed in big bucks . . ."

"How do you mean?"

"Louboutin shoes for one thing. The ones with the red soles.
They go for a thousand dollars a pop and I don't think they have
an outlet store in Freeport. Fancy gold watch too."

"Keep going."

"She sits at the bar a few seats down from Thorne. Orders a
vodka martini made with this expensive but kind of obscure
vodka called Double Cross. If she was trying to catch his interest,
it worked. While I'm making the martini for her, the two of them
start talking and after about a minute he slides down and sits next
to her and calls me over and says, 'I'll have what she's having.'"

"You mean like the line from the movie?" asked McCabe.

"Yeah. Except the funny thing was he'd never heard of it."

"Sounds like you could hear everything they were saying."

"I could. The place was dead quiet. Only other customers were
a young couple sitting where we're sitting now and they left a couple of minutes after the woman came in. Anyway, after he moves
in next to her, I was kind of curious if he'd have the nerve to ask
her if *she* wanted to go to the Regency."

"And did he?"

"He sure did. I mean, like right in front of me. Hands her exactly the same—excuse my language—bullshit he was handing me."

"Did she tell him her name?"

"Not her last name."

"How about her first."

"Yeah. She said it was Norah."

Chapter 13

MAGGIE TAPPED HER computer to life and entered a Google search using the words "Charles Loughlin," "Insurance," "Holden College" and "Connecticut." A couple of hundred hits popped up but the first one looked the most promising: a website for Northway Insurance/Loughlin Agency located at 921 Farmington Avenue in West Hartford.

Maggie clicked on a sublink titled *Meet Our People*. At the top of the new page was a head shot of an ordinary-looking guy wearing a dark suit, checked shirt and a red tie. He was gazing at the camera with what could only be described as a forced half smile. Probably didn't like having his picture taken. He looked to be about the same age as Josh Thorne. His sandy hair was brushed forward in an unsuccessful attempt to cover a receding hairline. Light blue eyes peered out from behind a pair of rimless glasses. He didn't look much like an ex–football player, but she supposed Division III football players probably didn't look much bigger or tougher than anyone else. On the other hand maybe Loughlin was bigger in person than he looked in the bio pic.

He didn't look much like a rapist either, but that didn't mean anything. Maggie knew from experience rapists came in all shapes, sizes and temperaments from bulldozers to choirboys. Or, for that matter, priests. The picture was captioned *Charles Loughlin, CEO*. Beneath that were office and cell numbers along with Loughlin's business e-mail address. His bio followed.

Charles Loughlin is President, Chief Executive Officer and Senior Partner of the Northway Insurance/Loughlin Agency. In addition to sales, Charlie's responsibilities include agency oversight and strategic management, information technology oversight and financial forecasting.

He began his career in 2002 as a Commercial and Personal Lines producer for the Northway/Peterson Agency. In 2006 he became Agency Manager and Lead Commercial Lines Producer for Northway/Peterson, the largest agency in the Northway Insurance group. He also holds the Certified Insurance Counselor Designation. He was named CEO in 2009.

Charlie earned a Bachelor of Science degree in Business from Holden College in 2002 where he was also a standout wide receiver on Holden's football team.

Charlie serves as President of the Rotary Club of West Hartford and the United Way of Hartford County. Charlie and his wife, Heather, are the parents of two handsome sons, Josh and Cameron. Charlie and his family enjoy hiking, mountain biking and skiing.

All in all a portrait of the ideal family man. Maggie wondered if son Josh had been named after Joshua Thorne. She also wondered if Charlie's wife had any inkling her standout wide receiver husband also stood out as an accused rapist. Be interesting to find out what, if anything, he'd told her about that. Maggie decided to try the office number first. At four-thirty on a Wednesday afternoon that seemed where he'd likely be.

"Northway Insurance. This is Anne Bailey. How can I help you?"

"I'd like to speak to Charles Loughlin, please."

There was a brief silence on the other end before Ms. Bailey responded. "I'm afraid that won't be possible. May I ask who's calling?"

"Can you tell me where I can reach Mr. Loughlin?"

There was an audible sigh on the other end. "I guess you haven't heard the news. You can't reach him."

"Why not?" Maggie had a feeling she already knew the answer.

"We sent out notices to all of Charlie's clients. I guess you didn't get one."

"Has he left his job?"

"In a manner of speaking, yes. Mr. Loughlin is dead. He died last week in a terrible accident. We're all still in a state of shock."

"You say this happened last week?"

"Yes. On Monday. About ten in the evening. While he was on his way home from a dinner meeting. Would you like to speak to . . ."

Maggie didn't wait for the woman to finish. She broke the connection, turned to her computer and found the website for the West Hartford Police Department. Clicked on the Detective Division. Thumbprint-sized photos and direct numbers were provided for each of the dozen detectives in the department. Changing over to her landline so caller ID would identify the call as coming from the Portland PD, Maggie tapped in the number for a Detective Antoinette Bernstein, one of the three women listed and the one who looked more experienced than the other two. Maggie usually found female detectives more willing to help their female counterparts than a lot of the guys. Especially in cases involving rape.

A woman with a husky smoker's voice answered. "Bernstein."

Maggie kicked off her shoes and leaned back.

"Detective Bernstein, this is Detective Margaret Savage of the Portland Maine Police Department."

"Okay. How can I help you?"

"We're investigating the disappearance and possible murder of a man named Joshua Thorne."

"By *possible* murder do you mean the death might have been an accident?"

"No. What I mean is the guy's missing. We haven't found a body yet, but I've got a strong feeling it won't be long."

"What do you need from me?"

"During the course of our investigation the name Charles Loughlin came up."

"The same Charlie Loughlin who just happened to end up dead here last week?"

"One and the same."

A few seconds passed before Bernstein asked, "Are we talking coincidence or connection?"

"Connection. Loughlin was an old friend and fraternity brother of the guy who's gone missing here."

"Now I'm interested. How did you know the Loughlin case was assigned to me?"

"I didn't. I picked your name from the list on your department's website."

"Well, you picked the right name. I'm the one looking into Loughlin's death."

"Can I ask you a few questions?"

"Long as I can ask you some."

"Fair enough. The woman who answered the phone at Loughlin's office said he died in what she called a terrible accident."

"Well, so far that's the party line. The one his family and colleagues are handing out as well."

"Any reason to think Loughlin's death might have been anything else?"

"There is. The 'anything else' possibly but probably not being suicide, or maybe, just maybe, murder. At the moment my boss and I are the only ones who think murder's the most likely. I'd like to pursue it but the chief keeps telling us not to start down that road without a damned good reason, aka hard evidence. Which means, of course, he'd let us go after it if that hard evidence happened to fall in my lap from an unexpected source in, oh, for argument's sake, let's say Portland, Maine."

Maggie smiled and decided she liked Bernstein. "Okay," she asked, "what makes you think Loughlin's death might not be the accident everybody else is saying it is?"

"Well, for starters, if it *was* an accident it was a damned peculiar one. The guy pulls his car off an empty road he had no reason being on onto a scenic overlook at the top of a sixty-foot dropoff with nothing but rock face below. It was a little before twelve o'clock at night."

"A little dark to be admiring the scenery."

"Especially on a freezing cold, overcast night. Temps down in the teens. Anyway, Charlie gets out of the car, walks to the edge and then either falls, jumps or maybe gets pushed over the edge."

"No guardrail?"

"An average-sized one . . . thirty-four inches. More than high enough to keep him from falling over it accidentally."

"Could he have tripped over it in the dark?"

"Possible since he was drunk as a skunk at the time, but given the height of the rail I have a hard time buying it. However it happened, his body was found the next morning at the bottom of the ravine. The fall fractured his skull and severed his spine. According to the ME he died immediately."

"Anything else?"

"Yeah. Like I said he was drunk. An empty bottle of Maker's Mark bourbon with Charlie's fingerprints all over it and his saliva on the rim was found in his car. He had a blood alcohol level of .22, which, in a hundred and eighty pound male, suggests he'd knocked back pretty much the whole bottle. I'm surprised Charlie could even walk when he went over the side."

"So he had to be drinking the bourbon as he was driving."

"Or after pulling off the road to admire the view. His wife denies it, but his friends and clients tell us our boy liked his booze. The general opinion is that the fact that he was drunk explains his tumbling over the guardrail."

"Do they have any explanations about what he was doing at the overlook in the first place?"

"Their most popular explanation is that he pulled over and got out of the car to take a leak. Thought it might be fun to piss over the side but being drunk he wasn't too steady on his pins. He supposedly slipped on some ice and went over while peeing. His fly was open with his pecker hanging out when they found the body. That's the accident theory. The one the DA's subscribing to as well. At least until we can prove otherwise."

"What about the suicide theory?"

"That one goes he drank the booze to give himself the courage to take the leap."

"Can anyone think of any reason he might want to kill himself?"

"Nope. And that's a problem. The question that comes up whenever anyone mentions the word *suicide* is motive. What would make a guy like Charlie Loughlin kill himself? People who knew him insisted he was a happy guy. Pretty wife. A couple of good-looking kids. A fancy house. A successful business. Living the American dream."

"Except for the fact he was a drunk?"

"Yeah. Except for that. And the fact that a couple of people who used to work for him told me that underneath Loughlin's smiley-face salesman's persona, the guy was a selfish, demanding prick. The kind of sweetheart who chose Christmas Eve to fire two of his salespeople who weren't producing the way he wanted them to. One who had a wife dying of metastatic breast cancer and probably wasn't producing because he was spending too much time taking care of her and their kids. Apparently stuff like that didn't count with Charlie. Bastard couldn't even wait till the wife died, which she did the second week in January, before dumping the guy. But hey, nobody's perfect."

"Not exactly the kind of tormented soul you'd figure who'd off himself."

"Not to me. Which is one of the reasons I think murder is the most likely possibility."

"Does the fired husband have an alibi?"

"Yeah. He was home with his sick wife."

"Alone?"

"No. There was a hospice nurse there and three of the wife's good friends dropped by at different times during the evening to visit. They all vouch for him."

Maggie thought about that. Loughlin definitely didn't sound like the type to jump off a cliff out of remorse because a woman he raped twelve years earlier in college had herself recently committed suicide. Just wouldn't happen. More importantly, given the coincidental timing of their deaths, the idea that both Loughlin and Thorne were killed, one after the other, as payback for the twelve-year-old rape and subsequent suicide was beginning to seem a whole lot more likely.

"Hey, Savage, you still there?"

"Yeah, I'm here. I'm just trying to wrap my head around all this."

Bernstein went on. "My personal theory is that somebody who had a bone to pick with Charlie forced him, maybe at gunpoint, to drive to the overlook, guzzle the booze and walk to the edge. That's when they gave him a shove."

"But you say your department isn't buying that?"

"My department's buying it. My boss is buying it. The chief is buying it. But so far the DA isn't."

"Why not?"

"Just looking out for himself. He's a young guy with major political ambitions. The rumor goes he's planning on running for attorney general in November and the last thing he wants or needs is an unsolved murder of a successful businessman he doesn't think we're likely to clear before the voters go to the polls. He's not willing to call it murder unless and until I find something or somebody that provides the kind of incontrovertible proof that'll lead both to a quick arrest and the kind of slam-dunk conviction that'll make him look good to the voters come election day. Like I said, I'm kinda hoping you might be the somebody with the proof."

"Well, to tell you the truth, I just might be," said Maggie.

"Okay. I think it's my turn with the questions. Why don't you start by telling me why you think Loughlin's death could be connected with your missing person?"

"A couple of months back, right after the holidays, Loughlin called our guy, who happens to be an old teammate and fraternity brother of his . . ." Maggie went on and told Toni Bernstein everything Rachel Thorne had said about her husband's disappearance and Josh and Charlie Loughlin's involvement in the Holden College rape. She also told her about the Christmas Eve suicide of the woman who had been raped. How she suspected the suicide might have been the trigger that led to the disappearance and possible murders of Loughlin and Thorne.

"The motive being revenge for the rape?" Bernstein asked when Maggie had finished.

"Yes. And also for the suicide. Possible suspects might include the dead woman's husband or lover if she had one. Her parents. Possibly her siblings or close friends. Anyone who might have been brooding about the rape and/or the suicide and looking for payback."

"The frat boys waited their turn and climbed aboard, huh?"

"That's how Thorne described it to his wife."

"And a good time was had by all."

"I guess. Except for the victim."

"Funny. Even mean as he was, I wouldn't have guessed Charlie would've been involved in something as ugly as that."

"Well, maybe he wouldn't have without Thorne's encouragement. When they played football together Josh was the quarter-back."

"And the quarterback calls the plays? Still it all happened quite a while ago."

"Twelve years. But it's only been about three months since the rape victim killed herself. This is all pure conjecture on my part but what seems likely to me is that PTSD resulting from a vicious gang rape, even that long after the event, could have been haunting her ever since and ended up triggering her death. At least, I want to look into that possibility. Talk to her shrink if she had one. Her family. People she worked with."

"Seems like a long time after the event for her to have had that kind of reaction?"

"It happens. Just look at the suicide statistics among vets suffering PTSD years after leaving the combat zone. Nearly happened to my own kid brother a couple of years after he got back from Iraq. Rape could easily lead to the same ending. Suicide among rape survivors is not uncommon."

"I guess. How come Loughlin, Thorne and the others were never prosecuted?"

"I don't know. I've got to talk to the people at the college about that. What Thorne told his wife after she bullied him into talking about it was that he and Loughlin and four other guys, currently nameless, did have sex with the girl. But he insisted that the girl was drunk and the sex was consensual."

Toni Bernstein snorted loudly on the other end of the phone. "Yeah. I've heard that one before."

"Haven't we all? But sometimes it's true. In this case Thorne told his wife he'd even made an audio tape recording of the girl saying yes."

"You telling me Thorne or Charlie or somebody just happened to have a tape recorder handy at the rape site? And he just happened to turn it on so he could capture the girl's verbal consent for posterity?"

"That's what the wife told us."

"Handy to have if she decided to accuse them of rape. In fact, a little too handy, don't you think?"

"I do."

"Anyone collect a rape kit or test the girl for roofies?"

"I don't know but I'd guess not. So far everything I've got comes literally fourth hand from Thorne's wife. What she told us was that the victim didn't report the rape until four months after the fact. Who knows why? Shame. Guilt. Not wanting to testify publically about an embarrassing sexual experience. My next call's to Holden College to see if I can get some hard information about exactly what happened. The truth is I don't even have a name for the victim yet."

There was a short silence on the other end so Maggie jumped in with another question. "You said Charlie had no business being on the road he was on. What did you mean by that?"

"He was coming from a dinner meeting with some clients. That particular road doesn't take him home from the restaurant. Doesn't really take him anywhere he's likely to want to go. He had no reason being there."

"But it is dark and lonely?" asked Maggie.

"Dark and lonely with very little traffic. Especially at a few minutes to twelve on a brutally cold winter's night."

While she listened Maggie looked at the photo of Josh Thorne tied to the bed. She wondered if they'd eventually find Josh's body at the bottom of a scenic overlook. Or maybe at the bottom of a lake. Or, more likely in Maine, not find his body at all because it was at the bottom of the ocean providing nutritious meals for some hungry lobsters. "Who were the last people to see Charlie alive?"

"We only know the next to last people. The two insurance clients he was having dinner with. They both say Charlie only had one bourbon before dinner and a couple of glasses of wine while they were eating. They both rightly insist it wasn't nearly enough to get him as stinking drunk as we found him."

"Did the three of them all leave together?"

"Yes. And this is where things get more interesting. One of the clients, a guy named Jeff Purdy, said that when they went out into the parking lot Charlie was called over by some woman who may or may not have known him but addressed him by name."

"What do you mean by she 'may or may not have known him'?"

"According to Purdy she called out, *"Charlie Loughlin?"* with a question mark on the end so it sounded like she wasn't sure it was him. Could have been she knew him, but couldn't see who it was walking by real well. Or it could have been that she didn't know him and she wanted to make sure she had the right guy. Anyway, he said yeah, he was Loughlin and she asked if she could talk to him for a minute. Charlie squinted into the darkness and asked, *'Who are you?'* Purdy says he heard her say her name was Norah Wilcox . . ."

A jolt of adrenaline shot through Maggie. She sat up straight. "Norah Wilcox?"

"Yeah. Why? You know the name?"

"Absolutely. Thorne's wife received an e-mail last night." Maggie described the bondage photograph to Bernstein. "The e-mail was signed by Norah Wilcox. As far as we know she was the last person to see Thorne either dead or alive. Now it sounds like she was the last one to see Loughlin alive."

"Don't get too excited, Savage. I've been tracking down possible Norah Wilcoxes since the night Charlie died and come up with zip. I think the name's a phony."

"Yeah, but the same name both times? That should be enough to convince your DA Loughlin was murdered. Hell, it convinces me that Thorne was. Charlie's clients hear this Wilcox woman say anything else?"

"Just that she asked if she could have a minute of Charlie's time. He said sure and walked over to where she was standing. Purdy and the other guy, a guy named Will Wattman, both waved goodnight and left."

"Could either one describe what Wilcox looked like?"

"Nah. I worked that hard. Neither got much of a look at her. It was a cold night and she was bundled up in a black parka with a fur hood. Nothing sticking out of the hood but her nose. Purdy did say her voice sounded young to him, but since he's seventy-four years old, young to his ears could be twenty or it could be fifty. No way of knowing."

"Find any other witnesses?"

"No. We canvassed people at the restaurant and also people in the area. No one could remember seeing her."

"Did your people look for this Norah Wilcox?"

"As best we could before the DA, Elliot Morgan, called the investigation off and stamped accidental death on the file. Neither Loughlin's wife nor any of his employees or friends had ever heard her name. There was no record of anybody by that name in either Charlie's business or home computers. Checked people in the area with that name or, given that Purdy's hearing might not be so good, people with similar sounding names. Hotel and motel registrations. Car registrations. Car rentals. Didn't come up with anything that looked remotely likely. That's when the DA told us to give it a rest, stop wasting resources and put it down as an accidental death."

Maggie sat quietly for a minute trying to figure out what her logical next step ought to be.

Bernstein interrupted her musing. "Your guy tell his wife anything else?"

"Just that the victim didn't scream rape until four months after it happened. By which time she would have been clean. Roofies or any other drug undetectable. The wife says when the girl finally did report the rape, the people at the college discouraged her from going to the police and the guys weren't punished in any way."

"Interesting. And you don't have a name for the girl who was raped?"

"I'm hoping somebody at the college will tell us who she was. We also have some people checking both news and police reports for a thirty-something-year-old woman who attended Holden College committing suicide just before Christmas. So far nothing but they've only just gotten started."

"Ah, yes, Christmas. A favorite time of year for depressives to act on bad impulses."

"Yeah. In the meantime, I think maybe we should both talk to Mrs. Loughlin."

"Okay by me. Given Thorne's disappearance I think talking to her in person would be better than by phone. Any way you can come down here?"

"Practically on my way. Just need to pack a few things. It's a little over three hours from here to there. Not sure what time I'll get there but it'd be great if we could meet with her tonight. If she says it's too late, then first thing in the morning. Let me know what works."

"Okay. I'll tell Heather Loughlin we may have some new information. What's your cell?"

Chapter 14

"WOULD YOU LIKE a drink or anything?" Andie Barrett asked Mc-Cabe. "I'll be happy to fix you something." She then mouthed the words, "On the house."

McCabe smiled. Considering the long line of top tier single malts on the shelf behind the bar, under other circumstances McCabe might have been tempted. But in the end he simply said, "Thanks but no thanks. Not while I'm working."

"Okay. Maybe some other time."

"Yeah, maybe some other time," he said to Andie, and left it at that. It was time to change the subject. "Now do you happen to remember if this Norah told Joshua Thorne her last name?"

"No. She didn't," she finally said. "Just told him her name was Norah and that she lived in New York City and worked for an ad agency down there."

"Did she tell him the name of the agency?"

"No."

"Was she here on business?"

"Didn't sound like it. She told Thorne she owned a house in

Portland. In fact, she suggested that instead of going to the bar at the Regency they ought to go there. To her house. Something about having more privacy. Pretty stupid if you ask me. I mean, this Thorne guy looked okay—in fact, he looked great—but she'd never met him before and after, like, ten minutes' bar chatter she's asking him if he wants to go home with her." Andie held both hands up, palms forward, in a silent *go figure* gesture. After a minute, she asked, "To tell you the truth it all seemed like it might be some kind of setup. Did Thorne do something to her? Or vice versa? I mean, is that why you guys are interested?"

Pictures of the missing Joshua Thorne would probably be circulating on TV and online soon enough but McCabe didn't want word of Josh's disappearance getting out before that happened.

"We just need to find him and talk to him. Norah said she owned this house? She wasn't renting?"

"Yeah. She definitely said she owned it. Said she'd inherited it from her parents."

"Did she say where the house was?"

"The only thing I heard her say was that it was only a few minutes away."

He knew 339 Hartley Street was in Portland. A few minutes away if ten counted as a few.

"I don't know if she meant by car or on foot."

McCabe stood up. "Okay. Thank you for your help, Andie. I think I've got what I need." He handed her a card. "If you think of anything else, please give me a call."

She pocketed the card.

"In the meantime, I wonder if you'd mind spending an hour or so over at headquarters working with David Ishkowitz, our sketch specialist." Ishkowitz didn't actually draw his sketches. He was a computer artist who used a software program called Identi-Kit 7 that was capable of producing excellent likenesses based on witness descriptions. "We'd like you to help Dave develop a picture of what this Norah woman looked like."

"Now?"

"Now would be great if you can. I can set it up with Ishkowitz."

"Gee, sure, I guess, if Sarah will let me." Andie seemed excited at the idea of taking part in a police investigation. "I'll have to ask her if somebody else can cover the bar."

"Let me talk to her about that. I need to ask her a couple of other questions anyway."

Andie said okay and then wrote something down on a cocktail napkin and handed it to him. McCabe glanced down at a phone number and pocketed it. They rose from the table. Andie disappeared toward the back of the restaurant.

McCabe didn't know if the Port Grill had a surveillance camera hidden in the bar or not and there was a good chance Andie wouldn't either. One reason restaurants install cameras is to see if their bartenders or other help are stealing from the till. Not likely at a place like the Port Grill but you never knew.

Sarah Jackson appeared. "Hi. How can I help you, Detective?"

McCabe asked if they could "borrow" Andie for an hour or so.

"I don't know."

"It *is* important."

"Just for an hour? I guess I can find somebody to cover for her for an hour," Sarah said.

"Also, do you happen to know if the owners keep a security camera anywhere in the bar."

"Yes," she said after a moment's hesitation. "As a matter of fact, we do. In case of robberies or some kind of trouble in the bar. Most of the staff aren't aware of it."

"I see. Do you record what the camera sees?"

"Yes. We keep the video for twenty-four hours, then we erase it."

"Can I borrow the disk from last night? From, say, nine P.M. until closing."

Sarah made a face like this was something she'd really rather not do.

"Like I said it is important. It involves a possible murder investigation. I can get a warrant if need be but I'd rather not waste the time."

"I have no problem, but I'll have to check with one of the owners." She took out a cell phone and speed dialed a number. She briefly explained McCabe's request to the person on the other end.

"Okay," she said into the phone. "Okay, fine." She ended the call and said to McCabe, "It's fine with them. Come with me."

As soon as he was back on the street with the video in his pocket, McCabe called Dave Ishkowitz and told him to expect a visit from a young woman named Andie Barrett. "Make the sketch of this Wilcox woman a priority and get it to me as soon as you can."

Ishkowitz agreed. McCabe ended the call and, as he walked, he punched in the number for the City of Portland tax assessor's office. At 5:45 he hoped someone would still be there.

He lifted his collar against the chill. A cold drizzle had started to fall and Fore Street was filled with cars—Portland's excuse for rush hour traffic—most heading for Franklin Arterial, the quickest way to the interstate from this side of town.

"Tax office. This is Joan Dempsey."

McCabe talked as he walked. "Ms. Dempsey, this is Detective Sergeant Michael McCabe of the Portland PD. I'm in the middle of an investigation and I wonder if you could check a couple of things for me."

"I'll try."

"First can you give me the name of the owners of a house at 339 Hartley Street?"

"That's easy. Just hold on a minute."

Dempsey was back in considerably less than a minute. "That address shows husband and wife as co-owners. A couple named Bickle. Bob and Brenda Bickle."

Not Norah Wilcox. Bob and Brenda Bickle. Sounded to McCabe like the start of a tongue twister. *Bob and Brenda Bickle bite basketfuls of biscuits.* "Do you have a phone number for the Bickles?"

"There's a couple of local numbers. They're listed as cell phones."

Dempsey read off both. McCabe had no need to write either down. The numbers would be etched in his memory more or less forever.

"Thank you," he said. "One more favor. Could you see if you can find a residential property in Portland owned by someone named Norah Wilcox. W-I-L-C-O-X."

Another minute went by.

"Okay, I show four properties owned by people named Wilcox," said the clerk, "but there doesn't seem to be any Norah. Could ownership be listed under another name? First or last?"

Norah Wilcox had told Thorne she inherited the property. McCabe supposed it could be listed under her parents' names. Or Wilcox might be a married name. Or, more likely, it was a name she just made up for the benefit of Joshua Thorne.

"I don't think so but could you e-mail me the addresses for all four Wilcox properties? And the full names of the owners?" he asked. "And could you copy Detective Margaret Savage on the e-mail?"

Joan Dempsey said she would and McCabe provided both e-mail addresses.

He then tried calling the Bickles. Both calls went to voice mail and McCabe left his number and asked them please to return the call. He told them it was important.

Chapter 15

THE HOLDEN COLLEGE website informed Maggie that Holden was a small, private liberal arts school, founded in 1836 and located in upstate New York in a town called Willardville. It boasted an active Greek life and a Division III football team, nicknamed the Warriors, whose opponents included Maine's Colby, Bates and Bowdoin colleges. Maggie glanced at the school's main number. She didn't know how much information she'd be able to get by cold calling, but as she was increasingly certain Thorne wasn't missing but dead, she'd push as hard as she could. Again Maggie used the department landline instead of her cell and punched in the college's main number.

She was pleasantly surprised when a live female answered instead of a computer asking her to press 1 for English or 2 for Spanish. "Holden College. How may I direct your call?"

Might as well start at the top. "The president's office, please."

"Thanks. I'll connect you."

A few seconds later another, younger-sounding female came on the line. "President Nixon's office."

Suppressing an urge to ask the woman if Tricky Dick had come back to life and was hanging out in upstate New York, Maggie asked to speak to the president.

"May I ask who's calling and what this is in reference to?"

"Yes. This is Detective Margaret Savage. I'm a detective with the Portland Police Department. I need to talk to the president regarding a homicide investigation that may involve several Holden alumni."

There was an audible intake of breath before the woman responded, "Homicide? You mean as in murder?"

"That's right, as in murder."

"Oh wow. I'll see if she's available," said the assistant.

So President Nixon was a woman. As with Toni Bernstein, that might turn out to be an advantage when considering accusations of rape.

"This is Ann Nixon. To whom am I speaking?"

Nixon's voice was deep, her accent distinctly upper crust. The kind McCabe liked to call Locust Valley Lockjaw. It made her sound like a youngish version of Katharine Hepburn, back when the now dead actress was maybe in her forties.

"Ms. Nixon, this is Detective Margaret Savage of the Portland Police Department. I'm investigating the possible murders of two Holden College alumni. I believe one of the murders may have taken place about ten days ago in Connecticut, the other just last night here in Portland, and I need your help."

Maggie knew that without a body or other proof she was skating on thin ice describing either Thorne's disappearance or Loughlin's so-called accidental death as murders. But she was certain doing so would get her the information she needed a lot faster than telling Nixon that Thorne was still officially a missing person or that Loughlin was officially a drunk who might have taken a nasty fall.

"I'm disturbed to hear that. How can I help?"

"A man named Joshua Thorne, who graduated from Holden in 2002, has been reported missing. Since we haven't found his body yet I can't say with certainty that Thorne is dead, just that I believe that to be the case. We happen to know one of Thorne's classmates and fraternity brothers, Charles Loughlin, is dead."

"Murdered?"

Maggie didn't want to lie. Nixon might check with other sources. She left her response as "Most likely."

"But not definitely? Perhaps you'd like to explain."

"We've been told by a witness that back in the fall of 2001 or perhaps early winter of 2002 both Thorne and Loughlin were accused of raping a female freshman at a fraternity party that took place on the Holden campus at the Alpha Chi Delta house. The victim of the rape recently killed herself."

"I'm sorry to hear that. How recently?"

"Last Christmas. It seems likely what happened to Thorne and Loughlin is related to that rape and subsequent suicide."

"Retribution?"

"Exactly. It's possible some other former students, also fraternity brothers, might have participated in the rape and therefore might also now be in danger. We need your help in confirming that Thorne and Loughlin were charged with rape and the name of the girl who claimed she was the victim. I'll also need a list of all members of the Alpha Chi Delta fraternity in the fall of 2001 both to confirm what supposedly happened and to warn other potential victims."

"So what you're telling me is that you don't even know the

name of the student who was supposedly raped, nor the names of others who might have been involved?"

"Yes, ma'am. That's why I need your help."

"May I ask who this so-called witness is?"

Maggie had a strong feeling that unless she told Ann Nixon as much as she could, the president was likely to stonewall her. She might just stonewall her anyway. "Our witness is Joshua Thorne's wife. According to Mrs. Thorne, Loughlin called her husband right after the holidays and told him about the suicide. Mrs. Thorne overheard the conversation. Afterward she questioned her husband, asking what it was all about. After some hesitation Thorne admitted having had sex with the girl. He also told his wife that Loughlin and several other members of the fraternity had sex with her as well. But he insisted it was all consensual. Police forces in both Portland and West Hartford, Connecticut, need your help in confirming or possibly refuting Mrs. Thorne's account of the events."

There was only silence on the other end. "President Nixon, are you still there?"

"I'm here. But I must tell you, Ms. Savage . . ."

"Detective Savage."

"Detective Savage . . . that this all seems very flimsy. Based on nothing more than a secondhand account of something that may or may not have happened twelve years ago. And in addition to not knowing if Joshua Thorne is, in fact, dead you also don't even know the supposed rape victim's name."

Maggie had a feeling she'd made a major tactical blunder in calling Nixon instead of the dean of students in the first place. But since she had, her only option was to press on.

"No. The only names we have are Thorne and Loughlin. We

know Loughlin died under suspicious circumstances and we have strong physical evidence that Thorne has at least been kidnapped if not murdered. That is not a coincidence. It's essential that we find out if these events are, as you suggested, retribution for a rape that may have taken place in the fall of 2001. That's why I'm calling."

"Before this goes any further, I have to ask you, how do I know you're really a police officer and this isn't just some kind of weird prank or publicity stunt?"

"Don't you have caller ID?"

"Not on calls that come through the main switchboard."

"I see. In that case I suggest we hang up and you place a call to the Portland Police Department. When you get through, ask for me, Detective Margaret Savage. S-A-V-A-G-E. I'm a senior investigator on all violent crimes that take place within the city of Portland."

Nixon agreed. They both hung up. A minute later Maggie's phone rang. "President Nixon?"

"Yes."

"Is there any way you can give me the information I need?"

"I'm thinking about it—2001 was a long time ago. Well, before my time here. If there was a rape or even an accusation of rape, wouldn't it have been reported to the Willardville police and wouldn't they have the information you need?"

"My understanding is that the victim only reported the incident to Holden College administrators and was urged by them not to go to the police."

"That's a very serious allegation."

"Rape is a very serious crime. Ms. Nixon, this is very important. The lives of other men . . ."

"Who may be rapists. Or not."

"That's not for us to judge without investigating further. In any case their lives may depend on whether or not we can warn them of the possible danger and capture a murderer before there are any more victims."

After a brief silence, Ann Nixon told Maggie she'd see what she could find out. "Our records are quite good and our dean of students has been in the job for over twenty years. I'll get some answers and call you back."

"If you don't mind I'd rather talk to the dean myself."

"I'm afraid I do mind. I want to speak to the dean before you talk to him or anyone else here at Holden. And if you want my cooperation, I'd suggest you don't try calling him behind my back."

Maggie thought about arguing but in the end decided it wouldn't get her anywhere. "Okay. Fine. But please call back as soon as you can."

"I'll let you know."

She and Ann Nixon exchanged cell numbers and e-mail addresses and Maggie hung up.

Chapter 16

MAGGIE LOOKED UP to find McCabe standing by her desk. They both said, "Guess what?" at pretty much the same time.

"You first," said Maggie.

"The Port Grill maintains video surveillance of the bar."

"Really? That's good news. I wouldn't have thought that likely."

"Me either. But I've got last night's disk right here. Video only. No sound. Also last night's bartender, a woman named Andie Barrett, remembers both Thorne and Wilcox well. Ishkowitz is working with her on an Identi-Kit sketch of Wilcox right now."

"That's good news."

"Yeah. Let's go see what we can see on the video."

They both headed for the conference room. McCabe stuck the disk into the DVD player and was about to press Play.

"Before you do that," said Maggie.

"What?"

Maggie spent the next ten minutes replaying her conversations with Detective Toni Bernstein and Ann Nixon. "If Bernstein can set up a meeting, I'm heading down to West Hartford tonight to talk to Loughlin's wife and maybe the two guys who were with Loughlin the night he was killed."

"And, of course, staying at Motel 6?"

"Sadly."

"At least we'll find out if Tom Bodett is telling the truth or not."

"What do you mean?"

"Y'know." McCabe lowered his voice. "'This is Tom Bodett for Motel 6 and we'll leave the light on for you.'"

"Did it ever occur to you, McCabe, that the fact you remember not just complete scripts of old movies but also every commercial ever written can be a real pain in the butt for people who don't care about that stuff?"

McCabe grinned. "Yeah, I know. Anyway, what do you think Mrs. Loughlin can add to the brew?"

"We'll see if Charlie told her more about the rape than Josh told Rachel. If we're lucky she'll have the names of some of the other frat brothers who followed Loughlin in the roughriders club. After that, whether or not Nixon cooperates, I'll most likely continue on to Willardville first thing in the morning and start asking questions. Maybe take Bernstein with me."

McCabe listened and then nodded. "Okay. Works for me." He then gave her a quick summary of his conversation with Andie Barrett. "Now let's go look at the video. Maybe we'll get to see what Norah Wilcox looks like."

The screen came to life. A down angle shot of a modestly crowded bar. Both the color and video resolution were surprisingly good for a surveillance camera but mostly all they could see was tops of heads and backs and partial side views of the faces of people sitting at a crowded bar. Andie Barrett, the sole bartender, could be seen working the bar, smiling and chatting as she filled orders. The time code on the bottom left read 5:52:30 P.M.

McCabe jumped to 9:30:00 P.M. The bar had emptied out and Andie had started tidying up. At 9:32:17 Joshua Thorne entered frame. He walked to the corner barstool, removed his suit jacket and draped it over the back of the stool and sat down. Since the far end of the Port Grill bar turned a ninety-degree curve, the camera provided Maggie and McCabe with a decent view of Thorne's face. Andie approached. He smiled and gave her his order. She turned, grabbed a bottle of what looked like Grey Goose vodka. Threw some ice cubes into a cocktail shaker and poured what looked like a generous measure of booze. Josh spoke, Andie shrugged, grinned and added a second measure. She shook the drink and then poured it into a martini glass and placed it in front of him along with a bowl of what looked like nuts. She set the shaker, which probably still contained a decent slug of booze, under the bar where Thorne was sitting.

Thorne raised his glass, took a sip, licked his lips and said something to Andie, who was still standing nearby. Complimenting her on her mixology skills? Possibly. Andie leaned in and for the next ten minutes they talked.

"He's asking her if she wants to meet him at the Regency after she closes up," said McCabe.

"Yeah, he's on the make, all right," said Maggie. "And from her body language I'd say if he wants her, he's got her."

Thorne finished what was in his glass. Andie refilled it from the shaker under the bar. He picked up the refilled glass and toasted her with a tilt of the head.

"Yeah, she's an eager little thing," said McCabe. "Offered me a drink on the house when I was over there asking her questions."

"Cute freckle-faced bartender meets handsome hunk of a cop?" asked Maggie. "How could she resist? I mean, really, McCabe, how could any girl?"

McCabe gave Maggie a wicked smile and handed her the cocktail napkin with Andic's phone number on it. "She even slipped this in my pocket."

Maggie just rolled her eyes and tossed the napkin in the trash.

Meanwhile the video kept playing. When the time code reached 9:55:42 Thorne's eyes shifted away from Andie toward the entrance. The camera caught the side and then the back of an elegant blonde entering the frame. Andie turned to see what or who had distracted her wannabe friend's attention. The blonde's head turned slightly toward Thorne and then away. She took off her jacket and slipped it over a barstool three down from Thorne. Throughout the sequence no more than a sliver of her face was visible.

"Okay," said McCabe, "so far all we can tell is Norah's blonde, dresses chic, has great legs and a good figure. At least from the rear."

"All of which Andie already told you."

"Yup."

Norah sat down. Andie came over. Josh turned in the direction of the camera as he focused his attention on what they were saying. Andie nodded, said something, probably warning Norah that the Port Grill was closing in twenty-five minutes. She then grabbed a rectangular bottle from the lineup at the back of the bar and started making a Double Cross martini for Wilcox. Thorne finished his drink and came around the bar to where

Norah was seated. As she turned toward him her face completely disappeared from view. All they could see was shoulder-length blond hair.

Thorne and Wilcox talked for a minute. Andie made Thorne a drink with the Double Cross vodka. Norah raised her glass to clink Thorne's. There was no wedding band on Wilcox's left hand. Just what looked like a fancy gold watch on her wrist. "So far none of this is helpful," said McCabe. "Given the clarity of the shot, I'd hoped we'd at least get a look at her face. It's almost like she knows the damned camera's there."

"No. It's just the natural angle given that Thorne's sitting to her left."

"Let's fast-forward and see if we can get a face shot when they get up to go." It only took a few seconds to reach 10:22:36 on the video. Norah was putting on her jacket. Thorne was fetching his. And then they both started toward the exit. The best they could do was a less than one-quarter view of her left cheek just before she exited frame. McCabe moved the video to the frame that gave them the best look and froze it there.

"Not great."

"Okay. She's a dirty blonde. I guess in both senses of the word. She has expensive taste in clothes and, I think, high cheekbones. We ought to see what Starbucks can do to give us anything more specific."

"I doubt there's a whole lot more for him to get. Let's see how Dave is doing with his sketch."

McCabe called. Ishkowitz told him he was just finishing up with Andie. "She's done a real good job. Notices facial details a whole lot better than most people."

McCabe suspected Andie had also studied Norah's face last

night in the bar a whole lot more than most people. "E-mail me the sketch, would you, Dave?"

They went back to McCabe's desk. Maggie pulled her chair over and sat beside him as McCabe downloaded the image attached to Ishkowitz's e-mail. A full face drawing of an attractive blonde woman with light colored eyes and a long, narrow face was looking back at them.

McCabe studied the image. "Gillian Anderson," he said.

"What?"

McCabe didn't answer, just grabbed his phone and called Ishkowitz back. "Did Andie Barrett leave yet?"

"Nope. But she's just about to."

"Would you ask her if she could stop up here for a minute? You come too."

He could hear Ishkowitz asking and Andie saying sure.

"What was that all about," asked Maggie after McCabe hung up.

"From this drawing Norah looks a lot like Gillian Anderson. You know, the actress from *The X-Files*?"

McCabe Googled Anderson's name and pulled up a straight-on head shot. He took a screen grab of the Anderson shot and put the two images side by side on the screen. The resemblance was obvious. Wilcox's blonde hair framed her face in the same graceful waves as Anderson's. She had the same straight features and light colored eyes.

The elevator doors opened and Andie stepped out and looked around. McCabe called her over.

"Where's Dave?"

"He said he'd be right up."

McCabe made introductions, then got up and asked Andie to sit in his chair.

"What do you see?" asked McCabe

"That's Gillian Anderson, right? The actress. From *The X-Files*."

"Remind you of anyone else?" asked McCabe.

Andie leaned in toward the screen and studied the Anderson photo. "Yeah," she said with a big smile. "Norah Wilcox."

"You think that really is a picture of Norah?"

"No. There are some differences but it's pretty damned close. That *is* Gillian Anderson, isn't it?"

"Would you say the face is exactly like Norah's?"

"No. It's not like they're twins or anything. But the shape of their faces is nearly the same. But Norah's cheeks are very slightly fuller. And her cheekbones more pronounced."

Dave Ishkowitz moved in behind McCabe.

"Then the mouth. Norah's lips are fuller than Anderson's. But the smile is very similar. And the hair's the right color and the cut's pretty close."

"How about differences?"

"Norah has higher cheekbones. Not a lot higher. Just a little. Also I'd say Norah looks younger. At least in that photo, which must be pretty recent."

"A lot younger?"

Andie shrugged. "No. I don't know when that picture was taken but I think Gillian Anderson has got to be forty-something by now."

"Forty-six," said McCabe. "You think if someone saw that photo they'd think it was Norah?"

"I don't know. Like I said, they're not twins. But the photo looks a lot more like Norah than the sketch."

"Partly that's because it's a photo," said Ishkowitz, "and not a computer sketch."

"Anyway, I've gotta go," said Andie. "I've already been here longer than you told Sarah."

McCabe walked her to the elevator.

"When do you get off work tonight?" he asked.

Andie smiled. "Around eleven. Call me."

"You're free?"

"I am."

"Then I will call," said McCabe. "I want you to come back here and do some more work helping Dave Photoshop that image."

"Oh," said Andie, trying to hide her disappointment. "Sure, I guess so." The elevator doors closed over Andie's face just as her smile morphed into a frown.

McCabe went back to where Maggie and Ishkowitz were still comparing the Identi-Kit sketch with the photo of Anderson. "Dave, I just asked Andie to come back here when she finishes work tonight at eleven. I need you to take the Anderson pic and Photoshop it till we get to a point where Andie says, 'Hey, that's not Gillian Anderson, that's Norah Wilcox!' If it works we put it out as the photo of our suspect."

Chapter 17

MAGGIE SAID SHE was going home to pack a bag for her road trip. McCabe told her to check in when she got there. After she left he gave the Bickles' cell numbers another try. There was still no answer from Bob Bickle's phone. But Brenda picked up hers.

"Hello. Who's this?" The voice sounded like Brenda was at least in her seventies. Maybe older.

"Is this Mrs. Bickle?"

"Yeah. Who's this?"

"Detective Sergeant Michael McCabe of the Portland Police Department."

"Cops?"

"That's right. I need to ask you some questions."

"What kinda questions?"

"Are you and your husband the owners of the house located at 339 Hartley Street in Portland?"

"Oh, crap. Bobby, it's the cops from Portland. Somethin' about the house. What, did somebody try to break in or something?"

"Are you and your husband the owners of the house at 339 Hartley Street?"

"Yeah, we own the place. Has that busybody O'Malley been bitching about noise again?"

As he suspected, Joan O'Malley had a history of excessive noise complaints. Maybe Hartley Street wasn't going to lead anywhere. "Mrs. O'Malley heard some yelling and screaming coming from what she thought was your house last night. One of our officers got no response when they knocked on your door. I'd like your permission to enter the premises and make sure nothing is wrong."

"Jesus Christ. That damned woman has no life of her own so she just wants to butt her nose into everybody else's. Every time some kid yells in the street she calls the cops and blames us."

McCabe tried to make his long sigh inaudible. "Nobody's blaming anybody, Mrs. Bickle. We would simply like to check the house and make sure everything is okay. Make sure there've been no break-ins or any damage to your property. You can either meet us at the house and let us in or give us permission to enter and check it out."

In the background McCabe could hear an irritated male voice. "Brenda, what the hell is going on. Gimme the goddamned phone." Then much closer. "This is Robert Bickle. Who is this and what do you want?"

Putting a check on an impulse to snap back at Bickle's aggressiveness, McCabe drew a deep breath and said once again, "This is Detective Sergeant Michael McCabe. Portland Police Department."

"Portland cops, huh? Then you must know my nephew. Jess Fardella? Brenda's sister's kid. He worked with you guys till he retired a couple of years back."

Jess Fardella had been a community policing officer. McCabe had worked with him once or twice over the years. "Jess? Yeah, I knew him. Good cop. What's he up to these days?"

"Bought himself a bar and grill out in Standish. Nice little place. Doin' good, I hear."

"Good to know," said McCabe. "Tell him Mike McCabe says hello next time you talk to him. Anyway, we've had a complaint of excessive noise coming from the house at 339 Hartley Street. That's your place, right?"

"We don't live there anymore," Bickle interrupted. "Haven't for ten years. Not since I retired. We only come up occasionally in the summer. Mostly to make sure the place is still in one piece. We're down in Florida now. At The Villages . . ."

McCabe had heard of The Villages. In fact, some friends of his mother had moved there. Place was a vast retirement community with more than five thousand homes for seniors and, rumor had it, one of the fastest growing rates of STDs in the country. The idea of horny baby boomers bringing the sexual revolution they started back in the '60s with them into their golden years always made McCabe chuckle.

"But you still own the house in Portland?"

"Yeah, we own it but we use it strictly as a rental property."

"Oh yeah? Full-time tenants?"

"Nah. We rent it furnished on a weekly basis. Mostly in summer. June to October. Occasionally other times."

"Anybody there now?"

"Why do you want to know?"

"Please just tell me if renters are currently in the house."

"Yeah. It's rented. Just for this week. Saturday to Saturday so the renter should still be there. Did you try knocking on the door?"

"One of our officers did. There was no answer. Who did you rent it to?"

"Some woman named Wilcox. Norah Wilcox."

McCabe felt a flash of excitement.

"She didn't burn the place down or anything, did she?" asked Bickle.

"No, nothing like that," he said, keeping his voice calm and relaxed.

"What, then? She doin' something illegal in the house? Selling drugs or something?"

McCabe decided not to elaborate. "Yeah, that's possible. Once we check it out I can let you know more specifically. You have an address for Ms. Wilcox?"

"Goddammit. I knew that deal was too damned good to be true."

"What do you mean?"

There was a long sigh on the other end. "This Wilcox woman calls us direct like two weeks ago," said Bickle. "Tells me she's coming to Portland on business. Says she doesn't like hotels and so she looked for a place online. Y'know? On the website. Vacation Rentals Online? VROL? Anyway, she saw our ad and wanted to rent the house for a week."

"Why did you think it was too good to be true?"

"Well, when she told me she wanted to rent the place, I said fine, just send us a check for one week's rent plus a five hundred dollar security deposit and we'll e-mail you a rental agreement that you can fill out and e-mail back. She says no, she'd rather send cash than a check and not fill out any paperwork. I say I'm not sure about that. She then says if we do it her way, in addition to the rent, we can keep the security deposit and she'll throw in another five hundred besides. Altogether that's fifteen hundred in cash for a place that's okay but sure as hell ain't no palace. Honestly, it's kind of crummy. Only one decent bedroom. The second one's used mostly for storage. Naturally, I get suspicious so before I agree I ask her what's going on. Why would she be willing to pay more'n twice as much?"

"And what does she say?"

"Well, her voice gets real low like she doesn't want anybody else hearing what she's going to tell me. She asks if I can keep a secret. If she can trust me."

"Go on."

"I'm gettin' more and more curious so I say, yeah, sure, I can keep a secret as well as the next guy. That's when this Norah tells me she's coming to Portland to meet some guy and wants to stay with him at the house, and I say, 'Yeah, so? What's the big deal about that?'

"She says both she and this guy are married to other people so they want to meet in a place where nobody's gonna know them and nobody's gonna be able to track them down. I don't say nothing back so she keeps talkin'. Says it's gotta be a secret because her husband and his wife are real suspicious of what they're up to. I still say nothin'. She goes on and tells me her husband'll dump her if he finds out she's having an affair, and since he's real rich there's no way she wants to risk him divorcing her for adultery. Anyway, she says that's the reason she wants to pay cash and not sign any lease. She says she can't afford to leave any kind of paper trail 'cause for all she knows the husband may already have hired a private detective to keep an eye on them.

"While she's talkin,' I'm sitting here thinking this woman's already offered me fifteen hundred in cash for a two-bedroom place, one of which I use for storage and isn't included in the rental, that only rents for six hundred a week even in July, so I figure what the hell, a little negotiating won't hurt. I tell her if she makes it two thousand she's got a deal. If she says no, I'm ready to back down and take the fifteen. But nope, all she says is two thousand is fine. So I say fine back. I tell her where to send the money. When I get it I'll call her back and tell her how to get into the house. But she won't give me her number and says she'll call me back."

Okay, thought McCabe. There was no question now—339 Hartley Street was the house Norah Wilcox invited Joshua Thorne to visit. The place where she tied him to the bed and took the nude photo, then e-mailed it to his wife. Possibly the place where she went on to kill him. One crime confirmed. One suspected. "Did you ever get any kind of information about this Norah Wilcox?"

"Yeah. Like I said, I told her she could have the place but that she at least had to give me an address and a phone number in case there was any damage. Told her I'd just write it down and put it in a folder. And that I wouldn't show it to her husband or to a private eye or anybody else. After a little back and forth, she finally says okay."

"You still have the address and phone number she gave you?"

"Yeah. Like I told her, I wrote the information down and put it in the file folder I keep for the rentals."

"Can you let me have it?"

Bickle hesitated for a minute, then said, "I told her I'd keep her info private, but hey, if she committed a crime there . . ."

"It's looking that way."

"Okay. Sure. For an old pal of Jess's I guess so. Lemme go into my office and dig it out."

"No problem. I'll wait."

It was a couple of minutes before Bickle picked up the phone again. "Yeah, I've got it right here," he said. "Name's Norah Wilcox. Norah with an *H* at the end. Address is 851 West 94th Street, Apartment 6G, New York, NY 10025."

McCabe knew the streets of Manhattan's Upper West Side well enough to know that while the zip code was legit, the number 851 on West 94th Street, would put Norah's apartment right in the middle of the Hudson River. Or maybe even atop the Jersey shoreline.

"How about the phone number?"

"212-555-7390."

McCabe figured that was a phony too but he'd check it out. "What happened next?" he asked.

"Next? She sent me the money. A priority mail envelope filled with twenty brand-new Franklins tucked inside a piece of white paper."

"What did you do with the cash?" McCabe was pretty sure Bickle would have avoided depositing the money so he wouldn't have to pay taxes on it.

"Spent a couple of hundred. I still have the rest."

"How about the paper they were wrapped in?"

"I tossed the paper. The money's still inside the cardboard envelope."

"Have you or anyone else touched it?"

"'Course I touched it. How am I supposed to get the money out or count the bills if I don't touch it?"

"Anyone else touch it? Like your wife?"

"The mailman touched the outer envelope, I guess. I didn't tell Brenda about the cash or it woulda been gone as fast as she could get to the nearest mall. Poof. Just like that. Don't tell her I said that."

"Mr. Bickle, it looks like a serious crime may have been committed in your house. I'm going to have to ask the local police department down there to check the envelope and remaining bills for fingerprints. They'll also need to take your fingerprints since we know you also touched the money."

"Ah geez, is that really necessary?"

"Totally necessary."

"Will I get my money back?"

"We'll have to keep the bills for evidence. However, I'll see if I can arrange to have a check sent to you to reimburse you for the amount."

"Can't you guys give me cash?"

McCabe smiled. "Sorry, Bob. I'm afraid you'll have to give Uncle Sam his share. Now I'd appreciate it if you would give me permission to enter the premises and search it for evidence."

"Jesus. Okay. Yeah. I guess so. That's fine."

"Do you have a smartphone?"

"Yeah."

"Okay, just write down your permission for me to enter. Sign it and take a photo of the page with your smartphone. Then just text the photo to me." He gave Bickle his name and cell number. "When I get there how do I get in?"

"You'll see a lockbox on the left-hand side of the porch facing the house. The combination is 7490. There should be a key to the front door inside."

"How big is the house?"

"Not big. Living room, kitchen and dining room downstairs. Two bedrooms and a bath upstairs. Like I said, only one of the bedrooms, the one to the right as you go up the stairs, is included in the rental. Bathroom's in the middle. The storage bedroom to the left."

"Any basement or attic space?"

"Nope."

"What do you store in the second bedroom?"

"Crap we shoulda thrown out years ago. Plus there's a one-car garage attached to the house. We added that ourselves back in the late '70s. Door from the garage goes into the kitchen. Would you do me one favor?"

"What?"

"Would you let me know if anything's wrong or been damaged?"

"We'll let you know."

McCabe hung up and thought about next steps. Did Bob Bickle's permission allow him to legally enter the house on Hartley Street? Maybe not by itself. Technically, as a renter, Norah Wilcox had a legal expectation of privacy till ten A.M. Saturday morning when the rental expired. If the case ever went to trial, Norah's defense lawyer would definitely argue that McCabe's entering the house without a warrant constituted an illegal search and any evidence found inside might therefore be inadmissible in court.

McCabe figured he had more than enough probable cause to get a judge to issue a warrant. On the other hand, with Joshua Thorne's life definitely at risk, McCabe didn't want to wait too long to get one. The photo Norah e-mailed to Rachel Thorne offered probable cause to believe that not only had a crime been committed on the premises but that Joshua Thorne might, even now, be in mortal danger. Still some judges could be tricky and the idea of blowing a case on a technicality? Well, it had happened before and he swore he'd never let it happen again. If he could get it done fast he'd get the damned warrant.

McCabe decided to call District Court Judge Paula Washburn,

who he knew could and would act fast if she agreed with him that the matter was urgent. She also lived in town on Danforth Street just minutes away. He punched in her cell number, still stored in his memory bank five years after she'd first given it to him in the Lucas Kane case. He just hoped Washburn hadn't changed her number and that she had her phone turned on.

She hadn't and she did. "Well, good evening, Sergeant. May I ask why you're calling me in the middle of my sacred martini hour?"

McCabe gave Washburn the two-minute version of what was going on.

"So you think you're going to find Joshua Thorne in that house?" she asked.

"I do."

"Which way? Dead or alive?"

"I'm willing to bet on dead but I don't really know. I may also find the suspect. Most likely alive."

"Okay. Just so I'm sure I've got this straight. First, an unknown woman calling herself Norah Wilcox rents the house at 339 Hartley Street from its owners, Bob and Brenda Bickle. However, Ms. Wilcox refuses to sign a lease. Instead, she pays Mr. Bickle in cash four times as much as Bickle is asking and she gives him a phony address and phone number. Secondly, a woman also calling herself Norah Wilcox allows herself to be picked up by Joshua Thorne in the bar at the Port Grill and suggests they go to a house she supposedly inherited from her parents that was quote 'only a few minutes away' unquote. Thirdly, there are no houses in the city of Portland owned by anybody named Norah Wilcox. Fourth, or is it fourthly? On the same night a woman also calling herself Norah Wilcox e-mails Joshua Thorne's wife a photograph of Mr. Thorne, naked, blindfolded and tied to a filthy mattress you can't imagine anyone willingly lying on. And fifthly, again if there is such a word, Mr. Thorne doesn't show up this morning for an important business meeting and nobody knows where he is. Does that pretty much sum it up?"

"Perfectly, Your Honor."

"All right. I'm signing your warrant. Stop by as soon as you get it written up."

"Thank you, Your Honor."

Chapter 18

As HE SLOWLY returned to consciousness Joshua Thorne wondered if a needle was still stuck in his thigh. Wondered what kind of drug Norah had stuck him with. Whatever it was it hadn't left him with the same kind of headache the first drug had.

He remembered the needle going in, the dizziness, the blacking out. But he had no idea how much time had passed since then. An hour? A couple of hours? Jesus, maybe even a whole day. Thorne tried and failed to open his eyes. The blindfold was still in place. The ropes still bound his wrists to the bed frame. He told himself to ignore the burning pain in his wrists he could still feel from his failed attempts to escape the first time around. Ignore the fact that his body still ached from having been tied in one position for what seemed like days. Ignore the fact that he was incredibly thirsty, his mouth feeling as dry and rough as sandpaper.

On the plus side, at least the headache was gone. Thank God for small favors. The absence of pain might help him assess his situation more clearly and logically instead of just hysterically shrieking into the void like he had before. The shrieking hadn't gotten him anywhere before and going nuts one more time again would not now get him free.

What Josh needed to do was come up with a plan. If anyone was capable of smart planning, it was him. He'd earned a well-deserved reputation as one of the smartest, cagiest deal makers, not just at Harris Brumfield, but anywhere on the Street. Hell, if he decided to leave Floyd in the lurch he knew he could land a half dozen job offers as easily as snapping his fingers. Headhunters called him all the time. He always told them he might be interested in moving. And then gave them a comp number that made them gasp. So far, nobody had come up with the number.

Anyway, he told himself, *stop telling yourself how cool and smart you are and concentrate on coming up with a plan.* Any damned plan that would get him out of here.

First things first. What Josh had to do now was stop fantasizing about beating the shit out of Norah and start figuring out how to convince her to let him go. He didn't really know her. Didn't know how she thought. What was important to her? What kind of offer might work? They'd never met before last night. He'd never even seen her. Yet she'd come into the bar not just willing to hook up but actually inviting him to come to her place (assuming this shithole actually belonged to a woman who wore a Patek Philippe watch, which he seriously doubted). The question was why. The first possibility, maybe the only possibility, was that someone had paid her a lot of money to do what she did. Which included screwing him. Which meant she was nothing more than a high-class whore. Maybe the simplest tactic, possibly the only tactic when dealing with whores, was to pay more than the other guy. He didn't really give a shit how much it'd take to get out of here. The key was to make it an amount she'd find believable yet tempting enough to take the chance to let him go. Top of the line escorts could easily demand three or four grand an hour for their services so she wasn't broke. A fact that the expensive watch on her wrist corroborated. He'd paid some really prime talent five grand himself. And Norah was without question prime talent. So what would it take to convince her to do something as potentially risky as double-crossing whoever had hired her by cutting the ropes that bound him. A million dollars for five minutes work with a knife? Way too much. She'd never believe it. But a hundred thousand? He considered that. Yes, he'd definitely go that high. And yes, she'd probably go for it. But wouldn't it be smarter to start lower? Maybe make fifty the opening bid and see how she reacted.

The trickier part of the equation was A) convincing her he wouldn't hurt her if she did cut the ropes. And B) convincing her that he really would pay up. He was a good salesman. Hell, he was a great salesman and, in this instance, he had a great case to make. All she had to do was cut the blindfold over his eyes so he could see what he was doing and then cut the rope holding his right hand. After that she could just take off while he was still tied to the bed and unable to give chase. With his right hand free he was sure he could work his way out of the rest of the ropes himself while she got herself out of harm's way. Second, even if he did meet with her at some later date to deliver the money, why on earth would he want to hurt her then and have the whole crazy nightmare end up going public? Probably with cops and courts and God only knew what. His boss would find out. His wife would find out. Potential future employers would find out. His reputation would be ruined. And so would his career. He thought about it and found the argument compelling. A hundred thou for her coupled with his need to keep the whole incident quiet. Okay. Settled. That was the pitch. Now all he needed was for her to come back.

He lay his head back down on the pillow and tried to breathe calmly and regularly. However long it took he wouldn't lose his temper again. It was just as he was telling himself that for maybe the fiftieth time that the silence was broken by a noise. A bang. Sounded like a small caliber gunshot from downstairs. Suddenly alert, Josh wondered what the hell was going on. Had someone come back in the house and shot Norah? Had she shot someone else? Could it just have been someone slamming a door? Or a fire-cracker going off on the street? He supposed any and all were possible.

"Norah?" he called again, keeping his voice calm, not angry, hoping against hope there would be some kind, any kind, of response.

Finally, to his surprise there was. Nothing verbal. Just the sound of feet climbing creaky stairs. Thank God, she was coming back. He'd make his pitch and soon he would be free.

The door to the bedroom opened. Warmer air from the hallway wafted across his body. Josh took in a deep breath.

"Norah? Is that you?" he asked in the pleasantest voice he could muster. "Where have you been? I was getting worried."

There was no answer. But there was definitely someone else in the room. No question about it. He could hear soft gentle breathing at the side of the bed. If only he could reach out and touch her. "So you came back?" he said. "That's great. Listen, there's something we should really talk about. Something that would benefit both of us greatly."

She still offered no response. But Josh could hear what sounded like her stocking or maybe bare feet moving across the room toward the end of the bed.

He turned his head in the direction the sound seemed to be coming from. "Well, I hope you've enjoyed yourself, Norah, but it's time to let me go. It really is. And you know what? I will pay you . . . are you listening . . . fifty thousand dollars in cash to simply cut the rope holding my right hand to the bed and remove the blindfold. I know, you're probably thinking if you cut the ropes I might hurt you in some way. But you know something? If you only cut the rope holding my right hand you could take off and I wouldn't be able to hit you or even touch you in any way."

There was still no response. Josh could still hear her breathing. Then he felt her hand lift his penis and hold it. Then she stroked his balls. What the fuck was going on? Did she want to have sex again? Weird. He wondered if she was still naked. Maybe she was just some kind of crazy sex addict. Maybe that's all this whole crazy thing was about.

"I won't hurt you," he said. "I promise I won't. Just cut the rope and let me go and I'll give you fifty thousand tax-free dollars no questions asked, no answers needed."

She started sliding her hand up and down his penis, her fingers tickling his balls. He felt himself growing hard. "Hey, listen, if you want to fool around again, well, we can do that."

The only response was a soft chuckle.

"Norah? What are you doing?" he asked as calmly as he could.

The hand between his legs began moving faster. Josh lay back, his breath coming more rapidly now, his mind too confused to object to something that even under the current circumstances still felt good.

"I hope you're enjoying your hand job, Josh. Because I'm afraid it's going to be the last one you'll ever get."

And just as Josh's body arched up in his final urgent sexual climax, he felt hands untying the blindfold and removing it from his eyes.

"I also want you to have one last look at me."

Josh opened his eyes and stared up in both shock and horror as the cold, sharp steel of a twelve-inch butcher's knife was raised high above his body and thrust deeply between his legs. He began screaming. But his screams of pain at what was happening were abruptly cut short as the point of the now bloodied knife, having done its work between his legs, was next pushed deeply into his neck and pulled across his throat, severing first his trachea, then his carotid artery and finally his jugular.

Before the self-proclaimed prince of Wall Street, the self-made millionaire, the hot-shit stud whose charms no woman could resist, before he could gather his wits enough to understand what the fuck was going on or even why, before he could begin to mentally process the horror of it all, Joshua Thorne's conscious mind blanked out. His breathing slowed. His life's blood, which had first flowed from the agonizing wounds of castration, now poured out, first in bursts and then in a torrent from his nearly severed neck. In less than a minute both the bleeding and Josh's breathing stopped for the very last time.

Chapter 19

MAGGIE HAD JUST crossed the Massachusetts line into Connecticut on I-84 when Toni Bernstein called. She said Heather Loughlin was willing—in fact, anxious—to meet with them tonight. As soon as Maggie could get there.

"At first she was reluctant," said Bernstein. "Went into the usual 'I've already told you everything I know' routine. Didn't know what business a cop from Portland had butting in blah-blah-blah. But as soon as I mentioned Joshua Thorne's name and told her he'd been declared missing, she turned on a dime and said she'd meet with us tonight. Whatever time you got here. She sounded not so much shook up . . . I don't know, almost excited hearing that something might have happened to him. Said she knew him from college."

"Heather went to Holden?"

"That's what she said."

"Did you get the feeling she might know something about Thorne's disappearance?"

"No. I don't think so. She sounded genuinely surprised to hear his name. What I do think is hearing about Thorne disappearing, just a week after Charlie's death, was proof to her that Charlie didn't kill himself. Proof he was murdered. Which I'd guess was her second choice from the beginning."

"Second choice?"

"Yeah. It makes a weird kind of sense. I think an accident would have been her first choice, but if the death wasn't accidental, maybe it's more comforting for the grieving widow to think some bad guy killed her husband than believing that the guy hated his life and his marriage so much he would kill himself to end it. At least if it's murder you don't spend the rest of your life wondering what you did wrong or what you might have done differently. So yeah. Bad as it is, murder is better than suicide. But we can talk more about that later, after you meet Heather. How long before you get here?" she asked.

"Forty-five minutes, give or take."

"Have your GPS take you to 67 Schuyler Road. Once you get close, you'll take a right off Albany onto Schuyler. Loughlin's house is about a quarter mile down on the right. Big stone Tudor. More ostentatious than beautiful. I'll be in a black unmarked Taurus parked right out front. Pull in behind me."

Maggie ended the call and asked Siri to take her to the Schuyler Road address. Siri told Maggie it would be her pleasure.

A little over half an hour later, she pulled her red TrailBlazer behind Bernstein's car and flashed her lights twice to announce her presence. Bernstein exited, ground out a cigarette, bent over and picked up the filter and stuck it in her jacket pocket. She lit another cigarette and walked back to the driver's side of Maggie's Chevy sucking in smoke. Maggie lowered the window and a wave of tobacco smoke blew in.

"Savage?"

"Call me Maggie. I take it you're Toni Bernstein."

"That's me."

"You always chain-smoke?"

"Pretty much. But if it bothers you I'll try to refrain."

"I can handle it."

Bernstein went around to the passenger's side and climbed up into the TrailBlazer. She was a big-boned woman, nearly as tall as Maggie and probably thirty pounds heavier. Not much of it looked like fat. Maggie guessed she was in her midforties. Her graying dark hair cut short. Even aided by careful makeup remnants of scars from what must have been a vicious case of teenage acne were still visible.

After exchanging some pleasantries about the drive down, Bernstein said, "Well, this is Charlie's house."

The large stone Tudor was set back maybe two hundred feet from the road. Both the house and the brick driveway leading to the three-car garage were well-lit with floods.

"Looks like the insurance business pays well. What's a place like this go for?"

Bernstein shrugged. "Today's market? Probably a million five. Give or take a hundred thou."

"So Charlie was making plenty of money."

"Oh yeah. More than you and me put together. Maybe not in the Wall Street class but Charlie was doing okay."

"What kind of insurance did he handle?"

"Mostly commercial. Charlie insured most of the small businesses in and around West Hartford. Quite a few of the bigger ones too."

"Tell me about the wife."

"A classic Heather. You know what I mean? One of those pretty blonde homecoming queen types I always hated in high school when I couldn't get a date and she had all the guys drooling over her. She and Charlie met in college."

"Does Heather have a career?"

"She used to do the weather on the Fox station out of Hartford back before her kids were born. Didn't know shit about meteorology but she looked good reading the teleprompter. Last six years, she's been a full-time mom with the help of a part-time nanny. Which means she gets to play golf and tennis as much as she wants and have lunch with her pals at the country club a couple of times a week. She also helps run a couple of local causes."

"Like what?"

"Local animal shelter. And the historic preservation society. But mostly she took care of her hubby, who I guess was as demanding of her as he was of his employees."

"Sexually demanding?"

"Maybe, but judging by her clothes, jewelry and the Mercedes SUV she drives, Mrs. Charlie had a pretty good gig while it lasted. Of course she was devastated by his death. Or so she says."

"Aside from the money, did she seem happy with her marriage?"

"If she wasn't she didn't let on. The two times I interviewed her she seemed pretty broken up by his death. You mind if we get out of the car? I could use another cigarette."

"It's okay. Just open your window and blow the smoke that way."

Bernstein tapped another Camel out of the pack and lit it. "You haven't asked me yet how much insurance Charlie carried."

"How much?"

"I don't know but I imagine a lot."

"Millions?"

"Probably. One of the folks at the Northway office wouldn't put a number on it, but he said Charlie quote 'arranged well for his family' unquote. Started going on about a bunch of fancy policies and trust arrangements most of which I couldn't make heads nor tails of. Not my area of expertise."

"Anybody else look into it?"

"Nobody has, thanks to the DA's hands-off order. But I have a feeling Heather the widow's going to be a whole lot richer than Heather the wife. Just has to find herself a willing boy toy."

"Any possibility she was the woman in the black parka?"

"Nope. She has a rock solid alibi for the night he was killed."

"Like what?"

"Dinner and girl talk with three friends at one of their houses. All three corroborate. Left about eleven. When she got home she told the seventeen-year-old babysitter she wanted her to call her mother and let her know she was spending the night. Said the roads were icy and dangerous and the girl had only been driving for a couple of months. Both the babysitter and the mother confirm the story. The two boys, Josh and Cameron, were both asleep. Heather says she had a glass of wine, watched *Letterman* with the sitter for an hour and then went to bed. Woke up at two in the morning when the youngest one, three-year-old Cameron, got frightened about something and climbed into bed with her."

Maggie held up both hands in surrender. "And I'll bet even Cameron corroborates the story. Right?"

Bernstein didn't laugh. "When Heather noticed Charlie wasn't there, she tried reaching him by phone. When she couldn't, she called 911. And yes, for what it's worth, Cameron vouches for his mother. At least, when asked the question 'Did you get in bed with Mommy last night?' he nods solemnly. So no. Heather Loughlin did not kill her husband. Guaranteed. How about Thorne's wife? What was she up to the night he disappeared? She have an alibi?"

"Three hundred miles away in Brooklyn, New York, going to a movie and having dinner with a friend. The friend corroborates. When did they find Charlie's body?"

"Next morning around eight. A man driving to work stopped at the overlook to take a pee behind the bushes."

"Popular pastime."

"Certainly seems so. Wish us girls had it so easy. Anyway, the guy checks out Charlie's empty car. Then looks over the edge, sees Charlie lying there and calls us."

Maggie frowned. "If Charlie was pushed over the edge and Charlie's car was still there, how did the pusher leave the scene?"

"Good question. We checked and nobody called a cab. So either an accomplice picked the killer up or Wilcox, if it was Wilcox, must have gone on foot."

"How far?"

"About five miles from the restaurant parking lot. Assuming that's where Norah left her vehicle."

Maggie thought about that. Five miles was easily walkable. Even on a cold winter night.

Bernstein read her mind. "For what it's worth, nobody reported seeing any walkers on that road at that hour."

Maggie filed the question away in her mind and changed the subject. "Did you ever ask Heather about Charlie being accused of rape in college?"

"It never came up. And I didn't mention it when I made the date with her tonight. Just told her Joshua Thorne had gone missing up in Portland. That you were investigating the case and thought there might be some connection with Charlie's death. She didn't ask what kind of connection, which I found a little curious. I have no idea what, if anything, she knows about the college rape or about the victim's suicide."

Bernstein ground out her third cigarette in ten minutes. Pocketed the filter. "Let's head up to the house," she said. "I'll make preliminary intros and then you take it from there."

Maggie nodded. "Works for me. Let's go."

The two detectives walked up the driveway and then along a long bluestone path to a large Tudor-style front door that was rounded at the top and looked like it had been crafted from solid oak planks. Bernstein used a big black knocker rather than ring the bell.

After a minute or so the door was opened by a woman in her early thirties with a good figure, regular features and the kind of bland blonde good looks that seem to be de rigueur for female reporters on cable news stations. Except, at the moment, this particular blonde had her shoulder-length hair tied back in a ponytail. She was dressed casually in jeans, a blue sweatshirt with the letters *KP* on it and a pair of expensive running shoes. She opened the door wider and peered past them into the darkness. "No reporters or news trucks hanging around out there?" she asked.

"No. Have they been bothering you?"

"Yeah. Constantly right after Charlie died. Not so much the last few days. Not since the DA decided it was an accident."

She signaled them inside. "Come on in. I'm Heather Loughlin."

Maggie held out her hand. "Detective Margaret Savage. Portland Police Department."

Mrs. Loughlin looked down at the outstretched hand and hesitated for a split second before taking and shaking it. "I'm sure you're who you say you are but may I see some identification?

What with the reporters and other creeps who've been banging on the door, I like to know for sure who I'm talking to."

Maggie flipped open her badge wallet and handed it to Heather Loughlin, who examined both the gold badge and the photo ID.

"Mrs. Loughlin," said Maggie.

"Please call me Heather."

"Okay, Heather, I'm Maggie. Thanks for meeting with us so late."

"Late is actually better. We just got the boys off to sleep. Why don't we talk in the den? It's quieter back there and we're less likely to wake them up." Without waiting for a response, Heather Loughlin led them through a large center hall that boasted polished hardwood floors covered with oriental rugs, past a grandiose staircase and through a large modern kitchen that seemed to Maggie to have been taken right out of the pages of *Maine Home and Design* or, she supposed in Heather's case, Connecticut Home and Design, if such a magazine existed. Beyond the kitchen was an even larger room with a vaulted ceiling and glass doors that opened onto a patio and at least a half an acre of backyard lit with floods. Maggie noted a huge flat-screen TV that was turned on but muted. Built-in bookcases in dark wood dominated one wall and a floor-to-ceiling stone fireplace another. A gas fire burned in the hearth. In the center of the room a pair of large overstuffed love seats faced each other with a matching ottoman in between. Everything looked expensive. Tasteful but expensive.

Heather sat in one of the love seats and signaled Bernstein and Maggie to take the one opposite her. She took a sip from a large glass of red wine that was on the table next to her. There was a mostly empty bottle next to that. Maggie wondered how much she'd had to drink prior to their arrival.

"Can I offer you some wine? Or perhaps coffee? Or tea?"

"No thank you. Nothing," said Maggie.

Bernstein continued. "Like I told you, Maggie is investigating a missing-person case in Portland."

"Yes. Joshua Thorne."

Maggie picked up the questioning. "You know Thorne?"

"Not since college." Heather shook her head and spoke, more to herself than to the two detectives. "Jesus Christ, first Charlie's dead and now, like two weeks later, Josh Thorne goes missing? What the hell is going on?"

"But you did know Thorne?"

"Of course I knew him. We all went to college together. Holden College up in Willardville, New York. That's where Charlie and I met. Charlie and Josh were good buddies back then. Fraternity brothers. Teammates on the football team. Lacrosse team as well."

"When was the last time you saw Josh? Or spoke to him?"

"Me personally? Not for ages. Four or five years at least. Charlie and Josh haven't seen much of each other lately either. I think the last time was back at their tenth reunion two years ago."

"Did you go to the reunion?"

"No. I was class of '03. One year behind them. But other than that, all I know about Josh these days is what Charlie told me. That he was making a zillion bucks a year and swaggering around like he owned the world and everything in it. The way Charlie described it, Josh kinda thought of himself as the Wolf of Wall Street? Y'know the movie? With Leo DiCaprio? Said Josh thought he could buy anything or anyone he wanted."

Maggie frowned. If Charlie described Josh that way it had to be recently because the movie only came out last Christmas. She knew because she'd seen it with Charles Kraft the night she and

Kraft broke up. Just before New Year's Eve. She'd ended up toasting the New Year in the back booth at Tallulah's with McCabe, who was also on his own at the time.

"At the reunion Charlie tried to pitch Brumfield Harris's insurance business and Josh blew him off. Said he didn't handle the company's insurance stuff and then shut the conversation off. Charlie got kind of pissed about that. Said as an old friend and fraternity brother Josh could at least have offered to make some introductions to whoever did handle the company's insurance. It'd take minimal effort on Josh's part. But getting into the New York financial market would have been a big deal for Charlie."

"So Charlie was angry with Josh?"

"I think hurt or wounded would be more accurate. In any case, I think that's why they haven't talked to each other since."

"You said you met Charlie at college?"

"Yeah. I met him a couple of months after I got there but didn't start dating him seriously till spring semester of my sophomore, his junior, year."

"How about Josh? Did you ever date him? Before Charlie, I mean."

Heather offered a small smile. "Joshua Thorne? I think every girl on campus had the hots for him. I mean, have you ever seen Thorne? The guy is Hollywood handsome. Least he was back then. Smart too."

"Were you one of the girls who had 'the hots'?"

Heather poured what was left of the wine into her glass.

"Yeah, sort of. I mean, if he showed any interest before Charlie and I got together I probably would have jumped at the chance.

But he never did. And then the thing with Charlie started and I fell in love with him. He asked me to marry him his senior year." A sad smile crossed Heather's face. "He proposed March 21. First day of spring. He thought that would be a romantic day to get engaged. 'Course in upstate New York, March 21 is still the middle of winter so when he got down on his knee he was kneeling in twelve inches of snow. Gave me one of the smallest diamonds you ever saw." Maggie checked the diamond currently on Heather's finger. Definitely not the smallest she'd ever seen. Heather must have traded the first one in somewhere along the way. "Charlie's family didn't have much money. Ring cost him his entire savings from his summer job."

Heather seemed lost in memories of what Maggie supposed were happier times and she decided to let her ramble on. "We were married the following year after I graduated. Josh was one of the groomsmen. After college Charlie got a job selling insurance here in West Hartford. I'd majored in voice and theater and I'd wanted to go to New York and see if I could get anywhere as an actress. Instead, because Charlie was already working for Northway and he was—" Heather used her fingers to make air quotes "'—the man in the family,' his ambitions were more important than mine. In the end I looked for a job in Hartford and became the weather girl for the local Fox station. Reporting live from the scene on multicar accidents during winter storms was as close to theater as I ever got aside from some local amateur productions. Then, of course, the kids came along and Charlie convinced me becoming a full-time mom was—" more finger quotes "'—the right thing to do.'" Heather downed the last of her wine, got up and pulled a new bottle from a wine rack under one of the bookcases. She opened it and poured a glass. "Sure you guys won't join me? I kind of hate drinking alone."

Maggie shook her head. "No can do. Not while we're working but thanks anyway."

Heather sat and sipped quietly for a minute. "Still think I could have been a damned good actress if I'd let myself take a chance." There was more than a hint of self-pity in her voice now. "If I hadn't let Charlie talk me out of it. Too late now. For all of us."

Chapter 20

AT ABOUT THE same time that Maggie pulled in behind Toni Bernstein's Taurus, McCabe turned his own unmarked Ford Interceptor off Stevens Avenue and onto Hartley Street, a search warrant signed by Judge Washburn tucked securely in his breast pocket. He parked on the far side of the street, half a dozen houses down from 339. The spot gave him a good view of the place without much chance of being spotted by anyone inside. He sat quietly for ten minutes waiting for lights to go on, or shades to go up, or any other signs of activity. He saw none. The house seemed uninhabited.

Deciding he'd waited long enough, he fished a pair of latex gloves and Tyvek booties from the center console and stuffed them in the side pocket of his black overcoat, an older and shabbier version of the coat Mark Christensen had worn this morning, a relic from McCabe's New York days working homicide for the NYPD. He exited the car and walked up the far side of the street, passing three or four parked cars, keeping an eye out for dog walkers, runners, any pedestrians at all. When he reached a point directly opposite 339, he looked both ways. Seeing nothing suspicious, he crossed over. Walked up the redbrick path and climbed three wooden steps badly in need of a paint job to a house that, from the outside, looked both unloved and uncared for. No wonder Bickle could only get six hundred bucks a week for it even in high season.

The lockbox was attached to a wrought-iron railing on the left side of the landing where Bickle said it would be. McCabe pulled on the gloves and slid the booties over his shoes. Then he lifted the lockbox and, being careful not to smudge possible fingerprints, released the catch to a small sliding panel and pushed it up. Underneath were four numbered rotors, the numbers just visible in the faint glow of a streetlamp. Using the tip of a pen, he pushed each rotor carefully to the appropriate number. The box popped open. Empty. No key inside. He hadn't expected that. Could Norah have simply taken the key with her when she left? Or thrown it away? Or was she still in residence? Technically the place was hers till Saturday so maybe she'd just gone out to buy groceries. Or to a restaurant. Or, for all McCabe knew, maybe he and Maggie were wrong about Thorne being dead. Instead maybe Josh and Norah were upstairs in bed fucking their brains out or, given the bondage shot, maybe Mistress Norah was giving Josh the spanking of his life and Josh was loving it.

There was also another, more lethal possibility. That Thorne was in the house either dead and still tied up, but that Norah hadn't left yet. She was hunkered down inside, hiding in the dark, holding a gun and patiently waiting for the asshole on the porch to come bumbling through the door before blowing his head off.

Standing off to one side, McCabe rang the bell. In response there was nothing but silence from inside. As he debated going in and checking the place out, McCabe could hear the familiar little voice in his head reminding him that one of the first things every cop learns is to never, ever enter a potentially dangerous situation without backup. There were rules against it in pretty much every department in the world. Rules McCabe had broken more times than he cared to admit or even remember. But rules that were, nevertheless, there for a reason.

In the end he said, as he almost always did, the hell with the rules. He didn't want to waste any more time. Especially if Thorne was still alive. McCabe pressed his back against the vinyl siding and moved silently to the edge of the door. He leaned in as close as he could and listened for sounds from within. There were none. If Norah or anyone else was waiting on the other side, they were doing so in total silence. McCabe slid his Glock from its holster. Squatting low, he reached across and turned the knob on the off chance it would open and he wouldn't have to waste time picking the lock. To his surprise, it did open and McCabe pushed it in about six inches. The hinges emitted a small squeak, but no shots rang out in response. No shouts for help came from a wounded Joshua Thorne. He supposed it was possible Wilcox had left in such a hurry she hadn't bothered either to lock the door or return the key. On the other hand it remained equally possible she was kneeling in the dark, waiting for him to present himself as an easy target.

He took a deep breath. Let it out slowly. Then moved in fast and low, sweeping his gun in a wide arc across the room. No shots rang out. No bullets tore into him. Nothing moved. Silently he closed the door, rose and looked around.

The room was cloaked in darkness, pieces of furniture appearing as little more than shadows. He stood motionless, waiting for his eyes to adjust to the gloom. After a minute the shadows began forming themselves into more tangible shapes. He found himself in a small sparsely furnished living room. He could see the side of a brown corduroy sofa in front of him and a low coffee table in front of that. Some sort of cabinet was pushed against the wall to his left. What looked like a bookcase dominated the wall to the right. A couple of straight-back chairs in the corners. On the coffee table, McCabe could just make out the shapes of what looked like two empty martini glasses, one turned over on its side. If Norah's lips had sipped from one, her DNA should still be on it. Careless if she was about to commit murder. McCabe figured everybody in America who watched enough episodes of *CSI* would know they shouldn't leave evidence like that behind.

Maybe Norah didn't watch TV. Maybe she preferred picking up men in bars and tying them to beds. He'd collect both glasses on his way out. Or have Jacoby do it. A precaution in case she was planning on coming back after he left and cleaning up.

Under his feet, the floor was covered in something soft. He flicked on the flashlight app and pointed it down. Shag carpeting. Faded orange. The same style and color his mother still had on the living room floor in his childhood home. The height of fashion in Irish neighborhoods in the north Bronx thirty years ago. Brother Bobby had offered to replace the old shag half a dozen times. But Rosie McCabe always gave him the same answer. She wanted to keep the place the way it was when her husband, Tom McCabe Sr., had been alive and the kids lived at home. She said Dad always liked the feel of the rug under his feet. And so did she.

Keeping his back as close as he could to the wall, McCabe shuffled quickly around the room, careful not to bump into anything or knock anything over. He passed a pair of windows covered with orange curtains. Under the curtains, closed venetian blinds. He raised a slat and peered out. No one approaching. No one watching from the street. He dropped the slat and continued around the room. Went around the bookcase that contained more touristy knickknacks than books. Relics, he supposed, from Bickle vacations taken years before. Beyond the bookcase, a TV stand with a thirty-two-inch flat-screen set on top. Beyond the TV he found a closed door. Reaching across, pulled it open and peered in. No hidden shooters inside. Just a coat closet with no coats. Just half a dozen metal hangers on the cross bar and a canister vacuum cleaner on the floor with what looked like a dark lump behind it. He pointed the phone light at the lump and it turned into a pile of men's clothes. He bent down and pulled out the top piece. A finely tailored men's suit jacket. Exactly like the one Thorne wore in the surveillance video. In the breast pocket was a leather wallet. The rest of Joshua Thorne's clothes, including his underwear, were piled under the jacket. Unless he'd left the house buck-naked he was still here. McCabe returned the jacket to the pile and left the clothes where he found them. He'd go through Thorne's wallet later.

McCabe shut the closet door and started moving again. Reaching an open entryway, he ran his light around an empty dining room. The matched dining room set looked like thirty-year-old relics from Bob's Discount Stores or whatever the '80s equivalent was. Blinds were pulled down over the windows and closed tight. A repro print on one wall featured a brown-skinned girl in Mexican garb dancing while in the background a guy wearing a sombrero and serape strummed a guitar. A mirror in a wood frame hung on the other wall.

McCabe guessed no one had eaten in this room anytime recently. It was about as inviting as eating in a morgue. Beyond the dining room, to his right, a steep, narrow staircase led up to a second-floor landing. McCabe debated going upstairs to see if he could find the bedroom where the bondage photo of Josh had been taken but self-preservation told him it was smarter to clear the rest of the downstairs first. Make sure no one was down here, hiding in the kitchen or possibly in the attached garage. Maggie would never forgive him if he let himself get shot in the back in the process of climbing upstairs to look for someone who was probably already dead. Nope. She'd never, ever let him hear the end of something as stupid as that.

He headed for the kitchen. Moved in fast and found neither armed assailants, nor dead or dying bankers. Just an empty, ordinary kitchen with appliances that were old, plain and white. Formica countertops, a beige linoleum floor and a small wooden table with a pair of chairs completed the accessories.

McCabe moved to a door with two rows of checked gingham curtains covering glass panels. He pushed the curtains aside and flashed his light out into a small, windowless one-car garage. A tan late-model Nissan Altima was parked inside. He opened the door and went in fast, checking to make sure no one was crouching down on the other side of the car or in any of the dark corners of the garage. No one was. He glanced back at the car. It had Maine plates but bore no bumper stickers, window stickers or other identifying marks. He pulled open the driver's side door. No dead bodies or live killers lurking inside. Just a set of keys with a plastic Avis tag lying in the center console and beside them a book. A well-worn leather Day Runner. The kind of appointment book most people had stopped using back when they got their first smartphone or tablet. But also the kind that, unlike their electronic cousins, left no permanent or traceable records behind. McCabe picked up the Day Runner and stuffed it in his overcoat pocket to be examined after he'd finished searching the house. Other than that there was nothing. No coffee cups in the holders. No footprints on the rubber floor mats. No Burger King wrappers or other detritus lying around. Still, nobody drives a car even a short way without leaving some trace evidence. Hair, fingerprints, bits of dry skin, whatever. McCabe would leave that particular search to Bill Jacoby and his evidence techs who would do a much better job of finding whatever was there, which would probably include traces of previous drivers as well as some from Norah Wilcox.

Bending down on the driver's side of the car, McCabe found a trunk release button and pressed it. The latch popped open.

He scurried low to the back of the car, wondering if there was any way the body of a six foot three, two hundred and ten pound guy like Joshua Thorne could fit into the trunk of a Nissan. According to McCabe's father, a much decorated veteran of thirty plus years on the NYPD, the New York mob traditionally used the oversized trunks of 1980s Lincoln town cars to transport the bodies of their generally shorter but mostly fatter victims. Tom McCabe senior had even entertained the guests at one of his parents' Saturday night dinner parties regaling them with a case in which two short, fat and very dead wiseguys had been stuffed together in what looked like a compromising position inside the trunk of a single town car. A Nissan Altima wasn't, however, a town car.

McCabe lifted the trunk lid and stared. A dead body was indeed tucked inside. Just not the dead body he'd been expecting. Instead of the former Holden College quarterback and current Wall Street millionaire, the car's trunk contained the mortal remains of one very beautiful, very blonde and very dead hooker who just happened to bear a striking resemblance to the actress Gillian Anderson. Though the resemblance was hard to see with her hands and slender wrists reaching outward toward McCabe in a vain attempt to stop the bullet that had left a small hole almost perfectly centered in the middle of her forehead. McCabe flipped on his light and played it quickly over her body. She was still dressed exactly as she'd been in the video from the Port Grill. A black down coat was pushed in behind her. From the positioning of the body, McCabe guessed that the killer had forced Norah to climb into the trunk herself, no doubt at gunpoint, no doubt promising not to kill her if she cooperated. Norah's empty eyes were open, starting to cloud over but still reflecting the bright light from McCabe's phone back at him. He didn't think she'd been dead very long. Risking the wrath of Jacoby, he stripped off a glove and laid a single bare finger on her neck just under her jawbone. Even lying in the cold of the garage, her skin temperature still retained some warmth. Dead no more than an hour and probably less. Which meant he may have just missed catching the killer. Whoever the killer was. Joshua Thorne? Maybe. Somebody else? A third person? Just as likely. Maybe even more so.

McCabe put his glove back on and once again looked down at the dead woman. He knew it was way past time to stop playing Lone Ranger and call in the cavalry before he got his own ass shot off. Still gazing into the trunk, he pulled his phone from his pocket and started to make the call.

Thinking about it later, he wondered why he didn't hear the footsteps coming up behind him. Maybe it was because his mind was too focused on trying to figure out why Norah had been murdered. Or who had done it. Or maybe Maggie was right when she insisted that his hearing was going. Especially when he couldn't hear a thing she said when they sat across from each other in the back booth on a crowded night at Tallulah's. Whichever it was, the simple fact was that McCabe neither heard nor sensed the person approaching from behind. At least, not until he felt the barrel of a small handgun thrust into the left side of his neck. He instantly dropped and started turning in an effort to grab the hand holding the gun before the shooter could fire. But it was all in vain. Just as he began the turn something hard and heavy slammed into the right side of his head.

McCabe stumbled first to his knees and then facedown on the hard concrete floor. His world turned black. Michael McCabe, whose only experience in the ring was occasionally sparring with Brian Cleary at the Portland Boxing Club, was knocked out just as quickly and just as cold as if, for some idiotic reason, he tried going fifteen rounds with Evander Holyfield.

Chapter 21

MAGGIE FIGURED SHE'D listened to about as much as she could take of Heather's sob story about her unfulfilled dreams of theatrical stardom. Even worse, thanks to her fourth or maybe it was her fifth glass of wine, the wannabe actress was starting to slur her words. While the alcohol might help loosen her tongue, Maggie needed the words that came out of her mouth to be at least minimally coherent. It was time to cut to the chase. Past time, in fact. Maggie got up from the love seat, walked behind it and stood, resting her hands on the back. A dominant position, especially given that she was nearly six feet tall, from which she could look down at Heather Loughlin as she grilled her. "Okay, Heather. It's time for you to tell me everything you know about the girl your husband and Joshua Thorne and maybe some other fraternity brothers raped their senior year in college."

Heather stared up at Maggie, abruptly alert to unexpected danger. She suddenly seemed less drunk. "I don't know what you're talking about?"

"Come on, Heather. Of course you know. The freshman girl

Charlie and Josh Thorne and, from what I hear, a bunch of other Holden College Warriors—that's their nickname, isn't it, the Warriors?—the girl they gang-raped at a fraternity party in the fall of their senior year."

Heather stared blankly as if the question had struck her dumb.

"Don't just sit there and say nothing, Heather. You and Charlie were dating back then, weren't you? Hell, you must have been. It was only a few months before he gave you—what did you call it?—the world's smallest diamond. And it *was* a Saturday night so wouldn't you, the almost fiancée, have been with him? Or at least nearby when it happened? You were at that party, weren't you?"

"I don't know what you're talking about. Charlie would never rape anyone."

"Bullshit."

Heather reached across to get her glass from the side table. She missed. It tipped. Some wine spilled on her jeans.

"Oh, shit." She got up to wipe it off.

"Sit down, Heather," Maggie commanded. "Put the glass down. Your jeans can wait. This investigation into your husband's murder can't."

"Charlie died in a terrible accident . . ."

"Wake up, Heather. Charlie's death was no accident. I'll say it as plainly as I can. I believe, and Detective Bernstein agrees with me, that your husband was murdered ten days ago in retaliation for the recent suicide of the freshman girl he attacked and raped at Holden College in the fall of his senior year. Joshua Thorne may also have been murdered for the same reason."

Heather paled. "I don't know anything about that."

"Jesus Christ, Heather, please don't give me any more of this bullshit. Josh told his wife and his wife told us that it was Josh who raped the girl first, that Charlie went second and who knows how many others came next. No pun intended. It took the girl, who was just a seventeen-year-old freshman, a few months to work up the courage to go to the college administrators and charge these two big, strong football hotshots with forcible sexual assault. In other words, rape. She had passed out by the time the others took their turns so Josh and your soon-to-be fiancé were the only ones she could name."

Heather looked up. Her face squeezed itself into a distorted rage. "You shut up, you fucking bitch!" she screamed. "You're shitting on the memory of a man I loved and just buried and everything you're saying is just bullshit!"

Maggie leaned in further, still resting her hands on the back of the love seat and wishing she could get closer. Wishing she could get right in Heather's face. "Bullshit?" asked Maggie. "Really? The college told the girl, the one Josh and your husband raped, that she couldn't press charges because she'd waited too long to come forward. There was no longer any physical evidence to prove her case. And maybe more important to the college administrators, the men who did it, the rapists, were big-deal athletes. Football and lacrosse stars. The publicity backlash if it went public would have been murderous. Contributions from wealthy alumni would probably take a dive. Especially alumni who were football fans. And maybe even well-heeled female alumnae who didn't like hearing about gang rapes by star athletes. And then, of course, who knows how many smart high school seniors would suddenly change their minds and decide their first choice college was Bates or Hamilton or who knows where. But anywhere other than Rape Central.

"So the deans told the girl to forget about it. Told her to shut up and pretend it never happened. But that was kind of tough for her to do. Because by this time the rumor mill was in high gear and word of the rape had spread all over campus. So even if Charlie didn't tell you about it himself, a whole lot of somebody else's would have. Holden's a small school. Less than two thousand students. No way you could have avoided hearing the rumors of what your husband did."

By this time, Heather was rigid with anger. "I told you to shut the fuck up!"

But Maggie kept pressing. "So don't sit there and try to hand me any more of your crap about this being the first time you ever heard about it."

Heather pushed herself up on wobbly legs. "Leave me alone, you fucking bitch!" she screamed. And as she screamed, she picked up her half-full glass of red wine, reared back and hurled it at Maggie's head. Maggie barely managed to dodge the missile, which flew past her left ear and smashed into the seventy-five-inch flat-screen TV where it shattered into a million pieces. The muted screen went dark.

"Get out of here!" Heather screamed, her hands covering her face. "I don't want you in my house! Get out! Get out! Get out!"

Maggie calmly wiped red wine from her face with the sleeve of her jacket. Didn't make much difference to the jacket. The wine stains wouldn't come out anyway. It was time to let up a little. Lowering her voice to a calm, friendly tone, she said, "Heather, I really think you'd feel a lot better if . . ."

But Heather wasn't done. Before Maggie could finish speaking, Heather charged Maggie, her fists clenched. She drew back her right arm to throw a fist at Maggie's face. Moving fast for a woman her size, Toni Bernstein was up and on her, grabbing Heather from behind before the fist could land. Toni turned her and pushed her down until her body was doubled over the arm of the love seat. Bernstein then pulled both of Heather's arms up behind her and, with the practiced ease of the veteran cop she was, snapped a pair of cuffs around the struggling woman's wrists. Then with one hand on the back of Heather's neck she pushed her face down into the cushions of the love seat.

Heather struggled, arching her body, first left, then right. Trying desperately to free herself from Bernstein's grasp. "Let me go," she snarled. "Let me go, you fucking bull dyke bitch!"

But Bernstein was too strong and Heather knew it. After a minute she simply let herself go limp.

Bernstein pulled her to her feet and frog-walked her back to her own seat and sat her down. "All right, Mrs. Loughlin. Because I know you've been under a lot of stress," she said in a quietly controlled voice, "I'm going to give you two choices. Choice number one, you can stop drinking right now, sit quietly in your seat and do your best to answer Detective Savage's questions like a responsible adult. If you promise to do that, I'll remove the handcuffs and we can continue. But if you don't, and this is your second option, I'm going to place you under arrest for assaulting a police officer, take you down to the station and lock you in an interview room where you can either answer Detective Savage's questions or, if you don't want to, you can submit to a body cavity search, change into a jumpsuit and have your cute little rear end tossed in a jail cell. The choice is yours. But if you decide to choose door number two, let me know now so I can read you your Miranda rights before we load you into my car to head downtown."

Chapter 22

HEATHER LOUGHLIN SUCKED in a series of deep breaths and let them out slowly. She looked from one detective to the other before finally saying in a quiet voice, "Okay. I'm sorry. I'm sorry for being rude."

"Rude?" asked Maggie, stifling a laugh. "You'd place your violent behavior under the category of being rude?"

"Yes. It was rude. And yes, also violent. But you must know I'm very upset by Charlie's death and I guess it's obvious I've had too much to drink. It won't happen again. If you would please remove the handcuffs I'll answer your questions as best I can."

Maggie nodded at Bernstein and Bernstein pulled Heather to her feet and unlocked the cuffs. Heather sat back down and rubbed her wrists. "By the way," she said to Maggie, "let me pay you for your jacket. That wine's probably ruined it."

"I'd rather you just answered my questions. I need you to tell me what you know about the rape and how you know it." Maggie took a small digital recording device from her jacket pocket. "I'm going to record what you say."

Heather blinked her eyes, saying nothing, apparently debating how best to tell the tale. "I should tell you I learned some of this back in 2001, the year it happened. A few of the details I only learned recently."

"How recently?"

"Early January. A man I'd never met visited me and filled in parts of the story I didn't know about. Anyway, the rape happened in the fall of my junior year at Holden. Charlie and Josh's senior year. A Saturday night in October about a month after 9/11. I think everybody in America remembers those days after the attacks so clearly because it was all so awful and the atmosphere was so tense. Anyway, that particular Saturday night there was a rush party at the fraternity both Charlie and Josh belonged to, Alpha Chi Delta. It was considered one of the two or three best houses on campus. A lot of the football players and other athletes belonged to it."

"A rush party?"

"Yes. Any freshman boys who were interested in rushing Alpha Chi were told that if they wanted to be considered for membership they'd have to show up at this party to be evaluated. Part of the evaluation was that they have to bring at least one freshman girl to the party who was good-looking enough to pass muster. If they brought two girls, it made their chances of getting in and maybe getting a bid even better."

"Who decides who's good-looking enough?" asked Maggie.

"One of the senior brothers, usually a football player, is stationed at the door and he makes the decision. The idea is that anybody who wants to become a brother has to be cool enough to bring, as they put it, one or two hot-looking babes. Otherwise they get turned away."

"Sounds like my husband would've been out of luck," said Bernstein. "Leastways, if he'd brought me."

Heather actually smiled at the remark. "I don't know. Depends what you looked like when you were eighteen."

"Like I look now. Only thirty years younger. Anyway, keep going with your story."

"There were probably a hundred people there. Dancing. Drinking beer. Making out. Just about all the girls who were there were freshmen who'd come with one or another of the potential rushees. Other than that there were probably a few local high school girls."

"But you're saying you weren't there?"

"No. I wasn't. The only time I ever went to an Alpha Chi rush party was my freshman year. It's where I met Charlie so I know how the party goes. The upper classmen immediately start birddogging the best-looking freshman girls the boys bring to the house. It's like the new girls on campus are, I don't know, an offering to the older brothers. Kind of a gift to gain admission."

"An *offering*?" Maggie asked. "The freshman girls are supposed to be *offerings*? Is that what you called it?"

"Yeah. I know it sounds kind of crude but it's not really that bad. How it worked was that after they got there all the freshmen guys are herded upstairs and locked in this attic room where a couple of the upper classmen, the so-called rush committee, are stationed first to interview them and second to make sure they don't try to escape. Meanwhile the rest of the upper classmen . . ."

"How many?"

Heather shrugged. "Forty or fifty. They're at the party downstairs trying to get to meet the 'new talent,' as they called it. Senior boys get first pick of the best-looking girls. Juniors go second and so on."

"What are you telling me? That *all* the girls got raped?"

"Of course not. It wasn't like that. I'm sure the boys all would have loved to have gotten laid with one or another of the freshmen girls but I don't think many, if any of them, actually did. The party had nothing to do with rape. Mostly they just danced and drank and, if they wanted to, they made out. If some had sex, and some probably did, as far as I know it was totally consensual."

"Keep going."

"I never heard anything about Charlie being involved in any accusations of rape until much later. The beginning of winter term after Christmas break. All I know is when we got back to campus for winter trimester, there were all these rumors swirling around campus that some freshman girl was accusing Josh and Charlie, who were well-known on campus 'cause they were the two biggest stars on both the football and lacrosse teams, and also accusing some of their other fraternity brothers of gang-raping her at Alpha Chi's October rush party. It was all anybody on campus was talking about."

"And everybody knew what the girl's name was?"

"Yes. Hannah Reindel. She'd gone to the dean of students and accused Josh and Charlie of raping her at the rush party. She claimed Josh put drugs in her drink. Roofies, I guess. Or maybe something else. Anyway, when she started getting groggy, she said he dragged her upstairs to a room where Charlie and some other guys were supposedly waiting. She claimed that Charlie was the one who ripped her clothes off but that Josh raped her first. After that Charlie took his turn. Then a bunch of others. She said she was too groggy from the drugs by that time to remember who or how many others there were. She just said she was sure there were a bunch of them. The only names she remembered were Charlie and Josh. Maybe because they were well-known athletes or maybe because they went first. Before she passed out."

Chapter 23

McCabe wasn't sure how much time had passed before he slowly regained consciousness and staggered to his feet. All he knew was that he had a bitch of a headache, the side of his face felt hot and swollen, the garage door was open, cold wet air was blowing in and the car that held Norah Wilcox's body was gone. And so was the cell phone he'd been about to use to call for help when his world went black.

When McCabe felt steady enough to remain upright without holding on to anything he went through all his pockets looking for the phone, not really expecting to find it, which he didn't. Not in the pocket he usually kept it in. Not in any of the others. Next he checked to see if his Glock was still in its holster. Happily it was. But first things first. McCabe needed help and that meant he had to find the phone before he did anything else.

It was possible it had fallen from his hand when he went down. Or perhaps when he was being dragged across the floor? It was too damned dark in the garage to see much of anything especially now that he didn't have the help of the iPhone flashlight. He got down on his knees and started checking the floor around him, sweeping his hand from left to right, starting from where he'd regained consciousness to where he figured he must have been standing when he was looking at Norah's body in the trunk. He couldn't find the phone anywhere. Nothing but a whole lot of dirt and what felt like a gooey oil stain.

Okay, he told himself, ignore the pain. Think clearly. The killer was gone. Probably to dump the body. And McCabe needed to find his phone. No reason he could think of not to turn on the lights. He pushed himself back onto his feet, half walked, half staggered toward the kitchen door. After thirty seconds of stroking the wall he found the switch and turned it on.

McCabe waited a few seconds while his eyes adjusted to the light. Then he searched every inch of the garage floor. No luck. No phone. Not even one smashed to smithereens by having car wheels roll over it as it backed out of the garage. The killer must have taken it with him. A smart, if temporary, way to keep McCabe from calling for help.

At least whoever had whacked him had been considerate enough to have dragged or rolled McCabe's unconscious body over to the kitchen side of the garage before backing out. More thoughtful than driving over him. Possibly he or maybe she had no interest in killing people who weren't involved in any rapes. On the other hand, they'd put that bullet in Norah Wilcox's brain and as far as McCabe knew Norah hadn't raped anyone.

Heading back into the kitchen, McCabe couldn't shake the image of Norah's dead eyes staring blankly up into his, as if pleading with him to find and punish whoever it was who'd taken her life. He offered up a silent promise that he would.

McCabe turned on a light in the kitchen. In a drawer under

a whiskey glass that held the drying remains of what looked and smelled like Scotch, McCabe found a pile of dishtowels. He took one and opened the freezer door. The first thing he noticed inside was a clear rectangular bottle lying on its side. The glass bottle was marked by what looked like an upside down *T* atop a second upright *T*. Beneath the double *T* logo, at the bottom of the bottle, was the brand name. *Double Cross.* He left the bottle where it was and filled the towel with a handful of ice cubes and pressed them against the side of his head.

Leaning against a kitchen counter, McCabe held the icy towel in place with one hand and held his Glock with the other, guarding against possible invasions that might possibly come from either the garage or the living room doors. As he stood waiting for the ice to do its magic, he considered the possibility, even probability, that it was Joshua Thorne who had killed Norah. If that's what had happened Thorne must have somehow convinced Norah to untie the ropes that were binding him to the bed. He probably promised not to hurt her if she did. Probably promised her money. He sure as hell had plenty of it. The guy was a Wall Street millionaire. Money was his stock in trade. Prostitutes are by definition greedy so, for argument's sake, say she buys his bullshit. She cuts the ropes and frees him from the bed. When she does, wham! He leaps up and grabs her. He's enraged at what she's done to him. Tying him naked to a filthy mattress. Blindfolding him. Photographing him that way and then e-mailing the photograph to Josh's wife. So enraged that once he's free he grabs a gun. Whose gun? His own? Unlikely. Hers? Possible. Even probable. A high-priced prostitute who makes a living going into strange men's homes and trading sex for money might well carry a gun for protection. Holding her gun on him would seem like a smart thing to do if she was cutting the ropes and freeing him. But despite the gun, when he's finally free, he goes for her. She wants to shoot but hesitates. Or maybe she fires and misses. But Josh doesn't. He's an athlete. Big, strong and fast. He grabs her and wrestles the gun away. Then he picks her up and hauls her down to the car where he tosses her in the trunk. She reaches out, pleading for her life. But Josh is too pissed about the whole bondage thing to listen to her pleas. He's got the gun in his hand. He uses it, and bang, just like that, Norah's dead. Then what? Josh is standing there naked so he goes back into the house to find his clothes. But that's when McCabe arrives. Josh hustles upstairs and waits, hoping McCabe will leave, or thinking maybe he'll have to shoot him if he doesn't. But McCabe doesn't leave. Instead he seems to be searching the house. He goes into the garage where he finds Norah's body. Josh doesn't know McCabe's a cop. Maybe he figures he's just a pal of Norah's. Who knows, maybe her pimp, so he'd better get the hell out of there. McCabe is bending down, looking at Norah and not toward the kitchen. Josh sneaks into the garage. If McCabe turns and sees him, Josh will have to kill him. But McCabe doesn't see him so there's no need to shoot. Instead Josh grabs something in the kitchen, sneaks up behind McCabe and clobbers him. Pausing only to steal McCabe's phone, he gets dressed and drives away. Dumps Norah's body and goes back to the Regency Hotel readying his story for the cops. *Yeah, I did pick this babe up at the Port Grill. Yeah, I did screw her. Yeah, she did tie me up and take that picture. But then she took off. It took me hours but I finally managed to free myself from the bed. So I got dressed and took off myself. Came back to the hotel.*

Still holding the ice pack against his head, McCabe headed to the closet to see if Thorne's clothes and wallet were still there. They were. Still balled up behind the vacuum cleaner. He wouldn't have fled the house naked but he might have found some of Bob Bickle's old clothes and put them on. Maybe Bickle was a big guy and his clothes would fit Josh. One way to find out. McCabe reached down and pulled out the suit jacket. He felt the breast pocket. The wallet was still there, and so no, Thorne wasn't Norah's killer. While he might have worn some of Bickle's clothes to flee, he never would have left his wallet behind.

McCabe debated his immediate options. He supposed he could go to his car and use the police radio to call for help. Or bang on Mrs. O'Malley's door, wake her up and ask to use her phone. But if Thorne wasn't the killer, there was at least a slim possibility he was still alive and still tied to the bed upstairs. That meant the first priority had to be going upstairs and finding him. If he wasn't dead, McCabe would do what he could to help him survive. If he was dead, he'd then head back to the car and use the radio to call for help.

McCabe headed toward the narrow stairwell that led up to the bedrooms. He climbed slowly, silently, keeping his body in a low crouch and listening for the slightest sound. When he reached a point where he could just peer over the top step, he stopped and scanned the scene from floor level. The second-floor landing consisted of a small, carpeted hallway with three doors. One to his right. One to his left. One dead ahead. He climbed the remaining steps in semidarkness, the landing lit only by reflected light from the kitchen. According to Bob Bickle the door to the left led to the unused storage bedroom. The room most likely to house an iron bedstead, a filthy mattress and a bound and blindfolded man.

McCabe put his makeshift ice bag on the floor, held his gun in two hands and pushed the door open with his foot. He waited. When no shots rang out in response, he moved into the room fast and silent, his weapon leading the way. The first thing he noticed was something wet and sticky under his booties. A faint but familiar smell tainting the air. He knew immediately what it was. Blood slowly congealing on the bare floor beneath his feet. McCabe looked up and saw a cord attached to an overhead light. He pulled on it and any doubts as to the fate or whereabouts of Joshua Thorne vanished. There he was. Still naked. Still bound to the bed frame by clothesline. Only the blindfold had been removed, suggesting, perhaps, that the killer wanted Thorne to witness his own death. And possibly to see who it was who was taking his life.

The killing of Joshua Thorne couldn't have been more different than the killing in the garage. The single shot to Norah's head was quick, efficient and about as impersonal as murder ever gets. Thorne's death was far more brutal. Savage, sadistic and sexually very angry.

McCabe supposed that the killer had taken out Norah first to make sure she couldn't finger him as the one who had hired her to lure the victim to this house. After she was dead, the killer had come upstairs and finished this sadistic business. McCabe studied the victim's body.

There was a deep ugly wound between Thorne's legs where his genitals had once been but were no longer. It seemed to McCabe from the amount of blood that had poured from that wound that Thorne had been both alive and likely conscious, his heart still pumping, when the killer castrated him. McCabe remembered Maggie once saying after they'd arrested a serial rapist, "They ought to cut this bastard's balls off," she'd said. "That'd fix him."

Well, this time they'd fixed him good. The idea that Thorne was still alive to witness the torture sent an involuntary shudder through McCabe's body. Despite a fair amount of blood staining the cardboard, the words *Rapists Get What Rapists Deserve* remained partially visible.

McCabe wondered if the killer, having completed the gruesome surgery, had stood in the room and listened to Joshua Thorne's screams. Maybe the same screams that prompted Mrs. O'Malley next door to call in her complaint of excessive noise. McCabe imagined the killer standing there watching the agony on the victim's face and listening to Thorne's cries with a sense of satisfaction before finishing the execution by cutting Thorne's throat from ear to ear. The cut across the neck was so deep that it had nearly severed the victim's head from his body.

McCabe quickly checked the other bedroom and the bathroom. Finding them both empty, he headed downstairs. Leaving the bloody booties by the door, he left the house and headed for his car. When he reached his car, he used the police radio to call in the murders. He also asked Dispatch to have someone ping his cell phone. He hoped it would still be in the killer's pocket. He then headed back to the house.

Chapter 24

WHILE MAGGIE WAS debating how much of Heather Loughlin's version of events to believe, her cell phone vibrated. Caller ID said *Holden College*. Maggie figured it had to be Ann Nixon getting back to her. She let it go to message. She'd return the call when she'd finished getting what she could from Heather.

"Why did the girl, this Hannah Reindel, wait four months before reporting the crime?" she asked.

"My opinion? Because there was no crime. It was all bullshit. No crime, no rape. She probably got a little or maybe a lot drunk and went upstairs with Josh. Who wouldn't have? He was unquestionably the best-looking and most desirable guy on campus. This Hannah girl then proceeded to have consensual sex not just with Josh but with half the football team because she was probably drunk as a skunk or high on weed or maybe both and these were mostly good-looking guys. Not just Josh but all of them. After she sobered up, she was ashamed of what she'd done so she didn't say a word about it to anyone. But guys talk and soon rumors were flying around campus about how this Hannah Reindel girl had fucked half the Alpha Chi house in one night. People started slut-shaming her. Calling her a whore. Strange guys calling her up and inviting her to their fraternity parties to quote 'do her thing.' She could barely go anywhere on campus without girls avoiding her and guys hitting on her, then and only then does she go to the dean's office and start screaming rape.

"When I first heard about it I badgered Charlie to tell me the truth, 'cause, Jesus Christ, I was already dating this guy and I sure as hell didn't want a boyfriend who might be a rapist. At first he denied ever touching her. But Charlie always was a lousy liar. I told him I didn't believe him. Said I couldn't see him anymore because he wasn't telling me the truth. He came to me a week later and begged for forgiveness. It was really hard for him, but finally he broke down and admitted that yes, he did have sex with this Hannah girl and he was sorry about that but so did Josh and a bunch of the others."

"How many others?" asked Maggie.

"I don't know. He just said a bunch. He swore to me that it was all consensual. It was the only time in my life I ever saw Char-lie cry. He said Hannah was begging for it, and yeah, she was drunk and the guys were being stupid but when a good-looking girl walks into a room filled with guys, does a striptease, then lies down and spreads her legs, hell, you can't blame a bunch of horny twenty-year-olds for taking her up on it."

"And you believed him when he said it was consensual?"

"I was pissed as hell that a guy I thought I was in love with could possibly be involved in something as sleazy as that, but yes, I believed him. And I still do. Charlie never raped anybody."

"How can you be so sure?" asked Bernstein.

"Because I know Charlie and he's not that stupid or cruel.

But not just that. He also had proof this Hannah girl was asking for it."

"What kind of proof?"

"Josh made an audio recording of her asking for sex, pleading with the guys to fuck her."

Maggie and Toni Bernstein exchanged glances, then stared at Heather Loughlin in silence for a full minute, maybe more. "An *audio* recording?" Maggie finally asked. "Whose idea was it to make this audio recording?"

"Josh's." Heather smiled. "He was the so-called—" she again made quote signs with her fingers "'—brains' of the bunch. Nobody ever accused Josh of being stupid."

"And why did Josh make this recording?"

"Isn't it obvious?"

"Possibly. But I want to hear you say it."

Heather sighed as if she was patiently explaining something totally obvious to someone who, just as obviously, wasn't very bright. "Josh made the recording as proof that this girl was asking for it. That she wanted the whole backfield and a couple of wide receivers to screw her. It was insurance in case she screamed rape. Which is exactly what she later did. And it worked."

"Oh yeah?" asked Bernstein. "How?"

"When Josh and Charlie were called into the dean's office and were told that a freshman girl was accusing them of rape, Josh played the tape for the dean and the others. Her voice shouting, 'Fuck me, fuck me, fuck me,' is why the whole thing was dropped."

"Have you ever listened to this tape?"

"No. Charlie wouldn't let me. I didn't want to anyway. The idea disgusts me."

"Does the tape still exist?"

"I have no idea. But I'll bet you Joshua Thorne does."

"You told us you learned more about Hannah Reindel from a man you spoke to after Christmas. Tell us about that."

Heather shook her head sadly. "It was the second week in January. Charlie was at work and the kids were already back in school. This guy called out of the blue."

"On your cell number?"

"No. Here at the house. On the landline."

"A listed number?"

"Yes. At first I thought it was a sales call or something and I wasn't going to talk to him. But he said he was the freshman guy who brought Hannah Reindel to that party and he had some information about what Charlie and Josh had done that he thought I'd want to know about. I said all that stuff had been dead and buried years ago and I intended to keep it that way. I was about to tell him to screw off and hang up when he told me that the girl, Hannah Reindel, had just recently committed suicide. He said her death was Josh's and Charlie's fault. He said she killed herself because of what happened the night of the party. I mean, come on, twelve years later? Wouldn't she have gotten over it in twelve years? It was just a drunken night of sex. Anyone would have."

Anyone would have? Maybe some people would have. But surely not anyone. Especially if Josh's tape was phony and seventeen-year-old Hannah Reindel had indeed been violently raped by "the entire backfield plus a couple of wide receivers." Trauma from something as violent as gang rape wasn't something you just got over. It stayed with many women forever, creating unmentionable fears, anxieties and vivid flashbacks of the event itself.

"Did this man say anything else?"

"Yes. He said he'd been suffering the guilt of what happened that night for over twelve years. From having brought Hannah to that party. He said he thought it was way past time for Charlie and Josh to suffer for what they had done as well."

"Did he make any specific threats?"

"No. I hung up before he could. I told Charlie about the call that night when he got home from work. He said not to worry about it. The guy had called him too. Charlie said he felt sorry for the guy but he wasn't going to listen to his bullshit. He just hung up on him. And now Charlie is dead. And maybe Josh is too."

"Did he tell you his name? Or where he lived?" asked Maggie.

"He said his name was Evan Fischer. I think he said something about living somewhere in New Hampshire."

TONI BERNSTEIN TAPPED out and lit one of her cigarettes as soon as Heather Loughlin's door closed behind them. As they walked back to the road, she sucked in a deep drag and blew it out into the cold night air. Maggie speed dialed McCabe. His phone rang four times, then went to voice mail. "McCabe, call me as soon as you get this. Our killer may be a guy named Evan Fischer. Husband of the girl who was raped at Holden College. The one who killed herself. We've got to find this Fischer guy and talk to him. Pronto."

Meanwhile Bernstein used her phone to see if she could find an Evan Fischer in New Hampshire. There were two. One spelled Fisher lived in Nashua. The other spelled Fischer lived in Durham, the town where the state university was located. A landline number was listed on SuperPages for the one in Durham. Bernstein punched in the number. After four rings a man's voice came on. *"Hi, this is Evan and Hannah. We can't take your call right now but if you leave your name and number we'll get back to you as soon as we can."*

"Voice mail for Evan and Hannah. I think we got our guy."

On the off chance he worked there and there'd be a computerized employee directory available on the phone, Maggie tried the main number for UNH. *"Welcome to the University of New Hampshire. If you know your party's extension, please dial it now. If not, please call back in the morning."*

Last call. The Durham, New Hampshire, PD. It took three rings for the call to be answered.

"Durham Police Department. This is Officer Heller. How may I help you?"

"Hi, this is Detective Margaret Savage of the Portland Police Department. I'm trying to locate a Durham resident named Evan Fischer. Are you familiar with Mr. Fischer?"

"Fischer? You mean the guy whose wife killed herself couple of months back?"

"That's right. I'm wondering if you might have a number where I could reach him."

"May I ask what your interest is? The guy's in pretty bad shape."

"He's a possible suspect in a murder case in Connecticut and another one in Portland."

"Murder? Jesus. Who'd he kill?"

"Can't tell you yet. But I do need to talk to him. Listed landline goes to voice mail."

"Then he's probably at his cabin. Hang on and let me try his cell for you. "

Maggie waited while Heller made the call. A minute later he was back on with Maggie. "He's not there either. Leastways he's not answering his phone. If we're talking something serious like murder . . ."

"That's what we're talking."

"All right, why don't I send a car over to the cabin and see if he's there. If he is, we'll sit with him till you get here. If not, I'll call you back and let you know. You in Portland now?"

"No. I'm in Connecticut. West Hartford. But if you do find him I'll head up to Durham tonight. Shouldn't take more than a couple of hours."

Maggie gave him her number and Heller said he'd let her know and the two detectives started back toward their cars. "Okay," asked Bernstein. "What do you want to do first?"

"Get something to eat and wait for this Heller guy to get back to me. If Fischer's at the cabin I'm off to the races."

"*We're* off to the races."

"Fair enough. If he's not there, I better find a cheap place to stay tonight. Either way I've got to let my boss know what's going on."

"Yeah. I know a terrific place you can both eat and sleep."

"Cheap?"

"Not only cheap, it's free. It's called Chez Bernstein."

"Your place?"

"My place. We've got an extra bedroom we keep all made up in case the prodigal son ever decides to visit. Which is next to never. An excellent bathroom and shower you can have all to yourself. And my husband's already put together a homemade lasagna that's just waiting for my call to be popped in the oven. And trust me, Lennie's lasagna is to die for. Work for you?"

"You sure your husband won't mind a strange woman turning up at eleven at night?"

"Nah. Lennie loves having guests. Loves having people tell him what a great cook he is."

Sounded a whole lot better than a Motel 6. Even if they did leave the lights on for you. "I think you've got a deal."

Chapter 25

Once back in the house McCabe headed straight for the closet where Thorne's clothes had been stuffed. He wanted a look at the wallet before Jacoby's people arrived and started doing their thing. Pulling on a fresh pair of gloves and holding the wallet carefully by the edges, McCabe pulled it from the jacket and opened it. Inside he found Joshua Thorne's New York State driver's license with a shot of a smiling Josh in the top slot. Born November 5, 1979. Died March 5, 2014. A Scorpio. Four months short of his thirty-fifth birthday. Below the license McCabe found an American Express Black Card with Thorne's name on it. A rich man's status symbol that charged a seven thousand five hundred dollar fee just for the privilege of applying for one. No surprise someone like Josh carried one. In the slot below that was a keycard for a room at the Regency. In a back slot he saw the white tops of what looked like a batch of business cards. He pulled them out and leafed through them. Most were for various real estate executives Thorne was presumably courting for deals. But one didn't fit the pattern. A card for someone named

Evan Fischer, Ph.D., who was, apparently, an associate professor of Behavioral Psychology at the University of New Hampshire in Durham. A strange card for Josh to be carrying. What sort of business would he have with a psychologist in New Hampshire? And why was he carrying the card in his wallet? Was Thorne planning on doing something that required the expertise of a psychologist? Didn't make much sense but McCabe figured it most likely didn't mean much. Still he committed Fischer's address, phone numbers and e-mail to memory and put the card back where he found it. He next checked the back pockets of the wallet. Nine hundred and sixty-two dollars in cash plus a couple more credit cards, a AAA card and a membership card for the Downtown Association, one of New York's most exclusive private clubs.

McCabe pushed the wallet back into the jacket pocket, closed the closet door and went back upstairs. He first did a quick check of the other bedroom and the bathroom. As expected both were empty and looked unused. He then went back to the scene of the crime and allowed himself a more thorough look around the room. A bunch of cardboard boxes labeled Earle W. Noyes & Sons, a local moving company, lined the walls. Filled, he supposed, with stuff the Bickles hadn't taken with them to Florida. Winter jackets and long underwear? Maybe. He'd leave all that to Jacoby's people to go through.

There was a closet door on the wall across from the foot of the bed. McCabe pulled it open. A few empty hangers swung on their hooks with the sudden rush of air but there was nothing else inside except another half dozen movers' boxes.

He closed the door and turned back to the end of the bed to view the corpse from the angle the original photo had been taken.

Had the killer taken a second shot? A postmortem photo of the surgical handiwork? If so, had it been e-mailed to Rachel Thorne? McCabe hoped not. Seeing what McCabe was seeing now might destroy her. Still Starbucks might find something in a new photo that could possibly provide some kind of clue.

Seconds later he heard the first of the sirens screaming their way up Forest Avenue toward Hartley Street. He went downstairs and out the front door to deploy the troops. The first responding officer climbed out of her cruiser.

"Sergeant McCabe, I'm Officer Willetts." Cleary was right. Willetts was "a babe." One of the best-looking female cops he'd ever seen and that included a certain six-foot-tall senior detective who looked pretty damned good herself. He doubted Brian would heed his advice about it not being smart to date other cops. No more than McCabe would have done back when he was Brian's age. Or even now when he was well past Brian's age. Well, good luck to that.

"What do you need me to do?" Willetts asked.

"First thing," he said, "let me borrow your cell phone."

The young cop looked puzzled but handed over her phone and gave him the pass code. He punched in his own number and listened for the ring, hoping it was somewhere in the house. He heard nothing.

While Willetts waited, her face paled as she looked first at McCabe's bruised and swollen face. But she said nothing. If she was ever going to make it to a senior level in the department she'd better learn to ask more questions.

"Can I keep this for a little while?" asked McCabe. "I need to make a few calls."

Willetts nodded. McCabe pocketed the phone. "I'll return it

as soon as I can. And I won't look at anything private," he added, wondering if anyone who'd made it through the Academy would be foolish enough to engage in sexting.

"Yessir. Thank you, sir."

McCabe first called Avis Rent-a-Car and after some back-and-forthing he managed to get the plate number for a Nissan Altima that had been rented to a Norah Wilcox. The car had been rented three days earlier at Portland Jetport. The renter was listed as arriving on a JetBlue flight from JFK. She'd turned down additional insurance and was the only driver authorized to operate the vehicle. Both the driver's license and credit card used for the rental had been issued to a woman named Norah Wilcox.

Three more units and the PPD Crime Scene van had already arrived by the time McCabe ended the call. The assembled uniforms were busy circling the house with yellow tape. McCabe directed a couple of them to keep the press and gawkers, who were already beginning to gather, as far back as possible. Before going back into the house he gave Jacoby and two of his Tyvek-suited techs a two-minute summary of what they'd find inside.

"I didn't see either murder weapon," he concluded. "But I didn't make a thorough search. I'm leaving that for you guys."

Jacoby grunted something about how he would find the weapons if they were there. "You oughta be more careful about letting killers sneak up behind you. You could just as easily have a bullet hole in your brain as a black and blue face. Which maybe you woulda deserved for general carelessness."

"Thanks, Bill. I appreciate your concern. Speaking of carelessness, I'm sure you'll be happy to know a bunch of the bloody footprints on the second floor and coming down the stairs are mine," he told Jacoby. "I stepped in the goo before I realized it was there. Still you may also find some prints from the bad guy."

Jacoby held up a plastic bag containing McCabe's bloody booties and grunted his displeasure at McCabe's screwing up the evidence search. "Next time, be more careful."

McCabe patted Jacoby's Tyvek-covered shoulder. "It's okay, Bill. You know I do my best."

Jacoby handed McCabe a fresh pair of booties and had one of his techs bag the bloody ones. Bill was getting grumpier every week. The guy was good at his job but McCabe wondered if it might not be time for him to consider retiring. He'd been doing this for over thirty years. Seemed like it was getting to him.

Back inside, McCabe pointed to the closet door. "You'll find the male victim's clothes in there. Rolled in a ball behind a vacuum cleaner. A leather wallet's in one pocket of the suit jacket. I looked through it but I was careful not to smudge any prints."

They walked across to the other side of the room. McCabe pointed at the coffee table. "Be sure to check those two martini glasses for DNA. I also noticed a mostly empty whiskey glass in the kitchen that needs checking too. We know our two victims were drinking martinis on the night of. I suspect it was the killer who drank the Scotch. I want prints and DNA on all three ASAP."

From the kitchen, they moved to the garage. "One of the bodies, the female, was out here in the trunk of a rented Nisson Altima. Whoever bopped me drove off in it. Assuming he came down to the garage and discovered me right after killing Thorne. Any bloody footprints showing shoes not booties would have been his."

Jacoby nodded without comment. Then he pointed to a wooden rolling pin on the floor. "Must have bopped you with that."

It seemed likely.

They went back inside and climbed the stairs to have a look at Joshua Thorne.

"Jesus Christ," said Jacoby, staring at the raw wound between Thorne's legs. "Somebody must have really hated this guy."

"I just now noticed," said McCabe, "there's what looks like dried semen on his thigh. Right where Thorne might have squirted."

"When he still had something to squirt with," said Jacoby.

"Make sure it came from him."

"Who else?" asked Jacoby.

"Could be the killer's. He, if I'm right and it was a he, might have found all this violence so stimulating he couldn't keep himself from jerking off out of sheer excitement."

"Make him a pretty weird fella, if you ask me. Any chance Thorne was gay? Or maybe swung both ways?"

"I don't think so. At least, not if what his wife told us about him is accurate."

"Anyway, you know me, McCabe. My team will go over this whole house with a fine-tooth comb. One tooth at a time."

"The semen DNA probably matches traces on one of the glasses downstairs. Of course we'll need all the DNA testing done ASAP."

"So what else is new?" said Jacoby. "I'll try to light a fire under Pines." Joe Pines was the DNA specialist at the Maine State Lab in Augusta. "He's begun using this new RapidHIT method. Gets you a usable read in just a couple of hours."

"Good."

"This the blindfold?" asked Jacoby. He was holding a silk necktie by a single gloved finger. "Found it at the foot of the bed."

McCabe took the tie. It was definitely similar in color and pattern to the blindfold covering Thorne's eyes in the photograph. Red silk Ferragamo with a herd of tiny gold elephants running downhill in diagonal rows. McCabe wondered again if the killer removed the blindfold not just to make Josh Thorne witness his own castration but also to let Thorne have a look at who was killing him.

"Hey, McCabe? You anywhere in the house?" Brian Cleary's distinctive bellow was coming from just inside the front door. Tasco was with him.

McCabe excused himself and went downstairs.

"Jesus," said Cleary, staring at him. "What happened to you?"

"Somebody hit me."

"Somebody hit you?" Cleary rolled his eyes. "No shit somebody hit you. Last time I looked that bad was the night I got the crap beat out of me by some Golden Gloves champ from the Bronx. It's what convinced me to give up boxing."

"I was coldcocked from behind. Had to be the killer."

"Got a hell of a punch if he did this with his fists."

"It was a wooden rolling pin. I went out like a light."

"Jesus, lucky he didn't kill you. Any broken bones?"

"I don't think so."

"Maybe you should check for concussion."

"I'll ask the EMTs to check when I go outside," said McCabe. "Anyway, I found Wilcox and Thorne."

"I take it they're both dead?"

"Very."

Bill Jacoby came downstairs and shooed them out of the house. "Okay. Why don't you people wait outside and stop contaminating my crime scene? With two murders we'll be at this for a while."

McCabe pulled off his gloves and booties. Jacoby took them and stuffed them in a plastic bag and the three detectives went outside. The temp had dropped at least ten degrees since McCabe had arrived and a light snow had started falling. Blue lights were flashing from one end of Hartley Street to the other. A couple of news vans had managed to squeeze in just beyond the cruisers and a gaggle of reporters stood on the other side of the yellow crime scene tape shouting out questions. Beyond the reporters a small scattering of neighbors, braving the cold with coats thrown on over their pajamas with most wearing slippers, watched the real life version of *Law and Order* play out on their own quiet street.

McCabe spotted a MedCu unit, went over and asked one of the medics to check his face for broken bones. The guy said he didn't think there were any but McCabe should have it checked by a doctor anyway. He swabbed the area with some antiseptic that stung like hell. Then gave him a proper ice pack to help bring down the swelling. McCabe then rejoined Tasco and Cleary and the three detectives headed over to Tasco's Honda CR-V, which he'd double-parked next to one of the cruisers. Inside the car it was still fairly warm. Tasco started the engine to keep it that way. It could be a long night.

McCabe brought the others up to speed on the location and condition of both bodies. Told them that the killer might be a psychology professor at UNH named Evan Fischer. There was no proof yet but it seemed like a possibility.

"You think it was a guy who cut off his balls?" asked Cleary.

Tasco shook his head. "I don't think so. I don't think any guy would ever do that to another guy. I mean, could you do that? No matter how much you hated the guy, you couldn't, could ya?"

McCabe just shrugged. Enough chatter. He told Cleary and Tasco he wanted them to take charge of the site. He started getting out of the car.

"Where you going?"

"Gotta let a few people know what's going on. I also have a book I want to read. Then I'm going to notify Mrs. Thorne of her husband's death."

Chapter 26

Maggie checked voice mail as soon as she got back in her car.

"Detective Savage. My name is Ian Landis. I'm dean of students at Holden College. President Nixon asked me to give you a call. I'm leaving the office now but you can call me at home up until midnight tonight. After that, I'm afraid your questions will have to wait until tomorrow morning."

Landis provided a number and Maggie jotted it down. She had about an hour to call before what she supposed was Dean Landis's bedtime.

She started her car, flashed her lights to signal she was ready to go and followed Toni Bernstein home. The drive took less than ten minutes. On the way a call came in from the Durham Police Department.

"Detective Savage, this is Officer Norm Heller from Durham. Just to let you know we had an officer stop by and Fischer's cabin is empty. No one in residence."

"Did the officer go inside?"

"No, ma'am. Need a search warrant to do that."

"Of course."

Maggie thanked him and followed Toni Bernstein as she turned into a town house community on Timberwood Road. At the second row of buildings Toni reached out the window and waved her arm, pointing Maggie to a parking area marked *Visitors*.

Toni waited at the door finishing yet another Camel as Maggie walked up carrying her briefcase and duffel bag.

"Let me just take a few more drags before we go in. The deal I made with Lennie is I can smoke as long as I don't smoke in the house."

"Ever tried quitting?"

"A million times. For years, Lennie kept hocking me to quit."

"Hocking?"

"Yiddish for *nagging*. I'd try but then a few days or a few weeks later I'd start again. Once I stayed off for a full two months. When I went back Lennie accused me of loving my Camels more than I loved him. When I told him he might have something there, he backed off and we made our deal. I still smoke but never in the house or in his car. He tells me he plans to have my tombstone carved into the shape of a large granite camel like the one on the pack. The epitaph will read, *Here lies Antoinette Bernstein. She loved her dromedaries more than she loved her life*."

"Sounds like my father," said Maggie. "Except the dromedaries he smokes are the short old-fashioned ones without the filter, which I have to believe are even worse for him."

"How old's your father?"

"Going on seventy-six. Still alive and kicking and still working as the sheriff of Washington County, Maine."

"Good for him. At his age, he's entitled." Toni snuffed out the cigarette and unlocked the door. The rich scent of garlic, tomatoes and cheese wafted out and Maggie followed Bernstein in.

"Wow, that smells wonderful."

Toni smiled. "Hey, there's nothing like coming home to a man who can make great food. My advice to you is don't worry about handsome or rich. All you gotta do is marry a man who loves to cook. I mean, Lennie and I have a deal. He cooks. I clean up. Works for both of us. Hey, Lennie, come on out and say hello to Maggie."

A heavyset man with a round face, a double chin and a pronounced beer belly pushing against a white apron that was spotted with red emerged from the kitchen. Obviously Lennie not only loved to cook, he loved to eat.

Maggie held out her hand. "Maggie Savage."

"Leonard Bernstein. Delighted to meet you and to answer your question before you ask it, no, I did not write the score to *West Side Story*."

"Well, it's nice to meet you anyway. And I'm sure the *West Side Story* guy could never have made anything that smells that delicious."

"Good. I hope you're hungry. Toni will show you your room and dinner can be ready in—" he looked at his watch "—fifteen minutes."

"I may need a bit more than that. I have to make a few calls that really can't wait. Why don't you two go ahead without me?"

Bernstein shook his head. "Not to worry. We'll wait. I have a nice bottle of Italian red that will keep us company while you make your calls."

Maggie thanked him and went up to the spare bedroom on the

second floor of the duplex. It was big, yet still felt cozy with thick carpeting, a queen-sized bed, a couple of comfy-looking chairs and a large bookcase filled mostly with paperback murder mysteries. Ian Rankin, Tess Gerritsen, Peter Robinson and a bunch more of Maggie's favorites. Best of all, it had a modern bathroom with one of those showers Maggie had never tried, the ones that hit you from six different directions all at once. She was almost sorry she couldn't hop in and try it out before doing anything else. But shower time would have to wait. Maggie dropped her duffel by the bed and her computer bag on the desk. Speed dialed McCabe again and left the same message she'd left before. It was unlike him not to respond to voice mail. If she didn't hear from him soon she'd call Fortier and sound the alarm. In the meantime, she figured she'd better call Landis to make sure she got him before he toddled off to bed.

She punched in the number he'd left on her voice mail. He answered on the first ring.

"Detective Savage?"

"Yes, Margaret Savage, Portland Maine Police Department."

"Ian Landis. Glad you caught me. I haven't been able to think about much else since I got the call from President Nixon."

"I'm glad as well. I should tell you before we start that I'm recording our conversation so that I'll be able to remember and review whatever you might be able to tell me."

"Also to use it against me in court?"

"I hope not."

"So do I. However, since I know I've done nothing wrong I won't worry about it. I hope you don't mind if I record the conversation as well. If anything comes of this discussion, I'll probably want to share it with Holden College's attorneys."

"Fair enough."

Landis started speaking before Maggie got a chance to ask a question. He sounded more than a little nervous to her ear. "Ann Nixon said you were investigating the death of one or perhaps even two of our alumni. Charles Loughlin and Joshua Thorne, two members of the Class of 2002. She said you thought Loughlin's death and Thorne's disappearance might be related to charges of rape against the two of them brought by a female freshman student in January 2002."

"Did she tell you that the 'female freshman' recently took her own life?"

"Yes, and I'm terribly sorry to hear that. I remember the girl and the incident well and before calling you I took the opportunity to refresh my memory by going over my notes. I took careful notes of everything that was said in the meetings we had. When this kind of thing comes up it's always a good idea to do that. I also told President Nixon as much of the story as I know. When she heard what I had to say, she asked me to fully cooperate with your investigation."

"Good. I'm delighted to hear that. Why don't you start by telling me what you remember about the incident? I'll interrupt with questions if there's anything I don't understand or need clarification on."

"Very well. At the start of the winter trimester in January 2002, a female freshman named Hannah Reindel made an appointment to speak to me about a sexual assault she said she'd suffered. Naturally I agreed to meet with her. A young man—another freshman named Evan Fischer—came with her to the meeting. Apparently he was the one who brought Hannah to the fraternity party where the incident took place. I asked if he was her boyfriend. She said no. Just a friend but she wanted him to attend. I asked if he'd been present during the alleged attack. He said no. He said he wasn't there but had found her later at the scene, undressed and in a state of shock. He helped her get dressed and brought her back to her dorm. I told them both that Fischer would have to wait outside. Neither of them seemed happy about that. The girl seemed nervous and upset. My guess was she was counting on him to corroborate her story.

"The meeting took place in my office at three P.M. on Tuesday, January 8, 2002. My assistant dean, a woman named Martha Kramer, sat in. I also asked one of our attorneys, a woman named Jocelyn Neal, to attend. It's standard procedure to have two or more people at conversations regarding accusations of sexual assault. Ideally, at least one and preferably two of them should be women. I had met Hannah once before during freshman week in early September and I was surprised when she arrived at my office that day by the physical changes in her."

"What sort of changes?"

"When I first met her at a reception for incoming freshmen in September I was struck not just by how pretty and vivacious she was but also how enthusiastic she seemed to be about beginning her studies. She wanted to major in Cultural Anthropology. Most incoming freshmen have never even heard of Cultural Anthropology. Or have much interest in it. "

"Do you remember all the students you meet at a freshmen reception?"

"No. Very few, in fact. But I was an anthropologist myself. Full professor and head of the department before accepting the dean of students job. And at that time I was still teaching one course in Sociolinguistics. I remember how eager and knowledgeable Hannah seemed. She spoke about wanting to someday teach anthropology at the college level. I thought how lucky Holden was to have attracted a student like her. I said perhaps someday she'd teach here. She said she'd be thrilled if things turned out that way."

"You mentioned physical changes," said Maggie. "What sort of physical changes?"

"For starters she'd lost a great deal of weight. She wasn't fat or even chubby when I first met her, but when she came to my office she was much, much thinner. Gaunt, really, with dark circles under her eyes. She wasn't eating. Or taking care of herself in any way. The energy and vitality that had impressed me so much in September was gone. Simply not there."

"What can you tell me about the meeting?"

"Hannah came in. I made introductions and suggested we sit around a small conference table. When we were seated I asked Hannah what it was about. She said, 'I want to report a rape. A whole bunch of rapes.'

"I asked her to tell us specifically what she was talking about. She said that she had been forcibly raped by at least two and possibly more male students after being dragged into a locked room at a party at the Alpha Chi Delta house. She only remembered two of the men specifically: Joshua Thorne and Charles Loughlin.

"She said the rapes had taken place in mid-October. I asked why it had taken her so long to come forward. She said it was because she was afraid. I asked her what she was afraid of. I remember she had a hard time looking at me when she spoke. But she did speak. She said she was afraid of being questioned by the police. Of being forced to testify publically in court. Afraid of people not believing what she said. Afraid of how her parents and friends might react. That everybody would blame her.

"Martha asked Hannah what made her decide to come in now. She said she couldn't live with it anymore. She wasn't eating. She wasn't sleeping. She was having nightmares and reliving the whole experience over and over again. She was planning to drop out of Holden anyway but before she did she wanted to make sure she went on the record with the truth about what Thorne and Loughlin had done to her. She said half the campus was whispering about it. Only the whisperers were saying it was her fault. That she got drunk and wanted to—pardon my language but I'm quoting her here— fuck everybody in sight."

Ian Landis went on for another five minutes or so describing what Hannah Reindel told him and the two women in attendance. "When she'd finished, the lawyer, Jocelyn, asked her if she'd reported the rape to the police. If a rape kit had been taken. She said no. She said Evan Fischer had taken her to the student health center and told the nurse there what happened. The nurse asked her if she had showered since the event. If she had cleaned herself . . . down there. She said she had. It was one of the first things she'd done. The nurse said she still had to go to the Champlain Valley Hospital in Plattsburgh where a rape kit would be collected. Hannah said she couldn't bear the idea of anyone touching her like that again and refused to go. She went back to her dorm room instead."

"Did you believe what she told you?"

"I did, yes. I knew Thorne better than I knew Loughlin and had always thought of him as a smug, self-satisfied egotist. But in cases like this, my personal feelings are irrelevant."

"What happened next?"

"I requested a meeting with Thorne and Loughlin. Kramer and Neal attended that meeting as well. The two men came in looking like the picture of injured innocence. I told them what they'd been accused of. They admitted that they'd both had sex with Hannah but insisted that the sex was consensual. They told me four other boys also had sex with Hannah that night, all of whom would swear, if it came to legal proceedings, that the sex was consensual. That she had said yes. But they adamantly refused to give me the names of the other four. They said they didn't want to hurt their reputations but that the four were willing to come forward if it proved necessary."

"In other words, you were faced with one *she said* versus six *he saids*?"

"Essentially, yes. Even though only two of the *he saids* were actually present. I expect the others would have come forward if Thorne and/or Loughlin were actually charged with rape. They also played an audio tape that they claimed proved Hannah had consented to having sex with them."

"Did you listen to the tape?"

"Of course. Several times. So did Martha and Jocelyn. It was Hannah's voice or it certainly sounded like it. She was saying things like 'I want it.' And 'Fuck me.' Again pardon my language. But . . ."

"But what . . ."

"In my view the tape was a phony. The things Hannah said were coerced out of her in bits and pieces while she was under the influence of drugs and the tape later spliced together to sound like it was all one continuous sequence. The breaks and blips were obvious to my ears. And I'm sure would have been obvious to anyone else's. Frankly I thought Thorne and Loughlin were guilty as sin."

"Did you tell them that?"

"No. I just thanked them for coming in and told them we'd get back to them."

"Then what?"

"Kramer, Neal and I discussed what we should do next. I wanted to pursue disciplinary action against the two men. Perhaps legal action as well. Jocelyn Neal said that as the college's attorney she strongly disagreed. She said too much time had passed. She said there was no physical evidence of rape. She agreed that the audiotape was fishy, that it had almost certainly been spliced together from bits and pieces, but that if we, as an institution, publically supported legal action for rape, it was unlikely we'd get a guilty verdict if the case went to trial or even any agreement to a plea deal if it didn't. At the same time she said we would be opening ourselves to civil litigation from Thorne and Loughlin and possibly from the others. Reluctantly, I backed down. Knowing what I know now, that Hannah recently took her own life, I have to believe the rapes were a contributing cause. I can't help but hold myself at least partially responsible for that. We told Hannah there was nothing we could do. That was the last time I saw her."

"Did you also talk to Evan Fischer about the allegations?"

"Yes. Separately. He told us that he was the first person to see Hannah after the event and that she was very upset and told him she had been raped."

"But you didn't do anything about it?"

"No. Neal said Fischer's testimony was secondhand hearsay. Nobody denied Hannah had had sex with all the men in that room. She reiterated that because of the time that had passed there was no proof of rape and since Hannah was not underage it still came down to a *he said, she said* situation. That even if the tape was shown to be phony, no wrongdoing could be proved. And, as I said, that would leave the college open to expensive lawsuits from both the Thorne and Loughlin families."

MAGGIE THANKED LANDIS and went downstairs where she was greeted by Lennie, no longer wearing the splotched apron. He rose from his chair to greet her. "Can I offer you a glass of wine?"

"That'd be very nice, thank you."

"White or red?"

She looked at the glass of red he was holding. "What are you drinking?"

"It's a very nice Capezzana Sangiovese. From Tuscany. Only ten bucks and really very good for the price. Here, have a taste."

Lennie offered Maggie his own glass and she took a small sip. "Mmm, it is good. Works for me."

He grabbed another glass, poured in at least eight ounces and handed it to her.

"Lennie knows more about Italian food and wines than any other Jewish guy I've ever met. He actually went over and took a month-long cooking course in Florence . . ."

"Firenze," he said, correcting his wife. "I think the English and by extension we Americans have a lot of gall thinking we can change the names of cities in other people's countries. The one that bugs me most is Livorno. It's a lovely city on the west coast of Tuscany that the Brits, in the glory years of the empire, decided they would call Leghorn. And if you look at old British maps that's just what they called it for centuries. It's an Italian city and the Italians named it Livorno. Where the hell did the Brits get Leghorn? That's a name for a rooster not a city. A cartoon rooster, in fact."

"Foghorn Leghorn?"

"Exactly. Anyway, dinner's ready. Nothing fancy. Just a basic lasagna and a green salad."

"Sounds perfect."

While they ate generous helpings of lasagna and salad, Maggie filled Toni Bernstein in on her conversation with Ian Landis. She said she didn't think a nine-hour round trip up to Willardville and back made sense at this point.

When Lennie headed into the kitchen to make three double espressos Maggie also mentioned to Bernstein how she'd been unable to reach her boss and was beginning to worry. She said it was unlike McCabe not to return her calls. "I don't mean to be rude but I think I better take my coffee upstairs with me and try to find out what's going on up in Portland now. Aside from anything else I want to see if we've got any meaningful leads on Joshua Thorne."

"Or maybe even a meaningful body."

"Maybe even. I also want to see what more I can find out about this Evan Fischer character."

"Yeah. I'll call my boss as well," said Toni. "Let him know about both Fischer and Thorne and that cute little sign he had on his chest. Maybe that'll be enough to convince the DA to get off his skinny ass and let us treat the Loughlin case as a murder."

Maggie thanked Lennie Bernstein for a fabulous dinner, excused herself and took her espresso upstairs to her room. She sat at the desk, took out her phone and tried McCabe again.

Chapter 27

As McCabe walked back to his car he heard the familiar strains of Ellington's "Take the A Train" emerging from the edge of Baxter Woods just to his right. He followed the sound, saw a light in the grass, bent down and found his phone just as the sound stopped and the call went to voice mail. The killer must have thrown the phone from the car window as he was driving away. McCabe checked recents and found three calls from Maggie. Figuring it had to be something important he called her right back.

"McCabe? Jesus Christ, where in hell have you been? I've been trying to reach you for hours. I've called you a bunch of times and all I got was voice mail. I thought maybe you were dead or something."

"Nope. Not dead. Just a little beat up. Is there something urgent you've got to tell me right now or can you give me a little time to get back to my car and check something out?"

"Something important?"

"Yeah. I've got a feeling it could be."

Maggie hesitated for a few seconds, debated whether she should let him hang up on her now that she finally had him on the phone. "How long?" she asked.

"I don't know. I'll call you soon as I can."

She finally said, "All right. Soon as you can."

"Scout's honor."

McCabe ended the call, went back to the house, found Willetts, gave her her phone back and then returned to his car.

He started the engine. Turned the heater up to high. Flipped on the interior lights and took Norah Wilcox's Day Runner from his pocket. He unzipped the well-thumbed book and started reading.

Basically the pages contained a bunch of men's names. At least, he assumed they were all men's, though a few could have gone either way. There were a couple of Chris's. One Alex. One Sam, who was probably not a Samantha. After each name was a notation of place, time and date. A sum of money was written in at the end of each entry. Most of the names had phone numbers or e-mail addresses scrawled next to them. Regular customers? It seemed likely. McCabe quickly scanned a couple of pages of names and the amounts of money she'd charged them for her favors, which ranged from fifteen hundred to ten thousand dollars. It seemed like Ms. Wilcox, the Gillian Anderson lookalike, must have been very, very good at what she did for a living. He wondered again how much she'd been paid to pick up Joshua Thorne in the Port Grill bar and lure him to this crummy little house on this modest little street in Portland, Maine.

McCabe started going through the book systematically, page by page, committing the whole thing to memory. He'd never heard of most of the names, but a few were definitely familiar. There were a couple of big-time businessmen and Wall Street types whose names he'd seen in the paper. There was one Republican senator from a southern state. And, just to even things out politically, one Democratic governor from a Midwestern one who, rumor had it, was considering a run for the White House. There were also a few celebrities of other kinds. A British Shakespearean actor and one-time Oscar winner who was currently getting great reviews playing Hamlet on Broadway. A well-known hip-hop artist. And a retired NBA power forward who was now providing color commentary on ESPN and, between games, McCabe supposed, having fun with Norah Wilcox.

As McCabe continued reading through the list, he realized he was hoping he'd find Peter Ingram's name among them. He would have loved to let his dear, sweet ex-wife know that *the wonderful man* she'd left him for spent at least some of his spare time consorting with a high class prostitute. On the other hand, he thought, wasn't a high class prostitute exactly what Sandy herself had become when she'd left him to marry Ingram for his money? Sadly, it seemed, there'd been no get-togethers between Norah and Ingram listed in Norah's not so little black book.

McCabe kept flipping through pages. Nothing in the book was organized in any way. Nothing was written in date order. Or any other kind of order. Norah might be great in bed, but she would have made a terrible secretary. Or executive assistant, as they called them these days. The book just contained a bunch of random notes for random dates with at least a hundred random men in random places scattered here and there. With this level of disorganization, McCabe wondered if Norah ever got her appointments mixed up and banged on the wrong hotel room door at the wrong time on the wrong date.

Most of the places listed for the illicit get-togethers looked like room numbers in high priced hotels in New York. He picked out one. *Edward Nealy, 11 P.M., 2/16/13, Room 1757, 4 Seasons, 57th Street, 629-555-1776. $3,000.* McCabe recognized 629 as an area code in Nashville, Tennessee, and just for the hell of it, he called the number.

"Hello."

"Is this Edward Nealy?"

"That's right. Who is this?" asked a male voice with a vaguely Southern accent.

"Who is it, Ed?" A woman's voice in the background. She had an even more pronounced accent.

"Mr. Nealy, this is Detective Sergeant Michael McCabe with the Portland Police Department. I'm trying to track down a woman named Norah Wilcox. You apparently spent some time with Ms. Wilcox last month in room 1757 at the Four Seasons Hotel in New York and I was wondering if you had any idea how I might reach her . . ."

"Is this some kind of joke?" There was a trace of panic in Nealy's voice.

"No, sir. No joke. Like I said, this is Detective . . ."

The phone went dead. McCabe smiled broadly. If they didn't find Norah's contact info first, he'd have one or more of his detectives follow up on each of the names in the book, starting with the politicians, hoping to find at least one who'd be eager to do his civic duty. If civic duty wasn't enough to convince them to help, threats of public exposure almost certainly would do the job. His guys were going to have a lot of fun embarrassing Ms. Wilcox's clients into providing information. McCabe might even give in to temptation and do some of the so-called grunt work himself.

A few of the paid assignations listed had taken place outside

New York at fancy hotels in Washington and also a couple in Boston. McCabe noticed that Norah didn't seem to work the well-trodden paths of sin out west in Las Vegas. Maybe what happened in Vegas stayed in Vegas. More likely, Norah had no need to travel so far or face so much heated local competition to get together with her well-heeled johns.

It also looked like she didn't just do business in hotel rooms. Unlike twenty-first-century doctors, it seemed twenty-first-century escorts also made house calls. Husbands at play when wifey's away? Probably. And to add insult to injury, he supposed a lot of them had their fun and games in the couples' marriage beds. Although, to be charitable, some of the johns might just be lonely rich guys who weren't married or in current relationships. Or maybe just sad sack goofballs who could never get it off with somebody who looked like Norah Wilcox without handing over a bundle of cash.

A variety of residential addresses were listed. Most were in Manhattan or the more fashionable neighborhoods in Brooklyn. A few were located in some of New York's tonier suburbs. Greenwich, Connecticut. Rye, New York. Far Hills, New Jersey.

When McCabe reached the back of the book he noticed a piece of lined notepaper sticking out from a flap on the inside back cover. He pulled it out and read: *Joshua Thorne. The Port Grill. 9:30 P.M. March 6, 2014. $25K.* Then, underneath, in pencil Norah had written in the name Evan Fischer along with the same New Hampshire cell phone number McCabe had found in Joshua Thorne's wallet. It was beginning to look like a pretty good bet this Fischer guy was the killer they were looking for. McCabe wondered for a minute about the nine-thirty time notation. He knew from the video that Norah hadn't walked into the bar until

9:58. Was she simply late? No, not late, he decided. More likely waiting outside the restaurant for the Trident people to leave before going in and making her play. Waiting outside also left her a backup option if Thorne decided to leave the restaurant with his clients and start walking back to his hotel. *Excuse me. I'm terribly lost. Can you tell me how to get to the Regency Hotel? Oh, you're going that way? Do you mind if I walk with you? It makes me a little nervous walking alone at night.*

Under the note that contained Norah's date with Joshua Thorne, McCabe also found a photograph, a recent headshot of Thorne smiling confidently into the camera. Probably a screen grab from the Harris Brumfield website. Supplied, no doubt, to make sure she picked up the right guy.

McCabe zipped up the book, put it back in his coat pocket and called Maggie.

"Okay, McCabe. Where are you and what the hell is going on?"

"I'm at 339 Hartley Street. I found Wilcox and Thorne. They're both dead."

"Both of them? Jesus. Who killed who?"

"Well, it looks like a third person killed both of them. And from where I'm sitting now it looks like it may just be a man named Evan Fischer."

"You said Evan Fischer?"

"Yeah. Why? You know the name?"

"Yes. Evan Fischer is the name of the man who was married to the woman who committed suicide. The one who was gang-raped by Thorne, Loughlin and the rest of them. What do you know about him?"

"Not a whole lot. I found his business card in Joshua Thorne's

wallet. He's a psych professor at UNH in Durham. More importantly I found his name again next to Josh Thorne's in the back of
Norah's Day Runner."

"Day Runner? Who the hell keeps a Day Runner anymore?"

"Apparently Norah did. What I wanted to do before calling
you back was to memorize the contents so I could give the book to
Jacoby for his evidence bag."

"Anything interesting?"

"Yes. Turns out Norah was a high priced New York hooker who
used the book to keep track of her dates. Lots of interesting names
and numbers in there. Including Evan Fischer's. His name and
contact info were in a pocket in the back along with a photo of
Joshua Thorne and right next to it the time and place for picking
up Thorne at the Port Grill. Plus an indication that he'd paid her
twenty-five K for the job."

McCabe filled Maggie in on some of the specifics he'd read in
the book and then went on to describe everything he had found in
the house on Hartley Street. The missing key. The open door. The
clothes rolled up in the closet. The martini and whiskey glasses.
The condition of the bodies. Where they were found. How they
were murdered. And finally how he'd been whacked from behind
and, while he was still out, how the car with Wilcox's body still in
the trunk was driven from the scene.

"Jesus, he hit you with a rolling pin? Are you okay?"

"Yeah, I'm fine. You always said I had a swelled head. At last
you're right."

"Stop with the jokes, please. Did you see who hit you?"

"Not really. I figure it has to have been Fischer but I couldn't
swear to it in court. I just caught a flash of movement as I started

to turn. Whoever it was he, or possibly she, had a slender body. Dressed in black. Not very tall. Maybe five-nine, five-ten. What do you know about this Fischer guy?"

"Like I said, he's Hannah Reindel's husband."

"Who's Hannah Reindel?"

"The girl on the bridge. The one Rachel told us about who jumped off and killed herself. The one Josh Thorne and Charlie Loughlin and some other guys raped twelve years ago."

"You learned all this in Connecticut?"

"I did." Maggie took her turn filling McCabe in on what she'd learned from Toni Bernstein, Heather Loughlin and Ian Landis.

"So Hannah Reindel ended up marrying this Fischer guy?"

"Yes," said Maggie. "Fischer was Hannah's date the night she was raped. The boy who took Hannah to the fraternity party. He also took her to the college health center afterward and four months later went with her to file the complaints against Thorne and Loughlin."

"Sounds like she was someone he really cared about."

"I think so. And he may have cared enough to take vengeance on the men who destroyed her life and, in a sense, ultimately killed her."

"Rape, suicide and revenge," said McCabe. "More than enough motive for him to murder Loughlin and Thorne."

"I agree," said Maggie. "The big question is why kill Norah Wilcox?"

"Presumably to get rid of a witness."

"I guess. But there's something odd about that."

"What?"

"Well, killing Loughlin and Thorne were crimes of rage and passion," said Maggie. "Revenge for the horrible things they'd done to Fischer's wife. And the condition of Thorne's body certainly confirms that rage. But Wilcox was killed execution-style. No emotion. Just cold-blooded murder. Just doesn't sound like the work of the same person."

"You're making assumptions about Fischer's state of mind when he killed Thorne, if in fact he's the one who killed Thorne. The attack was sadistic and vicious but sadism and viciousness don't necessarily imply rage."

"Still sounds to me like the reverse of Fischer's personality. At least it is if what Landis told me is accurate. He may have wanted vengeance, but from Dean Landis's description, he sure as hell didn't sound like any kind of sadist."

"I don't think we know enough yet to make that assumption."

"All right, I'll suspend disbelief for the moment," said Maggie. "I may come back to it later but, in the meantime, let me try to summarize our Fischer-as-killer hypothesis. We'll just say Fischer decides to get rid of the only witness to his crime. He tells Wilcox to climb in the trunk. She pleads for her life but instead of sparing her he puts a nice little hole in her head and closes the trunk. He then goes upstairs and does what he does to Thorne. After he's finished with Thorne but before he can flee, he hears you sneak into the house. He waits quietly upstairs for you to leave. Ready, of course, to shoot you if you come upstairs. Instead you go into the garage. He doesn't hear anything for a while and thinks maybe you've left. He sneaks downstairs, discovers you looking at dead Norah in the trunk. But instead of shooting you or cutting your throat, he bops you on the head with a rolling pin and gets the hell out of there. Why didn't he kill you as well?"

"Good question. Maybe he doesn't want to kill a cop."

"After what he's done to Thorne? Besides, how's he supposed to know you're a cop and not just a nosy neighbor? You're wearing street clothes."

"Okay. So what are you getting at?"

"I'm not sure. He brutally kills one person. Surgically kills another. Then takes the time and effort to drag you out of the way of the car so he doesn't roll over you? Something about that just doesn't compute for me. Let's drop it for now. Anything else I should know?"

"Not really. Just that I'm on my way to inform Rachel Thorne of her husband's death."

"Sounds like a nasty chore. Try not to be too explicit."

Chapter 28

IT WAS CLOSE to midnight by the time McCabe pulled into the small circular courtyard fronting the Regency Hotel. He parked conspicuously in front of a sign declaring the space was reserved for guests checking in. Tossing an *Official Police Business* card onto the dashboard, he emerged into yet another of the cold damp nights typical of the Maine coast this time of year. The snow had thankfully turned to drizzle or maybe more accurately sleet. Either way it didn't seem likely to stick.

McCabe pushed cold bare hands into the pockets of his overcoat and leaned back, propping himself against the side of the car, prepping himself on how best to handle what he was certain was going to be a difficult and perhaps ugly next-of-kin notification. Even if he didn't say a word about castration.

At this hour Rachel might already be asleep. There was an equally good chance, imagining Josh still unaccounted for, she'd be sitting up worrying and waiting for word that he'd been found. McCabe watched a few groups of bundled-up guests scurry into the landmark hotel after enjoying a show or dinner in one or another of Portland's late-closing restaurants.

Stalling on the NOK, McCabe studied the details of the old landmark building. Neoclassical in design with turrets at either end, he remembered reading it was built in 1895 as the State of Maine Armory and served as headquarters for the Maine National Guard until 1941 when, as American involvement in the war drew closer, the Guard was federalized.

After the war, the Guard never moved back and the building stood semiabandoned in what was then a down at the heels neighborhood. When the resurgence of the Old Port got going in the mid-'80s some smart developers bought the place and turned it into a luxury hotel.

A young parking valet approached. "May I help you, sir? Are you checking in?"

"No thanks." Pushing himself up from the side of the car, McCabe added, "Portland Police. I'm here on business. Could you just leave the car where it is until I get back?"

"Yessir. No problem," the kid said enthusiastically. Police business. Probably the most exciting words he'd heard all night. Or maybe all winter. McCabe crossed the courtyard, climbed a short flight of granite steps and entered the hotel. A middle-aged woman with graying black hair pulled back in a bun stood behind the reception desk. Her badge identified her as Mrs. Lopez. "How can I help you, sir?"

He showed her his ID. "I need the room number for one of your guests. Mrs. Rachel Thorne."

"I'm sorry. We don't give out room numbers. Not even for the police. However, if you just pick up the house phone over there and ask for her by name the operator will connect you."

McCabe walked to the phone. Whether he woke Rachel or not didn't really matter. There was no way he wanted her to find out about Josh's death from some chirpy newscaster on News Center 6. He picked up the phone and asked for Mrs. Thorne's room. The phone rang half a dozen times before she finally picked up.

"Yes?" An impatient voice.

"Rachel? Did I wake you?"

"No. I'm awake. Who is this?"

"McCabe. Sergeant Michael McCabe."

"Oh. No. I just got out of the shower."

"May I come up? There's something we need to talk about."

"Does that mean you found Josh?"

"Yes."

There was a sharp intake of breath on the other end. "Where is he?"

Okay, so Rachel hadn't been sent any postmortem photos. Or maybe she just had no way of checking her e-mails. "That's something we need to talk about."

"What? Why? Where is he?"

"What room are you in?"

There was a long silence. "Give me five minutes to get dressed and I can come down and meet you in the bar."

"Bar's closed by now. We can talk more privately in your room than the lobby. I think that might be better."

Another short silence.

"All right. I'm in something they call the Governor's Suite. Room 411. The door to your left on the fourth floor."

McCabe went down the steps to the elevator bank. Pressed the button for four and emerged into a small hall with only two doors.

The one marked 411 opened before he had a chance to knock.

Rachel stood in the doorway, dressed in a white terry-cloth robe bearing the Regency Hotel logo over the breast pocket. A white towel wrapped around her wet hair.

"Why don't I wait out here while you get dressed?" he said.

"No. You'd better come in. I need to know what's going on." She looked at the bruising. "What in God's name happened to your face?"

"Nothing serious. Just tripped on the ice."

"Tripped on the ice? Really?"

Rachel stood to one side and gestured him in. Walking through the door, he could hear a familiar little voice speaking to him in what his brain told him was perfect Italian: *"Lasciate ogne speranza, voi ch'intrate."* Abandon all hope, ye who enter here. Dante's warning to sinners passing through the gates of hell.

Room 411, the Governor's Suite, was a large and luxurious space. The living room was decorated with high-end repro furniture and rugs. A floor-to-ceiling redbrick fireplace dominated the wall to his left. A gas fire burning in the hearth was throwing a lot of heat into the room, which felt good. He pulled off his wet overcoat.

"Here, why don't you give me that and sit down?" Rachel took the coat and hung it over a half-opened closet door. Instead of sitting, McCabe walked across the room to a pair of glass doors opening onto a large terrace. Beyond the terrace he looked out on a long row of rooftops lining Fore Street. Above the roofs a narrower view of the harbor that lay beyond. He tried to figure out what words to use to tell her about the death of her husband.

"Do you want to sit down?" asked Rachel. "Or would you rather we did this standing up?"

He turned and headed back into the room, but didn't sit.

"Where is Josh?" she asked.

McCabe said nothing.

"You're not looking at me."

"No, I wasn't," said McCabe, turning to face her. "But I am now."

"Where is my husband?" Rachel's eyes narrowed. "Is he dead? He is, isn't he?"

"Yes. He's dead."

Rachel stared at McCabe for a long minute.

"That stupid bastard," she said.

Not the response he was expecting.

"That selfish, lying, cheating, stupid sonofabitching bastard. What in the fuck's name was the matter with him?"

No pretense of grief. No reaction, but a face drawn in rage. Arms wrapped around her body.

"Bet that bastard didn't die in an accident, did he? Wasn't struck down by some random heart attack? No. Not Josh. Josh didn't take his leave of our picture perfect marriage with his last thoughts focused on his loving wife. No. My asshole husband fucked himself to death with some slut he barely knew. That's right, isn't it?"

A brief silence McCabe wasn't sure how to fill.

"Well, he did, didn't he? Goddamn him, I am so fucking pissed off."

McCabe stood there and watched her rage play out.

Finally, in a calmer voice, "Who was he fucking this time?"

"Your husband was alone on the mattress when he was murdered. The same mattress you saw in the picture. Arms and legs still tied. I doubt Josh was thinking about much of anything but survival at the time."

"Funny. Probably the first time it ever occurred to him he

wasn't immortal. All that bastard ever thought about was making more money and fucking more women. I'm not sure he even
enjoyed it all that much. Just wanted to run up the score. Two million dollars here. Five more women there. Only difference being
that the money didn't have to look young and sexy and the women
did. So he was still tied to that filthy bed when she killed him?"

"Yes."

"Jesus Christ. Murdered while fucking some slut. Maybe that's
what I'll put on his tombstone. *Here lies the great Joshua Thorne.
Murdered while fucking.*"

McCabe thought of the dried semen on Josh's thigh. "Maybe
not while fucking but pretty close," he said.

Rachel sighed deeply. "Well, it's poetic justice, I guess. A suit-
able way for Josh to go. No need to lie either to myself or to you
any longer."

"What were you lying about?"

"Just that I can't count the number of women he screwed while
he was married to me. And those are just the ones I know about.
Sonofabitch just couldn't keep his pants on. Couldn't keep his
magnificent cock to himself. And you know what the weird thing
is? What truly makes me want to kill the bastard all over again?"

"What?"

"I know I'm a whole lot sexier, a whole lot smarter and a whole
lot better-looking than ninety percent of the bitches he screwed
around with. Of course, that's just the ninety percent I know
about. What about you, McCabe? Even all beat up it's easy to tell
you're a better-looking guy than most. And no wedding ring? Are
you really married and you just slip your ring into your pocket
whenever you're in the mood to go tomcatting around?"

"I'm not married."

"And you're not gay? No. I can tell. You're definitely not gay. You're just a normal horny guy who's better-looking than most. Would you behave like Josh if you were married? Married, let's say, to me? I could tell by the way you were looking at me this afternoon from the minute I walked out of that elevator that you liked what you saw. That you wanted me. I mean, you did, didn't you?"

"You're a beautiful woman. There's no way you can hide it. But no. That's not how I would behave if I were married. To you or anyone else." McCabe didn't bother explaining to Rachel that his attitude toward marital cheating had been defined eight years ago, the only difference being the guys his wife screwed around with didn't have to be good-looking. They just had to be rich.

"Well, then, what the fuck was Josh's problem? I want you to look at me." Rachel untied her robe, opened it wide and showed him her naked body. "Go ahead, don't be shy. I'm not. This is what Josh had available to him any time he wanted it. Wouldn't a woman who looked this good be enough for you? A woman who was also usually sensitive, generally thoughtful and loving. Would you have to screw around with some Norah Fucking Wilcox, whoever the hell she is?"

"Cover up, Rachel. You don't want to be doing this."

"No. I don't think you would but let's find out. This is a test. Not of you but of Josh. To see if it's all guys or just Josh who was as fucked up as he was."

Instead of covering up, she let the robe slip to the floor. Gazing at her large but perfectly shaped breasts, the body firmed by endless exercise, the narrow stripe of pubic hair pointing down almost like an arrow, McCabe felt his breath coming faster, felt himself growing hard.

"Come on, McCabe. Let's find out if you aren't really just like

Josh. Maybe all guys are. Wouldn't you like to fuck me now? You can if you want to. It'd serve my asshole husband right." She moved closer and stroked his wounded cheek. "Come on. Let's go to the bedroom, McCabe. Don't be shy. Fucking you might just be the most fun way I can think of to get even with one of the great fuck artists of all time. The most appropriate way for me to shit on the memory of my loving husband the same way he shit on me over and over again for seven years."

"Put your robe on, Rachel."

"Fuck my robe. If you won't come to the bedroom at least enjoy the view. I'm sure it's one of the best in Portland." She left the robe lying on the floor and walked over to a sideboard where she threw ice cubes into a pair of highball glasses. She filled both nearly to the top from a bottle of Johnnie Walker Black. Held one out to him. "Take it, McCabe. Come on in, the water's fine."

McCabe's heart was beating faster. The temptation was nearly overwhelming. Just to walk across the room, take the drink from her, take a long slug of it, then put it down and slide his hands all over her beautiful body and take her to the bedroom. But no matter how sexy she was, it wasn't something he could let himself do.

"Fuck me, McCabe. Do it for Josh. Do it for me. Hell, do it for yourself." Looking down at the growing bulge in his trousers, she reached out and put her hand on his hard dick and gently squeezed. As she squeezed she leaned in, slipped her other arm around his neck, pulled him close and brushed his lips with hers. "Feels like you really want to," she said softly, invitingly.

Rachel's siren song was nearly irresistible and unlike Odysseus he had no crew to tie him to the mast to keep him from straying into disaster. *"Abandon all hope, ye who enter here,"* the little voice said again, and this time McCabe listened. He pulled her hand from his crotch, turned and walked to the closet door. He took down his still-wet overcoat and slipped it on.

Rachel sipped her drink as she watched him go. "I'm sorry you don't want to celebrate Josh's death with me. It would have been such fun."

"We'll talk again tomorrow. When you've had some time to process everything. Maybe you'll have recovered your senses a little." He walked out and closed the door to the Governor's Suite quietly behind him. His heart was still beating faster than usual when he heard the crash of the whiskey glass as it shattered against the door. The elevator arrived to take him down.

Chapter 29

TEN MINUTES LATER McCabe was back in his empty condo on the Eastern Prom. He tossed his coat over a chair, turned on a single small lamp and headed straight for his favorite stash. A Waterford crystal whiskey glass, the last from a set of four his sister Fran had given him as a wedding present nearly twenty years ago. And in its place of pride on the top shelf, the "good stuff." The Scotch he saved for special occasions. Twenty-five-year-old Macallan single cask malt whiskey, which had set him back two hundred and seventy-nine dollars for just one bottle. Plus fifteen cents for the deposit. He checked the contents. About half a bottle left. Just about enough, if he drank it all, to relieve him of his angst if not his desire for a murder victim's wife.

Half a bottle would equal a one hundred and thirty-nine dollar and fifty cents bender. Not counting, of course, the fifteen cents he'd get back if he returned the bottle, which he never did. A serious and expensive night's drinking, especially on a cop's salary. But between being beaten up, dealing with Joshua Thorne's mutilated corpse and almost allowing himself to be seduced by

Thorne's widow he figured he'd earned himself a little leeway. He poured a generous double shot of the Scotch, took a long swallow, closed his eyes and savored the smooth warmth of the stuff as it slid down his throat. Savored the way it almost instantly eased his tension and produced a pleasant glow.

He took another smaller sip and then, leaving the bottle out on the counter for a possible return engagement, he took the glass with him to the bathroom where he flipped on the light and peered in the mirror. Jesus. The flesh around and above his eye was black and the eye itself almost swollen shut. He could see out of it but looking at the swelling he wasn't sure how. The skin on his upper cheek and above the eye was purple, both swollen and painful to the touch. Despite the therapeutic effects of the EMT's ice pack, his face still bore a more than passing resemblance to Robert De Niro's at the end of the big fight scene in *Raging Bull*. And unlike De Niro's face this wasn't the work of a Hollywood makeup artist. The idea that Rachel would even consider getting it on with some-body who looked like he currently did seemed preposterous. Tell-ing him with a straight face he was a good-looking guy more than ridiculous. She'd told him she wanted to fuck him to get back at her dead husband. Prove that two could play the same game and, at that particular moment, the bruised and battered McCabe pro-vided the only available opportunity for retribution. He knew, had he accepted the invitation, it almost certainly would have proved disastrous. To the case. To his career. To his life.

He took the drink and being careful not to spill a drop went back to the living room and climbed onto his favorite perch. A window seat that just fit his body as long as he kept his knees bent. He took another sip of the precious twenty-five and gazed out the window at the streetlights along the prom, the occasional car going by, the wintry whitecaps whipping across the surface of Casco Bay, the waves reflecting lights shining on the nearby islands.

He conjured up Rachel Thorne's nearly perfect body in his mind. McCabe had done some stupid things in his life but giving in to desire and having sex with the wife of a murder victim the night her husband had been murdered would have been without question the all-time, undefeated, unchallenged, stupidest thing McCabe had ever done. If she ever told anyone about it, he could kiss his career as a cop goodbye. And a whole lot of other things as well.

Still, try as he might, he couldn't get Rachel out of his mind. Standing there by the sideboard, holding out her hand to him, urging him to come to the bedroom. The question he had about the entire scene was why. Especially when half his "you're a good-looking guy" face was, at the time, the color of an unpeeled and not particularly good-looking eggplant.

Was it, as she said, a way to get even with her cheating husband? Or maybe Rachel, like Josh, was just an unrepentant sex addict, one who got uncontrollably turned on by cops with fucked-up faces. An idea so ridiculous it actually made him laugh, which, in turn, made him realize his face only hurt more when he laughed.

If he asked Rachel why she'd behaved the way she had, she'd probably tell him again it was just payback against Josh. That she was just getting back at him for all the times he'd cheated on her. Maybe even getting back at him for being a rapist. The fraternity rape at Holden College. Maybe other rapes as well. Maybe even spousal rapes she had denied just yesterday.

That's when one final possibility struck him. One he hadn't thought of. What if Rachel tried to get him into bed, not to get even with Josh, but because she herself had murdered him? Being intimate with the lead investigator, especially if they did it more than once, would compromise the investigation in ways he couldn't begin to imagine. For starters pillow talk would give her an inside track on the investigation. She'd know what he was thinking and why. She could probably even steer any suspicion of murder away from herself and on to somebody else. Evan Fischer, for example. If he were to arrest her and the case went to trial, any halfway competent defense lawyer would have a field day grilling him on cross, tearing his testimony to shreds.

Detective, isn't it true that you were involved in a sexual relationship with the victim's wife?

He couldn't lie. His DNA would be all over the bedroom in the Governor's Suite.

And isn't it true that you became angry when she broke off that sexual relationship?

And doesn't the fact of your anger cast just a shadow of a doubt on the veracity of your testimony against the defendant?

Having an affair with McCabe would give Rachel a weapon she could use to control him. Control his ability to investigate. No jury would ever convict. And there'd be no second chance to convict even if new evidence came to light. You can never be prosecuted for the same crime twice. She'd be safe. Her six million dollars in insurance money would be safe. And McCabe's career would forever be fucked.

Was she really being that manipulative when she'd tried to tempt him into her bed? Or was it, as she said, just the desire of a woman scorned not once but dozens of times to even the score with her constantly cheating husband. He had no way of knowing.

McCabe finished the Scotch in his glass. Deciding he didn't need any more he put the bottle back on its shelf, stripped off his clothes, took a shower, trying hard to keep the hot water off his bruises. He dried off and climbed into bed alone and fell into a deep sleep.

As he slept, he dreamt he saw Rachel Thorne standing at the end of his bed. Moonlight coming in through the oversized windows lit her perfect body in a shimmering glow. She was smiling down at him. "Don't you want me? Don't you want this?" she asked, her hands indicating her body.

"Yes. Yes, I do."

He looked at her. She moved to the bed and climbed on top of him and steered him into her moist warmth. They moved together in perfect rhythm and after they came she slid off him and tied his hands and feet to the bed with expensive silk scarves. He looked up at her as she produced a large kitchen knife, drew it back and thrust it down between his legs. McCabe woke with a sudden scream, his hands moving down to make sure all his working parts were still there.

When the horror of the dream finally faded and his breathing slowed, McCabe climbed out of bed. Walked to the kitchen and poured himself another stiff shot of the good stuff. He went back to his perch on the window seat to drink it.

Chapter 30

"CAN WE TALK? In private?" asked Rachel.

McCabe's tight grip on his phone at 109 reminded him how edgy he still was about last night's attempted seduction.

"Why don't you come here to headquarters?" he asked. "We've got plenty of private places to talk."

"I won't do that. There are some things you need to know about Josh's death," she continued. "And I don't want to be videotaped. Or have others listen in. There are also some things I want to ask you." After a short pause, she added an anxious, "Please."

"All right. As long as you promise to keep your clothes on," said McCabe, making his voice sound cold when he said it.

"That's one of the things I want to talk about. My behavior last night. I have to apologize for that and it's one of the things I'd rather not have on video. Or have that short detective with the pug dog face drooling over. He was practically salivating when I came in with Mark yesterday."

She was talking about Cleary. He'd never thought about Brian that way but it fit. He did have kind of a pug face.

"Have you had breakfast yet?" she asked.

"Nothing you could call breakfast."

"Well, why don't you meet me in the dining room here? They do breakfast and it's quite pleasant. I'm there now. But you'll have to bring my iPhone with you. There's something on it I need to play for you."

Given her tone, McCabe was sure he'd learn more from Rachel in the relaxed setting of the Regency dining room than in the windowless interview room at 109. He decided he'd play good cop for now. Bad cop could come later if she forced the issue. "Fine," he said. "I'll grab your phone and see you in ten minutes."

The hotel's restaurant was called Twenty Milk Street. McCabe had had dinner there a couple of times with his ex-girlfriend Kyra. They served a first class New York strip steak at night and had a decent selection of single malts but that was really all he knew about the place. The large room was mostly empty when he arrived. Rachel was waiting at a table in the corner, a discreet distance from the half dozen other diners. A bowl with a half-eaten order of yogurt and fruit mixed with some kind of grain sat in front of her. She rose and offered her hand. McCabe noticed that not only did she have her clothes on but that the clothes were all the same color. Black. Black woolen slacks. A black pullover. A black cardigan. Her hair was tied back with a black ribbon. Black patent leather shoes. It seemed she'd decided on widow's weeds. Everything she wore was black except the large diamond engagement ring and plain gold wedding band that circled the fourth finger of her left hand and the fancy-looking gold watch that circled her left wrist.

He allowed her to wait with her hand extended for a second before taking and shaking it. "Can we declare peace?" she asked before letting go.

"I guess that depends on whether or not you're planning any further hostilities."

"I'm not."

"Well, then, fine. Peace. At least for now." They sat down and when a waitress came by McCabe ordered a toasted bagel with cream cheese and black coffee. The waitress disappeared. McCabe waited for Rachel to begin.

"I have no real excuse for what happened last night other than to say I went more than a little crazy when you told me Josh had been murdered. I felt trapped between rage, grief and a desire to punish him for the stupidity of what he'd done. Including the rape . . . rapes plural actually. I wasn't ready to tell you about that as long as I thought he might be alive. Anyway, I'm very sorry about all that." She smiled a thin smile. "Even though, despite your bruises, you *are* a good-looking man. And a good one. Some guys wouldn't have been as restrained as you were last night."

McCabe let the comments and compliments pass. "Yesterday you swore to Detective Savage and me that there was no way your husband was a rapist. You insisted he was too charming. Too good-looking. It was too easy for him to attract any woman he wanted to ever need to rape anyone. Why did you decide to change your story today?"

"Yesterday I thought or at least hoped Josh was alive. That there was some chance our lives could get back to some semblance of normal. At the time protecting him from charges of rape seemed like the right thing to do. Today I know he's dead. Protecting his reputation is no longer the first priority. Finding his killer is." Rachel's pause was perfectly timed. "I think I may know who that is."

"Go ahead."

"A day or two after Josh got that call from Charlie Loughlin,

I was called by a man named Evan Fischer. Fischer told me he had information about a gang rape at a Holden College fraternity party back in the fall of 2001. Information he was sure I'd want to know. I told him what I told you yesterday. That I had heard about it and questioned Josh about it and he convinced me that the charges of rape were nothing but lies. The girl who was supposedly raped was the campus slut and the sex was consensual. Not just asking for it but practically begging."

"Rather like you last night?"

"It hurts when you say things like that."

"I'm sorry. Go ahead."

"I told Fischer that unless he was one of the rapists and could prove what happened I wasn't interested in listening to his stories. Fischer begged me to at least listen to what he had to say. That he had information he was sure would convince me it was Josh who wasn't telling the truth. At least, not the whole truth. He said he knew exactly what happened at this party and said it was even worse than I thought. I asked how he'd come by his information. He said he was there that night. If I agreed to meet with him, then he would tell me everything he knew. I thought at first that he might be one of the other rapists who supposedly 'climbed aboard.' I asked him if he had told Josh what he knew. He said he had and that Josh accused him of spreading lies. Threatened him with legal action and maybe worse if he continued to do so."

"Worse meaning physical violence?"

"I don't know. Maybe. Anyway, I decided to hear what Fischer had to say. I decided it was stupid to ask some man I'd never met or even heard of before to come to the apartment and tell me about how he had raped someone. I also didn't want to meet in some coffee shop or restaurant where we might be overheard. To make a long story short, I decided to take a sick day from school and asked if we could meet at one o'clock the next afternoon on the Brooklyn Heights Promenade, which is about a five-minute walk from my apartment. I knew there wouldn't be too many people hanging around in the middle of a Tuesday afternoon in January but there'd be enough for me to feel safe. The forecast for the next day was sunny with a high in the low thirties so if we dressed warmly it wouldn't even be particularly uncomfortable. I told him I'd get there early and wait for him on a specific bench."

"He agreed to the time and place?"

"He did."

"Can you tell me what he said?"

"I can do better than that. I recorded the entire conversation with my iPhone. Did you bring it?"

McCabe handed over the phone "He didn't know he was being recorded?"

"No. But in New York it's perfectly legal as long as one party in the conversation is doing the recording. I checked."

"I know that," said McCabe. "But why did you decide to record it?"

"To have a record. One I could confront Josh with if I ended up believing what Fischer had to say. If Fischer convinced me that Josh was lying, that he really was guilty of the gang rape, I had decided to divorce him."

"Where did you hide the recorder?"

"In plain sight. I got to the designated bench early and was sitting there fiddling with my phone . . . pretending to write some texts . . . when he arrived. I just clicked on the recording app and put the phone down on the bench between the two of us. I don't think he noticed or, if he did, he didn't care."

"How long is this recording?"

"It runs twenty minutes or so. I used an app called Voice Record Pro."

McCabe had the same app on his phone. It could record conversations of any length with pretty reasonable quality.

"Have you edited it in any way?"

"No. It's all there just as I recorded it." Rachel looked around. A few more people had entered the dining room. "Listen, it might be better if we listen to it in my room. I can't play it here. Too public. And no, I won't take my clothes off again."

A pair of aging biddies at a nearby table threw disapproving glances in their direction. Rachel smiled. "See, we *can* be overheard."

Did McCabe want to go back to Rachel's room? The other option was taking the recording back to 109 but Rachel would be more relaxed answering questions here. He seriously doubted she was planning an encore striptease.

When they got to the room Rachel sat demurely on the opposite side of the coffee table from him. She put her phone on the table and pressed Play. Initially, all McCabe heard was background noise. Wind blowing in from New York Harbor. A rumble of traffic from the Brooklyn Queens Expressway, which runs beneath the promenade. A barking dog or two. Occasional chatter from passersby. But when they started speaking Rachel's and Fischer's voices were loud and clear enough to hear every word. McCabe could feel Rachel watching him as he listened.

"Rachel Thorne?"

"Yes."

"May I sit down?"

"Of course."

"My name is Evan Fischer. I'm an assistant professor of Behavioral Psychology at the University of New Hampshire. My specialty is studying the effects of post-traumatic stress disorder, PTSD, among victims of violent attack."

"Like in Iraq?"

"No. I study trauma stemming from noncombat situations. Muggings. Home invasions. Heart attacks. But most specifically rape. I've published a number of papers on the subject if you're interested. I also happened to have been married to Hannah Reindel."

"Who is Hannah Reindel?"

"You're not familiar with the name?"

"No. I've never met anyone by that name."

"She's dead now but Hannah was the young woman your husband, Joshua Thorne, picked out of a crowd of freshman girls at a fraternity party at Holden College in 2001. He drugged her, dragged her to a room where five of his fraternity brothers were waiting and raped her. He picked her out of a sea of gyrating college kids like a shark homing in on its chosen prey."

"A shark? Come on, Professor, isn't that a little over the top?"

"I don't think so. He obviously saw someone he wanted to have sex with and he did whatever it took to get her."

"Josh can be very charming."

"This had nothing to do with charm. Your husband gave this young woman, who was a seventeen-year-old virgin at the time and who didn't drink alcohol, a glass of sweet fruit juice laced with drugs."

"Roofies?"

"No way of knowing for sure but I think it must have been something stronger from her description of the effect. When the drugs hit she could barely stand up. When she was sufficiently groggy not

to raise a ruckus, though the music was so loud raising a ruckus probably wouldn't have helped, he dragged her upstairs to a filthy bedroom where half a dozen other men, all football jocks like your husband, were waiting like a swarm of pilot fish eager for the great white to bring them what they were hungry for. They locked the door, ripped Hannah's clothes off and threw her down on a filthy bare mattress where they took turns raping her. Naturally the shark went first."

"The shark being Josh?"

"Yes. When he'd had his fill of her, the others climbed on."

"Do you know the names of the others?"

"Just one. Charles Loughlin. Hannah passed out after Loughlin finished with her and she was unable to identify the others. Needless to say they never came forward of their own accord. And your husband refused to provide their names. But she said there were four others. Which made six in all."

"How do you know this? Were you there?" asked Rachel.

"To my everlasting sorrow I was."

"Were you one of them? One of these pilot fish?"

"No. I wasn't in the room. If I was I might have been able to stop it."

"Physically?"

"Of course not. Look at me. Your husband or any of the other jocks could have beaten the shit out of me with one hand tied behind his back. But I could have called the campus cops. Threatened to report them. Sadly I wasn't in the room. But I was in the fraternity house. I was the one who brought Hannah to the party. It was a rush party and the rules stated that any freshman guy who wanted to rush the Alpha Chi house had to bring a pretty girl as his ticket for admission. Hannah was more than pretty. She was beautiful. And, at the time, a good friend. While she wasn't my girlfriend, af-

ter I practically begged her to come she finally agreed to be my ticket to the party. After we got there all the wannabe pledges including me were herded upstairs to a large attic room and we were locked in for hours of preliminary hazing from some of the sophomore brothers. The junior and senior brothers stayed downstairs and had their pick of the freshman girls. Your husband chose Hannah.

"When they finally unlocked the door to the chapter room and let me and the other freshmen boys out it was after two o'clock in the morning. The place was pretty much empty except for a few drunks or druggies sleeping it off on the floor and some sofas. After we were let out the other freshman boys all left. Some with the girls they brought. Some alone. I couldn't find Hannah but I didn't think she'd have left without me. She didn't have a ride or a heavy coat and it was freezing cold out."

"She might have gotten a ride with someone else."

"She might have but she didn't. Anyway, I figured I'd better search the place before leaving without her. I went from room to room and couldn't find her anywhere and was almost ready to give up. But then I did find her. I opened the door to one room that seemed to be used as a storage room and there she was. Lying naked and shivering, huddled into a fetal position on a dirty bare mattress. There was cum on her belly and buttocks and in her pubic hair. There were dried bloodstains on her legs."

"Blood?"

"Yes, blood. Hannah went into that room a seventeen-year-old virgin. She came out the severely traumatized victim of six vicious rapists. One after another after another. Actually, it was probably more than six. I'm sure some of these so-called gentlemen went after her more than once."

"Dear God."

McCabe looked across at Rachel. Found it hard to intuit what she was thinking. Her eyes were intently focused on the phone, her attention on the words she was listening to. Words she'd certainly heard more than once before.

"*I went around the room looking for her clothes and eventually found everything except her underpants. The clothes had all been lumped together in a ball and tossed into an otherwise empty closet. I don't know but my guess is somebody, maybe your husband, maybe one of the others, kept the underpants as some kind of sick souvenir. I helped Hannah get dressed and, because she was shivering uncontrollably, I put my winter jacket on her. We walked downstairs as best we could. She was hanging on to my arm like someone hanging on to a life preserver. The whole place was a shambles, but on the way down we didn't see anyone awake enough to ask or answer questions. Actually, I think it would have been worse for Hannah if we had. I drove her back to her dorm and took her up to her room. When we got there she just lay down on her bed in the same fetal position she'd been in before, staring blankly for hours at nothing in particular. Not really seeing anything. The look in her eyes scared me. I now know it's what traumatized combat veterans call the 'thousand-yard stare.'*"

"Did you ask her what happened?"

"Of course. But she wouldn't say anything. She was simply mute. It was weeks before she was able to talk to me about it. But even years later describing what happened that night caused her incredible pain. She never even told her parents about what had happened, because they were . . . are . . . the kind of people who wouldn't know how to handle what she had to say. They wouldn't have been able to talk about it. Not uncommon. When someone they love is viciously raped like Hannah was people don't know *how to address it. A lot try to act like everything's okay and it never really happened. I've run into people in my practice, well-meaning people, who behave exactly that way. Say things like, 'You have to try to get over it,' 'Don't dwell on it, try to think about your future and not what happened in that room.' And worst of all, some actually blame the victim. A lot of cops do that. They ask things like, 'Weren't you really asking for it?'*

"Most people who haven't experienced gang rape have no idea how traumatizing, how utterly disabling, an experience like that can be to a young and sensitive woman like Hannah.

"But even before she was able to talk about it to me, I was certain she'd been raped multiple times by multiple men. There was no way it could have been anything else. I wondered at the time if any of the other freshmun girls had been dragged into other rooms and raped that night or if Hannah was the only one. I think she must have been. Somebody told me later they call what happened to her winning the President's Award."

"Why did they call it that?"

"Because the president of the house gets to choose the victim."

"And Josh was president."

"Yes. Anyway, when I got her back to her dorm room, I sat there with her for a couple of hours waiting for her to show some signs of life. Waiting for her to tell me what happened. But she didn't. All she did was to take a shower, after which she lay back down on her bed. Finally I found her winter coat in her closet, put it on her and walked her back to my car. She hadn't even recovered enough to ask where we were going. But I drove her over to the student health center. At six A.M. on a Sunday morning there was only one nurse on duty there and I had to bang on the door to get her attention. When she finally let us in she asked Hannah what was the matter.

Hannah still wasn't responsive. So I told the nurse that, while I didn't know for sure, I thought Hannah had been raped. The nurse looked at me kind of squirrelly and asked if it was me who had raped her. That's when Hannah finally spoke. She looked up and said, 'No it wasn't Evan. He wasn't there. It was a bunch of other guys.'

"'How many?'

"'I don't know. A lot.'

"The nurse put her arm around Hannah's shoulders and tried to comfort her. She told her she was very sorry but there was nothing they could do for Hannah there. That she'd have to go to the hospital in Plattsburgh and have a rape kit done and that the police would have to be brought in. Hannah listened for a couple of minutes. But when the nurse was in the middle of explaining what a rape kit was and what Hannah would have to go through to get the evidence they'd need to prove the rapes she suddenly just turned around and walked out. I called for her to come back but she didn't. I followed her to my car. She was sitting in the passenger seat and told me to take her back to her dorm. I wanted to drive her to the hospital. She said no and we argued about it for a little while but in the end I listened to her. I know now that the hospital in Plattsburgh, the Champlain Valley Medical Center, is exactly where we should have gone if your husband or any of the others were ever going to be punished for their crimes. I also know that an invasive internal examination and questioning by detectives wasn't something that someone as sensitive as Hannah could have handled at the time. But back then I was just this innocent goofy kid who was hopelessly in love with this beautiful girl who didn't love him back and when she said, 'I'm not letting those people touch me. I'm not

going to let anyone touch me there again. Not ever. Take me back to my dorm,' I simply wasn't strong enough to argue with her so I did what she asked.

"I dropped her off outside her dorm room and watched her walk inside. I can still see every step she took vividly. Possibly the most painful thirty seconds I've ever experienced in my life. After she went through the door I sat in the car and began weeping. I blamed myself for everything that had happened to Hannah that night. Told myself it was my fault. I was the one who wanted to join this stupid fraternity. I was the one who asked . . . Christ, I actually begged Hannah to come to this party with me. I was, God forgive me, actually excited at first to see that the girl I'd brought to the party was dancing with the guy I knew was president of the fraternity and quarterback of the football team."

"You knew who Josh was?"

"Everybody on campus knew. He was a star. When I didn't see them anymore I stupidly thought she and Josh were together and Hannah was telling Josh what a cool guy I was and how they should make me a brother. Fat chance.

"Anyway, Hannah avoided me for the next couple of weeks and I was too shy and too consumed with guilt about what I had done to go anywhere near her. But finally she called me and asked me if I would come pick her up with my car and take her for a ride. We drove for a couple of hours mostly on back roads going nowhere in particular and, after swearing me to secrecy, she managed to tell me, in fits and starts, most of what went on in that room. At least the parts that happened before she passed out. I told her she had to go to the police. Rape is a crime and these people had to be arrested. She told me she couldn't handle standing up in public and *telling people—the police, lawyers, judges and others—what had happened to her."*

"But didn't she finally go to the dean and accuse Josh and Charlie Loughlin of rape? I mean, she did, didn't she?"

"Yes. It was your husband who finally drove her to do that."

"What do you mean?"

"Holden is a small campus. Whenever he'd see her walking on one of the paths, going to the library or to class or whatever, he'd catch up to her and start talking to her. Asking her if she wanted to go out on a date with him. Get together again is how he put it. 'Gee, I'm sorry about what happened the last time but I'd really like to see you again.' Each time he'd say something like that Hannah would panic. Imagine him coming after her. She wouldn't leave her room for days. Wouldn't go to class. After months of enduring that kind of bullshit, with my encouragement—no, at my insistence—she finally worked up the strength to go to the dean's office and accuse your husband and the others of rape."

"But they didn't believe her?"

"Oh, I think some of the people there probably believed her, maybe all of them did, but there was no proof. No physical evidence. Not four months after the fact. Loughlin and your husband swore it was all consensual and they're sticking with the story to this day. They even played some phony tape for the dean where Hannah was supposedly giving consent to having sex. And none of the other four guys ever came forward. Josh and Charlie never named them. To this day I don't know who they were. Shortly after that, Hannah dropped out of school and never came back.

"Again I blame myself for not going to Plattsburgh that Sunday morning. After four months had passed, not only was there no

DNA, there was no longer any proof of vaginal bruising, no tears or other evidence of forced penetration or the fact that she'd been a virgin. The only proof that anything had happened was that Hannah was pregnant."

"Oh, my God."

"She didn't even know which of the six was the father. Naturally she had an abortion."

"Wouldn't fetal DNA have proven who the father was?"

"Sure. But so what? They'd already admitted they had sex with her. It was all too late. I should have dragged her to the hospital to have a rape kit taken the morning it happened. But I didn't. In the end, twelve years later, Hannah punished me for my weakness in not doing that by jumping from a railroad bridge near our home into the freezing water of the river below."

"You said she didn't love you. Yet she loved you enough to marry you."

"Yes. We were married the year I graduated from Holden. I'd never wanted anyone else and I think eventually, in her own way, she came to love me as best she could. But her capacity for love and certainly for a normal sexual relationship between husband and wife had been severely diminished. Sex between us was difficult and occasional and, no matter how much I loved her, I'm sure she never enjoyed it. It was because of Hannah that I chose my specialty in Behavioral Psychology."

"Researching PTSD in rape victims?"

"Yes. And over the years Hannah continuously exhibited all the classic symptoms. Depression. Isolation. A sense of being dirty or disgusting. Flashbacks in which she relived the rapes as if she were experiencing the whole thing all over again. She suffered from re-

curring nightmares. Sudden rushes of intense fear for no apparent reason. And finally, of course, suicide, which is very common among women who've been as violently raped as she was."

"Even after twelve years."

"Yes. Listen, Rachel. I'm a good liberal and I normally don't believe in capital punishment but I believe your husband murdered my wife. I believe he deserves to die for what he has done."

There was about twenty to thirty seconds of silence on the recording. Nothing but the background sounds of the city.

"Are you planning on killing him?" Rachel finally asked.

"Who knows? Maybe I will."

There were a few more seconds of background sounds and then the recording stopped.

"After that he just got up and walked away," said Rachel. "I never saw or heard from him again. At the time I didn't take the threat of murder seriously. I thought it was just talk. But given what's happened it's obvious I was wrong. I think the man who killed my husband was Evan Fischer. It's your job to find him and arrest him."

"Why didn't you tell me about this recording during our interview yesterday?"

"Because I didn't know for sure that Josh was dead yesterday. If he wasn't, if he was just involved in some kinky sex thing somewhere or even if he had been kidnapped for ransom, I didn't want the details of what happened at Holden College to go public. That would have ruined both our lives. As it is, it's only ruined mine."

"It also ended his."

"Yes, it did." Rachel's voice was flat as she said this. Devoid of emotion or affect.

McCabe put Rachel's phone in his pocket. "I'll need to listen to this again. Have some other people listen to it as well. In any event, the recording constitutes material evidence in a murder case so we'll need to keep it. And we'll also need to talk to you again, so please don't leave Portland."

McCabe headed for the door of the suite and Rachel followed him. "Josh may bear some responsibility for the death of Fischer's wife," she said. "But that doesn't excuse Fischer's guilt for the murder of my husband. Or for the murder of Charles Loughlin. He should be punished for both these crimes."

"He will be if we can prove he did it. Is there a number I can use to reach you?"

"Yes," said Rachel. "I bought what your partner called a burner phone." She gave McCabe the number.

"Before you go," she said, "you never told me how Josh died?"

"He was killed with a knife."

"Stabbed?"

"Not exactly. His throat was cut. He bled to death. He was also castrated."

Rachel looked at McCabe blankly. "Well, I suppose that, in its own way, is a kind of justice."

Chapter 31

MCCABE TRIED BOTH of the numbers listed on Evan Fischer's business card. Neither answered. He next called the head of the Psychology Department at UNH. An assistant answered. "Professor Fischer has been on leave of absence since the death of his wife. I expect he mostly stays at home."

"I need to speak to him about a related investigation. He's not answering his phone. Do you happen to know where he lives?"

"I'm not sure Evan would welcome any intrusion given the grieving process he's been going through. In fact, I'm sure he wants to be left alone."

"I do think he'll want to hear what we have to tell him. It concerns the death of his wife."

"I see. Well, Evan and Hannah kept an apartment in town not far from campus: 1024 Madbury Road. But they spent most of their time at a small cabin they owned in the woods off Lee Hook Road about ten miles from town. If I had to guess, I expect you'd find him there. It's where he'd likely retreat. Where they were the night Hannah . . . died."

McCabe got directions to the cabin and, as he ended the call, Connie Davenport tossed a folder on his desk.

"Printouts of all the news reports I could find on Reindel's suicide," she said. "Figured this was the one you wanted even before you gave me Fischer's name."

"Anything useful?"

"Nothing about the rapes. More like obits than anything else. This should prove more helpful." She handed him a second folder. "The state police investigator's report on the death. I asked the New Hampshire Staties to send over a copy and they did."

"Thanks, Connie."

"Need anything else?"

"Let me look through this stuff first."

McCabe glanced through the few newspaper and Internet reports on the death. Most were local to the Durham, NH, area and, as Connie had said, none offered either many details or insights. He tossed the folder on his desk and picked up the police report.

McCabe opened it and started reading. The ME had listed hypothermia as the cause of death. Manner of death was suicide. Jumping off a bridge into a freezing river. Date of death December 24. Christmas Eve. Time of death 4:11 A.M.

The first officer on the scene was a local deputy sheriff who had to fight off Fischer's hysterical demands that they find his wife. "Professor Fischer looked about five minutes from death himself when I picked him up on the road. I called it in. Got a rescue team down to the river to see if they could find the wife. Then I drove him straight to the hospital. The docs there told me doing that saved his life."

Rescuers found Hannah's body about an hour later. She was still in the water, wedged up against a large rock. Seemed like the state police lead investigator, a Sergeant Wally Eckridge, had conducted a thorough investigation. Before accepting Fischer's story at face value he'd questioned him at length about why his wife might have taken her own life.

When McCabe finished reading Eckridge's report he decided to talk to Eckridge directly.

"What can you tell me about Hannah Reindel's suicide?" he asked after introducing himself.

"What's Portland's interest?"

"We had a messy homicide here in town two nights ago. We think there may be a direct link between our murder and Reindel's death."

"Oh yeah? What kind of link?"

"Our victim, a guy named Joshua Thorne, was accused of raping Reindel back in college. There was a reference to punishing rapists on a cardboard sign the killer left on the victim's chest. Note said 'rapists get what rapists deserve.' The victim was castrated before having his throat cut. My guess is he was conscious at the time."

"Charming. Okay. What do you need from me?"

"I read your report on Reindel's death. Right now, Reindel's husband, Evan Fischer, is a suspect for killing Thorne. Motive being revenge for her death."

"What kind of evidence do you have that he's your guy?"

"Aside from the obvious motive, we also have an audio recording made by Thorne's wife of Fischer threatening to kill her husband."

"Wife make the recording?"

"Yep. Fischer contacted her and arranged a meeting."

"And you're sure the voice on the recording is Fischer's?"

"Not yet. We'll have to authenticate that. But he may well admit it's his voice when we talk to him. He's also a suspect in the death of a second one of the accused rapists in Connecticut."

"Hard for me to see Fischer killing a guy the way you described. But I've got to admit he was and probably still is crazed about his wife's death."

"Crazed enough to have tried something like that?"

"I don't know. Maybe. I suppose it's possible."

"What can you tell me about Fischer? Your guys fished him from the water?"

"Not exactly. Local deputy found him waving his arms and screaming hysterically on a back road not far from the Lamprey River. Hundred yards or so downriver from the bridge where she supposedly jumped. Deputy thought Fischer was close to dying himself so he called for help to try to find the wife and then took Fischer to the hospital. He was there overnight coming down from a bad case of hypothermia, which is what killed her."

"What's Fischer like?"

"Well, he sure doesn't come across like a ruthless killer or rabid vengeance seeker. Or somebody who'd ever push his wife off a bridge. Or, for that matter, cut your victim's balls off. Evan Fischer is your classic mild-mannered professor. Teaches at UNH in Durham. He's a fairly small guy. Five nine or so. Skinny and kinda geeky-looking. On the other hand every cop in the world knows looks and manner can be deceiving."

McCabe considered the description. The fact that Fischer would never have been able to subdue someone like Josh Thorne directly might explain his use of a plan B. Using Thorne's weakness for sexy-looking women against him. Using Norah Wilcox, the high-priced escort, to lure Thorne into a helpless position. A handpicked Delilah hired to give Samson the haircut that neutralizes his strength.

"According to your report you guys thought Reindel's death might not have been suicide. You thought Fischer might have killed her."

"Yeah, we did briefly. What initially got me thinking that way was when I talked to him while he was still in the hospital. Admittedly he was a little hysterical but he kept blaming himself for Reindel's death. Kept saying over and over again that he was the one who killed her. Certainly sounded like a confession to me. Got me wondering if maybe he'd pushed her in and then jumped in after her. Murder/suicide scenario. Not that uncommon with unhappy married couples. After he left the hospital I put him in an interview room and hammered him for a while. Tried to get him to admit murdering her by throwing her in the river."

"His motive being?"

"Tired of living with and supporting a woman who by all accounts was suffering from mental illness. When we told him that's what we thought had happened, he looked at me like I was crazy. Said he would have died for Hannah but never in a million years could he have killed her. That wasn't what he meant when he said he felt guilty for having killed her.

"When Joe Murray, one of our detectives, got tough with him, told Fischer to cut the bullshit and tell the truth, the truth being that he'd tossed Hannah over the side of the bridge, Fischer lost it. Said that he wasn't responsible for Hannah's death. Murray tried to ask him if that wasn't what he meant, what the hell did he mean? Fischer started screaming at Murray. Told him he was just a dumb cop who'd never understand how much he loved his wife.

"Murray said, 'I love my wife but sometimes I feel like killing her.'

"Fischer started ranting and raving about the real killers of his wife being these six guys who raped her in college. He said what they did caused her to jump off a bridge twelve years later, which, frankly, seemed pretty damned far-fetched to me."

McCabe decided not to argue the point. Better to let Eckridge keep on talking.

"Fischer started telling us how much he wanted to kill the bastards for what they did to Hannah. He actually said, and you can watch him saying it on our video if you want, that he was gonna quote 'cut their fucking balls off.' Unquote."

"Did you ever check on his story about the rapes?"

"Yeah, I checked. The Willardville cops said they had no record of anything like that ever having been reported. Not in 2001. Not in 2002 or 2003 either. Campus cops also didn't have any record of what he was talking about."

Once again, McCabe didn't bother explaining why there was no record. He just asked Eckridge what happened next.

"Next? Not a damned thing except he lawyered up. One second he's yelling and screaming and ranting about killing the fuckers who killed his wife. The next second he goes totally quiet. Just sits there silently like he's lost the power of speech. Our guy keeps asking him questions. He keeps saying nothing. After a couple of minutes of that he asks for a lawyer. He called a guy named Richard Wyatt, who's an acquaintance of Fischer's. Got a cabin not far from Fischer's. Wyatt teaches criminal law at UNH law school over in Concord and has a big rep as one of the top criminal defense lawyers in the state.

"Wyatt was the one who told us about Reindel and Fischer's

history. He said Fischer had never been able to overcome his sense of guilt for having put Hannah in harm's way. When he said he'd killed her all he meant was that he was the one who took her to the party where the rapes occurred. He also told us Reindel's tried to kill herself a couple of times before. Once with pills. Once by slashing her wrists in the bath. Fischer saved her both times.

"We checked and both the EMTs who rescued her and the ER docs at the hospital confirmed the story. Wyatt said that's what Fischer was doing in the water when she jumped in this time. Trying to save her. He said that unless we were ready to arrest him for a murder he didn't commit, and for which we didn't have a shred of real evidence other than the rantings of a distraught man, we should let him go. He was right on all counts so we cut Fischer loose. Now maybe you can tell me what you need from me."

"I think Fischer *was* telling you the truth. Our evidence indicates that back in college Reindel *was* gang-raped by a bunch of jocks at a fraternity party. The rapes were never reported to the local or campus cops, but one of my detectives confirmed with college administrators that they in fact happened. Anyway, our murder victim was the head rapist. The guy who dragged Reindel into the room where the others were waiting. The guy who was probably murdered down in Connecticut ten days ago was the second."

"Jesus. Think he's going after numbers three through six?"

"I'm not sure but I don't think he knows their names. But I do have somebody trying to find out who they are and where they live now. At the same time we're looking at Fischer as a likely perp in our case and so are the Connecticut cops. We need to find him and talk to him. He's not answering either his office or cell phone and his boss says he's on compassionate leave. Thinks he's living in his cabin. I need directions how to get there."

Eckridge provided detailed instructions. "Want me to join you there?"

"Thanks for the offer, but I think the fewer cops the better when we talk to him. Last thing we need before we're sure he's our guy is a bunch of flashing blue lights."

"Probably a good call. He's not real fond of me at the moment. Just seeing my face would probably get him to lawyer up again."

"Okay. Thanks. When we're done with Fischer I may want to take a look at the bridge where Hannah took the leap. Just to get a sense of the place."

"Just give me a buzz when you're done talking and I'll run you over there."

McCabe told Wally Eckridge he would, hung up and called Maggie. "Where are you?" he asked. "Still in Connecticut?"

"No. Just got home. I'll dump my stuff and come on over."

"Stay where you are. I'll pick you up in ten. Professor Fischer's not answering his phone. We're going down to New Hampshire to pay him a visit."

"Can you pick up some coffee and doughnuts on the way? Haven't had breakfast yet."

"You got it."

On his way out, McCabe stopped by Brian Cleary's desk. "How're you guys making out with the Trident bunch?"

"Well, we made them all nervous as hell with news of Thorne's death. When I told them about the castration they all began covering their balls. Like they were worried about losing them."

"Can't say I blame them. They receive any specific threats or warnings?"

"Nothing I'd put much credence in. There've been a bunch of nasty notes and e-mails about the condo development. But these have been coming in for a while since the whole fight with the city went public. One anonymous handwritten note threatened to blow the thing to kingdom come if it ever gets built. We're trying to find the author through prints and DNA but it's probably a stretch. Beyond that nobody's been threatened with murder. Joe Bonner's hiring some bodyguards to cover his top execs. Waste of money if you ask me. I think this case is more about rape than it is about real estate."

"I'm pretty sure you're right. Leave Trident to Tom for the moment. I want you to bring Rachel Thorne in and find out what she was doing between four P.M. or so when she left here yesterday until I told her about Thorne's death last night near midnight."

"Didn't you go over that last night?"

"Never got around to it. She was too upset about the murder." McCabe figured Rachel would be smart enough not to mention the dropped robe episode. If not he'd just have to endure Cleary's smart-ass comments for a few days. At least he hadn't given in to foolish temptation.

"So I get to talk to the babe?" Cleary sounded pleased by the prospect.

"I wouldn't get your hopes up, Brian. You may think she's a babe. She thinks you look like a pug."

"Pug? As in pugilist?"

"No, I mean more the canine variety."

"Geez. She really said that?" Cleary looked genuinely hurt.

McCabe gave the little tough guy a smile. "Nah, I'm just pulling your chain. Anyway, here's how I want you to go about the conversation. Here's what I want you to ask her."

Chapter 32

WALLY ECKRIDGE'S INSTRUCTIONS included the fact that the two-mile dirt road leading to the cabin was narrow, rocky, steep in places and filled with potholes and hard-packed ice and snow. They took Maggie's red Chevy TrailBlazer since the four-wheel-drive, off-road vehicle seemed a smarter choice than one of the department's unmarked sedans. McCabe drove. The weather had cleared and the main roads were dry and lightly trafficked. McCabe took 295 to the turnpike, then headed south toward the Piscataqua River Bridge that separates Maine from coastal New Hampshire. On the way, Maggie plugged in a pair of earbuds and listened without comment to Rachel Thorne's recording of the conversation on the Brooklyn Heights Promenade. When it was over she listened to the whole thing again. A little more than an hour after leaving Portland, they found the turn off Lee's Hook Road right where Eckridge said it would be. They drove through deep woods on a bumpy and seldom used dirt road that made them thankful for the TrailBlazer's heavy-duty springs. The road ended a little over a mile in. A rusty Jeep Wrangler and a black

Dodge pickup were parked side by side at the end. McCabe pulled the TrailBlazer in behind the Jeep. To their right was a narrower and even rougher dirt path. A sturdy chain was strung between two trees blocking access. A sign hanging from the chain read *Private Property. Keep Out*. McCabe and Maggie ducked under the chain and started toward Fischer's cabin.

The path was uneven and heavily wooded on both sides. Mostly big pine and spruce with a scattering of birch and hardwoods. A dark brown log cabin was visible in a small cleared area about a hundred yards in. Wood smoke was drifting from a stone chimney and the scent of it filled the cold air. As they drew nearer, Mc-Cabe could see a man's face peering out of the window to the left of the door. Then the face disappeared and seconds later the door opened. A smallish, painfully thin man wearing jeans, work boots and a heavy wool shirt emerged cradling a deer rifle in his arms.

"Stop right where you are, whoever you are. If you could read you'd know this is private property."

"Please drop the weapon, sir. We're police officers, detectives, from Portland, Maine," said Maggie, holding up her gold shield and simultaneously walking a little closer to Fischer. "We need to talk to you about the deaths of Joshua Thorne and Charles Loughlin."

"Both of them dead?" Fischer looked at them with what might be real or possibly feigned surprise. "Well, holy shit and hallelujah. Maybe there's some justice in the world after all."

"Are you telling us you didn't know they were dead?" asked McCabe.

"That's what I'm telling you. But I'm certainly glad to hear the news. Couldn't have happened to a more deserving pair. How'd it happen?"

"They were both murdered. Loughlin a week ago. Thorne early yesterday morning. Now would you please put your weapon down. We're not looking for any trouble here. We just want to talk to you."

"Won't be any trouble at all if the two of you just turn around and get your rear ends out of here the same way you came in."

Fischer held the gun steady. As if by silent signal, Maggie and McCabe began to widen the distance between them.

Fischer's eyes went nervously from one to the other, the rifle still raised and aimed generally above and between the two of them. Neither Maggie nor McCabe had any sense he intended to fire.

"Look, all we want to do is to talk to you, Professor," said McCabe. "We believe you can help us find the killer or killers of these two men."

"So you can arrest them? Put them in prison?"

"Yes."

"Can you give me one good reason why I would want to help you do that? Hell, I hope whoever did it gets away scot-free. In my view killing those bastards was nothing more than just retribution for what they did to my wife. I just hope whoever did it made them suffer like they made Hannah suffer. Couldn't have happened to a scummier pair of individuals."

"Was it you, Evan?" asked Maggie. "Was it you who was seeking just retribution?"

Fischer didn't answer. Just stood looking at her, the rifle still in his hands.

"Did you?" Maggie continued. "Kill them, I mean?"

"If I had, I seriously doubt I'd be telling you about it."

"Can you can tell me where you were Tuesday night?"

"Where I've been most days and nights since Hannah's death and cremation. Right here in my cabin."

"Alone?"

"Of course alone. My wife's ashes are my only company."

"Did you see or talk to anyone?" asked McCabe.

"Only Hannah. I sometimes talk to her. A private conversation with her ashes. Sadly, a one-sided conversation, though I often imagine her talking back. But I'm not so far gone that I actually hear voices."

"Did you see or talk to anyone who can confirm that you were here on Tuesday night and early Wednesday morning?"

"No. Only Hannah."

"What have you been doing?" asked Maggie. "Between your chats with Hannah?"

"What have I been doing?" Fischer regarded the Portland cop with the same level of disdain he probably reserved for particularly dim students in one of his classes at the university. "Well, I've been drinking a whole lot more than I normally do. Probably gone through more bottles of whiskey in the last two months than I have in the last five years. Sadly not eating a whole lot either. Clothes don't fit too well these days. Have to get some new ones once they start falling off. But mostly I've been thinking about Hannah. The good times we had together. And the difficult ones. Mourning her loss. Reading a lot as well."

"What were you reading?" asked Maggie, hoping the innocuousness of the question might help drain some of the tension out of Fischer. Draw him into a conversational rather than confrontational mode.

"Mostly lightweight novels. Also some things she had written. She was a writer. I don't know if you knew that. Reading her words help me feel closer to her. They're her side of the conversation as it were."

As Fischer spoke, Maggie and McCabe kept walking almost but not quite imperceptibly toward him.

"Okay. I see what you're trying to do. Sneak up on me while I'm blathering on about my dead wife. That's far enough. I don't want to talk to you or anyone else. I just want the two of you to turn around and leave me alone with my wife. But before you do maybe you can tell me what a couple of cops from Portland, Maine, have to do with either Thorne's or Loughlin's deaths?"

"Joshua Thorne was murdered in Portland," said McCabe. "We're in charge of the investigation and we drove a long way to talk to you. We have reason to believe you may know more about these killings than you're letting on. Now, we can have this chat nice and friendly right in your cozy warm cabin or we can have you arrested for threatening police officers with what I have to assume is a loaded weapon. In which case we can have our chat at police headquarters up in Portland. Your choice."

Fischer looked from one to the other as if trying to decide what to do. "I don't think so," he finally said. "I know enough about what's legal and what's not. One of the things I know is two cops from Portland, Maine, don't have any authority to arrest me or anyone else here in New Hampshire."

"That's not totally accurate," said McCabe. "But in any case we're working with Sergeant Wally Eckridge of the New Hampshire State Police. I believe you've met Sergeant Eckridge. And if you'd rather have him arrest you than us, we can have him here in ten minutes. And if you don't put that weapon down now, I'll make damned sure he arrives with a fully armed SWAT team."

"Are you threatening me?"

"Yes, Professor, I'm afraid that's exactly what I'm doing. Now please put down your gun."

"If you're accusing me of killing Thorne and Loughlin, well, I didn't. I have to admit I thought a lot about that after Hannah's death. Even planned how I'd do it. Wish I was capable of actually doing something like that. Make me feel a lot better if it was me who killed them. But it wasn't."

"Professor Fischer," said Maggie, "we're not accusing you of killing anyone. At least not yet. But we do have to talk to you about Joshua Thorne and what he and Loughlin did twelve years ago at Holden College. There are strong signs retribution for rape was the motive for murder."

"I happen to be in mourning for my wife and at the moment I don't feel like talking to anyone about her death much less a pair of cops I don't know from Adam. But the real truth of the matter is that it was Thorne and Loughlin who killed her. Not directly. But what they and some others did to her ended up killing her in a much crueler way than merely shooting or stabbing her. Or throwing her off a bridge into a river." Fischer lowered the barrel of the rifle till it was pointing toward the ground. "Now, I'm not a violent man and I don't want to hurt anybody but I will if I have to. Like the sign says this is private property. I'm assuming cops can read. So I'm asking you, please just turn around, get off my land and leave me to mourn in peace."

Maggie and McCabe glanced at each other. McCabe nodded almost imperceptibly and the two of them started moving— McCabe to the left, Maggie to the right.

Which is when Fischer fired.

The bullet passed more or less equally between the two of them and way high. At least eight or ten feet over their heads. Either the guy had terrible aim or he just wanted to scare them with a warning shot. Either way they drew their weapons and crouched down for cover behind trees to either side of the path.

"Hold your fire," McCabe whispered to Maggie. Then, in a louder voice, he called out, "Professor Fischer, Evan, please put the gun down and put it down now."

"If you two are so sure I killed Loughlin and Thorne, why don't you just kill me now? Put me out of my misery and that'll be the end of that."

"We're not accusing you of killing anyone. We're not arresting you. But we do have to talk to you."

Fischer fired again. The second shot was just as off target as the first. It was obvious he had no desire to hit them. It occurred to McCabe that what Fischer might be trying was to goad them into shooting and killing him. Suicide by cop. A common enough phenomenon that seemed to be gaining in popularity. He didn't plan on offering the professor that particular way out.

"Cover me but don't fire unless you absolutely have to," McCabe said to Maggie in a loud whisper. "I'm going to try taking the gun away from him."

McCabe holstered his weapon, stood up, held his hands in the air and moved from behind the tree. He started walking toward Fischer.

"For Christ's sake, McCabe, don't be stupid," Maggie called out.

McCabe didn't respond. "Go ahead and shoot me if that's what you're planning to do, Professor," said McCabe in a quiet voice. "Otherwise, please put down your gun. We mean you no harm. But we do need to talk."

Fischer aimed the rifle directly at McCabe. "Stay right where you are," he shouted.

McCabe kept walking, open palms turned outward toward Fischer. About fifteen feet out he figured he was close enough that a round from Fischer's gun might hit him even if the professor was trying to miss. Given the guy's marksmanship, maybe especially if he was trying to miss.

"I know you don't want to hurt anyone," said McCabe softly. "And we certainly don't want to hurt you. We just need you to tell us what you know about the deaths of Joshua Thorne and Charles Loughlin."

"I don't know anything about their deaths. Now I'm asking you, please, please don't take another goddamned step." There was a hint of panic in Fischer's voice. "Please don't make me kill you."

Chapter 33

McCabe kept walking. Fischer looked panicky, studying McCabe, as if trying to decide what to do next. When McCabe was only about ten feet away Fischer lifted the rifle over his head with both hands and threw it at McCabe and, as he did, he turned and ran.

McCabe caught the weapon before it hit him and without a round going off.

"Stop," Maggie cried as she dashed out from behind the tree she was using for cover. "Dammit, stop, you sonofabitch, or I will shoot."

But Fischer kept going. He was already around the cabin and into the woods.

Maggie holstered her weapon and ran to the left around the cabin following Fischer into the woods.

McCabe ran around the other side and joined the chase.

Fischer was moving fast and probably knew the lay of the land like the back of his hand. For sure better than they did.

At first, it was easy to see the red of Fischer's plaid shirt flashing in and out between the green of the trees. But as the professor went deeper into the woods, they saw a lot more green and a lot less red. The guy was a runner. No question about that. His legs covered the ground over twisty and difficult paths surprisingly fast. The two detectives followed as best they could, the ground under them covered with jagged ice, hidden rocks and fallen branches, all waiting to trip them up. Fischer was opening the distance between them and McCabe figured it would only be seconds before he totally disappeared from view. That's when their luck turned. Fischer tripped on something and fell forward, landing flat on his face. He rose painfully to his feet but Maggie was almost on him. He ran right at her. Probably hoping to knock her out of the way and continue his flight.

But Mag was three inches taller and maybe twenty pounds heavier. She hit his gut with her shoulder, wrapped her arms around his legs and brought him down exactly the way her kid brother Harlan taught her to tackle back when he was playing middle linebacker at Machias Memorial High School. Fischer went down hard. A face-plant into rough ice and stone with Maggie still on top of him. He'd probably end up looking more bruised and battered than McCabe. Putting her knee in the small of his back she pulled Fischer's arms behind him and snapped a pair of cuffs onto both wrists. Then she flipped the professor over on his back.

"Evan Fischer?" Maggie asked, kneeling next to him.

"You know who I am. Why are you asking? I fired a gun at you. Why don't you just shoot me and be done with it?"

"You wanna die?" asked McCabe as he reached the spot. "You

want us to put a bullet in your brain and put you out of your misery? Well, tough shit, Professor. You're gonna have to leave this world on your own terms. We're not helping you out."

The fight went out of Fischer all at once. His body deflated. He lay strangely calm.

"Joining Hannah in death," he said, lying quietly on the frozen ground. "I've been thinking a lot about that lately. Having you do it for me would be so much easier than finding the courage to do it on my own." Fischer smiled bitterly.

McCabe patted him down to make sure he wasn't carrying any other weapons. He wasn't. "Now let's get up," said McCabe, hauling the smaller man to his feet. He started marching him back toward the cabin.

"Are you going to arrest me? For shooting at you?"

"I haven't decided. Depends whether or not you tell us the truth about who killed Joshua Thorne."

"If I talk to you, answer your questions as best I can, will you go away and leave me alone?"

"If you can convince us you had nothing to do with Joshua Thorne's or Charles Loughlin's deaths, then most likely yes."

McCabe pushed Fischer into the cabin ahead of him. Maggie picked up Fischer's rifle from the ground. She pulled out and emptied the magazine, put the rounds in her pocket, made sure the chamber was empty and followed them into the cabin and closed the door. "We're going to have to hang on to this rifle for a while," she said to Fischer.

He nodded. "I hope I get it back. I inherited it from my father so it has some sentimental value. He was a passionate hunter."

"Do you hunt?"

"Occasionally."

"What do you hunt?"

"Deer mostly. I'm not a bad shot. I could have hit you if I was trying."

"But you weren't?"

"No. I had no intention of that. Would you mind taking these handcuffs off if I promise not to attack?"

McCabe, deciding Fischer posed no immediate threat, unlocked the cuffs and handed them to Maggie, who put them back on her belt.

"Thank you."

"So you weren't trying to hit us out there?" Maggie asked.

"No. I'm a lousy shot but not that lousy. I'd have a hard time killing a human being. Even a cop."

"How about Joshua Thorne?"

"I have a hard time thinking of Thorne as human so I guess I could kill him given the opportunity. I wish I had, but no, I didn't do it. I would have loved to see both those bastards dead but I'm not the man you're looking for."

"Are there any other guns in the house?" asked Maggie.

"No. Well, yes, actually, one. About five years ago Hannah bought herself a handgun and took a course on how to use it. I took the course with her."

"You're telling me you knew your wife was suicidal. Tried to kill herself twice before she actually succeeded and you allowed her to keep a handgun in the house . . . not to mention the rifle?"

"I tried to talk her out of buying it but she wouldn't listen. She said if I didn't like the fact that she was a woman who wanted to protect herself, well, then, she was perfectly willing to leave me and find her own place to live. Rather than lose her, I gave in. I'm pretty sure if anybody had ever tried to rape her again she would have killed the rapist without a second thought. I like to think I would have too. But it would have been harder for me. But having the gun loaded and available made her feel safer."

Chapter 34

BRIAN CLEARY COULDN'T get the pug comment out of his head when Rachel Thorne settled herself in the same chair in the same small interview room she'd been in before. The insult irritated him, changing his perception of her from *babe* to *bitch*. He had a strong feeling that that was what McCabe had intended by telling him, but still it pissed him off.

"Sergeant McCabe asked me to go over a few details with you that we haven't covered yet," said Cleary.

"Fine." Rachel looked up at the light. "I suppose I'm back on video."

"You are. By the way, my condolences on your loss."

"Thank you."

"What I need you to tell me now, Mrs. Thorne, is where you've been and what you were doing from the time you left police headquarters yesterday until you heard about your husband's death last night."

"I spent the day worrying about Josh. Hoping he was all right."

"Just sitting alone in your hotel room?"

"No. I went out."

"Maybe you could provide some details. Where you went. What you did."

"Is that really necessary?"

"My boss thinks it is. As many details as you can recall."

"Fine." Rachel sighed audibly. "Well, let's see. First thing I did when I left here was to stop by Starbucks. I told my brother Mark I was going to stay in Portland until we'd found Josh. He said that was probably a good idea and that I should keep him informed. He said he was going to catch the next flight back to New York. He'd made a reservation for one that left at six o'clock and called for an Uber car to take him to the airport. I waited with him till it arrived ten minutes later. Then I walked over to the Regency Hotel. Since I thought I might be staying for a while I asked for the best suite they had. I checked in, took a look at the room."

"Room 411?"

"That's right. Then, since I'd brought absolutely nothing with me from New York except my shoulder bag and tablet, I went shopping."

"Shopping?"

"Yes. You know, shopping," said Rachel. "Going into stores and buying things. Surely you've tried it once or twice." Then looking him up and down, she added, "Then again, maybe you haven't."

Cleary managed to restrain himself from snapping back at the sarcasm. It wasn't easy.

"Where did you go and what did you buy?"

Rachel sighed loudly once again, signaling her impatience to Cleary. Letting him know she found this conversation about as interesting as filling out tax returns. "Is any of this really necessary?"

"Yes. I'm afraid it is, so you may as well relax and hang in till we're finished."

Rachel sighed again. "Initially I walked down Exchange Street. They have some nice shops there. I went into three. Tavecchia. Serendipity. Anthropologie. I mostly bought clothes. A couple of pairs of jeans. Some underwear. A couple of tops. Two pairs of wool trousers. A warm casual coat. A more formal coat. And, of course, a ball gown."

Cleary frowned. "A ball gown?"

"Yes. In case I get invited to any parties while I'm here."

Cleary's frown deepened.

"Sorry. Only kidding. Just wanted to see if you were actually paying attention to all this nonsense."

"I'd advise you to take this seriously, Mrs. Thorne. It's far from nonsense. This is a murder case and it's your husband who's been murdered."

"Yes. You're right. I'm sorry. Somehow it just seems so irrelevant. Especially knowing that Josh is dead."

"I understand. Did you buy anything else?"

"Yes. A backpack and a suitcase to carry everything in. Then I went back to the hotel and dumped all the stuff in my room. After that I went back down and asked the concierge where the nearest pharmacy was. He pointed me to a Rite-Aid on Congress Street. I walked over there and bought some basics and also what Detective Savage called a burner phone since you people still have both my cell phone and tablet."

"Can I have the number of the phone?"

Rachel gave it to him. "What else? Oh, yes. I bought some more stuff at a place called Fleet Feet. Running shoes. Some tights and tank tops and sweatshirts and a Gore-Tex jacket."

"What did you do then?"

"Changed into the running clothes and went for a run."

"What time?"

"Six . . . six-thirty."

"It would have been dark by then."

"I'm not afraid of the dark and running is what I do when I'm feeling tense or depressed. And at the time I was feeling both. Josh says I'm a little obsessive about it. Actually, I'm a lot obsessive about it. I run for pleasure as well as exercise. I've run a bunch of marathons including New York and Boston. I've been planning on running London this year at the end of March but what with Josh's death I guess that's off."

"What's your best time?"

"Is that relevant?"

"Just curious. I'm a runner myself."

"Two fifty-seven and change."

"Pretty good. How far did you run last night?"

"I did about ten miles. Maybe a little more."

"Where?"

"I ran from the hotel down to the trail that starts at the ferry terminal and ran east all the way past East End Beach, followed the trail up to Back Cove, went around the cove and then on some streets in that neighborhood for a while. I don't remember the names of the streets but they were mostly quiet residential streets and then I doubled back, ran around the cove again and then back here."

"Was one of the residential streets called Hartley Street?"

"I have no idea."

"How did you know where to go?"

"They gave me a trail map at the front desk."

"Did anybody see you while you were running?"

"Quite a few people considering the lousy weather. But nobody I know or could identify. The woman at the reception desk saw me return."

"What time did you get back to the hotel?"

"Quite late. Ten o'clock or thereabouts."

"More than three hours for ten miles? You've done twenty-six miles in less time than that."

"I wasn't pushing myself and I walked part of the way."

"Really? I thought the running was what relaxed you."

"It wasn't a race. I walked when I felt like walking."

"Fair enough. And then what?"

"I went back to my room. Lay down for a little while. Took a nap actually. I hadn't slept a wink worrying about Josh the night before. When I woke up I took a long, hot shower. After I got out of the shower is when Sergeant McCabe arrived and told me that Josh's body had been found."

"And what time was that?"

"I don't know. Sometime after eleven. Can you tell me anything more about the murder?"

"No more than Sergeant McCabe could. How long was he with you?"

"I don't know. Maybe half an hour. It was around eleven-thirty when he left."

"What did you do then?"

"I drank. I forgot to mention I also bought a bottle of Scotch when I was shopping. I was very upset with the news of Josh's death and I thought the booze would help. I had about three stiff drinks, which both relaxed me and made me a little drunk. Then I called my brother and told him about Josh. Asked him to let our parents know. And Josh's mother. I didn't think I could handle those particular conversations. I'm assuming the police have told Josh's clients here in Portland and his office in New York."

"We have. What did you do after that?"

"I went to bed but I couldn't sleep. I just kept imagining the pain Josh must have gone through before he died. So I got up and tried to read."

"Yeah? What were you reading?"

"A murder mystery. Bad choice, I suppose, under the circumstances. Didn't matter. I couldn't focus on the story anyway."

Cleary let a minute pass in silence to see what Rachel might bring up. She said nothing.

"Do you own a gun, Rachel?" he asked. "A small caliber handgun?"

Rachel looked surprised. "No. Not my thing."

"Does Josh own a gun?"

"Yes. A couple of them. I've always thought men liked guns because they're sort of like penises. What do you think?"

Cleary ignored the remark. "He owns handguns?" he asked.

"Yes. Two."

"What kind?"

"I don't know. Guns don't interest me all that much."

"Have you ever fired one?"

"Yes. Josh has taken me to a gun range a couple of times."

"Are you a good shot?"

"Not bad. I have good eye-hand coordination. I played tennis in college. Coach tennis at Charlton."

"Rachel." Cleary let a pregnant pause go by before continuing in an offhand manner. "Rachel, did you, by any chance, kill your husband?"

"I won't dignify that question with a response."

"Did you also kill the woman we're calling Norah Wilcox?"

Silence.

"Well, did you? While you were out on your run did you some-how track your husband to a small house on Hartley Street? Break in and kill both him and the woman he was having sex with? The woman first with a shot to the head? Your husband next, castrat-ing him with a butcher knife before cutting his throat?"

"I'm afraid this conversation has come to an end."

"You might get away with it, you know. Or at least have charges reduced to manslaughter. Catching your husband having sex with another woman. Crimes of passion and all that."

"If you have any further questions, you little pint-sized prick, you can refer them to my attorney."

"Who is your attorney?"

"I'll let you know when I choose one. Goodbye, Detective." Rachel got up and walked out of the room.

Chapter 35

"MIND IF I have a look around?" McCabe asked Fischer.

"Not much to see except books and magazines, but help yourself."

The cabin was small and simply furnished. There was a main room with a wood burning stove plus a small kitchen and dining area. A couple of chairs. A sofa. A few tables and lamps. And, as Fischer had said, books and magazines everywhere, covering pretty much every available surface. Hundreds or maybe thousands of them stuffed into rows of homemade bookshelves lining the walls, nothing more than pine planks held up by cinder blocks. More books were piled up in the corners and wherever space allowed on the furniture. In addition to the books, there were a number of psychology journals visible. Literary journals as well. Some of the names were familiar to McCabe. *Ploughshares, The Kenyon Review, The Paris Review.* But there were none he'd ever actually read.

An open door led to a bedroom. Standing in the doorway McCabe could see an unmade queen-sized bed, a pair of side tables

and a dresser. In addition to its own share of books and magazines, the bedroom was covered with piles of clothes all over the
floor. A dirty and mostly empty whiskey glass sat on one of the
bedside tables. A half-empty bottle of Dewar's next to it. Another
Scotch drinker. Like the third drinker at Hartley Street. Looking at the mess McCabe wondered if Fischer was simply a congenital slob who needed a living as well as a loving wife to pick
up after him or whether the mess was more a result of depression
brought on by Hannah's suicide. A second door from the main
room led to the bathroom. McCabe looked in. Again small, plain
and functional. Sink, toilet, some shelves to hold toiletries and a
metal shower enclosure.

"You and Hannah live out here most of the time?" he asked.

"Yes. She liked the isolation. I think she felt safer out here
alone than being surrounded by people in our apartment in town.
When she was there she always imagined someone climbing in
the window or picking the lock on the door or grabbing her while
she took out the garbage. Here, let me make some space for you
to sit down."

Fischer started moving piles of papers and magazines off the
sofa and one chair and laying them on top of some other piles that
occupied the floor. After a couple of minutes Maggie and McCabe
were able to share the sofa. Fischer sat opposite them.

Maggie told him since this had to be considered an official police interview, she was going to record the conversation. He nodded indifferently. She flipped on the recorder and went through
the required preliminaries. Date. Time and place of interview.
Names of those present. Then she asked a few general questions
designed to make Fischer forget he was being recorded. How long
had he owned the cabin? How did he like living out here in the

woods? How much time had he and Hannah spent here as op-posed to the apartment near the campus?

"I tried to talk her into staying in town except for weekends. But she preferred staying here."

"Why so?" she asked, wanting him to repeat for the record what he had told them a little earlier.

"Like I told you, she didn't think some random rapist would wander all the way out here searching for prey."

Sexual safety in the woods? McCabe wondered if either Fischer or Hannah had ever seen *Deliverance*. He didn't ask.

"It seemed to her much more likely to happen close to cam-pus where the apartment is. I think all those horny young college guys made her nervous. She was still an attractive, even beauti-ful woman. Even if she was a little old for them." Fischer handed them his phone with a photo on the screen. "This is her about a year ago." The picture showed Hannah seated on one of the chairs in a much neater version of this room. She had a round face with intelligent brown eyes and long dark hair that hung straight down. More than pretty enough to have attracted the likes of Joshua Thorne. Or some college kid in Durham.

"Being on campus reminded her too much of what happened at Holden. And that's in no way irrational. I mean, have either of you read the statistics on sexual assaults on college campuses these days?"

"We both have," said Maggie. "And they're appalling." The last numbers she had seen said over twenty percent, more than one in five female students, were victims of some level of sexual assault in college and nearly two-thirds of those attacks went unreported.

"Okay, so Hannah preferred living out here and you mostly stayed with her?"

"Yes. I didn't like leaving her here alone. She was intermittently suicidal. She'd tried to kill herself twice before it actually happened. Once with pills. Once by slitting her wrists in the bath. I managed to get her to the hospital in time to save her both times. I was constantly on guard for a third try. I was as much her guardian in this house as her husband. I was always concerned what might happen when I had to be on campus and she was here alone."

"And yet you left her here with a loaded gun."

"I told you why."

Maggie pointed to a laptop open on a desk, which was really just a rectangle of plywood supported by a pair of metal file drawers. "That computer yours?" she asked.

"No. Mine's in my briefcase. That's Hannah's. She used it for her writing on the days she could bring herself to work. I don't know if you knew she was a writer. Good one too. Published some wonderful short stories. She also made a little money writing pieces about gardening and house design for glossy magazines. She was nearly finished with a novel that she'd been working on for about five years now. Semiautobiographical. About a young woman who was raped in college and who, years later, hunts down her rapist and kills him."

"With a kitchen knife?" asked Maggie.

Fischer looked at her curiously for a second and then simply nodded. "Is that what happened to Thorne?"

Maggie didn't respond.

"I'm guessing from your silence that it is. Strange. Life imitating art."

"You've read Hannah's book?"

"Of course. A number of times. In a number of iterations. It was never quite finished but she almost got there. I may try to finish it myself and get it published anyway. More than anything else it represents her legacy."

"Anybody else read it?"

"Not when she was alive. She was nervous showing it to other people."

"Have you ever mentioned the content to other people?"

"No. Well, yes, actually. To one other person. After Hannah's death."

"Who?"

"Joshua Thorne's wife. Rachel Thorne."

"You've met Rachel Thorne?"

"Yes. After Hannah's death I wanted both Rachel and Josh to know how what he and his friends did to her in college had destroyed and ultimately ended her life. I contacted both of them. He refused to talk to me. Told me to fuck off and not to bother him again. But she agreed to meet with me. I brought a copy of the manuscript with me. I wanted her to read it. Give her a more intimate sense of the brutality of what her husband had done."

"Did she say she would read it?"

"Yes, she seemed quite eager to. But I don't know if she ever did."

After a brief silence Fischer began talking again. "Writing a story even loosely based on what happened to her at Holden was the most difficult thing Hannah ever attempted. It'd often get to be too much and she'd have to stop working on it. Sometimes for months at a time. Too emotionally difficult to constantly relive the situation. It provoked too many flashbacks. Which may have been a contributing factor in her suicide."

"Why did she want to do it?" asked McCabe.

"More a question of had to than wanting to. As difficult as it was, I think working on the book was, for the most part, therapeutic for her. It gave her life purpose. It seemed to offer a kind of catharsis and in spite of the difficulty I encouraged her to pursue it. Sadly, she was actively writing the night she went off that bridge, which makes me wonder how much working on the book might have pushed her to do it. Wonder if my encouraging her to write might have contributed to her suicide. Another source of guilt."

A look of utter devastation appeared on Fischer's face. And then as quickly and suddenly as it had come it changed. Like an actor playing two roles suddenly switching from one character to another. He looked up, smiling as if something had suddenly occurred to him. "Well, I must apologize for being such a terrible host. Hannah would give me hell for that. Can I offer either of you something to drink? Coffee? Tea? I've also got some cookies somewhere. Or alcohol? I've got wine or beer, if you prefer."

McCabe thanked him and declined but Maggie accepted the offer of coffee and cookies. As Fischer fiddled with the coffeemaker, notes from Duke Ellington's "Take the A Train" emerged from McCabe's jacket pocket. Caller ID indicated Bill Bacon on the other end. McCabe thought about letting the call go to voice mail but then changed his mind. Bacon knew where he was and what he and Maggie were doing. He wouldn't be calling unless it was important. Or at least pertinent. "Gotta take this call. Be right back."

McCabe zipped his jacket and left the warmth of the cabin, closing the door behind him.

Chapter 36

"Hi, Bill. What do you have?"

"Norah Wilcox. Truth of the matter is I've got two Norah Wilcoxes. One dead. Plus a second Norah who happens to be very much alive."

"Does the live one have anything to do with the case?"

"I think so. But first I ought to tell you dead Norah's body turned up a couple of hours ago. She was still in the trunk of the Altima. We found it parked in a legal spot on Lawn Avenue just off Deering. Patrol unit drove by the car three times before recognizing the number plate and calling it in. We pulled the trunk and there she was. Still dressed up like she was in the surveillance video from the bar. Except her body was pretty much frozen."

Frozen made sense. Temps hadn't gotten above thirty-two for some time. Another Lainie Goff, thought McCabe, recalling the completely frozen corpse of a young woman they'd found in the trunk of her own BMW. A case he and Mag had worked a couple of years back.

"Weird thing is," said Bacon, "he left the gun he used to shoot her right there in the trunk with her. A baby Sig."

The "baby Sig" Bacon was referring to was a Sig Sauer P238 Nitron. Powerful and small. Just five inches long and weighing less than a pound, McCabe always thought of it as a woman's gun and the company marketed it as such. Bacon was right. It was strange the killer just left it in with the body. Much smarter and just as easy to toss the murder weapon into the harbor where it'd never be found.

"You're sure you've got the right gun? Maybe the one you found was Norah's and she had it out trying to defend herself."

"Whoever it belonged to it's still the gun that killed her. I held off calling you until we had a ballistics match. No question. It's the right gun."

"Prints or DNA?" he asked.

"Some prints on the gun. Don't have a match for them yet. Jacoby's folks are still going over the car but so far they haven't come up with anything. Looks like whoever bopped you and drove out of the garage was careful about that. So far all the techs have found came either from Josh Thorne or the Norah in the trunk."

"You said something about two Norahs. Who's the second one?"

"An ex-classmate of Evan Fischer's. Fischer and Norah #2 went to high school together. Ridgewood, New Jersey. Class of '01. She still lives nearby. Town called Ho-Ho-Kus, which is a pretty silly name for a town if you ask me."

McCabe had passed through both Ridgewood and Ho-Ho-Kus a bunch of times. They were upscale commuter towns set right next to each other fifteen miles or so northwest of Manhattan via the George Washington Bridge.

"And she's not the woman in the trunk?"

"Nope. Totally different type. And, like I said, still very much alive."

"Has she been in touch with Fischer lately?"

"She says not. I called her and she says she remembers Evan Fischer quite well, but hasn't seen or heard from him in years. She's currently married with two kids and doesn't even use the name Wilcox anymore. She's Brightman now. Norah Brightman."

"So how'd you manage to dig that one out?"

"Didn't you know I'm a top detective just like you? Isn't that what us top detectives do?"

"So I've been told. Now tell me how you found her."

"When I ran out of likely or even remotely possible Norah Wilcoxes on the Internet and every other database I could think of, I decided to change tactics and check out people from both Fischer's and Rachel Thorne's past. One of the places I looked was Evan Fischer's high school yearbook."

"How'd you find his yearbook?"

"Holden College alumni office told me he'd graduated from Ridgewood High School, class of '01. So I called the school library and discovered they have copies of all their yearbooks. Librarian was nice enough to check an entry in the '01 book for me, and ta-da, there they both were. Evan Fischer and Norah Wilcox. I asked the librarian to scan the page with Wilcox's photo and e-mail it to me and she did."

"I take it Mrs. Brightman's never worked as a three thousand dollar a night escort in New York City?"

"Nah. Ridgewood Norah would have a tough time getting fifty bucks a throw."

"Cut the shit, Bill."

"Okay, sorry. Only kidding. She was kind of cute in her high school pic but current photos on Facebook and Instagram show her as a plain, plump and pleasant-looking mom. But in no way glamorous."

"And you managed to talk to her?"

"Yes. She currently works as an ER nurse at Valley Hospital in Ridgewood. She says she and Fischer were friends back in high school. Dated a couple of times but never anything serious. She hasn't seen or heard from him in years. She went to their tenth reunion but he wasn't there. However, she did say that she'd heard about Fischer's wife's suicide from another classmate and meant to write him a condolence note. But she hadn't gotten around to it yet. I figure that Fischer just picked a name from his past and told the fake Norah Wilcox to use it."

"Okay. That's good information. Getting back to dead Norah, do we know anything about her except what she did for a living? Like maybe her real name?"

"Nope. She's officially a Jane Doe. Can't even inform next of kin yet. I'm kind of out of ideas. What do you want me to try next?"

McCabe didn't say anything for a minute. Breaking the case would be easy if they could find out who hired dead Norah, aka Jane Doe, and promised to pay her twenty-five grand to lure Joshua Thorne to 339 Hartley Street. He was still thinking the killer was most likely Evan Fischer. But it could have been someone else.

Bill Bacon broke the silence. "I was thinking maybe we could publish that composite picture that Ishkowitz Photoshopped and see if anyone comes forward and IDs her?"

"No, I don't want to do that yet," said McCabe, figuring every whackadoo Gillian Anderson fan in the country would start calling in with hot tips. Hell, Anderson might even get pissed enough to make a fuss about it if she realized that they'd started the process with her image. "I assume you've Googled escort services in New York and looked for pictures of her?" asked McCabe.

"Yup. Every one of them. Least all the ones I could find online and on the pages of BackList. A lot of good-looking babes out there for three grand a night, even one asking five grand, but no Gillian Andersons."

"Okay, here's what I want you to do. I found dead Norah's Day Runner date book in the glove compartment of the Altima. I don't have it with me but I remember pretty much the whole thing." McCabe's eidetic memory would allow him to remember and repeat for Bacon's recorder every name, date and number he'd seen in Norah Wilcox's Day Runner. "I want you to go get a recorder and record this call. Let me know when you're ready."

A minute or two later, Bacon said, "Okay, McCabe, you're on the air."

"Okay. The book is filled with, oh, I don't know, maybe a hundred or more names of her clients, most with phone numbers and places and dates when they got together. A lot of repeat customers among them. I'm going to repeat them all to you and when I'm done I want you to start calling the johns."

It took him a little over fifteen minutes to recite them all. When he had finished, he said, "I want you to call them all. They won't know the Norah Wilcox name but if you tell them when and where they met with her, what her phone number is and how much they paid, they shouldn't have any problem remembering. I want you to get the name she used with them and also the name of whoever ran the escort service. Call the number and find out her real name if you can and any information about who she is and where she came from. Aside from anything else we're going to have to notify next of kin about her death."

"This ought to be interesting," said Bacon. "Think her clients will cooperate? Wouldn't do their reputations much good. Or their relationships if they're married."

"A lot will hang up on you. If they do, keep after them. Call them back, leave a message if necessary, and tell them if they don't cooperate and tell us what they know about Ms. Wilcox, we'll let the world . . . including wives and employers . . . know all about their secret adventures in the big city."

"Jesus, McCabe, I think that's called blackmail."

"I'm not sure it qualifies. In any case, I doubt they'll call the police."

"We *are* the police."

"So I've been told. Don't worry about it. Just tell them we'll give them total confidentiality if they help us out. If they refuse to tell us whatever they know about her, we go public. My bet is they'll start singing like canaries."

"Likely she didn't give them her real name either. Prostitutes like to stay as anonymous as possible."

"Maybe. But they should know how to contact her. Whoever was running her or maybe some of her coworkers might know her real name or at least have some usable background information. When you find one make a date with her."

"Really?"

"Really."

"Where and when?"

McCabe thought about appropriate hotels. "The Grand Hyatt

on 42nd Street. Tomorrow night, nine o'clock. Have Fortier arrange a credit card for you and make a reservation."

"So you want me to go down to New York and spend time hanging out with a high priced hooker?"

"No."

"No?"

"I'm gonna be the one hanging out with the high priced hooker."

"Damn. Why do you get to have all the fun?"

"Sorry, Bill. Rank has its privileges."

"Well, at least that'll make my wife happy. I'll start making calls soon as we hang up. Let you know what I find out."

Chapter 37

By the time McCabe went back into the cabin, Maggie was sitting with her boots off, her stocking feet tucked under her, sipping coffee and listening to Fischer tell her how much he'd loved his wife. How hard it was going to be to go on living without her.

"What made you want to call Thorne and Loughlin?" she asked.

"I thought they should know what happened to Hannah. How they destroyed the life of a beautiful and talented young woman. I called Loughlin first. Then Thorne. I told them both about Hannah's death. Tried to explain how Hannah's suicide was their fault. Instead of showing any contrition, Loughlin told me not to call again and hung up. Thorne had the gall to tell me the multiple rapes were my fault, not his."

"Why your fault?"

"I brought her to the party."

"He admitted they were rapes?"

"No. He called them Hannah's sexcapades. He claimed she was eager to play. Which is total bullshit. Anyway, after Loughlin and Thorne told me to fuck off I called their wives."

"Why?"

"I don't know. I wanted to hurt them by making their wives aware of what kind of scum they were married to. I guess I hoped when they found out they'd make their husbands' lives miserable for what they'd done to Hannah. I called Heather Loughlin first. She hung up even faster than Charlie did."

"But Rachel Thorne didn't hang up," said Maggie. "In fact, she agreed to meet with you. Isn't that right?"

"Yes. We arranged to meet in Brooklyn. I assume Rachel told you that."

"She did. Evan, did you have any idea Rachel was recording your conversation when you met with her?"

Fischer furrowed his brows. "No. No idea at all. Is that legal?"

"It is as long as one party to the conversation is aware of it."

"Did Rachel give you this recording to listen to?"

"Yes. She played it for Sergeant McCabe in Portland and I listened to it twice on the drive down here."

A frown line formed between Fischer's eyes. He was angry again. "I'm not sure why she'd want to record it or even why she'd want you to hear what we talked about that afternoon."

"Oh yeah? Why not?"

"Because we talked about murdering her husband."

Maggie looked at him oddly. "In light of what happened to him doesn't that conversation seem kind of relevant?"

Fischer rose from his chair without answering and began pacing back and forth in the small room, his face knotted in concentration. Was he trying to remember what he'd said to Rachel on the Brooklyn Heights Promenade? Maybe. Maggie began to ask another question but he waved her off. "Give me a minute, will you? I have to think something through."

Fischer continued to pace. Probably trying to remember not just what he'd said to Rachel but what might be incriminating. As he paced, Maggie watched him muttering and moving his hands about as if deeply involved in a complex conversation with himself. Or maybe repeating the conversation with Rachel. Then he stopped and looked at Maggie. "You said you listened to this recording?"

"That's right."

"Twice?"

"Right again."

"All while you were driving down here?"

"Yes. Why?"

"The drive from Portland takes about an hour."

"A little less. We drive fast."

"Then you couldn't have listened to it twice."

"And why is that?"

"Because my conversation with Rachel went on a lot longer than that. The first half hour or so we talked on a bench overlooking New York Harbor. Then we went back to her apartment. She said she was getting cold but we had a lot more to talk about. She suggested we continue talking there. I asked her if Josh was there. She said he was away on business. He was in Portland, as a matter of fact."

"So you went to the apartment?"

"Yes. Walking there took only a few minutes and we didn't talk about much of anything on the way. Just some small talk about Brooklyn becoming the hot place to live in New York. When we got there we took an elevator to the fifth floor."

"What was the apartment like?"

Fischer shrugged. "Modern. Expensive."

"Can you describe it?"

"Why is that relevant? You want proof I was actually there?"

"Something like that."

Fischer shrugged. "It was a duplex. Two stories. Entire fifth and sixth floors of the building. I didn't go upstairs where I guess the bedrooms are but the living room and kitchen were very modern. All white and glass furniture. Modern art on the walls. Looked original. SubZero fridge and a big Viking stove in the kitchen that had, like, six burners. I asked her if she liked to cook. She said no, she never cooked. They mostly ate out. Or ordered in. Ridiculous. What else? Let's see. There were big floor-to-ceiling windows from one end of the main room to the other. You could look out and see the Statue of Liberty and the Manhattan skyline. I don't know what places like that go for these days but I imagine it's got to be millions."

"What then?"

"She asked me if I wanted a drink."

"Did you?"

"Yes, I really did. I was so nervous about being in Joshua Thorne's apartment with Joshua Thorne's wife that I was shaking like a frigging leaf and not just from the cold. I asked her if she had any Scotch. She got out a bottle and poured one for me and one for herself. She had ice with hers. I don't take ice."

"What kind of Scotch?" asked McCabe.

"Oh Christ, I don't know. Something expensive. Johnnie Walker Black, I think. Does it really matter?"

"I was just curious," said McCabe.

Maggie took Rachel Thorne's iPhone from her pocket and set it on one of the magazines littering the table. "I'd like you to listen and tell us what's not here." She hit Play.

She watched Fischer's face while it played. Especially when it ended with him saying: "*Yes. Listen, Rachel, I'm a good liberal and I normally don't believe in capital punishment but I believe your husband murdered my wife. I believe he deserves to die for what he has done.*"

"*Are you planning on killing him?*"

"*Who knows? Maybe I will.*"

The recording stopped. "Is that it?" asked Fischer. "Is that all you've got?"

"That's it. You said there was more to the conversation than that."

"Yes. That's when Rachel suggested we go to the apartment. She didn't record what we said there?"

"Not that we know of," said McCabe. "I take it you didn't either."

"No. I did a lot of drinking and a lot of talking about Hannah and how she had died. Rachel seemed very sympathetic. She also seemed majorly pissed about Josh. Not just the rapes but what kind of person he was. She said she'd been thinking about divorcing him. Starting over. That kind of thing. I told her that would just free the bastard to rape more women. She said he didn't need to rely on rape. When he was really hot to get laid he would only use force to save time."

"He only used force to save time?" Maggie looked incredulous. "She actually said that to you?"

"Yes. I'd already had my second drink and remarks like that were making me wish he actually was there so I could shoot the bastard on the spot. Rid the world of a sociopathic monster."

"Did you have a gun with you?"

"Yes. I had Hannah's handgun with me."

"What kind of gun is it?" asked McCabe.

"A small Sig Sauer. I told you both Hannah and I went to a range and learned how to use it."

"And you wanted to kill Joshua Thorne?"

"Yes. Loughlin too. And maybe the others. But mostly it was Thorne I wanted to kill."

"Did you? Kill him, I mean?" Maggie asked as if simply curious. "Not in New York but two nights ago in Portland?"

"No, I did not. I'd have liked to but I didn't. I think maybe she's the one who killed him. Rachel, I mean. She's a hell of a lot tougher than me and she had plenty of motive. Joshua Thorne wouldn't be the first guy murdered by his wife."

"Where is this gun?" asked McCabe.

"That's another thing. It's gone. I think she may have stolen it. When I showed it to her, she took it and handled it. Looked like she knew what she was doing."

"It was stolen before or after your trip to New York?"

"Definitely after. I remember clearly putting it back in the drawer when I got home. And then one night a week later I looked in the drawer and it wasn't there."

"The cabin wasn't locked?"

"No. I never lock the place. Hannah was always adamant about locking up. Even had new locks installed. But after she died I reverted to old habits and never bothered. I reported the theft to the Durham police. They took down all the information but I don't think they ever did anything about it."

"Who knew you had this gun?"

"Lots of people. I discussed the fact that Hannah wanted to buy a gun with several of my colleagues in the Psych Department. We agreed if she decided to take her own life she probably wouldn't do it by blowing her brains out. Turned out we were right. The gun was there and she didn't use it."

"Who else knew you had the gun?"

"I told you Rachel did. I told her how I fantasized using it to kill her husband."

"Did you tell her where you kept it?"

Fischer frowned as if trying to remember. "I don't remember. I was pretty drunk by that time. I might have."

"And you told her where you were living?"

"I told her I worked at UNH. Gave her a business card. But I don't remember if I told her about the cabin. But c'mon, Detective, even if I did, it's a long haul from Brooklyn, New York, just to steal a gun. These days even crazy people can buy a gun pretty much anywhere. Including on the Internet."

True, thought McCabe. Unless you were a crazy person who wanted a specific gun with a specific serial number that just happened to belong to someone with a strong reason for wanting to kill your husband.

"Do you still have the receipt from when you purchased the gun?"

Fischer nodded.

"Would you show it to me?"

Fischer retrieved it from one of the file drawers that were holding up the desk and handed it over. A Sig Sauer Nitron purchased from a New Hampshire dealer four years earlier. Maggie made note of the serial number. McCabe simply committed it to memory.

"By the time we both had . . . God, I don't know how many drinks but really a lot . . . we started playing a game. Or what Rachel called a game. She named it Double Jeopardy. Like from the TV show."

"And how did this game go?" asked McCabe.

"She decided I was the contestant so I had to go first."

"Go first and do what?"

"Invent a way to kill Josh in which I wouldn't be caught. Of course I suggested something stupid. Like waiting for him to come home from work, hiding behind the door and blowing his brains out as he walked in. She laughed at that idea and said, 'Oh no, you've got to be a lot more clever than that. And I'm not sure I'd want all that blood and bits of Josh all over the apartment.'"

McCabe wondered if Fischer was making all this shit up. The whole game business sounded too stupid for words. On the other hand, he'd learned firsthand how much Rachel liked playing games. Dangerous games. He'd also learned she was a manipulative liar. So who the hell knew?

"I asked Rachel what she meant by 'clever.' She said if I didn't want to spend the rest of my life in jail I had to think up a way to kill Josh that nobody would figure out. 'Like what?' I asked.

"'Oh no,' she said. 'You're the contestant and I'm the moderator. You know? Like Alex Trebek. I make the rules and ask the questions. If you come up with the right answer you win the prize.'

"'And what is the prize?' I asked.

"'The ultimate one,' she said. 'At least for you. Revenge for the rape of your wife. For me a big pile of money. And not having to put up with a cheating husband anymore.'"

"And how well did you do in this game?" asked Maggie.

"Not very. I'm not very imaginative."

"When you were playing your game of How Do We Kill Josh, did Rachel ever suggest hiring a prostitute to lure Josh Thorne to his death?"

"No. I mentioned it. Remember, I was the contestant. She was the moderator. I came up with that idea in response to something she said. That there were only two things in the world that truly interested Josh. Money and fucking. I told her I didn't have access to the kind of money that would interest him. But fucking seemed like a good idea. So I suggested hiring a really hot woman to use as bait to lure him to a place where he could be killed anonymously. That turned out to be the only idea of mine she liked." A crooked grin spread across Fischer's face. "She gave me an A plus for it."

"An A plus?"

"Yes. I'm sure you know Rachel's a teacher. So am I. We both give out grades all the time."

"What happened next?"

"Nothing. It was already dark out and I had to leave to catch my bus back to New Hampshire. The whole trip back I was thinking she actually wanted me to do it. Kill her husband the way I dreamed up in the game. And maybe she did. That way, I would be the one who'd have to go to jail. And she could play the mourning wife and collect millions in insurance."

"Did you talk about Hannah's book? Her novel?" asked Maggie.

"Yes. Like I told you I gave her a copy to read. Certainly appropriate since it was about a victim murdering a rapist."

"In the book, neither the husband of the victim nor the wife of the rapist are the killers, are they?" asked Maggie.

"No. In the book it's the victim herself. She plans the murder and carries it out."

"How does she do it?"

"I told you. With a knife."

"Yes, you said that. But what does she do with the knife?"

"She castrates the rapist and then cuts his throat. I think that's how Hannah always fantasized getting back at Thorne."

"Did you tell Rachel how the rapist was murdered in the book?"

"No. But if she read it she would know."

"Would you let me read the book?"

"I don't know. I'd hate doing that without Hannah's permission, which at this point she can't give. The parts about the murder are pretty brutal."

"You let Rachel read it."

"Yes. I wanted her to know in a much stronger, more immediate way than I could possibly describe what her husband and the others had done to Hannah. And how she'd suffered from it ever since. I guess I wanted her to want to kill Josh every bit as much as I did. Or as Hannah did."

"Do you think Rachel killed her husband?"

"I don't know. I think she may have."

"But you didn't do it?"

"No. I didn't do it."

"Because you didn't want to spend the rest of your life behind bars."

"That part doesn't bother me." Evan Fischer laughed a small bitter laugh. "The rest of my life may well be very short."

Maggie threw McCabe a look he understood immediately. She wanted to take Fischer in under protective custody. He was clearly a danger to his own life. McCabe merely nodded.

"Can I see the book?" asked Maggie.

"It's in the computer. I'll e-mail it to you."

"Would you do that now?" Maggie handed him her card. Fisher went to the laptop, and attached a word document to an e-mail addressed to Maggie. He hit Send.

While Fischer was writing and sending the e-mail, McCabe went outside and called Bill Bacon. Asked Bill to take down the serial number of Fischer's gun and compare it to the one they'd found in the trunk.

"Now?"

"Yeah, do it now, Bill. I'll hang on."

Two minutes later Bacon was back on the phone. "You got it, McCabe. Same serial number. Same gun. It's the one that killed the woman in the trunk. Whoever she was. FBI has no record of her fingerprints. Or her DNA."

McCabe came back in the cabin.

"I need to talk to you for a couple of minutes," he said to Maggie. Turning to Fischer he added, "And I need you to stay right where you are."

Maggie headed for the door. As she was leaving she noticed Fischer pouring himself a large glass of Scotch. No ice.

Chapter 38

McCabe shut the door behind them and they walked far enough away from the cabin so there was no chance Fischer might overhear what they were saying. But close enough that they could keep an eye on the door.

For the next five minutes, McCabe filled Maggie in on his phone conversation with Bill Bacon. He told her about the discovery of the Altima on Lawn Avenue. Norah's near frozen body still in the trunk. The gun that killed her right beside her.

"Bill checked the serial numbers. Fischer's gun killed Wilcox. Which as far as I'm concerned pretty much seals it. Mild-mannered professor or not, Fischer's got to be our guy."

"What about Rachel driving up here to steal the gun?"

"To use to murder a woman Fischer had nothing against? I can't see even someone as devious as Rachel driving twelve hours round trip just to get her hands on Fischer's gun. Too easy just to take one of Josh's and throw it in the ocean after the deed is done."

"She might do the drive if she wanted to seal the deal against Evan."

"Mabe, but I think we go back to the cabin now, put the cuffs on the professor, let Wally Eckridge know what we're doing and take Fischer back to Portland. Then we put our mild-mannered professor in an interview room and not let him out until he confesses to all three murders or until we find at least a shred of hard evidence that it was Rachel who did the deed."

Maggie sighed and shook her head. "Maybe you're right. But I still don't think the guy has it in him to be that kind of killer. Maybe of Thorne and Loughlin. But no way would he kill a bystander like Wilcox. And even if he did, why would he be stupid enough to leave his gun sitting in the trunk right next to the body?"

"I don't know. Because he's the nervous type? Panicky. Probably forgot he left it there when he dumped the car."

"Even if I grant you that," said Maggie, "why compound the stupidity by handing two cops the receipt for the gun purchase with the serial number printed on it when he could just as easily have told us he'd thrown the receipt away?"

"Again I don't know, Mag. Because he's careless? And not very good at being a murderer? Because I surprised and panicked him by showing up unexpectedly at the house on Hartley Street? Maybe Fischer was hiding upstairs admiring his surgery when I came in. When he hears me open the trunk of the car and discover Wilcox lying there dead, he sneaks down, bops me on the side of the head and drives off. If it had been Rachel there'd have been no bop on the head. She would have just gunned me down without shedding a tear. Then chuckled when she rolled the car over my corpse on the way out."

Maggie nodded. She was inclined to agree with that. "Okay. Maybe. But I'm still not convinced. Aside from anything else, do you honestly think Evan Fischer would have a clue how to hire an expensive prostitute? Even for sex, let alone to lure Thorne to his deathbed? I just don't see it."

"What about the fact that Evan Fischer just happened to have asked a girl named Norah Wilcox to the senior prom. How the hell was Rachel Thorne supposed to find that out?"

"The same way Bill did. By researching the guy. Don't you see what's bugging me, McCabe? It's just too goddamned perfect. Using the Norah Wilcox name was just another little piece of the frame-up."

"Even if I grant you that, what about the Day Runner? Dead Norah kept a very thorough date book, which I went through page by page, and you know me, I remember every name, date and place written in that book. Evan Fischer's name was written in right next to the time and place for picking up Josh and delivering him for the kill."

"Rachel could have written that in and left it for us to find."

"Look, Maggie, all the evidence we've got points straight to Fischer. All of it. The gun. The Day Runner. The audio recording of him saying he wants to kill Joshua Thorne. Hell, even the method, castration and cutting Thorne's throat, came right out of Hannah's book."

"And none of this so-called solid evidence points to Rachel?"

"That's right. All we've got on Rachel is Fischer telling us that she invited him to her apartment where in her role as Lady Macbeth she lures him into playing a game the objective of which was to come up with a clever way to murder her husband."

"Yeah. And isn't it interesting that she didn't record that portion of the conversation?"

"Maybe because it never happened," said McCabe. "Maybe

Fischer made the whole thing up. Maybe the conversation ended like Rachel said on the Brooklyn Heights Promenade."

"Then how do you explain him describing what her apartment looks like. I doubt he'd make up details like that. Too easy to check. He even noticed what kind of Scotch she keeps there."

"All right," said McCabe. "You've got me on that one. We'll have to ask her about that."

"I'm sure she'll have thought up some clever explanation."

"Really? Like what?"

"I don't know. But she's thought of everything else. I'm sure she'll have some kind of explanation ready."

"I'll give you that one. He was even right about her brand of Scotch. She had a bottle of Johnnie Walker Black in her room when I did the NOK notification. She drank some herself and offered me some."

"Which I assume you turned down."

"I did." Remembering the scene in the Governor's Suite, McCabe felt himself begin to blush. He wondered if it showed or if the bruises on his face provided adequate camouflage.

Maggie didn't respond. She just looked at him like she was trying to figure something out.

"Look," said McCabe, "I know you don't like her . . ."

"Really? Not like her? How could that be? Is it just because she's a selfish, lying bitch who likes to flirt with you and probably every other good-looking guy in the world and has a nasty attitude toward me and probably every other woman she considers a competitor? None of that stuff means I don't like Rachel. It means I absolutely detest her. However, I can assure you my personal feelings about the woman are totally beside the point."

"The point being?"

"I think she killed her husband."

"I'll grant you Rachel may have had a motive for killing Josh . . ."

"Six million motives."

"Okay, six million motives. However, I can't think of a single one why she'd want to kill Charlie Loughlin. Fischer had a motive for killing Loughlin but Rachel barely knew the guy and I just don't see the selfish rich girl as you describe her taking on the role as the avenging angel of all rapists."

"Sure she had a motive. And you're demonstrating it right now. The easiest way for her to frame Fischer for killing her husband was to link that murder to the killing of a man she barely knew and had no reason to kill."

"You really think she's that much of a psycho?"

"Yeah, I do."

McCabe took a deep breath. "I don't know. Maybe you're right. But we don't have a shred of either physical or circumstantial evidence linking Rachel to either killing. No prosecutor in his right mind would take her to court on what we've got. On the other hand, Fischer? A slam dunk. If the DNA from the whiskey glass I found in the house on Hartley Street matches Fischer's, which I'm willing to bet it will, we've got a conviction. In fact, I think we ought to go back to the cabin and take him with us right now."

"I agree. Let's take him with us."

"You agree?"

"Yeah. I agree."

"Why the change of heart?"

"Because of Fischer. I keep thinking what he said. *'The way I feel now the rest of my life may well be very short.'*"

"And you think he meant it?"

"Yeah. I do. We take him in. We place him under suicide watch."

"You want me to do the honors?" asked McCabe.

"No. You scare him too much."

Maggie went back to the cabin and asked Evan Fischer to stand up and turn around. Then she cuffed him.

"What's this for?" asked Fischer.

"Evan Fischer, I'm placing you under arrest for the murder of Joshua Thorne and for the murder of an unidentified woman we're calling Jane Doe. Oh, and also for firing a loaded gun at two police officers." Maggie read Fischer his Miranda rights and walked him out to the TrailBlazer.

Before leaving, McCabe called Wally Eckridge, told him about the arrest and asked him if he could possibly have a team of evidence techs go over the place for any trace of a woman named Rachel Thorne. On the way back to Portland, McCabe drove. Maggie sat in the back with Fischer. And no one, including Evan Fischer, said a word. He just sat quietly in the backseat and stared blankly out of the window watching New Hampshire and then Maine roll by.

Chapter 39

McCabe called Rachel Thorne late Friday from 109 using his cell phone rather than the department's landline. That way only his name would show up on her caller ID.

"McCabe, Michael," she answered. "I wasn't sure when, if ever, I was going to hear from you again. Do you have any news for me?"

"Yes. I thought you'd want to know. We have Evan Fischer in custody."

"Well, thank God for that."

"We haven't gone public yet so I'd like you to keep that information confidential for now."

"Why?"

"It will help us get a conviction."

"All right." Rachel sounded puzzled. "But thank you for telling me. I was sure he was the guy. I was sure there was something wrong with that creep when we met in Brooklyn. I only wish I'd called the cops on him then when he first threatened to kill Josh. It was my fault, really, for not taking him seriously."

McCabe decided it was time to change the subject. "How are you holding up?"

"Better than yesterday. And definitely less crazy than I was Wednesday night. I really have to apologize again for my behavior. You must have thought I was out of my mind."

"Hey, listen, everybody reacts to traumatic news in unpredictable and sometimes dramatic ways." McCabe chuckled. "Though I have to admit yours was more unpredictable and dramatic than most."

There was a soft laugh in response on the other end of the phone. "Well, I hope you enjoyed the show."

"Listen," said McCabe, "there are some details we have to pin down about your meeting with Fischer in Brooklyn if we're ever going to get a conviction. Can you stop by headquarters tomorrow, say, at ten o'clock?"

McCABE WATCHED RACHEL emerge from the elevator at 109 at 10:10. She was once again dressed in newly purchased black. A grieving gesture for her loss? More likely a show for the benefit of the video camera she knew would be pointing at her from the light fixture in the interview room. She wore a black silk shirt open at the neck complemented by a simple strand of pearls. A black skirt that ended just below the knees. Black pumps with two-inch heels. Plain diamond studs pierced the lobes of her ears. She wore the same gold and diamond wristwatch she'd worn when she'd played him the recording of her conversation with Fischer. It was perhaps the only thing that didn't fit with the modesty of the outfit.

He met her at the elevator and led her across the floor, the eyes of half a dozen male detectives watching her with unfeigned interest. Maggie just watching. They went into the same small interview room where they'd met three days earlier. He sat across from her and waited in silence.

"Your partner's not joining us?"

"I thought we'd do this alone."

"Good. I'm glad. What is it you wanted to talk about?"

"I was just wondering if you're a congenital liar or if your lies just seemed like a good idea at the time?"

McCabe was staring directly into Rachel's eyes, waiting for even the slightest tell. The slightest hint of nerves or discomfort. A blink. A twitch. A glance toward the video camera or the door. There was none.

"Your face looks much better," she said. "The swelling's gone down quite a lot. You know you really are quite an attractive man. Though someone should take the time to dress you better."

"Answer the question, Rachel."

"I have no idea what your question was about," she said.

"I want to know why you lied to me about your conversation with Evan Fischer."

"Lied to you? How could I have lied to you? It was all there on the recording. Every word we said."

"Fischer doesn't think so. I played it for him and he says less than half of it is there. He says you turned the recording off when you left the bench on the prom. And didn't turn it on again while the two of you went to your apartment to continue talking."

"Really? Well, then, I'm afraid you've got the wrong liar. I'm not in the habit of inviting strange men back to my apartment. And even you have to admit Mr. Fischer is more than a little strange."

McCabe pressed Play on the digital recorder. "This is Fischer telling us what you talked about in your apartment."

"*By the time we both had . . . God, I don't know how many drinks*

*but really a lot . . . we started playing a game. Or what Rachel called
a game. She named it Double Jeopardy. Like from the TV show."

"And how did this game go?"

"She decided I was the contestant so I had to go first."

"Go first and do what?"

*"Invent a way to kill Josh in which I wouldn't be caught. Of
course I suggested something stupid. Like waiting for him to come
home from work, hiding behind the door and blowing his brains out
as he walked in. She laughed at that idea and said, 'Oh no, you've
got to be a lot more clever than that. And I'm not sure I'd want all
that blood and bits of Josh all over the apartment.'*

*"I asked Rachel what she meant by 'clever.' She said that if I
didn't want to spend the rest of my life in jail I had to think up a
way to kill Josh that nobody would figure out. 'Like what?' I asked.*

*"'Oh no,' she said. 'You're the contestant and I'm the moderator.
You know? Like Alex Trebek. I make the rules and ask the questions. If you come up with the right answer you win the prize.'*

"'And what is the prize?' I asked.

*"'The ultimate one,' she said. 'At least for you. Revenge for the
rape and death of your wife. For me a big pile of money. And not
having to put up with a cheating husband anymore.'"*

"And how well did you do in this game?" Maggie's voice.

"Not very. I'm not very imaginative."

*"When you were playing your game of How Do We Kill Josh,
did Rachel ever suggest hiring a prostitute to lure Josh Thorne to his
death?"* Again Maggie was speaking.

*"No. I mentioned it. Remember, I was the contestant. She was
the moderator. I came up with that idea in response to something
she said. That there were only two things in the world that truly
interested Josh. Money and fucking. I told her I didn't have access*

*to the kind of money that would interest him. But fucking seemed
like a good idea. So I suggested hiring a really hot woman to use as
bait to lure him to a place where he could be killed anonymously.
That turned out to be the only idea of mine she liked. She gave me
an A plus for it."*

McCabe hit the OFF button.

"A complete and utter lie from beginning to end," said Rachel.
"He's making the whole thing up."

"Would you describe your condo in Brooklyn Heights?"

"Did he describe it? Is that why you think I'm lying?"

"Describe the apartment."

Rachel did. And while her description contained far more detail, it pretty much matched everything Fischer had said.

"Maybe you could explain to me, if Fisher is lying, why his description of your apartment almost exactly matches your own?"

"*MetroLife*. The August 2013 issue."

"What?"

"*MetroLife*. It's sort of an upscale New York shelter magazine.
They did a special issue on the lifestyles of what they called Wall
Street's Young Guns. They ran three pages of photos showing our
apartment in detail. They also had profile descriptions of Josh and
myself. Our favorite artists. Our favorite restaurants. The place
we rent in the Hamptons. Photos of both of us. Including one I
assume you'll find interesting of me by the pool in East Hampton
in a particularly teeny-tiny bikini."

McCabe stared at her. The bitch—and that's how he'd begun to
think of her—had an answer for everything. He'd check the magazine but he was sure the photos would be there and that they'd
contain images of everything Fischer had described. He didn't
know where to take it from here.

"Of course there's another possibility," said Rachel. "One I didn't think of at first because I just didn't make the connection. It was New Year's weekend. Josh and I were skiing in Killington. We left after work Friday and got home late Monday night and when I got home things weren't quite how I leave them. Especially in my closet and my dresser drawers. My underwear drawers. I'm not quite OCD but pretty close. I fold things a certain way, line them up a certain way. The things were all there but they were folded differently. It really creeped me out. Josh pooh-poohed it. Said I'd probably just packed for Killington in a hurry. But I knew I hadn't."

"Anything taken?"

"No. We have some original art and a fair amount of expensive jewelry as well as a lot of electronics and none of it was touched."

Including, thought McCabe, a fancy gold and diamond wristwatch.

"Patek Philippe?" he asked, pointing at it.

"Yes. A birthday present from Josh. And that would have been there at the time."

"Did you report the break-in to the police?"

"No. Josh said there was no point since nothing was taken. No evidence of forced entry. No proof anybody really had broken in. But I was kind of shaken up. I don't like the idea of some creep pawing through my underwear."

"But you didn't do anything about it?"

"We did. At my insistence. Josh had a fancy security system installed. We didn't have one before."

"No idea how the guy got in?"

"I assume he must have picked the lock. I'm told that's not particularly hard." Rachel paused. A frown line appeared between her eyes. "Why are you staring at my watch?"

McCabe shook his head. "I'm sorry. I wasn't really. I was just thinking how pretty it was. How lucky you were to have been married to a man who would have given you something as beautiful as that. How terrible you must feel about your loss."

Rachel gave McCabe an odd look. "Thank you. I think."

Chapter 40

BILL BACON WAS getting both a sore ass and a sore ear sitting at his desk calling the johns listed in Norah Wilcox's Day Runner. So far he'd called twenty-seven of the big spenders and struck out twenty-seven times. A shitty batting average in anybody's league. Of the twenty-seven he'd called so far, fourteen hung up when he told them who he was and what he wanted. He called all fourteen back three times and left the same voice mail each time. *"This is Detective William Bacon of the Portland Police Department. We're working on a murder case and need the name and contact information for a woman you met with on such and such a date in such and such a room in such and such a hotel. We will keep both your name and any information you provide absolutely confidential."*

He hadn't yet tried McCabe's tactic of threatening to tell their wives but if this kept up he might be forced to give it a go. After completing his third voice mail to john number twenty-seven, Bacon got up and refilled his coffee cup with liquid that, after four hours in the carafe, looked and tasted more like black mud than anything else. Then he went back to his desk and tried number twenty-eight, Herbert Kaslow, whose area code indicated he was located in Pittsburgh.

A woman answered. "Mr. Kaslow's office."

"Is Mr. Kaslow in?"

"May I ask who's calling?"

"Detective William Bacon of the Portland Police Department."

"I'll see if he can take the call."

A few seconds later, "This is Kaslow. What can I help you with?"

"This is Detective . . ."

"Yeah, yeah, Mavis already told me who you were. Whaddya want?"

"Last December 4 you stayed in room 1505 of the Essex House Hotel in New York."

"What about it?"

"At approximately ten-thirty P.M. a young woman, an escort, came to your room."

"What the hell business is that of a cop from Oregon?"

"Maine."

"What?"

"Portland, Maine. Not Oregon."

"Oregon. Maine. Whatever. What business is it of yours who I meet with?"

"The woman you met with on December 4 was murdered here in Portland late last Tuesday night."

"Jesus Christ, you're kidding."

"Not kidding."

"Whaddya think? I had something to do with it?"

"No. We don't think you had anything at all to do with it. I just need you to give me the name of the woman you met with and what number you called to arrange your date with her."

"What? You don't even have her name? How the hell did you find me?"

"The name we have for her is a phony. An alias. We found your name and number listed in her date book. Also the date and time of your meeting at the hotel."

"Jesus Christ. That poor kid. I only know her as Hallie. No last name. Just Hallie. Probably not her real name either. She works—pardon me, worked—for a group called Elegant Escorts. I see her pretty regular when I go to New York. And you know something? I really liked her. I mean, as a person and not just for, you know . . . other things. I'm really sorry to hear what happened." There was a long sigh from Herb Kaslow. "Just a minute, let me get you the number. But please, you gotta promise me you won't tell them it was me who gave it to you. I got a feeling they won't like knowing I gave it to a cop. Even a cop from Maine."

AFTER RACHEL LEFT 109, McCabe took a walk around the Old Port. There was something about the gold watch on Rachel's wrist that was scratching at his brain, a sense that it was important, but he couldn't figure out what the hell it was. Or why it mattered. He walked to the bottom of Exchange Street, then crossed over to the other side and started walking back up.

In his mind he re-created the exact moment when the elevator doors opened and he first laid eyes on Rachel Thorne. He could see the gray slacks she wore, the gray cashmere pullover, the dark blue leather jacket. He remembered the wedding and engagement rings on her left hand. But the damned jacket she wore had covered her wrist. She might have been wearing the watch but there was no way he could be sure. And she'd kept the jacket on the whole time they were talking. He went through the entire conversation line by line. He remembered a few times when the left sleeve of the jacket rode up. There'd been no flashes of gold. None at all. Still, could he be sure? And even if she hadn't been wearing it, maybe she just had the damned thing stowed away in her shoulder bag.

That's when it hit him. McCabe turned around and headed straight back to 109 and then to Starbucks's cube on the second floor.

"Sergeant McCabe. How can I help you?"

"The video from the Port Grill. You still have it?"

"Of course. I copied it into my computer."

"Run it for me, will you?"

Starbucks booted up one of his computers, his long fingers dancing amazingly fast across the keyboard. The video came to life.

"Jump to where the woman comes into the bar."

Starbucks did and Norah Wilcox entered the scene.

"Now slow it down. I want to go through all of it frame by frame."

McCabe watched Norah walk across to the seat three down from Joshua Thorne. "Keep going. Stop on each and every frame where we can see her left wrist."

Norah's wrist came into view as she turned to hang her jacket on the back of her barstool. Starbucks froze the scene. Then moved it forward and then back again one frame at a time, finally stopping on one where Norah's wrist was pointed in the direction of the surveillance camera.

She was definitely wearing something gold. Maybe a watch. Maybe just a bracelet. "Push in on her wrist. Tight as you can without losing focus totally."

Starbucks enlarged the frame by minuscule degrees. The gold

flash on Norah Wilcox's left wrist became blurrier and blurrier but also revealed some marks McCabe felt certain was the face of a watch. Surrounded on each side by what just might be small diamonds. Not perfect but not bad.

"All right, let's go through the rest of the scene. See if there are any frames where we get a better look at that watch."

McCabe stood over Starbucks's shoulder as they watched Norah, moving in time lapse fashion, climb up onto the barstool. As she rested her hand on the bar the watch slipped beneath the cuff of her blouse and disappeared. Andie walked over to take her order. Joshua Thorne's head turned to get a better look at Norah. Andie turned away to make Norah's drink. Norah's wrist disappeared from view. Thorne said something. Then he got up and walked toward Norah. As Thorne approached, Norah turned slightly on her stool to her left to face him. Her left arm went up onto the back of the barstool, the sleeve of the blouse rose slightly and for just a frame or two the face of the watch was pointing directly at the lens of the camera. They couldn't ask for a better angle. Or more clarity. Starbucks moved in on the watch and the image became progressively blurrier.

"How much can you improve the resolution? I need to be able to identify that watch as accurately as possible."

"The quality of the original footage is surprisingly good for a restaurant surveillance camera," said Starbucks. "Definitely high def. Probably 1,920 by 1,080 pixels. I might be able to get a little closer and make it a bit clearer. But I don't think you'll ever be able to read the brand name of the watch or tell what time it is."

"Just do your best."

"Okay. Give me some time. Say, twenty minutes to fuss with it."

McCabe nodded. "Call me when it's as good as you can make it."

McCabe went back to his desk and went to the Patek Philippe webpage. He went through their selection of women's watches, which ranged in price from ten thousand bucks to over a hundred and forty. He went through the lineup and found a model that looked identical to the one Rachel had been wearing. And as best he could tell also pretty damned close to the one on Norah's wrist in the video. Solid gold. Two vertical rows of diamonds on either side of the rectangular face. Diamonds instead of numbers on the face. A list price of $41,800. For those interested in a bargain, McCabe found an online jeweler willing to sell it for a mere $36,780. McCabe shook his head in a display of democratic disgust. That little trinket on Rachel's wrist cost more than most families in Maine made in a year. More than some families made in two years. McCabe printed out an image of the watch and took it with him back down to Starbucks.

"This is the best I can do, Sergeant."

Starbucks's best was pretty damned good. The face of the watch nearly filled the screen and, while still pretty blurry, McCabe was certain the watch Norah was wearing at the Port Grill was identical to the one Rachel was wearing this morning. And while it was remotely possible they both might own the same watch, the odds against that had to be ridiculously high. He was also sure that the left wrist on the body in the trunk of the Nissan had been unadorned, which might mean that by taking the watch from Norah's wrist Rachel was simply reclaiming her own property. On the other hand if it *was* Rachel's watch, one Josh had given her for her birthday, wouldn't Josh have been suspicious when he saw Norah wearing an identical one in the bar? It didn't make much sense.

McCabe asked Starbucks to e-mail him the frame that offered

the best image of the watch. The question that kept bugging McCabe as he headed back to the fourth floor was had Rachel stolen the watch from the wrist of her dead victim? Or had Rachel lent it to Norah for the occasion? And if so, why?

Bill Bacon stopped at McCabe's desk. "Can we talk?"

McCabe put his computer to sleep and followed Bacon into the conference room. "Any luck?"

"Yeah, it took a while but after twenty-seven no answers and no callbacks a guy named Herb Kaslow from Pittsburgh finally talked to me. Seems Norah's regular working name is Hallie. No last name. At least none that Kaslow knows and I'm pretty sure Hallie's a phony name as well. Anyway, she works for a group that calls itself Elegant Escorts. When I called the number Kaslow gave me, a woman named Monica answered. I told Monica I was a high roller from Cleveland and wanted to set up a date with Hallie. She said she was sorry but Hallie wasn't available but all their escorts provided excellent company. I said I was particularly interested in Hallie and asked when she might be available. She said she wasn't sure. Hallie was traveling. I asked if Hallie had any good friends whose company I might enjoy as much. She asked what I had in mind. I said dinner at the hotel and some titillating conversation."

"Titillating?"

"Sorry, boss. Couldn't resist it. Neither could Monica. She laughed and told me that Elegant Escorts was a small company and while all their girls were titillating she thought I might find Hallie's best friend, Tara, the most titillating of all. I asked if Tara really was a friend and Monica said yes, the two of them were very close. We set up a time and I gave her the credit card Fortier set up for me and made the date. She charged the card a thousand bucks for the agency fee and said any further gifts I might want to give Tara were strictly between her and me."

"What name am I using?"

"Barry Simpson."

"Barry Simpson, huh? How come you didn't tell her my name was Bart?"

"I resisted temptation. I told Monica I was president of a steel tube manufacturing company in Cleveland."

"Okay. Good. Where and when am I meeting Ms. Tara?" asked McCabe.

"Suite 3015 at the Grand Hyatt."

"Suite?"

"Yeah. I figured it'd be better if you didn't talk to Tara about her friend's murder in a bedroom. Room's all paid for. Tara's going to meet you in the room at exactly eight o'clock."

McCabe checked the time. It was already three-thirty.

"I made reservations for you on the four-thirty Delta flight to LaGuardia. You should be able to make it no problem."

McCabe locked his weapon in his desk drawer. He was already late and didn't have time to fill out and hand in the paperwork that was required for him to carry it on the plane.

Chapter 41

THE KNOCK ON the door of McCabe's suite at the Grand Hyatt came precisely at eight o'clock. McCabe opened the door to a smiling twenty-something wearing a low-cut blue minidress covered with spangles and blue stiletto heels. She was a very pretty brunette with large and definitely titillating breasts.

"Mr. Simpson?"

"Yes."

"Hi, I'm Tara. May I come in?"

McCabe opened the door wider. When Tara was inside he put the *Privacy Please* sign on the door, flipped both interior locks and followed her in.

Tara looked around the place approvingly. Instantly spotting what seemed to be a familiar bottle chilling in a silver ice bucket, she smiled broadly. "Mmm, my fave. May I have a glass?"

McCabe popped the cork from the bottle of Veuve Cliquot. He filled one of two champagne flutes and handed it to Tara.

"You're not having any?"

"In a little while."

Tara took the drink to a small club chair. Crossed one leg over the other, making sure he couldn't miss the fact that she'd arrived commando-style.

"Well, Barry, what would you like to do this evening?"

"Talk."

"And after we talk?"

"Well, why don't we play that by ear?"

"Don't you have a little present for me?" she asked with a coy smile.

"What I have for you is some sad news. Hallie worked with you at Elegant Escorts and she was your friend, is that right?"

The coy smile disappeared.

"She is my friend. We share an apartment." The crossed legs tightened, cutting off McCabe's view. "Who are you and what do you want?"

"I'm a homicide cop from Portland, Maine. Sergeant Michael McCabe." McCabe flipped his badge wallet onto the table between them. Tara started to get up. McCabe blocked her exit. "Sit down, please. I'm not after you. I'm investigating the murder of this woman."

He handed Tara a postmortem photo showing Norah Wilcox from the neck up. The bullet hole in the middle of her forehead looked very black and very ugly. Norah herself looked very dead.

Tara sat back down on the edge of the chair and stared at the picture, wide-eyed. "Oh my God. Poor Hallie. I told her that whole fucking deal was too good to be true."

"I need you to tell me about 'the whole fucking deal.' Was Hallie her real name?"

"No. It was Sheila. Sheila Wachowski. She was from Chicago. South Side. Same neighborhood I come from."

"Her family still live there?" McCabe would have to inform the Chicago PD. Ask them to locate and inform next of kin.

"I don't know. I don't think she got on real well with her family."

"And what was the deal? The one that was too good to be true?"

"I really don't know that much about it. Just that she was gonna get twenty-five thou for one night in Maine."

"Tara, your friend has been murdered. I'm sure you want us to catch the person who did this."

Tara nodded tearfully, black mascara lines forming under her eyes. "All I know is that the date was supposed to be a birthday present for some rich guy. But he wasn't supposed to know about it. Hallie was supposed to go up to Portland and pick up this guy in a bar and spend time with him. Then take him to this rental house and show him a good time. And she was going to get twenty-five thousand dollars for that. I told her for that kind of money there had to be a catch. Hallie just smiled at me when I said that, and said, 'There sure as hell is.' I asked her what but she wouldn't tell me. Said it was supersecret. She couldn't tell anyone. But that she knew what she was doing. That's all I know."

"Can you tell me who hired her?"

Tara shrugged. "Somebody rich."

"Was it a man or a woman?"

"I dunno. Why would a woman arrange something like that? Hallie was supposed to be a surprise birthday present for the guy so I figured it was probably one of his rich buddies."

"You think Monica would know?"

"I don't think so. Sheila just told Monica that she had to be away for a few days. That there'd been a death in the family. Funny."

"What?"

"Her saying there'd been a death in the family. That turned out to be the truth. She just didn't know the death was going to be hers."

"Did Sheila have any other friends or maybe a boyfriend she might have told more about it?"

"I don't think so. She was very secretive about the whole thing. Would you do me a favor?"

"What?"

"If you catch the fucking guy who murdered my friend would you please let me know?"

McCabe took her cell number and said that he would. He also asked her for her real name.

"Jen O'Leary."

"Here, Jen." McCabe held out the envelope containing ten one hundred dollar bills that Fortier had grudgingly approved for the project. She took it. Started for the door. Stopped and turned and handed it back to him.

"I can't take this. It feels too much like blood money."

McCabe nodded. "Your call."

Chapter 42

McCabe's eleven o'clock flight back to Portland was delayed forty minutes due to lousy weather. He passed the time nursing a Dewar's on the rocks in a typical airport bar in Terminal C at LaGuardia. To his surprise the place actually had Macallan 12 but to his further surprise they wanted twenty-two bucks for a single shot and no way he was going to pay that. Mostly because it was ridiculous but also because there was no way Fortier would reimburse him for what Bill considered his extravagant tastes. On the other hand Bill would be overjoyed that he still had the envelope with the thousand bucks in it that he'd carried just in case Tara aka Jen O'Leary had wanted to make a deal for information. Sadly she had no information to bargain with other than the fact that Norah Wilcox's working name was Hallie and her real name was Sheila Wachowski. He'd learned nothing at all he could use to prove whether it was Rachel Thorne or Evan Fischer, or maybe both of them working in tandem, who'd been responsible for any or all of the three murders.

The woman at Gate C14 announced over her loudspeaker that

Flight 2334 to Portland would be delayed an additional fifteen minutes.

He called Maggie.

"How'd you do?"

"I struck out."

"Totally?"

"Not totally. At least I got Norah's real name. Sheila Wachowski. But Ms. Wachowski revealed none of the details of her secret assignment to either her best friend, Tara, or her employer, Monica. Basically I got bupkes except that Norah's assignment took her to Portland and that her next of kin notification will have to go to the Wachowskis, who apparently live somewhere on the south side of Chicago."

"Norah didn't even slip up and reveal the gender of her client with a careless *he* or *she* reference?"

"Nope. Nothing. Just that she was being paid twenty-five thousand dollars for basically one night's work in Maine."

"Okay. So what do we do now?"

"I haven't got a single idea in my head except maybe that I've got time for one more Scotch."

"Okay, fine. But don't come back drunk."

"I won't. See you in Portland."

McCabe ordered a refill on the Dewar's and stared with minimal interest at an NBA game between the Brooklyn Nets and the Cleveland Cavaliers. The Nets were getting creamed.

He sat there staring blankly at the screen and toting up what he knew and how he might be able to use it.

He'd learned Norah's working name. Hallie. Her boss's name. Monica. The fact that they both worked for an outfit that called itself Elegant Escorts. And that someone had paid Norah/Hallie

$25K to seduce Josh Thorne, tie him to a bed and shoot a photo of him, which she then e-mailed to New York. Pretty thin. On the other hand, as a seasoned poker player, he knew that sometimes a better option than folding a bad hand was a bluff. A bluff designed to convince Rachel Thorne that he was holding more and better cards than he actually was. He took out his phone and began composing a text to Rachel.

On my way back from New York where I had very informative conversations with Monica, Norah Wilcox's boss at Elegant Escorts, and a young hooker who calls herself Tara (real name Jen O'Leary). Hallie and Tara shared an apartment, shared clothes and shared practically everything else including clients and information about who had signed her up and paid for her fatal trip to Portland, Maine ($25K). I think it'll be in your long-term interest if you help me fill in the few holes that are left in this investigation. Please meet me first thing tomorrow morning at my office.

McCabe read the text over two or three times. He wasn't sure the fish would go for the bait, but he figured what the hell; he didn't have any other good ideas at the moment. Just as his flight was called for boarding, he hit Send.

Thanks mostly to the hour and the time of year, Delta's late flight back to Portland was more than half empty and McCabe got to stretch out by himself in one of the exit row seats. Just as the flight lifted off from the runway McCabe closed his eyes and fell into a deep sleep. He didn't wake up until he was on the ground again, this time in Portland.

Once out of the plane he headed across the road to the short-term parking lot where his prize possession, a classic '57 Ford Thunderbird convertible, was waiting to take him home to his condo on Portland's Eastern Prom.

Chapter 43

IT WAS NEARLY one in the morning on yet another cold, wet and overcast Maine night when McCabe parked the T-Bird in its assigned space. He climbed out and looked up. All the windows on all three floors of his building at 324 Eastern Prom were dark, the inhabitants likely enjoying a warm and probably well-deserved sleep. It had been a long, tiring and not particularly successful day and he was eager to join them in slumber. He locked the car. Found the key for the outer door of the building and slipped it in the lock.

He didn't see the slender figure moving to the door just behind him.

He pulled the door open and stepped inside. It wasn't until he reached the fourth stair on his way up that he realized that the familiar click of the door's automatic closing mechanism had come a few seconds late. He turned and saw Rachel Thorne standing at the bottom of the stairs. She was dressed in black tights and a black Gore-Tex jacket, her face and body dimly lit by the inadequate hall light. But the light was not nearly dim or inadequate enough for McCabe to miss the fact that she was pointing a gun at him. A Glock 26. The so-called Baby Glock. Small. Light. Easy to conceal. And, at this range, very, very deadly. Especially in the hands of an experienced shooter. It seemed Rachel had fallen for his bluff. Unfortunately not quite in the way he'd hoped.

"Put both hands behind your head and continue climbing the stairs. Any sudden and unexpected moves on your part and not only will you die but so will any and all of your neighbors curious enough and stupid enough to come out to see what's going on."

McCabe did as he was told. As he reached the third-floor landing she told him to stop and take off his overcoat and lay it gently on the floor. He briefly considered taking off the coat and tossing it toward her, simultaneously rushing down to grab the gun from her hand. But he had a feeling Rachel was a steady and competent marksman. He'd most likely be dead before the coat left his hand. Again he did as he was told and let the coat slide to the floor.

"Now your sports jacket."

He dropped that on top of the overcoat. There was no holster resting against his hip.

"Where's your gun?" asked Rachel.

"I'm not armed."

"Bullshit. Cops are always armed."

"Not when they're rushing to catch a last-minute flight to New York. Too much paperwork to fill out and not enough time to get it done."

She looked at him like he was lying. "Lift each of your trouser legs one at a time."

He did. There was no ankle holster on either side.

"Empty your pockets and turn them inside out."

"What? Do you think I'm carrying a knife?"

"I think it's possible."

Again he did as he was told.

"Now take off the rest of your clothes and leave them on the floor."

"Are you planning to rape me?"

"Don't get your hopes up. I just happen to think you're less dangerous naked than you are dressed."

Rachel was right again. Nudity tended to inhibit aggressive countermeasures. Or attempts to escape.

When he was totally undressed she looked down and smiled for the first time. "I was right. You are a good-looking man. In every respect. I'm kind of sorry you didn't take me up on my offer the other night. What stopped you?"

"Simple. You weren't worth it. In fact, I've been wondering why you attempted that particular seduction."

"Don't play stupid, McCabe. If you'd slept with me, even just once, no way would a jury ever have believed your testimony against me. Oh, and by the way, my brand-new iPhone was all set up and aimed at the bed to video the entire episode."

"Jesus. You and Josh made quite a pair, didn't you? One a moral leper, the other an out-of-control psychopath."

"Trying to irritate me, McCabe, simply isn't a good idea. Particularly in your current state. Now stretch forward and lean your hands against the side wall."

McCabe leaned in at about a forty-five-degree angle. He wondered if she'd ever had training at this kind of thing or if she was simply making it up as she went along. He opted for training. He heard her picking up his keys, unlocking the door to the apartment and going in.

"All right. Stand tall. Hands behind your head and come on in. Then close the door behind you."

McCabe closed the door and stood with his back to it. Rachel stood facing him. The Glock 26 pointing directly at his midsection.

"What exactly are you planning, Rachel?"

"I'm planning to kill you, McCabe."

"I got that part. But there's something else going on in that twisted little brain of yours."

Rachel smiled again. "There is indeed."

"Maybe you'd like to share it."

"Why not? I think you deserve to know how you'll be remembered. And how I plan on getting away with your murder. We're going to go into your kitchen and get a glass."

"We're going to share a last drink together?"

"No, there'll be only one glass. And there won't be any drinks."

"Okay, so what's the glass for?"

"You're going to jerk off into the glass."

McCabe frowned. He wasn't sure where she was going with this.

"And when you've successfully squirted your last, I'm going to shoot you. When you're dead, I'm going to take off my clothes. Perhaps rip them off would be a more accurate description. And then, and this is the part I'm not really happy about—"

"Don't tell me. Let me guess. You're going to hit yourself in the face. Not badly enough to do any serious damage but maybe just enough to leave a few nasty bruises. And then you're going to take my semen from the glass and put as much as you can up inside you."

"Very good, McCabe. I knew you were a smart boy."

"And then you're going to call the police and tell my erstwhile fellow officers how I raped you and how you just happened to have a gun and how rapists get what rapists deserve. How you killed the rapist McCabe in self-defense or perhaps, postrape, it might be called justifiable homicide?"

"Very good, McCabe. An A minus for you, Officer Friendly."

"Why not an A plus?"

"Because self-defense would work. You see, I only killed you when I realized you were about to rape me for a second time."

"Very good, Rachel. An A plus for you. Only one problem with your plan."

"Oh? And what's that?"

"What if I refuse to jerk off?"

"Then I'm afraid I'll just have to tie you to your bed and give you the best hand job you ever had."

"Like you gave Josh? Is that how the dried semen ended up on his leg?"

"A plus again."

McCabe glanced over Rachel's shoulder to the open door of the bedroom. Then quickly back at Rachel again. "Since it seems I'm going to die anyway, perhaps you'll be good enough to tell me why."

"Why what?"

"Why you killed not only Josh but the others. Charlie Loughlin and Norah Wilcox."

"Well, I had hoped that Fischer would do it for me. He certainly had reason enough. Unfortunately what he didn't have were the guts to carry out the job he helped me plan. So, in the end, I had to do it myself."

"Was it just for the money? The six million dollars in insurance money? And whatever else you and Josh had salted away?"

"Actually, money had very little to do with it. It was pure revenge. Josh was, to put it mildly, an abusive husband. Any time he felt like sex and I didn't want it, he'd beat the shit out of me and then spousal-rape me. Sometimes he'd just knock me around for the hell of it if he happened to be pissed about something. Which he was every other day. I wasn't going to put up with it anymore."

"Why didn't you call the police? Have a restraining order put on him?"

"And then what? Have him get so pissed off he'd kill me?"

Rachel was right. Restraining orders were at best a poor tool for violent husbands.

"But you killed two innocent people as well."

"Charlie Loughlin wasn't so innocent. He was a rapist as well. If you don't believe it read Hannah Reindel's book. As for the hooker, I'm sorry about her but I didn't see any way around it. I think we're reaching the end of question time."

"Just one more. The watch? You lent it to Norah, didn't you?"

"Yes."

"So how come Josh didn't recognize it when he picked up Norah at the Port Grill bar?"

"He never saw it before. It wasn't a gift from Josh. I bought it especially for the occasion and I wanted it back." Rachel sighed. "It really is too bad you wouldn't play with me that night. We both would have had a wonderful time."

A voice from behind Rachel spoke for the first time. "Unfortunately, Rachel, he's already taken." Maggie was standing in the open bedroom door, wearing the long T-shirt she usually slept in, with her Glock 17 trained at the middle of Rachel's back. "Now drop your gun."

Rachel Thorne reacted not by dropping the gun but by whirling around at the sound of the voice and aiming at Maggie. But her move was too late. Maggie's bullet entered Rachel's oh-so-beautiful face right between her perfect brown eyes and exited the back carrying bits of her twisted brain with it and spattering them against the wall and partly against McCabe.

"I think you better clean up and then get your clothes on," said Maggie. "We don't want the rest of the department seeing exactly what it is that makes you so irresistible to me."

Epilogue

THE NEXT DAY Evan Fischer was released from the Cumberland County jail and sent to Winter Haven Hospital for a complete psychiatric evaluation.

Detective Toni Bernstein of the West Hartford PD was informed of Rachel's confession that she was the "Norah Wilcox" who'd killed Charlie Loughlin.

And McCabe sent Jen O'Leary a text message telling her that Hallie's killer had been found and unfortunately shot to death resisting arrest.

Finally, the missing key to Bob and Brenda Bickle's house on Hartley Street turned up in a desk drawer in room 411, the Governor's Suite, of the Portland Regency Hotel.

Detective Margaret Savage was, of course, placed on temporary suspension while Portland Police Chief Thomas Shockley, Lieutenant Bill Fortier and Lieutenant Peter Gerlach, head of the PPD's Internal Affairs unit, investigated the circumstances of the shooting death of the suspect Rachel Christensen Thorne. Fortunately Maggie had recorded the entire conversation between

Rachel and McCabe with her cell phone while standing in the doorway so almost none of the facts were in question.

They were all sitting around the small conference table in Chief Shockley's office.

"I had no idea what time McCabe was coming home from New York and I was asleep when they got here," said Maggie. "The sound of their voices woke me. I could hear what they were saying so I obviously knew something was wrong. I slipped out of bed as quietly as I could, retrieved my weapon and my phone from the bedside table and went to the door, which was already ajar. I opened it further. Happily it doesn't squeak. Rachel's back was to me. McCabe was facing me. He saw me and I could tell he wanted me to hold off until he could pull a confession out of the suspect, Rachel Thorne. I wasn't so sure she wouldn't shoot him before finishing her confession." Maggie looked over at McCabe. "But we took the chance."

Shockley nodded. "The circumstances behind the killing of Mrs. Thorne are very clear from that recording and there won't be any need for further investigation into that. Do you agree, Gerlach?"

"I do. We should be able to reinstate Detective Savage to active duty very quickly."

"Good," said Shockley. "Then perhaps you and Lieutenant Fortier will excuse us. There's something I have to talk to Sergeant McCabe and Detective Savage about privately."

Fortier and Gerlach left.

When they were gone, he asked, "How long have the two of you been cohabiting?"

"I'm not entirely sure that's any of your business," said McCabe.

Maggie's look told McCabe to hold his tongue. "We're not exactly cohabiting," said Maggie. "I've kept my own apartment on Vesper Street. At least for the time being."

"But you do spend nights together?"

"Yes. Obviously. Quite a few," said McCabe. "Just as you and your girlfriend, Josie Tenant, have been doing for a couple of years."

"Unlike you and Savage, Tenant and I don't work together. I'm not her boss. And, unfortunately, the way this case ended makes it common knowledge that you and Maggie are living together. I don't think the public will particularly approve of two senior detectives living in sin. Particularly if one reports to the other."

"Living in sin?" said Maggie. "You must be joking. Everybody lives in sin these days. And trust me, there's nothing sinful about it."

"If you're asking us to end our relationship," said McCabe, "forget about it. It's taken us a long time to get here."

"We can have our resignations on your desk this afternoon," added Maggie.

"We've discussed setting up our own private investigations firm. McCabe and Savage."

"Or possibly Savage and McCabe," Maggie added with a smile.

Shockley stared unhappily at the two of them. "All right. Don't do anything hasty. Let me think about it."

McCabe and Savage left the office and headed toward the elevator.

"Want to get some lunch?" asked McCabe.

"Nah. I'd rather go back to the apartment and do a little more of that living in sin stuff."

McCabe smiled and kissed her as the elevator doors opened. Brian Cleary grinned at them as he exited. "Maybe you should give Willetts a call," McCabe called to him as he and Maggie got on.

When the doors closed, they kissed again.

Acknowledgments

There are many people I wish to thank for their contributions to this book. Former Portland Police detective Sergeant Tom Joyce's knowledge and insights regarding police procedure and the ins and outs of the Portland PD was, as always, immensely helpful. None of the McCabe/Savage books would have been possible without Tom's help.

I'd also like to thank my publisher, Dan Mallory, and editor, Emily Krump, from HarperCollins/William Morrow, and my agents Meg Ruley and Rebecca Scherer of the Jane Rotrosen Literary Agency, for their many significant contributions to the final version of this book.

Finally, writing *The Girl on the Bridge* would not have been possible without the insights provided by reading a number of memoirs written by brave women who have experienced and recovered from the horrendous psychological damage of violent rape. Chief among these is a book titled *After Silence: Rape & My Journey Back* by Nancy Venable Raine. I've never met nor spoken to Ms. Raine but I owe her a tremendous debt of gratitude.

ALSO BY JAMES HAYMAN

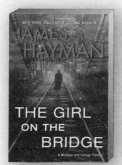

THE GIRL ON THE BRIDGE
A McCabe and Savage Thriller

Available in Paperback, E-Book, and Digital Audio

"A riveting police procedural that gripped me on page one and never let go. A first-rate story-teller at the top of his game." —Robert Dugoni, bestselling author of *My Sister's Grave*

THE GIRL IN THE GLASS
A McCabe and Savage Thriller

Available in Paperback, E-Book, and Digital Audio

"Had me guessing to the end. His plot crafting made me think of Martin Cruz Smith and Scott Turow at their best." —*Portland Press Herald*

DARKNESS FIRST
A McCabe and Savage Thriller

Available in Paperback, E-Book, and Digital Audio

"A deplorable villain, tantalizing characters, and a hint of romance mix with the twists. What more could a reader ask for?" —*Library Journal* (starred review)

THE CUTTING
A McCabe and Savage Thriller

Available in Paperback, E-Book, and Digital Audio

"Taut, deft and with a delicate sense of place, this is supremely accomplished storytelling—not just another depiction of a serial killer rampage." —*Daily Mail* (London)

THE CHILL OF NIGHT
A McCabe and Savage Thriller

Available in Paperback, E-Book, and Digital Audio

"Hayman creates an intricate plot, engaging regulars, and suspects that are convincing. The suspense is pulse lifting. This is a well-crafted thriller written to satisfy both men and women." —*Providence Journal*